D0819444

THE

McCONE FILES

BOOKS BY MARCIA MULLER

THE

McCONE FILES

BY

Marcia Muller

Norfolk, Virginia
Crippen & Landru Publishers
1996

Copyright © 1995 Marcia Muller

Cover copyright © 1995 Crippen & Landru Publishers

Cover painting by Carol Heyer; cover design by Deborah Miller

Crippen & Landru logo by Eric D. Greene

Third printing

ISBN (limited edition) 1-885941-04-8

ISBN (trade edition) 1-885941-05-6

Printed in the United States of America on acid-free paper

10 9 8 7 6 5 4 3

Crippen & Landru, Publishers
P. O. Box 9315
Norfolk, VA 23505-9315

CONTENTS

INTRODUCTION

Sharon McCone came into existence in 1971, when I was hiding out in what was to become her studio apartment on Guerrero Street in San Francisco's Mission district. Hiding out for a variety of reasons.

The city that had entranced me in the sixties was changing: the peace-and-love motif of the nearby Haight-Ashbury had given way to hard drugs-and-crime; people who used to attend free concerts in the park were heading for the singles bars; although many of us still wanted to save the whales and secure equal rights for women, gays, and minorities, we sensed something bad on the horizon. We did, after all, have Richard Nixon running for president.

In addition to the general societal malaise, I was contending with a failed journalistic career, a failing long-distance marriage, and the fact that I was such a terrible typist that the companies where I hired on as a temp never asked me back. Perhaps *not* contending is better phrasing; all I did was read mysteries for escape. Somehow novels about crime and criminals perfectly complemented my situation.

Every week I'd hop on the bus and travel to the main branch of the public library, where I'd check out as many mysteries as I could carry. Increasingly I found myself gravitating to those by the practitioners of the hardboiled school: Raymond Chandler, Dashiell Hammett, Ross Macdonald, John D. MacDonald, among others. More often than not the protagonists were private investigators: male, tough, disaffected loners. I would read the books and dream of going off into the night, free and unafraid, to right wrongs. I wanted to live them. Or did I want to *write* them?

When I found myself staring at the space on the library shelf where "Muller" would fit and dreaming of how my name would look in the company of my favorite crime writers, I knew the answer to that question.

I'd wanted to be a writer since I was old enough to read; now my future calling was decided. But through whose eyes would I live my stories? A private investigator's, yes. But not a man's; I didn't know anything about being a man. A San Franciscan's, for sure; it was the city I loved best. And she would have to be braver and think more quickly on her feet than her creator. She also needed a name.

Sharon McCone is first-named for one of my college roommates, Sharon Delano; she is last-named for a former head of the CIA, the late John McCone. My roommate was aware of the borrowing; John McCone was not until his niece wrote to ask why I'd used her family name and I admitted to my small private joke. Fortunately, Mr. McCone was amused. Sharon's physical appearance—a throwback to her Shoshone great-grandmother—mirrors that of a woman with whom I worked briefly at *Sunset* magazine. Her background is that of a friend in San Diego, with numerous events purloined from the life of yet another friend. Her personality, convictions, actions, and reactions are her own.

Of course, this individual did not spring to life fully formed. I struggled for years to bring her persona and circumstances into focus. Most of the private investigators I'd been reading about operated alone, frequently out of sleazy offices, and had very little personal life. I wanted McCone to be independent, yet exist within a world peopled by supporting characters. What sort of milieu would provide that framework?

All Souls Legal Cooperative was born out of a conference on women and the law held at University of California at Berkeley in the spring of 1972. While I was covering it as a final journalistic foray, I met a number of dedicated, energetic, and idealistic members of a southern California organization called Bar Sinisters. They were my introduction to the poverty law movement and provided McCone with what was to become her home base for the next twenty-two years. Once I created the co-op, I was able to begin writing.

I wrote. Hundreds of pages. Reams of paper. Truly awful stuff. The first McCone manuscript is so bad I keep it under lock and key. However, in writing the opening story of this collection, "The Last Open File," I was forced to go back and read parts of the manuscript in order to get the flavor of All Souls as I described it at the very beginning. It was a truly humbling experience in all respects save one: Sharon's voice was the same as it is today. Except for one detail—she had been a nurse before going to college: I suppose I presumed this would better enable her to deal with finding corpses—she was the same character who appeared in 1977 in *Edwin of the Iron Shoes*.

Over the seventeen years since that slim first novel, very little about McCone except her voice has remained the same, and the stories in this collection trace her development. In "The Last Open File," a prequel written especially for this volume, she is what a critic once referred to as "something of a cheerleader," rescued from destitution by her old friend Hank Zahn, who lures her into All Souls's employ with the promise of an intriguing case. And even her creator has to admit that in "Merrill-Go-Round"—written in 1978, but not improved enough for publication until 1981 (and further revised for this volume)—she is a little slow to pick up on the obvious clues. But by the time she investigates in "Wild Mustard," "The Broken Men," and "Deceptions," she is seeing a darker side to the world: the tragic consequences of human beings' foolish, stupid, or downright evil actions.

As she confronts these consequences, both in her short stories and her novels, McCone develops a cynical side. She is less willing to take people or situations at face value, and she finds her ideals are eroding. Not that they disappear; if anything, they arise inconveniently to complicate her life—as in "Final Resting Place," when against her better judgment she takes on an investigation for an old college friend, or "Deadly Fantasies," when she sets out to avenge a client she has let down. In "Somewhere in the City," set during the Loma Prieta earthquake of 1989, she is so profoundly affected that she risks her life to save a man she's never laid eyes on. Sharon and I both worked off a great deal of what psychologists term "survivor's guilt" with that tale.

In the 1991 novel *Where Echoes Live* McCone reaches a major emotional turning point, recognizing and beginning to deal with both her attraction to danger and her own potential for the rage and violence she deplores in others. While she accepts both as perfectly natural impulses, she knows she will be engaged in a lifetime struggle to control them. The effects of this self-knowledge are implied in the later stories, "Benny's Space" and "The Lost Coast."

The development of All Souls Legal Cooperative parallels that of McCone. A self-sacrificing group of liberals fueled by the ideals of the sixties gradually evolves into the largest legal-services plan in northern California, complete with an 800-number advice hotline. They're soon buying real estate, restructuring the organization and—eventually—squabbling among themselves. Even as dedicated a leftist as Hank Zahn admits that he likes good Scotch, designer suits, and being called in to consult with the city's deputy mayors. In fictional life, as in real life, change is inevitable, but finally McCone and her creator began to wonder if the co-op was a good place to work.

The answer was obvious, and with the 1994 publication of *Till the Butchers Cut Him Down*, McCone is on her own. She still can't cut the apron strings to All Souls, however, and maintains her offices there. In *A Wild and Lonely Place*, to be published in August of 1995, she is still tenuously tied to the past, but imagine my surprise when I heard her begin to grumble about the co-op. It's beginning to pale for her, she tells me. She doesn't like to have her clients come there, and she's sick of listening to the staff bicker. As she has so many times over the twenty-two years we've been together, McCone is dictating what direction the series will go.

Hence the final story in this collection, "File Closed," written as a companion to "The Last Open File." It is my way of rounding out McCone's tenure at All Souls, as well as paving the way for her future. If I've indulged in sentimentality there . . . well, leave-takings are sentimental occasions. But they also imply new beginnings, and who knows what awaits Sharon?

Certainly not her creator. As usual, I'll just have to wait till she tells me.

Marcia Muller
Petaluma, California
December 1994

THE LAST OPEN FILE

THE BIG Victorian slumped between its neighbors on a steeply sloping sidestreet in San Francisco's Bernal Heights district: tall, shabby, and strangely welcoming in spite of its sagging roofline and blistered chocolate paint. I got out of my battered red MG and studied the house for a moment, then cut across the weedy triangular park that bisected Coso Street and climbed the front steps. A line of pigeons roosted on the peak above the door; I glanced warily at them before slipping under and obeying a hand-lettered sign that told me to "Walk Right In!"

It seemed an unnecessary risk to leave one's door open in this low-rent area, but when I entered I came face-to-face with a man sitting at a desk. He had fine features and a goatee, and was dressed in the flannel-shirt-and-Levi's uniform of the predominantly gay Castro district; although his dark eyes were mild and friendly, he was scrutinizing me very carefully. I presented my business card—one of the thousand I'd had printed on credit at my friends Daphne's and Charlie's shop—and his expression became less guarded. "You're Sharon McCone, Hank's detective friend!" he exclaimed.

I nodded, although I didn't feel much like a detective any more. For the past few years I'd worked under the license of one of the city's large investigative firms; the day I'd received my own ticket from the state department of consumer affairs, my boss had fired me for insubordination. At first I'd seen it as an opportunity to strike out on my own, but operating out of my studio apartment on Guerrero Street was far from an ideal situation; jobs were few, I was about to run out of cards, and my rent was due next Thursday. Yesterday I'd run into Hank Zahn, a former housemate from my college days at U. C. Berkeley. He'd asked me to stop by his law firm for a talk.

I'd hoped the talk would be about a job, but from the looks of this place I doubted it.

The man at the desk seemed to be waiting for more of a response. Inanely I said, "Yes," to reinforce the nod.

He got up and stuck out his hand. "Ted Smalley—secretary, janitor, and—occasionally—court jester. Welcome to All Souls Legal Cooperative."

I clasped his slender fingers, liking his smile.

"Hank's in conference with a client right now," Ted went on. "Why don't you make yourself comfortable in the parlor." He motioned to his right, at a big blue room with a fireplace and a butt-sprung maroon sofa and chair. "I'll tell him you're here."

I went in there, noting an old-fashioned upright piano and a profusion of books and games on the coffee table. A tall schefflera grew in the window bay; its pot was a pink toilet. I sat on the couch and immediately a coil of spring prodded my rump. Moving over, I glared at where it pushed through the upholstery.

Make myself comfortable, indeed!

Ted Smalley had disappeared down the long central hall off the foyer. I looked around some more, wondering what the hell Hank was doing in such a place.

Hank Zahn was a Stanford grad and had been at the top of his law school class at Berkeley's Boalt Hall. When I'd last seen him he was packing his belongings prior to turning over his room in the brown-shingled house we'd shared on Durant Street to yet another of an ongoing chain of tenants that stretched back into the early sixties and for all I knew continued unbroken to this very day. At the time he was being courted by several prestigious law firms, and he'd joked that the salaries and benefits they offered were enough to make him sell out to the establishment. But Hank was a self-styled leftist and social reformer, a Vietnam vet weaned from the military on Berkeley's radical politics; selling out wasn't within his realm of possibility. I could envision him as a public defender or an ACLU lawyer or a loner in private practice, but what was this cooperative business?

As I waited in the parlor, though, I had to admit the place had the same feel as the house we'd shared in Berkeley: laid-back and homey, brimming with companionship, humming with energy and purpose. Several people came and went, nodding pleasantly to me but appearing focused and intense. I'd come away from the Berkeley house craving solitude as strongly as when I'd left my parents' rambling, sibling-crowded place in San Diego. Not so with Hank, apparently.

Voices in the hallway now. Hank's and Ted Smalley's. Hank hurried into the parlor, holding out his hands to me. A tall, lean man, so loose-jointed that his limbs seemed linked by paperclips, he had a wiry

Brillo pad of brown hair and thick hornrimmed glasses that magnified the intelligence in his eyes; in the type of cords and sweaters that he'd always favored he looked more the college teaching assistant than the attorney. He clasped my hands, pulled me to my feet and hugged me. "I see you've already done battle with the couch," he said, gesturing at the protruding spring.

"Where did you get that thing—the city dump?"

"Actually, somebody left it and the matching chair and hassock on the sidewalk on Sixteenth Street. I recognized a bargain and recycled them."

"And the piano?"

"Ted's find. Garage sale. The same with the schefflera."

"Well, you guys are nothing if not resourceful. You want to tell me about this place?"

"In a minute." He steered me to the hallway. "Wait till you see the kitchen."

It was at the rear of the house: a huge room equipped with ancient appliances and glass-fronted cupboards; dishes cluttered the drainboard of the sink, a stick of butter melted on its wrapper on the counter, and a long red phone cord snaked across the floor and disappeared under a round oak table by a window that gave a panoramic view of downtown. A book titled *White Trash Cooking* lay broken-spined on a chair. Hank motioned for me to sit, fetched coffee, and pulled up a chair opposite me.

"Great, isn't it?" he said.

"Sure."

"You're probably wondering what's going on here."

I nodded.

"All Souls Law Cooperative works like a medical plan. People who can't afford the bloated fees many of my colleagues charge buy a membership, its cost based on a scale according to their incomes. The membership gives them access to consul and legal services all the way from small claims to the U. S. Supreme Court. Legal services plans're the coming thing, an outgrowth of the poverty law movement."

"How many people're involved?"

"Seventeen, right now."

"You making any money?"

"Does it look like we are? No. But we sure are having fun. Most of us live on the premises—offices double as sleeping quarters, and there're some bedrooms on the second floor—and that offsets the paltry salaries. We pool expenses, barter services such as cooking and taking out the trash. There're parties and potlucks and poker games. Right now a Monopoly tournament's the big thing."

"Just like on Durant."

"Uh-huh. You remember Anne-Marie Altman?"

"Of course." She'd been an off-and-on resident at Durant, and a classmate of Hank's.

"Well, she's our tax attorney, and one of the people who helped me found the co-op."

"Why, Hank?"

"Why a co-op? Because it's the most concrete way I can make a difference in a world that doesn't give a rat's ass about the little people. I learned at Berkeley that bombs and bricks aren't going to do a damned thing for society; maybe practicing law the way it was meant to be practiced will."

He looked idealistic and earnest and—in spite of the years he had on me—very young. I said, "I hope so, Hank."

He must have sensed my doubt and felt a twinge of his own, because for a moment his gaze muddied. Then he said briskly, "So, how's business?"

I made a rueful face, glancing down at my ratty sweater and faded jeans. The heels on my leather boots were worn down, and the last time it rained, water leaked through the right sole. "Bad," I admitted.

"Thinking of looking for permanent employment?"

"With my references?" I snorted. "'Doesn't take direction well, nonresponsive to authority figures, inflexible and overly independent. Can be pushy, severe, and dominant.' That was my last review before the agency canned me. Forget it."

"Jesus, that could describe any one of us at All Souls."

"Maybe it's a generational flaw."

"Maybe, but it's us. You want a job here?"

"Do I want . . . *what*?"

"We're looking for a staff investigator."

"Since when?"

He grinned. "Since yesterday when I ran into you in front of City Hall and started thinking about all the nonlegal work we've been heaping on our paralegals."

"Such as?"

"Nothing all that exciting, I'm afraid. Filing documents; tracking down witnesses; interviewing same; locating people and serving subpoenas. Pretty dull work, when you get right down to it, but the after-hours company is good. We're all easygoing; we'd leave you alone to do your work in your own way."

"Salary?"

"Low. Benefits, practically nil."

"I couldn't live in; I've kind of o.d.'d on the communal stuff."

"We couldn't accommodate you, anyway. The only available space is a converted closet under the stairs—which, incidentally, would be your office. I might be able to raise the salary a little to help with your rent."

"What about expenses? My car—"

"Is a hunk of junk. But we'll pay mileage. Besides . . ." he paused, eyes dancing wickedly. "I can offer you a first case that'll intrigue the hell out of you."

A steady job, bosses who would leave me alone, a first case that would intrigue the hell out of me. What more was I looking for?

"You've got yourself an investigator," I told him.

✧

Hank's client, Marnie Morrison, was one of those soft, round young women who always remind me of puppy dogs—clingy and smiley and eager to please. A thinly veiled anxiety in her big blue eyes and the way most of her statements turned up as if she were asking a question told me that the puppy had been mistreated and wasn't too sure she wouldn't be mistreated again. She sat across from me at the round table and related her story—crossing and recrossing her bluejeaned legs, twisting a curl of fluffy blond hair around her finger, glancing up at Hank for approval. Her mannerisms were so distracting that it took me a few minutes to realize I'd read about her in the paper.

"His name, it was Jon Howard. I met him on the sorority ski trip to Mammouth over spring break. In the bar at the lodge where we were staying? He was there by himself and he looked nice and my roommate Terry, she kind of pushed me into going over and talking. He was kind of sweet? So we had some drinks and made a date to ski together the next day and after that we were together all the time."

"Jon was staying at the lodge?"

"No, this motel down the road. I thought it was kind of funny, since he told me he was a financier and sole owner of this company with holdings all over Europe and South America. I mean, the motel was cheap? But he said it was quieter there and he didn't like big crowds of people, he was a very private person. We spent a lot of time there because I was rooming with Terry at the lodge, and we did things like get take-out and drink wine?" Marnie glanced at Hank. He nodded encouragingly.

"Anyway, we fell in love. And I decided not to go back to USC after break. We came to San Francisco because it's our favorite city. And Jon was finalizing a big business deal, and after that we were going to get married." The hurt-puppy look became more pronounced. "Of course, we didn't."

"Back up a minute, if you would." I said. "What did you and Jon talk about while . . . you were falling in love?"

"Our childhoods? Mine was good—I mean, my parents are nice and we've always had enough money. But Jon's? It was awful. They were poor and he always had to work and he never finished high school. But he was self-taught and he'd built this company with all these holdings up from nothing."

"What kind of company?"

Frown lines appeared between her eyebrows. "Well, a financial company, you know? It owned . . . well, all kinds of stuff overseas."

"Okay," I said, "you arrived here in the city when?"

"Two months ago."

"And did what?"

"Checked into the St. Francis. We registered under my last name—Mr. and Mrs. Jon Morrison?"

"Why?"

"Because of Jon's business deal. He'd made some enemies, and he was afraid they'd get to him before he could wrap it up. Besides, the credit card we were using was in my name." Her mouth drooped. "The American Express card my father gave me when I went to college. I. . . guess that was the real reason?"

"So you registered at the St. Francis and . . . ?"

"Jon was on the phone a lot on account of his business deal? I got my hair done and shopped. Then he hired a limo and a driver and we started looking at houses. As soon as the deal was finalized and his money was wire-transferred from Europe we were going to buy one. We found the perfect place on Vallejo Street in Pacific Heights, only it needed a lot of remodeling, we wanted to put in an indoor pool and a tennis court? So Jon wrote a postdated deposit check and hired a contractor and a decorator and then we went shopping for artwork because Jon said it was a good investment. We bought some nice paintings at a gallery on Sutter Street and they were holding them for us until the check cleared."

"What then?"

"There were the cars? We ordered a Mercedes for me and a Porsche for Jon. And we looked at yachts and airplanes, but he decided we'd better wait on those."

"And Jon wrote postdated checks for the cars?"

Marnie nodded.

"And the rest went on your American Express card?"

"Uh-huh."

"How much did you charge?"

She bit her lip and glanced at Hank. "The hotel bill was ten thousand dollars. The limo and the driver were over five. And there was a lot of other stuff? A lot." She looked down at her hands.

I met Hank's eyes. He shrugged, as if to say, "I told you she was naive."

"What did your parents have to say about the credit-card charges?" I asked.

"They paid them, at least that's what the police said. Or else I'd be in jail now?"

"Have you spoken with your parents?"

She whispered something, still looking down.

"I'm sorry, I didn't catch that."

"I said, I can't face them."

"And what about Jon?" I recalled the conclusion of Marnie's tale from the newspaper account I'd read, but I wanted to hear her version.

"A week ago? They came to our hotel room—the real-estate agent and the decorator and the salesman from the gallery. The checks Jon wrote? They'd all bounced, and they wanted him to make good on them. Only Jon wasn't there. I thought he'd gone downstairs for breakfast while I was in the shower, but he wasn't anyplace in the hotel, he'd packed his things and gone. All that was left was a pink carnation on my pillow."

It was difficult to feel sorry for her; she had, after all, refused to recognize the blatant signs of a con job. But when she raised her head and I saw the tears slipping over her round cheeks, I could feel her pain. "So what do you want me to do, Marnie?"

"Find him."

"Aren't the police trying to do that?"

She shook her head. "Since the checks were postdated they were only like . . . promises to pay? The police say it's a civil matter, and all but one of the people Jon wrote them to have decided not to press charges. The decorator had already spent a lot of money out of pocket ordering fabric and stuff, so she hired a detective to trace Jon, but he's disappeared."

I thought for a moment. "Okay, Marnie, suppose I do locate Jon Howard. What then?"

"I'll go to him and get the money to pay my parents back. Then I can face them again."

"It doesn't sound as if he has any money."

"He must." To my astonished look she added, "All of this has been a terrible mistake. Maybe he ran away because his business rivals were after him? Maybe the big deal he was working on fell through and he was ashamed to tell me? When you find him, he'll explain everything."

"You sound as though you still believe in him."

"I do. I always will. I love him."

"She's got to be insane!" I said to Hank. Marnie Morrison had just left for the cheap residential hotel that was all she could afford on her temporary office worker's wages.

"No, she's naive and doesn't want to believe the great love of her life was a con artist. I figure meeting up with Jon Howard in his true incarnation'll cure her of that."

"Then you actually want me to find him?"

"Yeah. I'd like to get a look at him, find out what makes a guy like that tick."

As a matter of fact, so would I.

The recession-hungry merchants who had been taken in by the supposedly rich young couple were now engaged in various forms of face-saving.

Dealer Henry Richards of the Avant Gallery on Sutter Street: "Mr. Morrison was *very* knowledgeable about art. He asked all the right questions. He knew which paintings would appreciate and which would not. Had he followed through on the purchases, he would have had the beginnings of a top flight collection. He may not have been rich, but I could tell he was well educated, and there's no concealing good breeding."

Realtor Deborah Lakein of Bay Properties: "From the moment I set eyes on the Morrisons I knew something was wrong. At first I thought it was simply the silk-purse-out-of-sow's-ear effect: too much money, too little breeding. But they seemed serious and were very enthusiastic about the property—it's a gem, asking price one million three. In this market one doesn't pass up the opportunity to make such a sale. Of course his deposit check was postdated like the others he wrote all over town, and when I finally put it through it was returned for nonsufficient funds. The same was true of the checks to the contractor, decorator, and landscaper I recommended. Oh, I'm in hot water with them, I am!"

Salesman Donald Neditch of European Motors on Van Ness Avenue's auto row: "Well, our customers come in all varieties, if you know what I mean. You don't have to be a blueblood to drive one of these babies. All you need is the cash or the credit. The two of them were well dressed—casually but expensively—and they arrived in a limo. I could tell they hadn't had money for very long, though. He asked a lot of questions, but they were the kind you'd ask if you were buying a pre-owned model. About used cars, he was knowledgeable enough to sell them, but I'd bet the Mercedes for his wife was the first new car he ever looked at."

Claire Wallis, clerk in the billing office at the St. Francis Hotel: "No one questioned their charges because American Express was honoring them. There was a lot of room service, a lot of champagne and fine wines. Fresh flowers every day for the three weeks they stayed here. Generous tips added to each check, too. The personnel who had dealings with them tell me she was young and sweet; he was more rough at the edges, as you'd expect a self-made man to be, but very polite. Security had no complaints about loud partying, so I assume they were as well behaved in private as in public."

Wallis referred me to an inspector in the Fraud Division of the SFPD, who had taken a list of calls made from the "Morrisons's" suite and checked it out before it became apparent that no criminal statutes had been violated. The copy of the list the inspector provided me showed that Jon Howard had called car dealerships from San Rafael to Walnut Creek, a yacht broker in Sausalito, aircraft dealers near SFO and Oakland Airport. The numbers for the real-estate agency and art gallery appeared frequently, as did those of the contractor, decorator, and landscaper. Restaurants, theater-ticket agencies, beauty shops, and a tanning salon figured prominently. There were no calls to Marnie Morrison's parents, or to anyone who might have been a personal friend.

By now I realized that Jon Howard had covered his tracks very well. I had no photograph of him, no descriptions beyond the one Marnie provided—and that was highly romanticized at best. I didn't even know if he had used his real name. I made my way down to the list of places he'd called, though, visiting the yacht broker ("He didn't know shit about boats."), the aircraft sales agencies ("I told him he'd better take flying lessons first, but he just laughed and said he had a pilot on call."), and all the auto dealerships—including Ben Rudolph's Chevrolet in Walnut Creek, where Howard had called nearly every day, but no one had any recollection of either him or Marnie. Finally I reached Lou Petrocelli, driver for Golden West Limousine Service.

"Sure, I got to know him pretty well, driving him around for almost three weeks," Petrocelli told me. "He was . . . well, down-home, like a lot of the rock stars I've driven. When she came along he'd get in back with her and they'd hit the bar, watch some TV. When he was alone he'd hop up front and talk my ear off. Money, it was always money. Was this house in Pacific Heights a good investment? Did I think they oughta buy a van for the help to use for running errands? Which restaurants did the 'in' people eat at? Should he get season tickets for the opera? I thought it was funny, a guy who was supposed to be so rich and smart asking *me* for advice. He struck me as very insecure. But hell, I liked the guy. He was kind of wide-eyed and innocent in his way, and American Express was honoring the charges."

I asked Petrocelli to look over the list of establishments to which Howard had made phone calls. He confirmed he'd driven the couple to most of them, with the exception of the yacht brokers and the car dealership in Walnut Creek. They had traveled as far afield as the Napa Valley for wine tasting, and Marnie had insisted he share their hotel-catered picnic lunch. No, they'd never met with friends; Petrocelli didn't think they'd known anyone in the city except the merchants with whom they had dealings.

Around the time I reached the bottom of the list other cases began to claim my attention. I'd been ensconced long enough in the cubbyhole under the stairs that All Souls's attorneys believed I was there to stay and began heaping my desk with tasks. They ranged from filing documents with the recorder's office to serving subpoenas to interviewing a member of the San Francisco Mime Troupe about an accident he'd witnessed—no simple matter, since his replies to my questions were in pantomime. I made some effort on the Morrison case when I could, but Marnie had stopped calling to ask for reports. The last time I spoke with her she sounded so demoralized that three days later I stopped in at her hotel to see how she was doing; her room was empty, and the manager told me she'd checked out. Checked out in the company of a handsome young man driving an old Honda.

Jon Howard?

When I reported this latest development to Hank, he didn't seem surprised. "I had a call earlier," he said. "Some guy looking for Marnie. I was with a client, so Ted gave him her number."

"Then it probably was Howard. But how'd he know to call you?"

Hank shrugged. "You've been asking around about him, leaving your card. He could have talked to the limo driver, the real-estate broker—anybody."

"And of course she went away with him."

"She said she still loved him."

"I wonder if he plans to pull the same scam in some other city."

"Doubtful; he doesn't have her American Express card to bankroll it."

"What d'you suppose will happen to her?"

Hank shook his head. "Let's hope her dreams come true—whatever they might be."

✧

A year later I added a follow-up note to the Marnie Morrison file: her parents, whom Hank had contacted following her disappearance, reported that they'd begun receiving periodic money orders for a hundred dollars apiece, mailed from various Bay Area cities. They were convinced they came from Marnie, in repayment of the credit-card charges. Since they'd long before paid the bill, they wanted to give Hank a message to pass on to their daughter, should she contact him.

The message was that they loved her, she was forgiven and always welcome at home. Hank was never able to tell her.

A couple of years after that I appended a newspaper clipping to the file: the Morrisons had been killed in a fire that swept the southern California canyon where their home was located. The article rehashed the bizarre scam their daughter and her boyfriend had perpetrated and mentioned the money orders. A further footnote to the story ran a while later: the money orders were now arriving at the office of the executor of the Morrisons's estate, earmarked "for my parents' favorite charity."

When I saw this last item, I was intrigued and wished I could take the time to locate Marnie. But in those early days at All Souls my caseload was heavy and soon I was caught up in other equally intriguing matters.   The Morrison case still nagged at me, though; it was my first—and last—open file.

MERRILL-GO-ROUND

I CLUNG to the metal pole as the man in the red coat and straw hat pushed the lever forward. The blue pig with the bedraggled whisk-broom tail on which I sat moved upward to the strains of "And the Band Played On." As the carousel picked up speed, the pig rose and fell with a rocking motion and the faces of the bystanders became a blur.

I smiled, feeling more like a child that a thirty-year-old woman, enjoying the stir of the breeze on my long black hair. When the red-coated attendant stepped onto the platform and began taking tickets I got down from the pig—reluctantly. I followed him as he weaved his way through the lions and horses, ostriches and giraffes, continuing our earlier conversation.

"It was only yesterday," I shouted above the din of the music. "The little girl came in alone, at about three-thirty. Are you sure you don't remember her?"

The old man turned, clinging to a camel for support. His was the weathered face of one who has spent most of his life outdoors. "I'm sure, Miss McCone. Look at them." He motioned around at the other riders. "This is Monday, and still the place is packed with kids. On a Sunday we get ten times as many. How do you expect me to remember one, out of all the rest?"

"Please, take another look at the picture." I rummaged in my shoulder bag. When I looked up the man was several yards away, taking a ticket from the rider of a purple toad.

I hurried after him and thrust the picture into the old man's hand. "Surely this child would stand out, with all that curly red hair."

His eyes, in their web of wrinkles, narrowed. He squinted thoughtfully at the photo, then handed it back to me. "No," he said. "She's a beautiful kid, and I'm sorry she's missing, but I didn't see her."

"Is there any way out of here except for the regular exit?"

He shook his head. "The other doors're locked. There's no way that kid could've left except through the exit. If her mother claims she got on the carousel and disappeared, she's crazy. Either the kid never came inside or the mother missed her when she left, that's all." Done collecting tickets, he leaned against a pony, his expression severe. "She's crazy to let the kid ride alone, too."

"Merrill is ten, over the age when they have to be accompanied."

"Maybe so, but when you've seen as many kids get hurt as I have, it makes you think twice about the regulations. They get excited, they forget to hang on. They roughhouse with each other. That mother was a fool to let her little girl ride alone."

Silently I agreed. The carousel was dangerous in many ways. Merrill Smith, according to her mother, Evelyn, had gotten on it the previous afternoon and never gotten off.

Outside the round blue building that housed the carousel I crossed to where my client sat on a bench next to the ticket booth. Although the sun was shining, Evelyn Smith had drawn her coat tightly around her thin frame. Her dull red hair fluffed in curls over her upturned collar, and her lashless blue eyes regarded me solemnly as I approached. I marveled, not for the first time since Evelyn had given me Merrill's picture, that this homely woman could have produced such a beautiful child.

"Does the operator remember her?" Evelyn asked eagerly.

"There were so many kids here that he couldn't. I'll have to locate the woman who was in the ticket booth yesterday."

"But I bought Merrill's ticket for her."

"Just the same, she may remember seeing her." I sat down on the cold stone bench. "Look, Evelyn, don't you think it would be better if you went to the police? They have the resources for dealing with disappearances. I'm only one person, and—"

"No!" Her already pallid face whitened until it seemed nearly translucent. "No, Sharon. I want you to find her."

"But I'm not sure where to go next. You've already contacted Merrill's school and her friends. I can question the ticket-booth woman and the personnel at the children's playground, but I'm afraid their answers will be more of the same. And in the meantime your little girl has been missing—"

"No. Please."

I was silent for a moment. When I looked up, Evelyn's pale lashless eyes were focused intensely on my face. There was something coldly analytical about her gaze that didn't go with my image of a distressed mother. Quickly she looked away.

"All right," I said, "I'll give it a try. But I need your help. Try to think of someplace she might've gone on her own."

Evelyn closed her eyes in thought. "Well, there's the house where we used to live. Merrill was happy there; the woman in the first-floor flat was really nice to her. She might've gone back there; she doesn't like the new apartment."

I wrote down the address. "I'll try there, then, but if I haven't come up with anything by nightfall, promise me you'll go to the police."

She stood, a small smile curving her lips. "I promise, but I don't think that will be necessary."

Thrusting her hands deep in her pockets, she turned and walked away; I watched her weave through the brightly colored futuristic shapes of the new children's playground. Why the sudden conviction that the case was all but solved? I wondered.

I remained on the bench for a few minutes. Traffic whizzed by on the other side of the eucalyptus grove that screened this southeast corner of Golden Gate Park, but I scarcely noticed it.

My client was a new subscriber to All Souls Legal Cooperative, the legal-services plan for which I was a private investigator. She'd come in this morning, paid her fee, and told her story to my boss, Hank Zahn. After she'd refused to allow him to call the police, he'd sent her to me.

It was Evelyn's unreasonable avoidance of the authorities that bothered me most about this case. Any normal middle-class mother—and she appeared to be just that—would have been on the phone to the Park Station minutes after Merrill's disappearance. But Evelyn had spent yesterday evening phoning her daughter's friends, then slept on the problem and contacted a lawyer. Why? What wasn't she telling me?

Well, I decided, when a client comes to you with a story that seems less than candid, the best place to start is with that client's own life. Perhaps the neighbor at the old address could shed some light on Evelyn's strange behavior.

✦

By three that afternoon, almost twenty-four hours after Merrill's disappearance, I was still empty-handed. The old neighbor hadn't been home, and when I questioned the remaining park personnel, they couldn't tell me anything. Once again I drove to Evelyn's former address, on Fell Street across from the park's Panhandle—a decaying area that had gone further downhill after the hippies moved out and the hardcore addicts moved in. The house was a three-flat Victorian with a fire escape snaking up its facade. I rang the bell of the downstairs flat.

A young woman in running shorts answered. I identified myself and said Evelyn Smith had suggested I talk with her. "Her little girl has disappeared, and she thought she might've come back here."

"Evelyn? I haven't heard from her since she moved. You say Merrill's missing?"

I explained about her disappearance from the carousel. "So you haven't seen her?"

"No. I can't imagine why she'd come here."

"Her mother said Merrill had been happy here, and that you were nice to her."

"Well, I was, but as far as her being happy . . . Her *un*happiness was why I went out of my way with her."

"Why was she unhappy?"

"The usual. Evvie and Bob fought all the time. Then he moved out, and a few months later Evvie found a smaller place."

Evvie hadn't mentioned a former husband. "What did they fight about?"

"Toward the end, everything, but mainly about the kid." The woman hesitated. "You know, that's an odd thing. I haven't thought of it in ages. How could two such homely people have such a beautiful child? Evvie—so awkward and skinny. And Bob, with that awful complexion. It was Merrill being so beautiful that caused their problems."

"How so?"

"Bob adored her. And Evvie was jealous. At first she accused Bob of spoiling Merrill, but later the accusations turned nasty—unnatural relationship, if you know what I mean. *Then* she started taking it out on the kid. I tried to help, but there wasn't much I could do. Evvie Smith acted like she hated her own child."

"Have you found anything?" Evelyn asked.

I stepped into a small apartment in a bland modern building north of the park. "A little." But I wasn't ready to go into it yet, so I added, "I'd like to see Merrill's room."

She nodded and took me down the hallway. The room was decorated in yellow, with big felt cut-outs of animals on the walls. The bed was neatly made up with ruffled quilts, and everything was in place except for a second-grade reader that lay open on the desk. Merrill, I thought, was an unnaturally orderly child.

Evelyn was staring at a grinning stuffed tiger on the bookcase under the window. "She's crazy about animals," she said softly. "That's why she likes the merry-go-round so much."

I ignored the remark, flipping through the reader and studying Merrill's name where she'd printed it in block letters on the flyleaf. Then I shut the book and said, "Why didn't you tell me about your former husband?"

"I didn't think it was important. We were divorced over two years ago."

"Where does he live?"

"Here in the city, on a houseboat at Mission Creek."

"And you didn't think that was important?"

She was silent.

"Is he the reason you didn't call the police?"

No reply.

"You think he's snatched Merrill, don't you?"

She made a weary gesture and turned away from me. "All right, yes. My ex-husband is a deputy district attorney. Very powerful, and he has a lot of friends on the police force. I don't stand a chance of getting Merrill back."

"So why didn't you tell me all this at the beginning?"

More silence.

"You knew that any lawyer would advise you to bring in the police and the courts. You knew an investigator would balk at snatching her back. So you couldn't come right out and ask me to do that. Instead, you wanted me to find out where she was on my own and bring her back to you."

"She's mine! She's supposed to be with me!"

"I don't like being used this way."

She turned, panic in her eyes. "Then you won't help me?"

"I didn't say that."

She needed help—more help, perhaps, than I could give her.

The late-afternoon fog was creeping through the redwood and eucalyptus groves of the park by the time I reached the carousel. It was shut for the night, but in the ticket booth a gray-haired woman was counting cash into a bank-deposit bag. The cashier I'd talked with earlier had told me her replacement came on in mid afternoon.

"Yes," she said in answer to my initial question, "I worked yesterday."

I showed her Merrill's picture. "Do you remember this little girl?"

The woman smiled. "You don't forget such a beautiful child. She and her mother used to come here every Sunday afternoon and ride the carousel. The mother still comes. She sits on that bench over there and watches the children and looks sad as can be. Did her little girl die?"

It was more or less what I'd expected to hear.

"No," I said, "she didn't die."

It was dark by the time I parked at Mission Creek. All I could make out were the shapes of the boats moored along the ramshackle pier. Light from their windows reflected off the black water of the narrow channel, and waves sloshed against the pilings as I hurried along, my footsteps echoing loudly on the rough planking. Bob Smith's boat was near the end, between two hulking fishing craft. A dim bulb by its door highlighted its peeling blue paint, but little else. I knocked and waited.

The tye lines of the fishing craft creaked as the boats rose and fell on the tide. Behind me I heard a scurrying sound. Rats, maybe. I glanced over my shoulder, suddenly seized by the eerie sensation of being watched. No one—whom I could see.

Light footsteps sounded inside the houseboat. The little girl who answered the door had curly red-gold hair and widely spaced blue eyes, her t-shirt was grimy and there was a rip in the knee of her jeans, but in spite of it she was beautiful. Beautiful and a few years older than in the picture I had tucked in my bag. That picture had been taken around the time she printed her name in block letters in the second-grade reader her mother kept in the neat-as-a-pin room Merrill no longer occupied.

I said, "Hello, Merrill. Is your dad home?"

"Uh, yeah. Can I tell him who's here?"

"I'm a friend of your mom."

Wrong answer; she stiffened. Then she whirled and ran inside. I waited.

Bob Smith had shaggy dark-red hair and a complexion pitted by acne scars. His body was stocky, and his calloused hands and work clothes told me Evelyn had lied about his job and friends on the police force. I introduced myself, showed him my license, and explained that his former wife had hired me. "She claims your daughter disappeared from the carousel in Golden Gate Park yesterday afternoon."

He blinked. "That's crazy. We were no place near the park yesterday."

Merrill reappeared, an orange cat draped over her shoulder. She peered anxiously around her father at me.

"Evelyn seems to think you took Merrill from the park," I said to Smith.

"Took? As in snatched?"

I nodded.

"Jesus Christ, what'll she come up with next?"

"You do have custody?"

"Since a little while after the divorce. Evvie was . . ." He glanced down at his daughter.

The cat chose that moment to wriggle free from her and dart outside. Merrill ran after it calling, "Tigger! *Tigger!*"

"Evvie was slapping Merrill around," Smith went on. "I had to do something about it. Evvie isn't . . . too stable. She's got more problems than I could deal with, but she won't get help for them. Deep down, she loves Merrill, but . . . What did she do—ask you to kidnap her?"

"Not exactly. The way she went about it was complicated."

"Of course. With Evvie, it would be."

The orange cat brushed against my ankles—prodigal returned. Behind me Merrill said, "Dad, I'm hungry."

Smith opened his mouth to speak, but suddenly his features went rigid with shock.

I felt a rush of air and started to turn. Merrill cried out. I pivoted and saw Evelyn. She was clutching Merrill around the shoulders, pulling her back onto the pier.

"Daddy!"

Smith started forward. "Evvie, what the hell . . .?"

Evelyn's pale face was a soapstone sculpture; her lips barely moved when she said, "Don't come any closer, Bob."

Smith pushed around me.

Evelyn drew back and her right hand came up, clutching a long knife.

I grabbed Smith's arm and stopped him.

Evelyn began edging toward the end of the pier, dragging Merrill with her. The little girl's feet scraped on the planking; her body was rigid, her small face blank with terror.

Smith said, "Christ, do something!"

I moved past him. Evelyn and Merrill were almost to the railing where the pier deadended above the black water.

"Evvie," I called, "please come back."

"No!"

"You've got no place to go."

"No place but the water."

Slowly I began moving toward them. "You don't want to go into it. It's cold and—"

"Stay back!" The knife glinted in the light from the boats.

"I'll stay right where I am. We'll talk."

She pressed against the rail, tightening her grip on Merrill. The little girl hadn't made a sound, but her fingers clawed at her mother's arm.

"We'll talk," I said again.

"About what?"

"The animals."

"The *animals*?"

"Remember when you told me how much Merrill loved the animals on the carousel? How she loved to ride them?"

". . . Yes."

"If you go into the water and take her with you, she'll never ride them again."

Merrill's fingers stopped their frantic clawing. Even in the dim light I could see comprehension flood her features. She said, "Mom, what *about* the animals?"

Evelyn looked down at her daughter's head.

"What about the zebra, Mom? And the ostrich? What about the blue pig?"

I began edging closer.

"I *miss* the animals. I want to go see them again."

"Your father won't let you."

"Yes, he will. He will if I ask him. We could go on Sundays, just like we used to."

Closer.

"Would you really do that, honey? Ask him?"

"Uh-huh."

My foot slipped on the planking. Evelyn started and glanced up. She raised the knife and looked toward the water. Lowered it and looked back at me. "If he says yes, will you come with us? Just you, not Bob?"

"Of course."

She sighed and let the knife clatter to the planking. Then she let go of Merrill. I moved forward and kicked the knife into the water. Merrill began running toward her father, who stood frozen in front of his houseboat.

Then she stopped, looking back at her mother. Hesitated and reached out her hand. Evelyn stared at her for a moment before she went over and clasped it.

I took Evelyn's other hand and we began walking along the pier. "Are you okay, Merrill?" I asked.

"I'm all right. And I meant what I said about going to ride the carousel. If Mom's going to be okay. She is, isn't she?"

"Yes. Yes, she will be—soon."

WILD MUSTARD

THE FIRST time I saw the old Japanese woman, I was having brunch at the restaurant above the ruins of San Francisco's Sutro Baths. The woman squatted on the slope, halfway between its cypress-covered top and the flooded ruins of the old bathhouse. She was uprooting vegetation and stuffing it into a green plastic sack.

"I wonder what she's picking," I said to my friend Greg.

He glanced out the window, raising one dark-blond eyebrow, his homicide cop's eye assessing the scene. "Probably something edible that grows wild. She looks poor; it's a good way to save grocery money."

Indeed the woman did look like the indigent old ladies one sometimes saw in Japantown; she wore a shapeless jacket and trousers, and her feet were clad in sneakers. A gray scarf wound around her head.

"Have you ever been down there?" I asked Greg, motioning at the ruins. The once-elegant baths had been destroyed by fire. All that remained now were crumbling foundations, half submerged in water. Seagulls swam on its glossy surface and, beyond, the surf tossed against the rocks.

"No. You?"

"No. I've always meant to, but the path is steep and I never have the right shoes when I come here."

Greg smiled teasingly. "Sharon, you'd let your private eye's instincts be suppressed for lack of hiking boots?"

I shrugged. "Maybe I'm not really that interested."

"Maybe not."

Greg often teased me about my sleuthing instincts, but in reality I suspected he was proud of my profession. An investigator for All Souls Cooperative, the legal services plan, I had dealt with a full range of cases—from murder to the mystery of a redwood hot tub that didn't hold water. A couple of the murders I'd solved had been in Greg's bailiwick, and this had given rise to both rivalry and romance.

In the months that passed my interest in the old Japanese woman was piqued. Every Sunday that we came there—and we came often because the restaurant was a favorite—the woman was scouring the slope, scouring for . . . what?

One Sunday in early spring Greg and I sat in our window booth, watching the woman climb slowly down the dirt path. To complement the season, she had changed her gray headscarf for bright yellow. The slope swarmed with people, enjoying the release from the winter rains. On the far barren side where no vegetation had taken hold, an abandoned truck leaned at a precarious angle at the bottom of the cliff near the baths. People scrambled down, inspected the old truck, then went to walk on the concrete foundations or disappeared into a nearby cave.

When the waitress brought our check, I said, "I've watched long enough; let's go down there and explore."

Greg grinned, reaching in his pocket for change. "But you don't have the right shoes."

"Face it, I'll never have the right shoes. Let's go. We can ask the old woman what she's picking."

He stood up. "I'm glad you finally decided to investigate her. She might be up to something sinister."

"Don't be silly."

He ignored me. "Yeah, the private eye side of you has finally won out. Or is it your Indian blood? Tracking instinct, papoose?"

I glared at him, deciding that for that comment he deserved to pay the check. My one-eighth Shoshone ancestry—which for some reason had emerged to make me a black-haired throwback in a family of Scotch-Irish towheads—had prompted Greg's dubbing me "papoose." It was a nickname I did not favor.

We left the restaurant and passed through the chain link fence to the path. A strong wind whipped my long hair about my head, and I stopped to tie it back. The path wound in switchbacks past huge gnarled geranium plants and through a thicket. On the other side of it, the woman squatted, pulling up what looked like weeds. When I approached she smiled at me, a gold tooth flashing.

"Hello," I said. "We've been watching you and wondered what you were picking."

"Many good things grow here. This month it is the wild mustard." She held up a sprig. I took it, sniffing its pungency.

"You should try it," she added. "It is good for you."

"Maybe I will." I slipped the yellow flower through my buttonhole and turned to Greg.

"Fat chance," he said. "When do you ever eat anything healthy?"

"Only when you force me."

"I have to. Otherwise it would be Hershey Bars day in and day out."

"So what? I'm not in bad shape." It was true; even on this steep slope I wasn't winded.

Greg smiled, his eyes moving appreciatively over me. "No, you're not."

We continued down toward the ruins, past a sign that advised us:

CAUTION!
CLIFF AND SURF AREA
EXTREMELY DANGEROUS
PEOPLE HAVE BEEN SWEPT
FROM THE ROCKS AND DROWNED

I stopped, balancing with my hand on Greg's arm, and removed my shoes. "Better footsore than swept away."

We approached the abandoned truck, following the same impulse that had drawn other climbers. Its blue paint was rusted and there had been a fire in the engine compartment. Everything, including the seats and steering wheel, had been stripped.

"Somebody even tried to take the front axle," a voice beside me said, "but the fire had fused the bolts."

I turned to face a friendly-looking sunbrowned youth of about fifteen. He wore dirty jeans and a torn t-shirt.

"Yeah," another voice added. This boy was about the same age; a wispy attempt at a mustache sprouted on his upper lip. "There's hardly anything left, and it's only been here a few weeks."

The first boy nodded. "People hang around here and drink. Late at night they get bored." He motioned at a group of unsavory-looking men who were sitting on the edge of the baths with a couple of six-packs.

"Destruction's a very popular sport these days." Greg watched the men for a moment with a professional eye, then touched my elbow. We skirted the ruins and went toward the cave. I stopped at its entrance and listened to the roar of the surf.

"Come on," Greg said.

I followed him inside, feet sinking into coarse sand which quickly became packed mud. The cave was really a tunnel, about eight feet high. Through crevices in the wall on the ocean side I saw spray flung high from the roiling waves at the foot of the cliff. It would be fatal to be swept down through those jagged rocks.

Greg reached the other end. I hurried as fast as my bare feet would permit and stood next to him. The precipitous drop to the sea made me clutch at his arm. Above us, rocks towered.

"I guess if you were a good climber you could go up, and then back to the road," I said.

"Maybe, but I wouldn't chance it. Like the sign says . . ."

"Right." I turned, suddenly apprehensive. At the mouth of the tunnel, two of the disreputable men stood, beer cans in hand. "Let's go, Greg."

If he noticed the edge to my voice, he didn't comment. We walked in silence through the tunnel. The men vanished. When we emerged into the sunlight, they were back with the others, opening fresh beers. The boys we had spoken with earlier were perched on the abandoned truck, and they waved at us as we started up the path.

And so, through the spring, we continued to come to our favorite restaurant on Sundays, always waiting for a window booth. The old Japanese woman exchanged her yellow headscarf for a red one. The abandoned truck remained nose down toward the baths, provoking much criticism of the Park Service. People walked their dogs on the slope. Children balanced precariously on the ruins, in spite of the warning sign. The men lolled about and drank beer. The teenaged boys came every week and often were joined by friends at the truck.

Then one Sunday, the old woman failed to show.

"Where is she?" I asked Greg, glancing at my watch for the third time.

"Maybe she's picked everything there is to pick down there."

"Nonsense. There's always something to pick. We've watched her for almost a year. That old couple are down there walking their German Shepherd. The teenagers are here. That young couple we talked to last week are over by the tunnel. Where's the old Japanese woman?"

"She could be sick. There's a lot of flu going round. Hell, she might have died. She wasn't all that young."

The words made me lose my appetite for my chocolate cream pie. "Maybe we should check on her."

Greg sighed. "Sharon, save your sleuthing for paying clients. Don't make everything into a mystery."

Greg had often accused me of allowing what he referred to as my "woman's intuition" to rule my logic—something I hated even more than references to my "tracking instinct." I knew it was no such thing; I merely gave free rein to the hunches that every good investigator follows. It was not a subject I cared to argue at the moment, however, so I let it drop.

But the next morning—Monday—I sat in the converted closet that served as my office at All Souls, still puzzling over the woman's absence. A file on a particularly boring tenants' dispute lay open on the desk in front of me. Finally I shut it and clattered down the hall of the big brown Victorian toward the front door.

"I'll be back in a couple of hours," I told Ted, our secretary.

He nodded, his fingers never pausing as he plied his new Selectric. I gave the typewriter a resentful glance. It, to my mind, was an extravagance, and the money it was costing could have been better spent on salaries. All Souls, which charged clients on a sliding scale according to their incomes, paid so low that several of the attorneys and support staff were compensated by living in free rooms on the second floor. I lived in a studio apartment in the Mission District. It seemed to get smaller every day.

Grumbling to myself, I went out to my car and headed for the restaurant above Sutro Baths.

"The old woman who gathers wild mustard on the cliff," I said to the cashier, "was she here yesterday?"

He paused. "I think so. Yesterday was Sunday. She's always here on Sunday. I noticed her about eight, when we opened up. She always comes early and stays until about two."

But she had been gone at eleven. "Do you know her? Do you know where she lives?"

He looked curiously at me. "No, I don't."

I thanked him and went out. Feeling foolish, I stood beside the Great Highway for a moment, then started down the dirt path, toward where the wild mustard grew. Halfway there I met the two teenagers. Why weren't they in school? Dropouts, I guessed.

They started by, avoiding my eyes like kids will do. I stopped them. "Hey, you were here yesterday, right?"

The mustached one nodded.

"Did you see the old Japanese woman who picks the weeds?"

He frowned. "Don't remember her."

"When did you get here?"

"Oh, late. Really late. There was this party Saturday night."

"I don't remember seeing her either," the other one said, "but maybe she'd already gone by the time we got here."

I thanked them and headed down toward the ruins.

A little further on, in the dense thicket through which the path wound, something caught my eye and I came to an abrupt stop. A neat pile of green plastic bags lay there, and on top of them was a pair of scuffed black shoes. Obviously she had come here on the bus, wearing her street shoes, and had only switched to sneakers for her work. Why would she leave without changing her shoes?

I hurried through the thicket toward the patch of wild mustard.

There, deep in the weeds, its color blending with their foliage, was another bag. I opened it. It was a quarter full of wilting mustard greens. She hadn't had much time to forage, not much time at all.

Seriously worried now, I rushed up to the Great Highway. From the phone booth inside the restaurant, I dialed Greg's direct line at the SFPD. Busy. I retrieved my dime and called All Souls.

"Any calls?"

Ted's typewriter rattled in the background. "No, but Hank wants to talk to you."

Hank Zahn, my boss. With a sinking heart, I remembered the conference we had had scheduled for half an hour ago. He came on the line.

"Where the hell are you?"

"Uh, in a phone booth."

"What I mean is, why aren't you here?"

"I can explain—"

"I should have known."

"What?"

"Greg warned me you'd be off investigating something."

"Greg? When did you talk to him?"

"Fifteen minutes ago. He wants you to call. It's important."

"Thanks!"

"Wait a minute—"

I hung up and dialed Greg again. He answered, sounding rushed. Without preamble, I explained what I'd found in the wild mustard patch.

"That's why I called you." His voice was unusually gentle. "We got word this morning."

"What word?" My stomach knotted.

"An identification on a body that washed up near Devil's Slide yesterday evening. Apparently she went in at low tide, or she would have been swept much further to sea."

I was silent.

"Sharon?"

"Yes, I'm here."

"You know how it is out there. The signs warn against climbing. The current is bad."

But I'd never, in almost a year, seen the old Japanese woman near the sea. She was always up on the slope, where her weeds grew. "When was low tide, Greg?"

"Yesterday? Around eight in the morning."

Around the time the restaurant cashier had noticed her and several hours before the teenagers had arrived. And in between? What had happened out there?

I hung up and stood at the top of the slope, pondering. What should I look for? What could I possibly find?

I didn't know, but I felt certain the old woman had not gone into the sea by accident. She had scaled those cliffs with the best of them.

I started down, noting the shoes and the bags in the thicket, marching resolutely past the wild mustard toward the abandoned truck. I walked all around it, examining its exterior and interior, but it gave me no clues. Then I started toward the tunnel in the cliff.

The area, so crowded on Sundays, was sparsely populated now. San Franciscans were going about their usual business, and visitors from the tour buses parked at nearby Cliff House were leery of climbing down here. The teenagers were the only other people in sight. They stood by the mouth of the tunnel, watching me. Something in their postures told me they were afraid. I quickened my steps.

The boys inclined their heads toward one another. Then they whirled and ran into the mouth of the tunnel.

I went after them. Again, I had the wrong shoes. I kicked them off and ran through the coarse sand. The boys were halfway down the tunnel.

One of them paused, frantically surveying a rift in the wall. I prayed that he wouldn't go that way, into the boiling waves below.

He turned and ran after his companion. They disappeared at the end of the tunnel.

I hit the hard-packed dirt and increased my pace. Near the end, I slowed and approached more cautiously. At first I thought the boys had vanished, but then I looked down. They crouched on a ledge below. Their faces were scared and young, so young.

I stopped where they could see me, and made a calming motion. "Come on back up," I said. "I won't hurt you."

The mustached one shook his head.

Simultaneously they glanced down. They looked back at me and both shook their heads.

I took a step forward. "Whatever happened, it couldn't have—" Suddenly I felt the ground crumble. My foot slipped and I pitched forward. I fell to one knee, my arms frantically searching for a support.

"Oh, God!" the mustached boy cried. "Not you too!" He stood up, swaying, his arms outstretched.

I kept sliding. The boy reached up and caught me by the arm. He staggered back toward the edge and we both fell to the hard rocky ground. For a moment, we both lay there panting. When I finally sat up, I saw we were inches from the sheer drop to the surf.

The boy sat up too, his scared eyes on me. His companion was flattened against the cliff wall.

"It's okay," I said shakily.

"I thought you'd fall just like the old woman," the boy beside me said.

"It was an accident, wasn't it?"

He nodded. "We didn't mean for her to fall."

"Were you teasing her?"

"Yeah. We always did, for fun. But this time we went too far. We took her purse. She chased us."

"Through the tunnel, to here."

"Yes."

"And then she slipped."

The other boy moved away from the wall. "Honest, we didn't mean for it to happen. It was just that she was so old. She slipped."

"We watched her fall," his companion said. "We couldn't do anything."

"What did you do with the purse?"

"Threw it in after her. She only had two dollars. Two lousy dollars." His voice held a note of wonder. "Can you imagine, chasing us all the way down here for two bucks?"

I stood up, carefully grasping the rock for support. "Okay," I said. "Let's get out of here."

They looked at each other and then down at the surf.

"Come on. We'll talk some more. I know you didn't mean for her to die. And you saved my life."

They scrambled up, keeping their distance from me. Their faces were pale under their tans, their eyes afraid. They were so young. To them, products of the credit-card age, fighting to the death for two dollars was inconceivable. And the Japanese woman had been so old. For her, eking out a living with the wild mustard, two dollars had probably meant the difference between life and death.

I wondered if they'd ever understand.

THE BROKEN MEN

DAWN was breaking when I returned to the Diablo Valley Pavilion. The softly rounded hills that encircled the amphitheater were edged with pinkish gold, but their slopes were still dark and forbidding. They reminded me of a herd of humpbacked creatures huddling together while they waited for the warmth of the morning sun; I could imagine them stretching and sighing with relief when its rays finally touched them.

I would have given a lot to have daylight bring me that same sense of relief, but I doubted that would happen. It had been a long, anxious night since I'd arrived here the first time, over twelve hours before. Returning was a last-ditch measure, and a long shot at best.

I drove up the blacktop road to where it was blocked by a row of posts and got out of the car. The air was chill; I could see my breath. Somewhere in the distance a lone bird called, and there was a faint, monotonous whine that must have had something to do with the security lights that topped the chain link fence, but the overall silence was heavy, oppressive. I stuffed my hands into the pockets of my too-light suede jacket and started toward the main entrance next to the box office.

As I reached the fence, a stocky, dark-haired man stepped out of the adjacent security shack and began unlocking the gate. Roy Canfield, night supervisor for the pavilion. He'd been dubious about what I'd suggested when I'd called him from San Francisco three quarters of an hour ago, but had said he'd be glad to cooperate if I came back out here. Canfield swung the gate open and motioned me through one of the turnstiles that had admitted thousands to the Diablo Valley Clown Festival the night before.

He said, "You made good time from the city."

"There's no traffic at five a. m. I could set my own speed limit."

The security man's eyes moved over me appraisingly, reminding me of how rumpled and tired I must look. Canfield himself seemed as fresh and alert as when I met him before last night's performance. But then, *he* hadn't been chasing over half the Bay Area all night, hunting for a missing client.

"Of course," I added, "I was anxious to get here and see if Gary Fitzgerald might still be somewhere on the premises. Shall we take a look around?"

Canfield looked as dubious as he'd sounded on the phone. He shrugged and said, "Sure we can, but I don't think you'll find him. We check every inch of the place after the crowd leaves. No way anybody could still be inside when we lock up."

There had been a note of reproach in his words, as if he thought I was questioning his ability to do his job. Quickly I said, "It's not that I don't believe you, Mr. Canfield. I just don't have any place else left to look."

He merely grunted and motioned for me to proceed up the wide concrete steps. They led uphill from the entrance to a promenade whose arms curved out in opposite directions around the edge of the amphitheater. As I recalled from the night before, from the promenade the lawn sloped gently down to the starkly modernistic concert shell. Its stage was wide—roughly ninety degrees of the circle—with wings and dressing rooms built back into the hill behind it. The concrete roof, held aloft by two giant pillars, was a curving slab shaped like a warped arrowhead, its tip pointing to the northeast, slightly off center. Formal seating was limited to a few dozen rows in a semi-circle in front of the stage; the pavilion had been designed mainly for the casual type of concert-goer who prefers to lounge on a blanket on the lawn.

I reached the top of the steps and crossed the promenade to the edge of the bowl, then stopped in surprise.

The formerly pristine lawn was now mounded with trash. Paper bags, cups and plates, beer cans and wine bottles, wrappers and crumpled programs and other indefinable debris were scattered in a crazy-quilt pattern. Trash receptacles placed at strategic intervals along the promenade had overflowed, their contents cascading to the ground. On the low wall between the formal seating and the lawn stood a monumental pyramid of Budweiser cans. In some places the debris was only thinly scattered, but in others it lay deep, like dirty drifted snow.

Canfield came up behind me, breathing heavily from the climb. "A mess, isn't it?" he said.

"Yes. Is it always like this after a performance?"

"Depends. Shows like last night, where you get a lot of young people, families, picnickers, it gets pretty bad. A symphony concert, that's different."

"And your maintenance crew doesn't come on until morning?" I tried not to sound disapproving, but allowing such debris to lie there all night was faintly scandalous to a person like me, who had been raised to believe that not washing the supper dishes before going to bed might just constitute a cardinal sin.

"Cheaper that way—we'd have to pay overtime otherwise. And the job's easier when it's light anyhow."

As if in response to Canfield's words, daylight—more gold than pink now—spilled over the hills in the distance, slightly to the left of the stage. It disturbed the shadows on the lawn below us, making them assume distorted forms. Black became gray, gray became white; short shapes elongated, others were truncated; fuzzy lines came into sharp focus. And with the light a cold wind came gusting across the promenade.

I pulled my jacket closer, shivering. The wind rattled the fall-dry leaves of the young poplar trees—little more than saplings—planted along the edge of the promenade. It stirred the trash heaped around the receptacles, then swept down the lawn, scattering debris in its wake. Plastic bags and wads of paper rose in an eerie dance, settled again as the breeze passed. I watched the undulation—a paper wave upon a paper sea—as it rolled toward the windbreak of cypress trees to the east.

Somewhere in the roiling refuse down by the barrier between the lawn and the formal setting I spotted a splash of yellow. I leaned forward, peering toward it. Again I saw the yellow, then a blur of blue and then a flicker of white. The colors were there, then gone as the trash settled.

Had my eyes been playing tricks on me in the half-light? I didn't think so, because while I couldn't be sure of the colors, I was distinctly aware of a shape that the wind's passage had uncovered—long, angular, solid-looking. The debris had fallen in a way that didn't completely obscure it.

The dread that I had held in check all night spread through me. After a frozen moment, I began to scramble down the slope toward the spot I'd been staring at. Behind me, Canfield called out, but I ignored him.

The trash was deep down by the barrier, almost to my knees. I waded through the bottles, cans, and papers, pushing their insubstantial mass aside, shoveling with my hands to clear a path. Shoveled until my fingers encountered something more solid . . . .

I dropped to my knees and scooped up the last few layers of debris, hurling it over my shoulder.

He lay on his back, wrapped in his bright yellow cape, his baggy blue plaid pants and black patent leather shoes sticking out from underneath it. His black beret was pulled halfway down over his white clown's face, hiding his eyes. I couldn't see the red vest that made up the rest of the costume because the cape covered it, but there were faint red stains on the iridescent fabric that draped across his chest.

I yanked the cape aside and touched the vest. It felt sticky, and when I pulled my hand away it was red too. I stared at it, wiped it off on a scrap of newspaper. Then I felt for a pulse in his carotid artery, knowing all the time what a futile exercise it was.

"Oh, Jesus!" I said. For a moment my vision blurred and there was a faint buzzing in my ears.

Roy Canfield came thrashing up behind me, puffing with exertion. "What . . . Oh, my God!"

I continued staring down at the clown; he looked broken, an object that had been used up and tossed on a trash heap. After a moment, I touched my thumb to his cold cheek, brushed at the white makeup. I pushed the beret back, looked at the theatrically blackened eyes. Then I tugged off the flaxen wig. Finally I pulled the fake bulbous nose away.

"Gary Fitzgerald?" Canfield asked.

I looked up at him. His moonlike face creased in concern. Apparently the shock and bewilderment I was experiencing showed.

"Mr. Canfield," I said, "this man is wearing Gary's costume, but it's not him. I've never seen him before in my life."

The man I was looking for was half of an internationally famous clown act, Fitzgerald and Tilby. The world of clowning, like any other artistic realm, has its various levels—from the lowly rodeo clown whose chief function is to keep bull riders from being stomped on, to circus clowns such as Emmett Kelly and universally acclaimed mimes like Marcel Marceau. Fitzgerald and Tilby were not far below Kelly and Marceau in the hierarchy and gaining on them every day. Instead of merely employing the mute body language of the typical clown, the two Britishers combined it with a subtle and sophisticated verbal comedy routine. Their fame had spread beyond aficionados of clowning in the late seventies when they had made a series of artful and entertaining television commercials for one of the Japanese auto makers, and subsequent ads for, among others, a major U. S. airline, one of the big insurance companies, and a computer firm had assured them of a place in the hearts of humor-loving Americans.

My involvement with Fitzgerald and Tilby came about when they agreed to perform at the Diablo Valley Clown Festival, a charity benefit co-sponsored by the Contra Costa County Chamber of Commerce and KSUN, the radio station where my friend Don Del Boccio works as a disk jockey. The team's manager, Wayne Kabalka, had stipulated only two conditions to their performing for free: that they be given star billing, and that they be provided with a bodyguard. Since Don was to be emcee of the show, he was in on all the planning, and when he heard of Kabalka's second stipulation, he suggested me for the job.

As had been the case ever since I'd bought a house near the Glen Park district the spring before, I was short of money at the time. And All Souls Legal Cooperative, where I am staff investigator, had no qualms about me moonlighting, provided it didn't interfere with any of the co-op's cases. Since things had been slack at All Souls during September, I felt free to accept. Bodyguarding isn't my idea of challenging work, but I had always enjoyed Fitzgerald and Tilby, and the idea of meeting them intrigued me. Besides, I'd be part of the festival and get paid for my time, rather than attending on the free pass Don had promised me.

So on that hot Friday afternoon in late September, I met with Wayne Kabalka in the lounge of KSUN's San Francisco studios. As radio stations go, KSUN is a casual operation, and the lounge gives full expression to this orientation. It is full of mismatched Salvation Army reject furniture, the posters on the wall are torn and tattered, and the big coffee table is always littered with rumpled newspapers, empty Coke cans and coffee cups, and overflowing ashtrays. On the particular occasion, it was also graced with someone's half-eaten Big Mac.

When Don and I came in, Wayne Kabalka was seated on the very edge of one of the lumpy chairs, looking as if he were afraid it might have fleas. He saw us and jumped as if one had just bitten him. *His* orientation was anything but casual: in spite of the heat he wore a tan three-piece suit that almost matched his mane of tawny hair, and a brown striped tie peeked over the V of his vest. Kabalka and his clients might be based in L. A., but he sported none of the usual Hollywoodish accoutrements—gold chains, diamond rings, or Adidas running shoes. Perhaps his very correct appearance was designed to be in keeping with his clients, Englishmen with rumored connections to the aristocracy.

Don introduced us and we all sat down, Kabalka again doing his balancing act on the edge of his chair. Ignoring me, he said to Don, "I didn't realize the bodyguard you promised would be female."

Don shot me a look, his shaggy eyebrows raised a fraction of an inch.

I said, "Please don't let my gender worry you, Mr. Kabalka. I've been a private investigator for nine years, and before that I worked for a security firm. I'm fully qualified for the job."

To Don he said, "But has she done this kind of work before?"

Again Don looked at me.

I said, "Bodyguarding is only one of any number of types of assignments I've carried out. And one of the most routine."

Kabalka continued looking at Don. "Is she licensed to carry firearms?"

Don ran his fingers over his thick black mustache, trying to hide the beginnings of a grin. "I think," he said, "that I'd better let the two of you talk alone."

Kabalka put out a hand as if to stay his departure, but Don stood. "I'll be in the editing room if you need me."

I watched him walk down the hall, his gait surprisingly graceful for such a tall, stocky man. Then I turned back to Kabalka. "To answer your question, sir, yes, I'm firearms qualified."

He made a sound halfway between clearing his throat and a grunt. "Uh . . . then you have no objection to carrying a gun on this assignment?"

"Not if it's necessary. But before I can agree to that, I'll have to know why you feel your clients require an armed bodyguard."

"I'm sorry?"

"Is there some threat to them that indicates the guard should be armed?"

"Threat. Oh . . . no."

"Extraordinary circumstances, then?"

"Extraordinary circumstances. Well, they're quite famous, you know. The TV commercials—you've seen them?"

I nodded.

"Then you know what a gold mine we have here. We're due to sign for three more within the month. Bank of America, no less. General Foods is getting into the act. Mobil Oil is hedging, but they'll sign. Fitzgerald and Tilby are important properties; they must be protected."

Properties, I thought, not people. "That still doesn't tell me what I need to know."

Kabalka laced his well-manicured fingers together, flexing them rhythmically. Beads of perspiration stood out on his high forehead; no wonder, wearing that suit in this heat. Finally he said, "In the past couple of years we've experienced difficulty with fans when the boys have been on tour. In a few instances, the crowds got a little too rough."

"Why haven't you hired a permanent bodyguard, then? Put one on staff?"

"The boys were opposed to that. In spite of their aristocratic connections, they're men of the people. They don't want to put any more distance between them and their public than necessary."

The words rang false. I suspected the truth of the matter was that Kabalka was too cheap to hire a permanent guard. "In a place like the Diablo Valley Pavilion, the security is excellent, and I'm sure that's been explained to you. It hardly seems necessary to hire an armed guard when the pavilion personnel—"

He made a gesture of impatience. "Their security force will have dozens of performers to protect, including a number who will be wandering throughout the audience during the show. My clients need extra protection."

I was silent, watching him. He shifted his gaze from mine, looking around with disproportionate interest at the tattered wall posters. Finally I said, "Mr. Kabalka, I don't feel you're being frank with me. And I'm afraid I can't take on this assignment unless you are."

He looked back at me. His eyes were a pale blue, washed out—and worried. "The people here at the station speak highly of you," he said after a moment.

"I hope so. They—especially Mr. Del Boccio—know me well." Especially Don; we'd been lovers for more than six months now.

"When they told me they had a bodyguard lined up, all they said was that you were a first-rate investigator. If I was rude earlier because I was surprised by your being a woman, I apologize."

"Apology accepted."

"I assume by first-rate, one of the things they mean is that you are discreet."

"I don't talk about my cases, if that's what you want to know."

He nodded. "All right, I'm going to entrust you with some information. It's not common knowledge, and you're not to pass it on, gossip about it to your friends—"

Kabalka was beginning to annoy me. "Get on with it, Mr. Kabalka. Or find yourself another bodyguard." Not easy to do, when the performers needed to arrive at the pavilion in about three hours.

His face reddened, and he started to retort, but bit back the words. He looked at his fingers, still laced together and pressing against one another in a feverish rhythm. "All right. Once again I apologize. In my profession you get used to dealing with such scumbags that you lose perspective—"

"You were about to tell me . . . ?"

He looked up, squared his shoulders as if he were about to deliver a state secret to an enemy agent. "All right. There *is* a reason why my clients require special security precautions at the Diablo Valley Pavilion. They—Gary Fitzgerald and John Tilby—are originally from Contra Costa County."

"What? I thought they were British."

"Yes, of course you did. And so does almost everyone else. It's part of the mystique, the selling power."

"I don't understand."

"When I discovered the young men in the early seventies, they were performing in a cheap club in San Bernardino, in the valley east of L. A. They were cousins, fresh off the farm—the ranch, in their case. Tilby's father was a dairy rancher in the Contra Costa hills, near Clayton; he raised both boys—Gary's parents had died. When old Tilby died, the ranch was sold and the boys ran off to seek fortune and fame. Old story. And they'd found the glitter doesn't come easy. Another old story. But when I spotted them in that club, I could see they were good. Damned good. So I took them on and made them stars."

"The oldest story of all."

"Perhaps. But now and then it does come true."

"Why the British background?"

"It was the early seventies. The mystique still surrounded such singing groups as the Rolling Stones and the Beatles. What could be better than a British clown act with aristocratic origins? Besides they were already doing the British bit in their act when I discovered them, and it worked."

I nodded, amused by the machinations of show business. "So you're afraid someone who once knew them might get too close out at the pavilion tonight and recognize them?"

"Yes."

"Don't you think it's a long shot—after all these years?"

"They left here in sixty-nine. People don't change all that much in sixteen years."

That depended, but I wasn't about to debate the point with him. "But what about makeup? Won't that disguise them?" Fitzgerald and Tilby wore traditional clown white-face.

"They can't apply the makeup until they're about to go on—in other circumstances, it might be possible to put it on earlier, but not in this heat."

I nodded. It all made sense. But why did I feel there was something Kabalka wasn't telling me about his need for an armed guard? Perhaps it was the way his eyes had once again shifted from mine to the posters on the walls. Perhaps it was the nervous pressing of his laced fingers. Or maybe it was only that sixth sense that sometimes worked for me; what I called a detective's instinct and others—usually men—labeled woman's intuition.

"All right, Mr. Kabalka," I said, "I'll take the job."

I checked in with Don to find out when I should be back at the studios, then went home to change clothing. We would arrive at the pavilion around four; the show—an early one because of its appeal for children—would begin at six. And I was certain that the high temperatures—sure to have topped 100 in the Diablo Valley—would not drop until long after dark. Chambray pants and an abbreviated tank top, with my suede jacket to put on in case of a late evening chill were all I would need. That, and my .38 special, tucked in the outer compartment of my leather shoulderbag.

By three o'clock I was back at the KSUN studios. Don met me in the lobby and ushered me to the lounge where Kabalka, Gary Fitzgerald, and John Tilby waited.

The two clowns were about my age—a little over thirty. Their British accents might once have been a put-on, but they sounded as natural now as if they'd been born and raised in London. Gary Fitzgerald was tall and lanky, with straight dark hair, angular features that stopped just short of being homely, and a direct way of meeting one's eye. John Tilby was shorter, sandy haired—the type we used to refer to in high school as "cute." His shy demeanor was in sharp contrast to his cousin's straightforward greeting and handshake. They didn't really seem like relatives, but then neither do I in comparison to my four siblings and numerous cousins. All of them resemble one another—typical Scotch-Irish towheads—but I have inherited all the characteristics of our one-eighth Shoshone Indian blood. And none of us are similar in personality or outlook, save for the fact we care a great deal about one another.

Wayne Kabalka hovered in the background while the introductions were made. The first thing he said to me was, "Did you bring your gun?"

"Yes, I did. Everything's under control."

Kabalka wrung his hands together as if he only wished it were true. Then he said, "Do you have a car, Ms. McCone?"

"Yes."

"Then I suggest we take both yours and mine. I have to swing by the hotel and pick up my wife and John's girlfriend."

"All right. I have room for one passenger in mine. Don, what about you? How are you getting out there?"

"I'm going in the Wonder Bus."

I rolled my eyes. The Wonder Bus was a KSUN publicity ploy—a former schoolbus painted in rainbow hues and emblazoned with the station call letters. It traveled to all KSUN-sponsored events, plus to anything else where management deemed its presence might be beneficial. As far as I was concerned, it was the most outrageous in a panoply of the station's efforts at self-promotion, and I took every opportunity to expound that viewpoint to Don. Surprisingly Don—a quiet classical musician who hated rock-and-roll and the notoriety that went with being a D. J.—never cringed at riding the Wonder Bus. If anything, he took almost a perverse pleasure in the motorized monstrosity.

Secretly, I had a shameful desire to hitch a ride on the Wonder Bus myself.

Wayne Kabalka looked somewhat puzzled at Don's statement. "Wonder Bus?" he said to himself. Then, "Well, if everyone's ready, let's go."

I turned to Don and smiled in a superior fashion. "Enjoy your ride."

We trooped out into the parking lot. Heat shimmered off the concrete paving. Kabalka pulled a handkerchief from his pocket and wiped his brow. "Is it always this hot here in September?"

"This is the month we have our true summer in the city, but no, this is unusual." I went over and placed my bag carefully behind the driver's seat of my MG convertible.

When John Tilby saw the car, his eyes brightened; he came over to it, running a hand along one of its battle-scarred flanks as if it were a brand new Porsche. "I used to have one of these."

"I'll bet it was in better shape than this one."

"Not really." A shadow passed over his face and he continued to caress the car in spite of the fact that the metal must be burning hot to the touch.

"Look," I said, "if you want to drive it out to the pavilion, I wouldn't mind being a passenger for a change."

He hesitated, then said wistfully, "That's nice of you, but I can't. . . I don't drive. But I'd like to ride along—"

"John!" Kabalka's voice was impatient behind us. "Come on, we're keeping Corinne and Nicole waiting."

Tilby gave the car a last longing glance, then shrugged. "I guess I'd better ride out with Wayne and the girls." He turned and walked off to Kabalka's new-looking Seville that was parked at the other side of the lot.

Gary Fitzgerald appeared next to me, a small canvas bag in one hand, garment bag in the other. "I guess you're stuck with me," he said, smiling easily.

"That's not such a bad deal."

He glanced back at Tilby and Kabalka, who were climbing into the Cadillac. "Wayne's right to make John go with him. Nicole would be jealous if she saw him with another woman." His tone was slightly resentful. Of Nicole? I wondered. Perhaps the girlfriend had caused dissension between the cousins.

"Corinne is Wayne's wife?" I asked as we got into the MG.

"Yes. You'll meet both of them at the performance; they're never very far away." Again I heard the undertone of annoyance.

We got onto the freeway and crossed the Bay Bridge. Commuter traffic out of the city was already getting heavy; people left their offices early on hot Fridays in September. I wheeled the little car in and out from lane to lane, bypassing trucks and A. C. Transit buses. Fitzgerald didn't speak. I glanced at him a couple of times to see if my maneuvering bothered him, but he sat slumped against the door, his almost-homely features shadowed with thought. Pre-performance nerves, possibly.

From the bridge, I took Highway 24 east toward Walnut Creek. We passed through the outskirts of Oakland, smog-hazed and sprawling— ugly duckling of the Bay Area. Sophisticates from San Francisco scorned Oakland, repeating Gertrude Stein's overused phrase. "There is no there there," but lately there'd been a current of unease in their mockery.

Oakland's thriving port had stolen much of the shipping business from her sister city across the Bay; her politics were alive and spirited; and on the site of former slums, sleek new buildings had been put up. Oakland was at last shedding her pinfeathers, and it made many of my fellow San Franciscans nervous.

From there we began the long ascent through the Berkeley Hills to the Caldecott Tunnel. The MG's aged engine strained as we passed lumbering trucks and slower cars, and when we reached the tunnel—three tunnels, actually, two of them now open to accommodate the eastbound commuter rush—I shot into the far lane. At the top of the grade midway through the tunnel, I shifted into neutral to give the engine a rest. Arid heat assailed us as we emerged; the temperature in San Francisco had been nothing compared to this.

The freeway continued to descend, past brown sun-baked hills covered with live oak and eucalyptus. Then houses began to appear, tucked back among the trees. The air was scented with dry leaves and grass and dust. Fire danger, I thought. One spark and those houses become tinderboxes.

The town of Orinda appeared on the right. On the left, in the center of the freeway, a BART train was pulling out of the station. I accelerated and tried to outrace it, giving up when my speedometer hit eighty and waving at some schoolkids who were watching from the train. Then I dropped back to sixty and glanced at Fitzgerald, suddenly embarrassed by my childish display. He was sitting up straighter and grinning.

I said, "The temptation was overwhelming."

"I know the impulse."

Feeling more comfortable now that he seemed willing to talk, I said, "Did Mr. Kabalka tell you that he let me in on where you're really from?"

For a moment he looked startled, then nodded.

"Is this the first time you've been back here in Contra Costa County?"

"Yes."

"You'll find it changed."

"I guess so."

"Mainly there are more people. Places like Walnut Creek and Concord have grown by leaps and bounds in the last ten years."

The county stretched east from the ridge of hills we'd just passed through toward Mount Diablo, a nearby 4,000-foot peak which had been developed into a 15,000-acre state park. On the north side of the county was the Carquinez Strait and its oil refineries, Suisun Bay, and the San Jaoquin River which separated Contra Costa from Sacramento County and the Delta. The city of Richmond and environs, to the west, were also part of the county, and their inclusion had always struck me as odd. Besides being geographically separated by the expanse of Tilden Regional Park and San Pablo Reservoir, the mostly black industrial city was culturally light years away from the rest of the suburban, upwardly mobile county. With the exception of a few towns like Pittsburgh or Antioch, this was affluent, fast-developing land; I supposed one day even those north-county backwaters would fall victim to expensive residential tracts and shopping centers full of upscale boutiques.

When Fitzgerald didn't comment, I said, "Does it look different to you?"

"Not really."

"Wait till we get to Walnut Creek. The area around the BART station is all highrise buildings now. They're predicting it will become an urban center that will eventually rival San Francisco."

He grunted in disapproval.

"About the only thing they've managed to preserve out here is the area around Mount Diablo. I suppose you know it from when you were a kid."

"Yes."

"I went hiking in the park last spring, during wildflower season. It was really beautiful that time of year. They say if you climb high enough you can see thirty-five counties from the mountain."

"This pavilion," Fitzgerald said, "is part of the state park?"

For a moment I was surprised, then realized that the pavilion hadn't been in existence in 1969, when he'd left home. "No, but near it. The land around it is relatively unspoiled. Horse and cattle ranches, mostly. They built it about eight years ago, after the Concord Pavilion became such a success. I guess that's one index of how this part of the Bay Area has grown, that it can support two concert pavilions."

He nodded. "Do they ever have concerts going at the same time at both?"

"Sure."

"It must really echo off these hills."

"I imagine you can hear it all the way to Port Chicago." Port Chicago was where the Naval Weapons Station was located, on the edge of Suisun Bay.

"Well, maybe not all the way to Chicago."

I smiled at the feeble joke, thinking that for a clown, Fitzgerald really didn't have much of a sense of humor, then allowed him to lapse back into his moody silence.

When we arrived at the pavilion, the parking lot was already crowded, the gates having opened early so people could picnic before the show started. An orange-jacketed attendant directed us to a far corner of the lot which had been cordoned off for official parking near the performers' gate. Fitzgerald and I waited in the car for about fifteen minutes, the late afternoon sun beating down on us, until Wayne Kabalka's Seville pulled up alongside. With the manager and John Tilby were two women: a chic, fortyish redhead, and a small dark-haired woman in her twenties. Fitzgerald and I got out and went to them.

The redhead was Corinne Kabalka; her strong handshake and level gaze made me like her immediately. I was less sure about Nicole Leland; the younger woman was beautiful, with short black hair sculpted close to her head and exotic features, but her manner was very cold. She nodded curtly when introduced to me, then took Tilby's arm and led him off toward the performers' gate. The rest of us trailed behind.

Security was tight at the gate. We met Roy Canfield, who was personally superintending the check-in, and each of us was issued a pass. No one, Canfield told us, would be permitted backstage or through the gate without showing his pass. Security personnel would also be stationed in the audience to protect those clowns who, as part of the show, would be performing out on the lawn.

We were then shown to a large dressing room equipped with a couch, a folding card table and chairs. After everyone was settled there I took Kabalka aside and asked him if he would take charge of the group for about fifteen minutes while I checked the layout of the pavilion. He nodded distractedly and I went out front.

Stage personnel were scurrying around, setting up sound equipment and checking the lights. Don had already arrived, but he was conferring with one of the other KSUN jocks and didn't look as if he could be disturbed. The formal seating was empty, but the lawn was already crowded. People lounged on blankets, passing around food, drink and an occasional joint. Some of the picnics were elaborate—fine china, crystal wineglasses, ice buckets, and in one case, a set of lighted silver candelabra; others were of the paper-plate and plastic-cup variety. I spotted the familiar logos of Kentucky Fried Chicken and Jack-in-the-Box here and there. People called to friends, climbed up and down the hill to the rest-room and refreshment facilities, dropped by other groups' blankets to see what goodies they had to trade. Children ran through the crowd, an occasional frisbee sailed through the air. I noticed a wafting trail of irides-cent soap bubbles, and my eyes followed it to a young woman in a red halter top who was blowing them, her face aglow with childlike pleasure.

For a moment I felt a stab of envy, realizing that if I hadn't taken on this job I could be out front, courtesy of the free pass Don had promised me. I could have packed a picnic, perhaps brought along a woman friend, and Don could have dropped by to join us when he had time. But instead, I was bodyguarding a pair of clowns who—given the pavilion's elaborate security measures—probably didn't need me. And in addition to Fitzgerald and Tilby, I seemed to be responsible for an entire group. I could see why Kabalka might want to stick close to his clients, but why did the wife and girlfriend have to crowd into what was already a stuffy, hot dressing room? Why couldn't they go out front and enjoy the performance? It complicated my assignment, having to contend with an entourage, and the thought of those complications made me grumpy.

The grumpiness was probably due to the heat, I decided. Shrugging it off, I familiarized myself with the layout of the stage and the points at which someone could gain access. Satisfied that pavilion security could deal with any problems that might arise there, I made my way through the crowd—turning down two beers, a glass of wine, and a pretzel—and climbed to the promenade. From there I studied the stage once more, then raised my eyes to the sun-scorched hills to the east.

The slopes were barren, save for an occasional out-cropping of rock and live oak trees, and on them a number of horses with riders stood. They clustered together in groups of two, four, six, and even at this distance I sensed they shared the same camaraderie as the people on the lawn. They leaned toward one another, gestured, and occasionally passed objects back and forth—perhaps they were picnicking too.

What a great way to enjoy a free show, I thought. The sound, in this natural echo chamber, would easily carry to where the watchers were stationed. How much more peaceful it must be on the hill, free of crowds and security measures. Visibility, however, would not be very good . . . .

And then I saw a flare of reddish light and glanced over to where a lone horseman stood under the sheltering branches of a live oak. The light flashed again, and I realized he was holding binoculars which had caught the setting sun. Of course—with binoculars or opera glasses, visibility would not be bad at all. In fact, from such a high vantage point it might even be better than from many points on the lawn. My grumpiness returned; I'd have loved to be mounted on a horse on that hillside.

Reminding myself that I was here on business that would pay for part of the new bathroom tile, I turned back toward the stage, then started when I saw Gary Fitzgerald. He was standing on the lawn not more than six feet from me, looking around with one hand forming a visor over his eyes. When he saw me he started too, and then waved.

I rushed over to him and grabbed his arm. "What are you doing out here? You're supposed to stay backstage!"

"I just wanted to see what the place looks like."

"Are you out of your mind? Your manager is paying good money for me to see that people stay away from you. And here you are wandering through the crowd—"

He looked away, at a family on a blanket next to us. The father was wiping catsup from the smaller child's hands. "No one's bothering me."

"That's not the point." Still gripping his arm, I began steering him toward the stage. "Someone might recognize you, and that's precisely what Kabalka hired me to prevent."

"Oh, Wayne's being a worrywart about that. No one's going to recognize anybody after all this time. Besides, it's common knowledge in the trade that we're not what we're made out to be."

"In the trade, yes. But your manager's worried about the public." We got to the stage, showed our passes to the security guard, and went back to the dressing room.

At the door Fitzgerald stopped. "Sharon, would you mind not mentioning my going out there to Wayne?"

"Why shouldn't I?"

"Because it would only upset him, and he's nervous enough before a performance. Nothing happened—except that I was guilty of using bad judgment."

His smile was disarming, and I took the words as an apology. "All right. But you'd better go get into costume. There's only half an hour before the grand procession begins."

✧

The next few hours were uneventful. The grand procession—a parade through the crowd in which all the performers participated—went off smoothly. After they returned to the dressing room, Fitzgerald and Tilby removed their makeup—which was already running in the intense heat—and the Kabalkas fetched supper from the car—deli food packed in hampers by their hotel. There was a great deal of grumbling about the quality of the meal, which was not what one would have expected of the St. Francis, and Fitzgerald teased the others because he was staying at a small bed-and-breakfast in the Haight-Ashbury which had better food at half the price.

Nicole said, "Yes, but your hotel probably has bed-bugs."

Fitzgerald glared at her, and I was reminded of the disapproving tone of voice in which he'd first spoken of her. "Don't be ignorant. Urban chic has come to the Haight-Ashbury."

"Making it difficult for you to recapture your misspent youth there, no doubt."

"Nicole," Kabalka said.

"That was your intention in separating from the rest of us, wasn't it, Gary?" Nicole added.

Fitzgerald was silent.

"Well, Gary?"

He glanced at me. "You'll have to excuse us for letting our hostilities show."

Nicole smiled nastily. "Yes, when a man gets to a certain age, he must try to recapture—"

"Shut up, Nicole," Kabalka said.

She looked at him in surprise, then picked up her sandwich and nibbled daintily at it. I could understand why she had backed off; there was something in Kabalka's tone that said he would put up with no more from her.

After the remains of supper were packed up, everyone settled down. None of them displayed the slightest inclination to go out front and watch the show. Kabalka read—one of those slim volumes that claim you can make a financial killing in spite of the world economic crisis. Corinne crocheted—granny squares. Fitzgerald brooded. Tilby played solitaire. Nicole fidgeted. And while they engaged in these activities, they also seemed to be watching one another. The covert vigilant atmosphere puzzled me; after a while I concluded that maybe the reason they all stuck together was that each was afraid to leave the others alone. But why?

Time crawled. Outside, the show was going on; I could hear music, laughter, and—occasionally—Don's enthusiastic voice as he introduced the acts. Once more I began to regret taking this job.

After a while Tilby reshuffled the cards, and slapped them on the table. "Sharon, do you play gin rummy?"

"Yes."

"Good. Let's have a few hands."

Nicole frowned and made a small sound of protest.

Tilby said to her, "I offered to teach you. It's not my fault you refused."

I moved my chair over to the table and we played in silence for a while. Tilby was good, but I was better. After about half an hour, there was a roar from the crowd and Tilby raised his head. "Casey O'Connell must be going on."

"Who?" I said.

"One of our more famous circus clowns."

"There is really quite a variety among the performers in your profession, isn't there?"

"Yes, and quite a history: clowning is an old and honored art. They had clowns back in ancient Greece. Wandering entertainers, actually, who'd show up at a wealthy household and tell jokes, do acrobatics, or juggle for the price of a meal. Then in the Middle Ages, mimes appeared on the scene."

"That long ago?"

"Uh-huh. They were the cream of the crop back then. Most of the humor in the Middle Ages was kind of basic; they loved buffoons, jesters, simpletons, that sort of thing. But they served the purpose of making people see how silly we really are."

I took the deuce he'd just discarded, then lay down my hand to show I had gin. Tilby frowned and slapped down his cards; nothing matched. Then he grinned. "See what I mean—I'm silly to take this game so seriously."

I swept the cards together and began to shuffle. "You seem to know a good bit about the history of clowning."

"Well, I've done some reading along those lines. You've heard the term *commedia dell'arte*?"

"Yes."

"It appeared in the late 1500s, an Italian brand of the traveling comedy troupe. The comedians always played the same role—a Harlequin or a Pulcinella or a Pantalone. Easy for the audience to recognize."

"I know what a Harlequin is, but what are the other two?"

"Pantalone is a personification of the overbearing father figure. A stubborn, temperamental old geezer. Pulcinella was costumed all in white, usually with a dunce's cap; he assumed various roles in the comedy—lawyer, doctor, servant, whatever—and was usually greedy, sometimes pretty coarse. One of his favorite tricks was urinating onstage."

"Good Lord!"

"Fortunately we've become more refined since then. The British contributed a lot, further developing the Punch and Judy shows. And of course the French had their Figaro. The Indians created the *Vidushaka*—a form of court jester. The entertainers at the Chinese court were known as *Chous*, after the dynasty in which they originated. And Japan has a huge range of comic figures appearing in their *Kyogen* plays—the humorous counterpart of the *Noh* play."

"You really have done your homework."

"Well, clowning's my profession. Don't you know about the history of yours?"

"What I know is mostly fictional; private investigating is more interesting in books than in real life, I'm afraid."

"Gin." Tilby spread his cards on the table. "Your deal. But back to what I was saying, it's the more contemporary clowns that interest me. And I use the term 'clown' loosely."

"How so?"

"Well, do you think of Will Rogers as a clown?"

"No."

"I do. And Laurel and Hardy, Flip Wilson, Mae West, Woody Allen, Lucille Ball. As well as the more traditional figures like Emmett Kelly, Charlie Chaplin, and Marceau. There's a common denominator among all these people: they're funny and, more important, they all make the audience take a look at humanity's foibles. They're as much descended from those historical clowns as the white-faced circus performer."

"The whiteface is the typical circus clown, right?"

"Well, there are three basic types. Whiteface is your basic slaphappy fellow. The Auguste—who was created almost simultaneously in Germany and France—usually wears pink or blackface and is the one you see falling all over himself in the ring, often sopping wet from having buckets of water thrown at him. The Grotesque is usually a midget or a dwarf, or has some other distorted feature. And there are performers whom you can't classify because they have created something unique, such as Kelly's Weary Willie, or Russia's Popov, who is such an artist that he doesn't even need to wear makeup."

"It's fascinating. I never realized there was such variety. Or artistry."

"Most people don't. They think clowning is easy, but a lot of the time it's just plain hard work. Especially when you have to go on when you aren't feeling particularly funny." Tilby's mouth drooped as he spoke, and I wondered if tonight was one of those occasions for him.

I pulled a trey and said, "Gin," then tossed my hand on the table as he shuffled and dealt. We fell silent once more. The sounds of the show went on, but the only noise in the dressing room was the slap of the cards on the table. It was uncomfortably hot. Moths fluttered around the glaring bare bulbs of the dressing tables. At about ten-thirty, Fitzgerald stood up.

"Where are you going?" Kabalka said.

"The men's room. Do you mind?"

I said, "I'll go with you."

Fitzgerald smiled faintly. "Really, Sharon that's above and beyond the call of duty."

"I mean, just to the door."

He started to protest, then shrugged and picked up his canvas bag.

Kabalka said, "Why are you taking that?"

"There's something in it I need."

"What?"

"For Christ's sake, Wayne!" He snatched up his yellow cape, flung it over one shoulder.

Kabalka hesitated. "All right, go. But Sharon goes with you."

Fitzgerald went out into the hall and I followed. Behind me, Nicole said, "Probably Maalox or something like that for his queasy stomach. You can always count on Gary to puke at least once before a performance."

Kabalka said, "Shut up, Nicole."

Fitzgerald started off, muttering, "Yes, we're one big happy family."

I followed him and took up a position next to the men's room door. It was ten minutes before I realized he was taking too long a time, and when I did I asked one of the security guards to go in after him. Fitzgerald had vanished, apparently through an open window high off the floor—a trash receptacle had been moved beneath it, which would have allowed him to climb up there. The window opened onto the pavilion grounds rather than outside of the fence, but from there he could have gone in any one of a number of directions—including out the performers' gate.

From then on, all was confusion. I told Kabalka what had happened and again left him in charge of the others. With the help of the security personnel, I combed the backstage area—questioning the performers, stage personnel, Don and the other people from KSUN. No one had seen Fitzgerald. The guards in the audience were alerted, but no one in baggy plaid pants, a red vest, and a yellow cape was spotted. The security man on the performers' gate knew nothing; he'd only come on minutes ago, and the man he had relieved had left the grounds for a break.

Fitzgerald and Tilby were to be the last act to go on—at midnight, as the star attraction. As the hour approached, the others in their party grew frantic and Don and the KSUN people grew grim. I continued to search systematically. Finally I returned to the performers' gate; the guard had returned from his break and Kabalka had buttonholed him. I took over the questioning. Yes, he remembered Gary Fitzgerald. He'd left at about ten thirty, carrying his yellow cape and a small canvas bag. But wait—hadn't he returned just a few minutes ago, before Kabalka had come up and started asking questions? But maybe that wasn't the same man, there had been something different . . . .

Kabalka was on the edge of hysterical collapse. He yelled at the guard and only confused him further. Maybe the man who had just come in had been wearing a red cape . . . maybe the pants were green rather than blue . . . no, it wasn't the same man after all . . . .

Kabalka yelled louder, until one of the stage personnel told him to shut up, he could be heard out front. Corinne appeared and momentarily succeeded in quieting her husband. I left her to deal with him and went back to the dressing room. Tilby and Nicole were there. His face was pinched, white around the mouth. Nicole was pale and—oddly enough—had been crying. I told them what the security guard had said, cautioned them not to leave the dressing room.

As I turned to go, Tilby said, "Sharon, will you ask Wayne to come in here?"

"I don't think he's in any shape—"

"Please, it's important."

"All right. But why?"

Tilby looked at Nicole. She turned her tear-streaked face away toward the wall.

He said, "We have a decision to make about the act."

"I hardly think so. It's pretty clear cut. If Gary doesn't turn up, you simply can't go on."

He stared bleakly at me. "Just ask Wayne to come in here."

Of course the act didn't go on. The audience was disappointed, the KSUN people were irate, and the Fitzgerald and Tilby entourage were grim—a grimness that held a faint undercurrent of tightly-reined panic. No one could shed any light on where Fitzgerald might have gone, or why—at least, if anyone had suspicions, he was keeping them to himself. The one thing everyone agreed on was that the disappearance wasn't my fault; I hadn't been hired to prevent treachery within the ranks. I myself wasn't so sure of my lack of culpability.

So I'd spent the night chasing around, trying to find a trace of Fitzgerald. I'd gone to San Francisco: to his hotel in the Haight-Ashbury, to the St. Francis where the rest of the party were staying, even to the KSUN studios. Finally I went back to the Haight, to a number of the after-hours place I knew of, in the hopes Fitzgerald was there recapturing his youth, as Nicole had termed it earlier. And I still hadn't found a single clue to his whereabouts.

Until now. I hadn't located Gary Fitzgerald, but I'd found his clown costume. On another man. A dead man.

After the county sheriff's men had finished questioning me and said I could go, I decided to return to the St. Francis and talk to my clients once more. I wasn't sure if Kabalka would want me to keep searching for Fitzgerald now, but he—and the others—deserved to hear from me about the dead man in Gary's costume, before the authorities contacted them. Besides, there were things bothering me about Fitzgerald's disappearance, some of them obvious, some vague. I hoped talking to Kabalka and company once more would help me bring the vague ones into more clear focus.

It was after seven by the time I had parked under Union Square and entered the hotel's elegant dark-paneled lobby. The few early risers who clustered there seemed to be tourists, equipped with cameras and anxious to get on with the day's adventures. A dissipated-looking couple in evening clothes stood waiting for an elevator, and a few yards away in front of the first row of expensive shops, a maid in the hotel uniform was pushing a vacuum cleaner with desultory strokes. When the elevator came, the couple and I rode up in silence; they got off at the floor before I did.

Corinne Kabalka answered my knock on the door of the suite almost immediately. Her eyes were deeply shadowed, she wore the same white linen pantsuit—now severely rumpled—that she'd had on the night before, and in her hand she clutched her crocheting. When she saw me, her face registered disappointment.

"Oh," she said, "I thought . . ."

"You hoped it would be Gary."

"Yes. Well, any of them, really."

"Them? Are you alone?"

She nodded and crossed the sitting room to a couch under the heavily-draped windows, dropping into it with a sigh and setting down the crocheting.

"Where did they go?"

"Wayne's out looking for Gary. He refuses to believe he's just . . . vanished. I don't know where John is, but I suspect he's looking for Nicole."

"And Nicole?""

Anger flashed in her tired eyes. "Who knows?"

I was about to ask her more about Tilby's unpleasant girlfriend when a key rattled in the lock, and John and Nicole came in. His face was pulled into taut lines, reflecting a rage more sustained than Corinne's brief flare-up. Nicole looked haughty, tight-lipped, and a little defensive.

Corinne stood. "Where have you two been?"

Tilby said, "*I* was looking for Nicole. It occurred to me that we didn't want to lose another member of this happy party."

Corinne turned to Nicole. "And you?"

The younger woman sat on a spindly chair, studiously examining her plum-colored fingernails. "I was having breakfast."

"Breakfast?"

"I was hungry, after that disgusting supper last night. So I went around the corner to a coffee shop—"

"You could have ordered from room service. Or eaten downstairs where John could have found you more easily."

"I needed some air."

Now Corinne drew herself erect. "Always thinking of Nicole, aren't you?"

"Well, what of it? Someone around here has to act sensibly."

In their heated bickering, they all seemed to have forgotten I was there. I remained silent, taking advantage of the situation; one could learn very instructive things by listening to people's unguarded conversations.

Tilby said, "Nicole's right, Corinne. We can't all run around like Wayne, looking for Gary when we have no idea where to start."

"Yes, *you* would say that. You never did give a damn about him, or anyone. Look how you stole Nicole from your own cousin—"

"Good God, Corinne! You can't *steal* one person from another."

"You did. You stole her and then you wrecked—"

"Let's not go into this, Corinne. Especially in front of an outsider." Tilby motioned at me.

Corinne glanced my way and colored. "I'm sorry, Sharon. This must be embarrassing for you."

On the contrary, I wished they would go on. After all, if John had taken Nicole from his cousin, Gary would have had reason to resent him—perhaps even to want to destroy their act.

I said to Tilby, "Is that the reason Gary was staying at a different hotel—because of you and Nicole?"

He looked startled.

"How long have you two been together?" I asked.

"Long enough." He turned to Corinne. "Wayne hasn't come back or called, I take it?"

"I've heard nothing. He was terribly worried about Gary when he left."

Nicole said, "He's terribly worried about the TV commercials and his cut of them."

"Nicole!" Corinne whirled on her.

Nicole looked up, her delicate little face all innocence. "You know it's true. All Wayne cares about is money. I don't know why he's worried, though. He can always get someone to replace Gary. Wayne's good at doing that sort of thing—"

Corinne stepped forward and her hand lashed out at Nicole's face, connecting with a loud smack. Nicole put a hand to the reddening stain on her cheekbone, eyes widening; then she got up and ran from the room. Corinne watched her go, satisfaction spreading over her handsome features. When I glanced at Tilby, I was surprised to see he was smiling.

"Round one to Corinne," he said.

"She had it coming." The older woman went back to the couch and sat, smoothing her rumpled pantsuit. "Well, Sharon, once more you must excuse us. I assume you came here for a reason?"

"Yes." I sat down in the chair Nicole had vacated and told them about the dead man at the pavilion. As I spoke, the two exchanged glances that were at first puzzled, then worried, and finally panicky.

When I had finished, Corinne said, "But who on earth can the man in Gary's costume be?" The words sounded theatrical, false.

"The sheriff's department is trying to make an identification. Probably his fingerprints will be on file somewhere. In the meantime, there are a few distinctive things about him which may mean something to you or John."

John sat down next to Corinne. "Such as?"

"The man had been crippled, probably a number of years ago, according to the man from the medical examiner's officer. One arm was bent badly, and he wore a lift to compensate for a shortened leg. He would have walked with a limp."

The two of them looked at each other, and then Tilby said—too quickly—"I don't know anyone like that."

Corinne also shook her head, but she didn't meet my eyes.

I said, "Are you sure?"

"Of course we're sure." There was an edge of annoyance in Tilby's voice.

I hesitated, then went on, "The sheriff's man who examined the body theorizes that the dead man may have been from the countryside around there, because he had fragments of madrone and chaparral leaves caught in his shoes, as well as foxtails in the weave of his pants. Perhaps he's someone you knew when you lived in the area?"

"No, I don't remember anyone like that."

"He was about Gary's height and age, but with sandy hair. He must have been handsome once, in an elfin way, but his face was badly scarred."

"I said, I don't know who he is."

I was fairly certain he was lying, but accusing him would get me nowhere.

Corinne said, "Are you sure the costume was Gary's? Maybe this man was one of the other clowns and dressed similarly."

"That's what I suggested to the sheriff's man, but the dead man had Gary's pass in his vest pocket. We all signed our passes, remember?"

There was a long silence. "So what you're saying," Tilby finally said, "is that Gary *gave* his pass and costume to his man."

"It seems so."

"But why?"

"I don't know. I'd hoped you could provide me with some insight."

They both stared at me. I noticed Corinne's face had gone quite blank. Tilby was as white-lipped as when I'd come upon him and Nicole in his dressing room shortly after Fitzgerald's disappearance.

I said to Tilby, "I assume you each have more than one change of costume."

It was Corinne who answered. "We brought three on this tour. But I had the other two sent out to the cleaner when we arrived in San Francisco . . . Oh!"

"What is it?"

"I just remembered. Gary asked me about the other costumes yesterday morning. He called from that hotel where he was staying. And he was very upset when I told him they would be at the cleaner until this afternoon."

"So he planned it all along. Probably he hoped to give his extra costume to the man, and when he found he couldn't, he decided to make a switch." I remembered Fitzgerald's odd behavior immediately after we'd arrived at the pavilion—his sneaking off into the audience when he'd been told to stay backstage. Had he had a confederate out there? Someone to hand the things to? No. He couldn't have turned over either the costume or the pass to anyone, because the clothing was still backstage, and he'd needed his pass when we returned to the dressing room.

Tilby suddenly stood up. "The son of a bitch! After all we've done—"

"John!" Corinne touched his elbow with her hand.

"John," I said, "why was your cousin staying at the hotel in the Haight?"

He looked at me blankly for a moment. "What? Oh, I don't know. He claimed he wanted to see how it had changed since he'd lived there."

"I thought you grew up together on your father's ranch near Clayton and then went to Los Angeles."

"We did. Gary lived on the Haight before we left the Bay Area."

"I see. Now, you say he 'claimed' that was the reason. Was there something else?"

Tilby was silent, then looked at Corinne. She shrugged.

"I guess," he said finally, "he'd had about all he could take of us. As you may have noticed, we're not exactly a congenial group lately."

"Why is that?"

"Why is what?"

"That you're all at odds? It hasn't always been this way, has it?"

This time Tilby shrugged. Corinne was silent, looking down at her clasped hands.

I sighed, silently empathizing with Fitzgerald's desire to get away from these people. I myself was sick of their bickering, lies, backbiting, and evasions. And I knew I could get nowhere with them—at least not now. Better to wait until I could talk with Kabalka, see if he were willing to keep on employing me. Then, if he was, I could start fresh.

I stood up, saying, "The Contra Costa authorities will be contacting you. I'd advise you to be as frank as possible with them." To Corinne, I added, "Wayne will want a personal report from me when he comes back; ask him to call me at home." I took out a card with both my All Souls and home number, laid it on the coffee table, and started for the door.

As I let myself out, I glanced back at them. Tilby stood with his arms folded across his chest, looking down at Corinne. They were as still as statues, their eyes locked, their expressions bleak and helpless.

Of course, by the time I got home to my brown-shingled cottage the desire to sleep had left me. It was always that way when I harbored nagging unanswered questions. Instead of going to bed and forcing myself to rest, I made coffee and took a cup of it out on the back porch to think.

It was a sunny, clear morning and already getting hot. The neighborhood was Saturday noisy: to one side, my neighbors, the Halls, were doing something to their backyard shed that involved a lot of hammering; on the other side, the Curleys' dog was barking excitedly. Probably, I thought, my cat was deviling the dog by prancing along the top of the fence, just out of his reach. It was Watney's favorite game lately.

Sure enough, in a few minutes there was a thump as Wat dropped down from the fence onto an upturned half barrel I'd been meaning to make into a planter. His black-and-white spotted fur was full of foxtails; undoubtedly he'd been prowling around in the weeds at the back of the Curleys' lot.

"Come here, you," I said to him. He stared at me, tail swishing back and forth. "Come here!" He hesitated, then galloped up. I managed to pull one of the foxtails from the ruff of fur over his collar before he trotted off again, his belly swaying pendulously, a great big horse of a cat . . . .

I sat staring at the foxtail, rolling it between my thumb and forefinger, not really seeing it. Instead, I pictured the hills surrounding the pavilion as I'd seen them the night before. The hills that were dotted with oak and madrone and chaparral . . . that were sprinkled with people on horses . . . where a lone horseman had stood under the sheltering branches of a tree, his binoculars like a signal flare in the setting sun. . .

I got up and went inside to the phone. First I called the Contra Costa sheriff's deputy who had been in charge of the crime scene at the pavilion. No, he told me, the dead man hadn't been identified yet; the only personal item he had been carrying was a bus ticket—issued yesterday—from San Francisco to Concord which had been tucked into his shoe. While this indicated he was not a resident of the area, it told them nothing else. They were still hoping to get an identification on his fingerprints, however.

Next I called the pavilion and got the home phone of Jim Hayes, the guard who had been on the performers' gate when Fitzgerald had vanished. When Hayes answered my call, he sounded as if I'd woken him, but he was willing to answer a few questions.

"When Fitzgerald left he was wearing his costume, right?" I asked.

"Yes."

"What about makeup?"

"No. I'd have noticed that; it would have seemed strange, him leaving with his face all painted."

"Now, last night you said you thought he'd come back in a few minutes after you returned from your break. Did he show you his pass?"

"Yes, everyone had to show one. But—"

"Did you look at the name on it?"

"Not closely. I just checked to see if it was valid for that date. Now I wish I *had* looked, because I'm not sure it was Fitzgerald. The costume seemed the same, but I just don't know."

"Why?"

"Well, there was something different about the man who came in. He walked funny. The guy you found murdered, he was crippled."

So that observation might or might not be valid. The idea that the man walked "funny" could have been planted in Hayes' mind by his knowing the dead man was cripple. "Anything else?"

He hesitated. "I think . . . yes. You asked if Gary Fitzgerald was wearing makeup when he left. And he wasn't. But the guy who came in, he *was* made up. That's why I don't think it was Fitzgerald."

"Thank you, Mr. Hayes. That's all I need to know."

I hung up the phone, grabbed my bag and car keys, and drove back out to the pavilion in record time.

The heat-hazed parking lots were empty today, save for a couple of trucks that I assumed belonged to the maintenance crew. The gates were locked, the box office windows shuttered, and I could see no one. That didn't matter, however. What I was interested in lay outside the chain-link fence. I parked the MG near the trucks and went around the perimeter of the amphitheater to the area near the performers' gate, then looked up at the hill to the east. There was a fire break cut through the high wheat-colored grass, and I started up it.

Halfway to the top, I stopped, wiping sweat from my forehead and looking down at the pavilion. Visibility was good from here. Pivoting, I surveyed the surrounding area. To the west lay a monotonous grid-like pattern of tracts and shopping centers, broken here and there by hills and the upthrusting skyline of Walnut Creek. To the north I could see smoke billowing from the stacks of the paper plant at Antioch, and the bridge spanning the river toward the Sacramento Delta. Further east, the majestic bulk of Mount Diablo rose; between it and the foothill were more hills and hollows—ranch country.

The hill on which I stood was only lightly wooded, but there was an outcropping of rock surrounded by madrone and live oak about a hundred yards to the south on a direct line from the tree where the lone horseman with the signal-like binoculars had stood. I left the relatively easy footing of the fire break and waded through the dry grass toward it. It was cool and deeply shadowed under the branches of the trees, and the air smelled of vegetation gone dry and brittle. I stood still for a moment, wiping the sweat away once more, then began to look around. What I was searching for was wedged behind a low rock that formed a sort of table: a couple of tissues smeared with makeup. Black and red and white greasepaint—the theatrical makeup of a clown.

The dead man had probably used this rock as a dressing table, applying what Fitzgerald had brought him in the canvas bag. I remembered Gary's insistence on taking the bag with him to the men's room; of course he needed it; the makeup was a necessary prop to their plan. While Fitzgerald could leave the pavilion without his greasepaint, the other man couldn't enter un-madeup; there was too much of a risk that the guard might notice the face didn't match the costume or the name on the pass.

I looked down at the dry leaves beneath my feet. Oak, and madrone, and brittle needles of chaparral. And the foxtails would have been acquired while pushing through the high grass between here and the bottom of the hill. That told me the route the dead man had taken, but not what had happened to Fitzgerald. In order to find that out, I'd have to learn where one could rent a horse.

I stopped at a feed store in the little village of Hillside, nestled in a wooded hollow southeast of the pavilion. It was all you could expect of a country store, with wood floors and big sacks and bins of feed. The weatherbeaten old man in overalls who looked up from the saddle he was polishing completed the rustic picture.

He said, "Help you with something?"

I took a closer look at the saddle, then glanced around at the hand-tooled leather goods hanging from hooks on the far wall. "That's beautiful work. Do you do it yourself?"

"Sure do."

"How much does a saddle like that go for these days?" My experience with horses had ended with the lessons I'd taken in junior high school.

"Custom job like this, five hundred, thereabouts."

"Five hundred! That's more than I could get for my car."

"Well . . ." He glanced through the door at the MG.

"I know. You don't have to say another word."

"It runs, don't it?"

"Usually." Rapport established, I got down to business. "What I need is some information. I'm looking for a stable that rents horses."

"You want to set up a party or something?"

"I might."

"Well, there's MacMillan's, on the south side of town. I wouldn't recommend them, though. They've got some mean horses. This would be for a bunch of city folks?"

"I wasn't aware it showed."

"Doesn't, all that much. But I'm good at figuring out about folks. You don't look like a suburban lady, and you don't look country either." He smiled at me, and I nodded and smiled to compliment his deductive ability. "No," he went on. "I wouldn't recommend MacMillan's if you have folks along who maybe don't ride so good. Some of those horses are mean enough to kick a person from here to San Jose. The place to go is Wheeler's; they got some fine mounts."

"Where is Wheeler's?"

"South, too, a couple of miles beyond MacMillan's. You'll know it by the sign."

I thanked him and started out. "Hey!" he called after me. "When you have your party, bring your city friends by. I got a nice selection of handtooled belts and wallets."

I said I would, and waved at him as I drove off.

About a mile down the road on the south side of the little hamlet stood a tumble-down stable with a hand-lettered sign advertising horses for rent. The poorly recommended MacMillan's, no doubt. There wasn't an animal, mean or otherwise, in sight, but a large, jowly woman who resembled a bulldog greeted me, pitchfork in hand.

I told her the story that I'd hastily made up on the drive: a friend of mine had rented a horse the night before to ride up on the hill and watch the show at the Diablo Valley Pavilion. He had been impressed with the horse and the stable it had come from, but couldn't remember the name of the place. Had she, by any chance, rented to him? As I spoke, the woman began to frown, looking more and more like a pugnacious canine every minute.

"It's not honest," she said.

"I'm sorry?"

"It's not honest, people riding up there and watching for free. Stealing's stealing, no matter what name you put on it. Your Bible tells you that."

"Oh." I couldn't think of any reply to that, although she was probably right.

She eyed me severely, as if she suspected me of pagan practices. "In answer to your question, no, I wouldn't let a person near one of my horses if he was going to ride up there and watch."

"Well, I don't suppose my friend admitted what he planned to do—"

"Any decent person would be too ashamed to admit to a thing like that." She motioned aggressively with the pitchfork.

I took a step backwards. "But maybe you rented to him not knowing—"

"You going to do the same thing?"

"What?"

"Are you going to ride up there for tonight's concert?"

"Me? No, ma'am. I don't even ride all that well. I just wanted to find out if my friend had rented his horse from—"

"Well, he didn't rent the horse from here. We aren't even open evenings, don't want our horses out in the dark with people like you who can't ride. Besides, even if people don't plan it, those concerts are an awful temptation. And I can't sanction that sort of thing. I'm a born-again Christian, and I won't help people go against the Lord's word."

"You know," I said hastily, "I agree with you. And I'm going to talk with my friend about his behavior. But I still want to know where he got his horse. Are there any other stables around here besides yours?"

The woman looked somewhat mollified. "There's only Wheeler's. They do a big business—trail trips on Mount Diablo, hayrides in the fall. And, of course, folks who want to sneak up to that pavilion. They'd rent to a person who was going to rob a bank on horseback if there was enough money in it."

Stifling a grin, I started for my car. "Thanks for the information."

"You're welcome to it. But you remember to talk to your friend, tell him to mend his ways."

I smiled and got out of there in a hurry.

Next to MacMillan's, Wheeler's Riding Stables looked prosperous and attractive. The red barn was freshly painted, and a couple of dozen healthy, sleek horses, grazed within white rail fences. I rumbled down a dirt driveway and over a little bridge that spanned a gully, and parked in front of a door labeled OFFICE. Inside, a blond-haired man in faded Levi's and a t-shirt lounged in a canvas chair behind the counter, reading a copy of *Playboy*. He put it aside reluctantly when I came in.

I was tired of my manufactured story, and this man looked like someone I could be straightforward with. I showed him the photostat of my license and said, "I'm cooperating with the county sheriff's department on the death at the Diablo Valley Pavilion last night. You've heard about it?"

"Yes, it made the morning news."

"I have reason to believe that the dead man may have rented a horse prior to the show last night."

The man raised a sun-bleached eyebrow and waited, as economical with his words as the woman at MacMillan's had been spendthrift.

"Did you rent any horses last night?"

"Five. Four to a party, another later one."

"Who rented the single horse?"

"Tall, thin guy. Wore jeans and a plaid shirt. At first I thought I knew him."

"Why?"

"He looked familiar, like someone who used to live near here. But then I realized it couldn't be. His face was disfigured, his arm crippled up, and he limped. Had trouble getting on the horse, but once he was mounted, I could tell he was a good rider."

I felt a flash of excitement, the kind you get when things start coming together the way you've hoped they would. "That's the man who was killed."

"Well, that explains it."

"Explains what?"

"Horse came back this morning, riderless."

"What time?"

"Oh, around five, five thirty."

That didn't fit the way I wanted to. "Do you keep a record of who you rent the horses to?"

"Name and address. And we take a deposit that's returned when they bring the horses back."

"Can you look up the man's name?"

He grinned and reached under the counter for a looseleaf notebook. "I can, but I don't think it will help you identify him. I noted it at the time—Tom Smith. Sounded like a phony."

"But you still rented to him?"

"Sure. I just asked for double the deposit. He didn't look too prosperous, so I figured he'd be back. Besides, none of our horses are so terrific that anyone would trouble to steal one."

I stood there for a few seconds, tapping my fingers on the counter. "You said you thought he was someone you used to know."

"At first, but the guy I knew wasn't crippled. Must have been a chance resemblance."

"Who was he?"

"Fellow who lived on a ranch near here back in the late sixties. Gary Fitzgerald."

I stared at him.

"But like I said, Gary Fitzgerald wasn't crippled."

"Did this Gary have a cousin?" I asked.

"Yeah, John Tilby. Tilby's dad owned a dairy ranch. Gary lived with them."

"When did Gary leave here?"

"After the old man died. The ranch was sold to pay the debts and both Gary and John took off. For Southern California." He grinned again. "Probably had some cockeyed idea about getting into show business."

"By any chance, do you know who was starring on the bill at the pavilion last night?"

"Don't recall, no. It was some kind of kid show, wasn't it?"

"A clown festival."

"Oh." He shrugged. "Clowns don't interest me. Why?"

"No reason." Things definitely weren't fitting together the way I'd wanted them to. "You say the cousins took off together after John Tilby's father died."

"Yes."

"And went to Southern California."

"That's what I heard."

"Did Gary Fitzgerald ever live in the Haight-Ashbury?"

He hesitated. "Not unless they went there instead of L. A. But I can't see Gary in the Haight, especially back then. He was just a country boy, if you know what I mean. But what's all this about him and John? I thought—"

"How much to rent a horse?"

The man's curiosity was easily sidetracked by business. "Ten an hour. Twenty for the deposit."

"Do you have a gentle one?"

"You mean for you? Now?"

"Yes."

"Got all kinds, gentle or lively."

I took out my wallet and checked it. Luckily, I had a little under forty dollars. "I'll take the gentlest one."

The man pushed the looseleaf notebook at me, looking faintly surprised. "You sign the book, and then I'll go saddle up Whitefoot."

Once our transaction was completed, the stable man pointed out the bridle trail that led toward the pavilion, wished me a good ride, and left me atop one of the gentlest horses I'd ever encountered. Whitefoot—a roan who did indeed have one white fetlock—was so placid I was afraid he'd go to sleep. Recalling my few riding lessons, which had taken place sometime in my early teens, I made some encouraging clicking sounds and tapped his flanks with my heels. Whitefoot put his head down and began munching a clump of dry grass.

"Come on, big fellow," I said. Whitefoot continued to munch.

I shook the reins—gently but with authority.

No response. I stared disgustedly down the incline of his neck, which made me feel I was sitting at the top of a long slide. Then I repeated the clicking and tapping process. The horse ignored me.

"Look, you lazy bastard," I said in a low, menacing tone, "get a move on!"

The horse raised his head and shook it, glancing back at me with one sullen eye. Then he started down the bridle trail in a swaying, lumbering walk. I sat up straighter in correct horsewoman's posture, feeling smug.

The trail wound through a grove of eucalyptus, then began climbing uphill through grassland. The terrain was rough, full of rocky outcroppings and eroded gullies, and I was thankful for both the well-traveled path and Whitefoot's slovenly gait. After a few minutes I began to feel secure enough in the saddle to take stock of my surroundings, and when we reached the top of a rise, I stopped the horse and looked around.

To one side lay grazing land dotted with brown-and-white cattle. In the distance, I spotted a barn and a corral with horses. To the other side, the vegetation was thicker, giving onto a canyon choked with manzanita, scrub oak, and bay laurel. This was the type of terrain I was looking for—the kind where a man can easily become disoriented and lost. Still, there must be dozens of such canyons in the surrounding hills; to explore all of them would take days.

I had decided to ride further before plunging into rougher territory, when I noticed a movement under the leafy overhang at the edge of the canyon. Peering intently at the spot, I made out a tall figure in light-colored clothing. Before I could identify it as male or female, it slipped back into the shadows and disappeared from view.

Afraid that the person would see me, I reined the horse to one side, behind a large sandstone boulder a few yards away. Then I slipped from the saddle and peered around the rock toward the canyon. Nothing moved there. I glanced at Whitefoot and decided he would stay where he was without being tethered; true to form, he had lowered his head and was munching contentedly. After patting him once for reassurance, I crept through the tall grass to the underbrush. The air there was still and pungent with the scent of bay laurel—more reminiscent of curry powder than of the bay leaf I kept in a jar in my kitchen. I crouched behind the billowy bright green mat of a chapparal bush while my eyes became accustomed to the gloom. Still nothing stirred; it was as if the figure had been a creature of my imagination.

Ahead of me, the canyon narrowed between high rock walls. Moss coated them, and stunted trees grew out of their cracks. I came out of my shelter and started that way, over ground that was sloping and uneven. From my right came a trickling sound; I peered through the underbrush and saw a tiny stream of water falling over the outcropping. A mere dribble now, it would be a full cascade in the wet season.

The ground became even rougher, and at times I had difficulty finding a foothold. At a point where the mossy walls almost converged, I stopped, leaning against one of them, and listened. A sound, as if someone were thrashing through thick vegetation, came from the other side of the narrow space. I squeezed between the rocks and saw a heavily forested area. A tree branch a few feet from me looked as if it had recently been broken.

I started through the vegetation, following the sounds ahead of me. Pine boughs brushed at my face, and chapparal needles scratched my bare arms. After a few minutes, the thrashing sounds stopped. I stood still, wondering if the person I followed had heard me.

Everything was silent. Not even a bird stirred in the trees above me. I had no idea where I was in relation to either the pavilion or the stables. I wasn't even sure if I could find my way back to where I'd left the horse. Foolishly I realized the magnitude of the task I'd undertaken; such a search would be better accomplished with a helicopter than on horseback.

And then I heard the voices.

They came from the right, past a heavy screen of scrub oak. They were male, and from their rhythm I could tell they were angry. But I couldn't identify them or make out what they were saying. I edged around a clump of manzanilla and started through the trees, trying to make as little sound as possible.

On the other side of the trees was an outcropping that formed a flat rock shelf that appeared to drop off sharply after about twenty feet. I clambered up on it and flattened onto my stomach, then crept forward.

The voices were louder now, coming from straight ahead and below. I identified one as belonging to the man I knew as Gary Fitzgerald.

". . . didn't know he intended to blackmail anyone. I thought he just wanted to see John, make it up with him." The words were labored, twisted with pain.

"If that were the case, he could have come to the hotel." The second man was Wayne Kabalka. "He didn't have to go through all those elaborate machinations of sneaking into the pavilion."

"He told me he wanted to reconcile. After all, he was John's own cousin—"

"Come on, Elliott. You knew he had threatened us. You knew all about the pressure he'd put on us the past few weeks, ever since he found out the act would be coming to San Francisco."

I started at the strange name, even though I had known the missing man wasn't really Gary Fitzgerald. Elliott. Elliott who?

Elliott was silent.

I continued creeping forward, the mossy rock cold through my clothing. When I reached the edge of the shelf, I kept my head down until Kabalka spoke again. "You knew we were all afraid of Gary. That's why I hired the McCone woman; in case he tried anything, I wanted an armed guard there. I never counted on you playing the Judas."

Again Elliott was silent. I risked a look over the ledge.

There was a sheer drop of some fifteen or twenty feet to a gully full of jagged rocks. The man I'd known as Gary Fitzgerald lay at its bottom, propped into a sitting position, his right leg twisted at an unnatural angle. He was wearing a plaid shirt and jeans—the same clothing the man at the stables had described the dead man as having on. Kabalka stood in front of him, perhaps two yards from where I lay, his back to me. For a minute, I was afraid Elliott would see my head, but then I realized his eyes were glazed half blind with pain.

"What happened between John and Gary?" he asked.

Kabalka shifted his weight and put one arm behind his back, sliding his hand into his belt.

"Wayne, what happened?"

"Gary was found dead at the pavilion this morning. Stabbed. None of this would have happened if you hadn't connived to switch clothing so he could sneak backstage and threaten John."

Elliott's hand twitched, as if he wanted to cover his eyes but was too weak to lift it. "Dead." He paused. "I was afraid something awful had happened when he didn't come back to where I was waiting with the horse."

"Of course you were afraid. You knew what would happen."

"No . . ."

"You planned this for weeks, didn't you? The thing about staying at the fleabag in the Haight was a ploy, so you could turn over one of your costumes to Gary. But it didn't work, because Corinne had sent all but one to the cleaner. When did you come up with the scheme of sneaking out and trading places?"

Elliott didn't answer.

"I suppose it doesn't matter when. But why, Elliott? For God's sake, *why?*"

When he finally answered, Elliott's voice was weary. "Maybe I was sick of what you'd done to him. What we'd *all* done. He was so pathetic when he called me in L. A. And when I saw him . . . I thought maybe that if John saw him too, he might persuade you to help Gary."

"And instead he killed him."

"No. I can't believe that. John loved Gary."

"John loved Gary so much he took Nicole away from him. And then he got into a drunken quarrel with him and crashed the car they were riding in and crippled him for life."

"Yes, but John's genuinely guilty over the accident. And he hates you for sending Gary away and replacing him with me. What a fraud we've all perpetrated—"

Kabalka's body tensed and he began balancing aggressively on the balls of his feet. "That fraud had made us a lot of money. Would have made us more until you pulled this stunt. Sooner or later they'll identify Gary's body and then it will all come out. John will be tried for the murder—"

"I still don't believe he killed him. I want to ask him about it."

Slowly Kabalka slipped his hand from his belt—and I saw the knife. He held it behind his back in his clenched fingers and took a step toward Elliott.

I pushed with my palms against the rock. The motion caught Elliott's eye and he looked around in alarm. Kabalka must have taken the look to be aimed at him because he brought the knife up.

I didn't hesitate. I jumped off the ledge. For what seemed like an eternity I was falling toward the jagged rocks below. Then I landed heavily—directly on top of Kabalka.

As he hit the ground, I heard the distinctive sound of cracking bone. He went limp, and I rolled off him—unhurt, because his body had cushioned my fall. Kabalka lay unconscious, his head against a rock. When I looked at Elliott, I saw he had passed out from pain and shock.

❖

The room at John Muir Hospital in Walnut Creek was antiseptic white, with bright touches of red and blue in the curtains and a colorful spray of fall flowers on the bureau. Elliott Larson—I'd found out that was his full name—lay on the bed with his right leg in traction. John Tilby stood by the door, his hands clasped formally behind his back, looking shy and afraid to come any further into the room. I sat on a chair by the bed, sharing a split of smuggled-in wine with Elliott.

I'd arrived at the same time as Tilby, who had brought the flowers. He'd seemed unsure of a welcome, and even though Elliott had acted glad to see him, he was still keeping his distance. But after a few awkward minutes, he had agreed to answer some questions and had told me about the drunken auto accident five years ago in which he had been thrown clear of his MG and the real Gary Fitzgerald had been crippled. And about how Wayne Kabalka had sent Gary away with what the manager had termed an "ample settlement"—and which would have been except for Gary's mounting medical expenses, which eventually ate up all his funds and forced him to live on welfare in a cheap San Francisco hotel. Determined not to lose the bright financial future the comedy team had promised him, Kabalka had looked around for a replacement for Gary and found Elliott performing in a seedy Haight-Ashbury club. He'd put him into the act, never telling the advertisers who were clamoring for Fitzgerald and Tilby's services that one of the men in the whiteface was not the clown they had contracted with. And he'd insisted Elliott totally assume Gary's identity.

"At first," Elliott said, "it wasn't so bad. When Wayne found me, I was on a downslide. I was heavy into drugs, and I'd been kicked out of my place in the Haight and was crashing with whatever friends would let me. At first it was great making all that money, but after a while I began to realize I'd never be anything more than the shadow of a broken man."

"And then," I said, "Gary reappeared."

"Yes. He needed some sort of operation and he contacted Wayne in L. A. Over the years Wayne had been sending him money—hush money, I guess you could call it—but it was barely enough to cover his minimum expenses. Gary had been seeing all the ads on TV, reading about how well we were doing, and he was angry and demanding a cut."

"And rightly so," Tilby added. "I'd always thought Gary was well provided for, because Wayne took part of my earnings and said he was sending it to him. Now I know most of it was going into Wayne's pocket."

"Did Wayne refuse to give Gary the money for the operation?" I asked.

Tilby nodded. "There was a time when Gary would merely have crept back into the woodwork when Wayne refused him. But by then his anger and hurt had festered, and he wasn't taking no for an answer. He threatened Wayne, and continued to make daily threats by phone. We were all on edge, afraid of what he might do. Corinne kept urging Wayne to give him the money, especially because we had contracted to come to San Francisco, where Gary was, for the clown festival. But Wayne was too stubborn to give in."

Thinking of Corinne, I said, "How's she taking it, anyway?"

"Badly," Tilby said. "But she's a tough lady. She'll pull through."

"And Nicole?"

"Nicole has vanished. Was packed and gone by the time I went back to the hotel after Wayne's arrest." He seemed unconcerned; five years with Nicole had probably been enough.

I said, "I talked to the sheriff's department. Wayne hasn't confessed." After I'd revived Elliott out there in the canyon, I'd given him my gun and made my way back to where I'd left the horse. Then I'd ridden—probably the most energetic ride of old Whitefoot's life—back to the stables and summoned the sheriff's men. When we'd arrived at the gully, Wayne had regained consciousness and was attempting to buy Elliott off. Elliott seemed to be enjoying bargaining and then refusing.

Remembering the conversation I'd overheard between the two men, I said to Elliott, "Did Wayne have it right about you intending to loan Gary one of your spare costumes?"

"Yes. When I found I didn't have an extra costume to give him, Gary came up with the plan of signaling me from a horse on the hill. He knew the area from when he lived there and had seen a piece in the paper about how people would ride up on the hill to watch the concerts. You guessed about the signal?"

"I saw it happen. I just didn't put it together until later, when I thought about the fragments of leaves and needles they found in Gary's clothing." No need to explain about the catalyst to my thought process—the horse of a cat named Watney.

"Well," Elliott said, "that was how it worked. The signal with the field glasses was to tell me Gary had been able to get a horse and show me where he'd be waiting. At the prearranged time, I made the excuse about going to the men's room, climbed out the window, and left the pavilion. Gary changed and got himself into white face in a clump of trees with the aid of a flashlight. I put on his clothes and took the horse and waited, but he never came back. Finally the crowd was streaming out of the pavilion, and then the lights went out; I tried to ride down there, but I'm not a very good horseman, and I got turned around in the dark. Then something scared the horse and it threw me into that ravine and bolted. As soon as I hit the rocks I knew my leg was broken."

"And you lay there all night."

"Yes, half frozen. And in the morning I heard Wayne thrashing through the underbrush. I don't know if he intended to kill me at first, or if he planned to try to convince me that John had killed Gary and we should cover it up."

"Probably the latter, at least initially." I turned to Tilby. "What happened at the pavilion with Gary?"

"He came into the dressing room. Right off I knew it was him, by the limp. He was angry, wanted money. I told him I was willing to give him whatever he needed, but that Wayne would have to arrange for it. Gary hid in the dressing room closet and when you came in there, I asked you to get Wayne. He took Gary away, out into the audience, and when he came back, he said he'd fixed everything." He paused, lips twisting bitterly. "And he certainly had."

We were silent for a moment. Then Elliott said to me, "Were you surprised to find out I wasn't really Gary Fitzgerald?"

"Yes and no. I had a funny feeling about you all along."

"Why?"

"Well, first there was the fact you and John just didn't look as though you were related. And then when we were driving through Contra Costa County, you didn't display much interest in it—not the kind of curiosity a man would have when returning home after so many years. And there was one other thing."

"What?"

"I said something about sound from the two pavilions being audible all the way to Port Chicago. That's the place where the Naval Weapons Station is, up on the Strait. And you said, 'Not all the way to Chicago.'"

You didn't know where Port Chicago was, but I took it to mean you were making a joke. I remember thinking that for a clown, you didn't have much of a sense of humor."

"Thanks a lot." But he grinned, unoffended.

I stood up. "So now what? Even if Wayne never confesses, they've got a solid case against him. You're out a manager, so you'll have to handle your own future plans."

They shrugged almost simultaneously.

"You've got a terrific act," I said. "There'll be some adverse publicity, but you can probably weather it."

Tilby said, "A couple of advertisers have already called to withdraw their offers."

"Others will be calling with new ones."

He moved hesitantly toward the chair I'd vacated. "Maybe."

"You can count on it. A squeaky clean reputation isn't always an asset in show business; your notoriety will hurt in some ways, but help you in others." Picked up my bag and squeezed Elliott's arm, went toward the door, touching Tilby briefly on the shoulder. "At least think about keeping the act going."

As I went out, I looked back at them. Tilby had sat down in the chair. His posture was rigid, tentative, as if he might flee at any moment. Elliott looked uncertain, but hopeful.

What was it, I thought, that John had said to me about clowns when we were playing gin in the dressing room at the pavilion? Something to the effect that they were all funny but, more important, that they all made people look at their own foibles. John Tilby and Elliott Larson—in a sense both broken men like Gary Fitzgerald—knew more about those foibles than most people. Maybe there was a way they could continue to turn that sad knowledge into humor.

DECEPTIONS

SAN FRANCISCO'S Golden Gate Bridge is deceptively fragile-looking, especially when fog swirls across its high span. But from where I was standing, almost beneath it at the south end, even the mist couldn't disguise the massiveness of its concrete piers and the taut strength of its cables. I tipped my head back and looked up the tower to where it disappeared into the drifting grayness, thinking about the other ways the bridge is deceptive.

For one thing, its color isn't gold, but rust red, reminiscent of dried blood. And though the bridge is a marvel of engineering, it is also plagued by maintenance problems that keep the Bridge District in constant danger of financial collapse. For a reputedly romantic structure, it has seen more than its fair share of tragedy: some eight hundred-odd lost souls have jumped to their deaths from its deck.

Today I was there to try to find out if that figure should be raised by one. So far I'd met with little success.

I was standing next to my car in the parking lot of Fort Point, a historic fortification at the mouth of the San Francisco Bay. Where the pavement stopped, the land fell away to jagged black rocks; waves smashed against them, sending up geysers of salty spray. Beyond the rocks the water was choppy, and Angel Island and Alcatraz were mere humpbacked shapes in the mist. I shivered, wishing I'd worn something heavier than my poplin jacket, and started toward the fort.

This was the last stop on a journey that had taken me from the toll booths and Bridge District offices to Vista Point at the Marin County end of the span, and back to the National Parks Services headquarters down the road from the fort. None of the Parks Service or bridge personnel—including a group of maintenance workers near the north tower—had seen the slender dark-haired woman in the picture I'd shown them, walking south on the pedestrian sidewalk about four yesterday afternoon. None of them had seen her jump.

It was for that reason—plus the facts that her parents had revealed about twenty-two-year-old Vanessa DiCesare—that made me tend to doubt she actually had committed suicide, in spite of the note she'd left taped to the dashboard of the Honda she'd abandoned at Vista Point. Surely at four o'clock on a Monday afternoon *someone* would have noticed her. Still, I had to follow up every possibility, and the people at the Parks Service station had suggested I check with the rangers at Fort Point.

I entered the dark-brick structure through a long, low tunnel—called a sally port, the sign said—which was flanked at either end by massive wooden doors with iron studding. Years before I'd visited the fort, and now I recalled that it was more or less typical of harbor fortifications built in the Civil War era: a ground floor topped by two tiers of working and living quarters, encircling a central courtyard.

I emerged into the court and looked up at the west side; the tiers were a series of brick archways, their openings as black as empty eyesockets, each roped off by a narrow strip of plastic strung across it at waist level. There was construction gear in the courtyard; the entire west side was under renovation and probably off limits to the public.

As I stood there trying to remember the layout of the place and wondering which way to go, I became aware of a hollow metallic clanking that echoed in the circular enclosure. The noise drew my eyes upward to the wooden watchtower atop the west tiers, and then to the red arch of the bridge's girders directly above it. The clanking seemed to have something to do with cars passing over the roadbed, and it was underlaid by a constant grumbling rush of tires on pavement. The sounds, coupled with the soaring height of the fog-laced girders, made me feel very small and insignificant. I shivered again and turned to my left, looking for one of the rangers.

The man who came out of a nearby doorway startled me, more because of his costume than the suddenness of his appearance. Instead of the Parks Service uniform I remembered the rangers wearing on my previous visit, he was clad in what looked like an old Union Army uniform: a dark blue frock coat, lighter blue trousers, and a wide-brimmed hat with a red plume. The long saber strapped to his waist made him look thoroughly authentic.

He smiled at my obvious surprise and came over to me, bushy eyebrows lifted inquiringly. "Can I help you, ma'am?"

I reached into my bag and took out my private investigator's license and showed it to him. "I'm Sharon McCone, from All Souls Legal Cooperative. Do you have a minute to answer some questions?"

He frowned, the way people often do when confronted by a private detective, probably trying to remember whether he'd done anything lately that would warrant investigation. Then he said, "Sure," and motioned for me to step into the shelter of the sally port.

"I'm investigating a disappearance, a possible suicide from the bridge," I said. "It would have happened about four yesterday afternoon. Were you on duty then?"

He shook his head. "Monday's my day off."

"Is there anyone else here who might have been working then?"

"You could check with Lee—Lee Gottschalk, the other ranger on this shift."

"Where can I find him?"

He moved into the courtyard and looked around. "I saw him start taking a couple of tourists around just a few minutes ago. People are crazy: they'll come out in any kind of weather."

"Can you tell me which way he went?"

The ranger gestured to our right. "Along this side. When he's done down here, he'll take them up that iron stairway to the first tier, but I can't say how far he's gotten yet."

I thanked him and started off in the direction he'd indicated.

There were open doors in the cement wall between the sally port and the iron staircase. I glanced through the first and saw no one. The second led into a dark hallway; when I was halfway down it, I saw that this was the fort's jail. One cell was set up as a display, complete with a mannequin prisoner; the other, beyond an archway that was not much taller than my own five-foot-six, was unrestored. Its waterstained walls were covered with graffiti, and a metal railing protected a two-foot-square iron grid on the floor in one corner. A sign said that it was a cistern with a forty-thousand-gallon capacity.

Well, I thought, that's interesting, but playing tourist isn't helping me catch up with Lee Gottschalk. Quickly I left the jail and hurried up the iron staircase the first ranger had indicated. At its top, I turned left and bumped into a chain link fence that blocked access to the area under renovation. Warning myself to watch where I was going, I went the other way, toward the east tier. The archways there were fenced off with similar chain link so no one could fall, and doors opened off the gallery into what I supposed had been the soldiers' living quarters. I pushed through the first one and stepped into a small museum.

The room was high-ceilinged, with tall, narrow windows in the outside wall. No ranger or tourists were in sight. I looked toward an interior door that led to the next room and saw a series of mirror images: one door within another leading off into the distance, each diminishing in size until the last seemed very tiny. I had the unpleasant sensation that if I walked along there, I would become progressively smaller and eventually disappear.

From somewhere down there came the sound of voices. I followed it, passing through more museum displays until I came to a room containing an old-fashioned bedstead and footlocker. A ranger, dressed the same as the man downstairs except that he was bearded and wore granny glasses, stood beyond the bedstead lecturing to a man and a woman who were bundled to their chins in bulky sweaters.

"You'll notice that the fireplaces are very small," he was saying, motioning to the one on the wall next to the bed, "and you can imagine how cold it could get for the soldiers stationed here. They didn't have a heated employees' lounge like we do." Smiling at his own little joke, he glanced at me. "Do you want to join the tour?"

I shook my head and stepped over by the footlocker. "Are you Lee Gottschalk?"

"Yes." He spoke the word a shade warily.

"I have a few questions I'd like to ask you. How long will the rest of the tour take?"

"At least half an hour. These folks want to see the unrestored rooms on the third floor."

I didn't want to wait around that long, so I said, "Could you take a couple of minutes and talk with me now?"

He moved his head so the light from the windows caught his granny glasses and I couldn't see the expression in his eyes, but his mouth tightened in a way that might have been annoyance. After a moment he said, "Well, the rest of tour on this floor is pretty much self-guided." To the tourists, he added, "Why don't you go on ahead and I'll catch up after I talk with this lady."

They nodded agreeably and moved on into the next room. Lee Gottschalk folded his arms across his chest and leaned against the small fireplace. "Now what can I do for you?"

I introduced myself and showed him my license. His mouth twitched briefly in surprise, but he didn't comment. I said, "At about four yesterday afternoon, a young woman left her car at Vista Point with a suicide note in it. I'm trying to locate a witness who saw her jump." I took out the photograph I'd been showing to people and handed it to him. By now I had Vanessa DiCesare's features memorized: high forehead, straight nose, full lips, glossy wings of dark-brown hair curling inward at the jawbone. It was a strong face, not beautiful but striking—and a face I'd recognize anywhere.

Gottschalk studied the photo, then handed it back to me. "I read about her in the morning paper. Why are you trying to find a witness?"

"Her parents have hired me to look into it."

"The paper said her father is some big politician here in the city."

I didn't see any harm in discussing what had already appeared in print. "Yes, Ernest DiCesare—he's on the Board of Supes and likely to be our next mayor."

"And she was a law student, engaged to some hotshot lawyer who ran her father's last political campaign."

"Right again."

He shook his head, lips pushing out in bewilderment. "Sounds like she had a lot going for her. Why would she kill herself? Did that note taped inside her car explain it?"

I'd seen the note, but its contents were confidential. "No. Did you happen to see anything unusual yesterday afternoon?"

"No. But if I'd seen anyone jump, I'd have reported it to the Coast Guard station so they could try to recover the body before the current carried it out to sea."

"What about someone standing by the bridge railing, acting strangely, perhaps?"

"If I'd noticed anyone like that, I'd have reported it to the bridge offices so they could send out a suicide prevention and rescue team." He stared almost combatively at me, as if I'd accused him of some kind of wrongdoing, then seemed to relent a little. "Come outside," he said, "and I'll show you something."

We went through the door to the gallery, and he guided me to the chain link barrier in the archway and pointed up. "Look at the angle of the bridge, and the distance we are from it. You couldn't spot anyone standing at the rail from here, at least not well enough to tell if they were acting upset. And a jumper would have to hurl herself way out before she'd be noticeable."

"And there's nowhere else in the fort from where a jumper would be clearly visible?"

"Maybe one of the watchtowers on the extreme west side. But they're off limits to the public, and we only give them one routine check at closing."

Satisfied now, I said, "Well, that about does it. I appreciate your taking the time."

He nodded and we started along the gallery. When we reached the other end, where an enclosed staircase spiraled up and down, I thanked him again and we parted company.

The way the facts looked to me now, Vanessa DiCesare had faked this suicide and just walked away—away from her wealthy old-line Italian family, from her up-and-coming liberal lawyer, from a life that either had become too much or hadn't been enough. Vanessa was over twenty-one; she had a legal right to disappear if she wanted to. But her parents and her fiancé loved her, and they also had a right to know she was alive and well. If I could locate her and reassure them without ruining whatever new life she planned to create for herself, I could feel I'd performed the job I'd been hired to do. But right now I was weary, chilled to the bone, and out of leads. I decided to go back to All Souls and consider my next moves in warmth and comfort.

All Souls Legal Cooperative is housed in a ramshackle Victorian on one of the steeply sloping side-streets of Bernal Heights, a working-class district in the southern part of the city. The co-op caters mainly to clients who live in the area: people with low to middle incomes who don't have much extra money for expensive lawyers. The sliding fee scale allows them to obtain quality legal assistance at reasonable prices—a concept that is probably outdated in the self-centered 1980s, but is kept alive by the people who staff All Souls. It's a place where the lawyers care about their clients and a good place to work.

I left my MG at the curb and hurried up the front steps through the blowing fog. The warmth inside was almost a shock after the chilliness at Fort Point; I unbuttoned my jacket and went down the long deserted hallway to the big country kitchen at the rear. There I found my boss, Hank Zahn, stirring up a mug of the navy grog he often concocts on cold November nights like this one.

He looked at me, pointed to the rum bottle, and said, "Shall I make you one?" When I nodded, he reached for another mug.

I went to the round oak table by the windows, moved a pile of newspapers from one of the chairs, and sat down. Hank added lemon juice, hot water, and sugar syrup to the rum; dusted it artistically with nutmeg; and set it in front of me with a flourish. I sampled it as he sat down across from me, then nodded my approval.

He said, "How's it going with the DiCesare investigation?"

Hank had a personal interest in the case; Vanessa's fiancé, Gary Stornetta, was a long-time friend of his, which was why I, rather than one of the large investigative firms her father normally favored, had been asked to look into it. I said, "Everything I've come up with points to it being a disappearance, not a suicide."

"Just as Gary and her parents suspected."

"Yes. I've covered the entire area around the bridge. There are absolutely no witnesses, except for the tour bus driver who saw her park her car at four, got suspicious when it was still there are seven, and reported it. But even he didn't see her walk off toward the bridge." I drank some more grog, felt its warmth, and began to relax.

Behind his thick horn-rimmed glasses, Hank's eyes became concerned. "Did the DiCesares or Gary give you any idea why she would have done such a thing?"

"When I talked with Ernest and Sylvia this morning, they said Vanessa had changed her mind about marrying Gary. He's not admitting to that, but he doesn't speak of Vanessa the way a happy husband-to-be would. And it seems an unlikely match to me—he's close to twenty years older than she."

"More like fifteen," Hank said. "Gary's father was Ernest's best friend, and after Ron Stornetta died, Ernest more or less took him on as a protégé. Ernest was delighted that their families were finally going to be joined."

"Oh, he was delighted all right. He admitted to me that he'd practically arranged the marriage. 'Girl didn't know what was good for her,' he said. 'Needed a strong older man to guide her.'" I snorted.

Hank smiled faintly. He's a feminist, but over the years his sense of outrage has mellowed; mine still has a hair trigger.

"Anyway," I said, "when Vanessa first announced she was backing out of the engagement, Ernest told her he would cut off her funds for law school if she didn't go through with the wedding."

"Jesus, I had no idea he was capable of such . . . Neanderthal tactics."

"Well, he is. After that Vanessa went ahead and set the wedding date. But Sylvia said she suspected she wouldn't go through with it. Vanessa talked of quitting law school and moving out of their home. And she'd been seeing other men; she and her father had a bad quarrel about it just last week. Anyway, all of that, plus the fact that one of her suitcases and some clothing are missing, made them highly suspicious of the suicide."

Hank reached for my mug and went to get us more grog. I began thumbing through the copy of the morning paper that I'd moved off the chair, looking for the story on Vanessa. I found it on page three.

> The daughter of Supervisor Ernest DiCesare apparently committed suicide by jumping from the Golden Gate Bridge late yesterday afternoon.
>
> Vanessa DiCesare, 22, abandoned her 1985 Honda Civic at Vista Point at approximately four p. m., police said. There were no witnesses to her jump, and the body has not been recovered. The contents of a suicide note found in her car have not been disclosed.
>
> Ms. DiCesare, a first-year student at Hastings College of Law, is the only child of the supervisor and his wife, Sylvia. She planned to be married next month to San Francisco attorney Gary R. Stornetta, a political associate of her father . . . .

Strange how routine it all sounded when reduced to journalistic language. And yet how mysterious—the "undisclosed contents" of the suicide note, for instance.

"You know," I said as Hank came back to the table and set down the fresh mugs of grog, "that note is another factor that makes me believe she staged the whole thing. It was so formal and controlled. If they had samples of suicide notes in etiquette books, I'd say she looked one up and copied it."

He ran his fingers through his wiry brown hair. "What I don't understand is why she didn't just break off the engagement and move out of the house. So what if her father cut off her money? There are lots worse things than working your way through law school."

"Oh, but this way she gets back at everyone, and has the advantage of actually being alive to gloat over it. Imagine her parents' and Gary's grief and guilt—it's the ultimate way of getting even."

"She must be a very angry young woman."

"Yes. After I talked with Ernest and Sylvia and Gary, I spoke briefly with Vanessa's best friend, a law student named Kathy Graves. Kathy told me that Vanessa was furious with her father for making her go through with the marriage. And she'd come to hate Gary because she'd decided he was only marrying her for her family's money and political power."

"Oh, come on. Gary's ambitious, sure. But you can't tell me he doesn't genuinely care for Vanessa."

"I'm only giving you her side of the story."

"So now what do you plan to do?"

"Talk with Gary and the DiCesares again. See if I can't come up with some bit of information that will help me find her."

"And then?"

"Then it's up to them to work it out."

The DiCesare home was mock-Tudor, brick and half-timber, set on a corner knoll in the exclusive area of St. Francis Wood. When I'd first come there that morning, I'd been slightly awed; now the house had lost its power to impress me. After delving into the lives of the family who lived there, I knew that it was merely a pile of brick and mortar and wood that contained more than the usual amount of misery.

The DiCesares and Gary Stornetta were waiting for me in the living room, a strangely formal place with several groups of furniture and expensive-looking knickknacks laid out in precise patterns on the tables. Vanessa's parents and fiancé—like the house—seemed diminished since my previous visit: Sylvia huddled in an armchair by the fireplace, her gray-blond hair straggling from its elegant coiffure; Ernest stood behind her, haggard-faced, one hand protectively on her shoulder. Gary paced, smoking and clawing at his hair with his other hand. Occasionally he dropped ashes on the thick wall-to-wall carpeting, but no one called it to his attention.

They listened to what I had to report without interruption. When I finished, there was a long silence. Then Sylvia put a hand over her eyes and said, "How she must hate us to do a thing like this!"

Ernest tightened his grip on his wife's shoulder. His face was a conflict of anger, bewilderment, and sorrow.

There was no question of which emotion had hold of Gary; he smashed out his cigarette in an ashtray, lit another, and resumed pacing. But while his movements before had merely been nervous, now his tall, lean body was rigid with loosely controlled fury. "Damn her!" he said. "Damn her anyway!"

"Gary." There was a warning note in Ernest's voice.

Gary glanced at him, then at Sylvia. "Sorry."

I said, "The question now is, do you want me to continue looking for her?"

In shocked tones, Sylvia said, "Of course we do!" Then she tipped her head back and looked at her husband.

Ernest was silent, his fingers pressing hard against the black wool of her dress.

"Ernest?" Now Sylvia's voice held a note of panic.

"Of course we do," he said. But his words somehow lacked conviction.

I took out my notebook and pencil, glancing at Gary. He had stopped pacing and was watching the DiCesares. His craggy face was still mottled with anger, and I sensed he shared Ernest's uncertainty.

Opening the notebook, I said, "I need more details about Vanessa, what her life was like the past month or so. Perhaps something will occur to one of you that didn't this morning."

"Ms. McCone," Ernest said, "I don't think Sylvia's up to this right now. Why don't you and Gary talk, and then if there's anything else, I'll be glad to help you."

"Fine." Gary was the one I was primarily interested in questioning, anyway. I waited until Ernest and Sylvia had left the room, then turned to him.

When the door shut behind them, he hurled his cigarette into the empty fireplace. "Goddamn little bitch!" he said.

I said, "Why don't you sit down."

He looked at me for a few seconds, obviously wanting to keep on pacing, but then he flopped into the chair Sylvia had vacated. When I'd first met with Gary this morning, he'd been controlled and immaculately groomed, and he had seemed more solicitous of the DiCesares than concerned with his own feelings. Now his clothing was disheveled, his graying hair tousled, and he looked to be on the brink of a rage that would flatten anyone in its path.

Unfortunately, what I had to ask him would probably fan that rage. I braced myself and said, "Now tell me about Vanessa. And not all the stuff about her being a lovely young woman and a brilliant student. I heard all that this morning—but now we both know it isn't the whole truth, don't we?"

Surprisingly he reached for a cigarette and lit it slowly, using the time to calm himself. When he spoke, his voice was as level as my own. "All right, it's not the whole truth. Vanessa *is* lovely and brilliant. She'll make a top-notch lawyer. There's a hardness in her; she gets it from Ernest. It took guts to fake this suicide . . . ."

"What do you think she hopes to gain from it?"

"Freedom. From me. From Ernest's domination. She's probably taken off somewhere for a good time. When she's ready she'll come back and make her demands."

"And what will they be?"

"Enough money to move into a place of her own and finish law school. And she'll get it, too. She's all her parents have."

"You don't think she's set out to make a new life for herself?"

"Hell, no. That would mean giving up all this." The sweep of his arm encompassed the house and all the DiCesares's privileged world.

But there was one factor that made me doubt his assessment. I said, "What about the other men in her life?"

He tried to look surprised, but an angry muscle twitched in his jaw.

"Come on, Gary," I said, "you know there were other men. Even Ernest and Sylvia were aware of that."

"Ah, Christ!" He popped out of the chair and began pacing again. "All right, there were other men. It started a few months ago. I didn't understand it: things had been good with us; they still *were* good physically. But I thought, okay, she's young, this is only natural. So I decided to give her some rope, let her get it out of her system. She didn't throw it in my face, didn't embarrass me in front of my friends. Why shouldn't she have a last fling?"

"And then?"

"She began making noises about breaking off the engagement. And Ernest started that shit about not footing the bill for law school. Like a fool I went along with it, and she seemed to cave in from the pressure. But a few weeks later, it all started up again—only this time it was purposeful, cruel."

"In what way?"

"She'd know I was meeting political associates for lunch or dinner, and she'd show up at the restaurant with a date. Later she'd claim he was just a friend, but you couldn't prove it from the way they acted. We'd go to a party and she'd flirt with every man there. She got sly and secretive about where she'd been, what she'd been doing."

I had pictured Vanessa as a very angry young woman; now I realized she was not a particularly kind one, either.

Gary was saying, ". . . the last straw was on Halloween. We went to a costume party given by one of her friends from Hastings. I didn't want to go—costumes, young crowd, not my kind of thing—and so she was angry with me to begin with. Anyway, she walked out with another man, some jerk in a soldier outfit. They were dancing . . . ."

I sat up straighter. "Describe the costume."

"An old-fashioned soldier outfit. Wide-brimmed hat with a plume, frock coat, sword."

"What did the man look like?"

"Youngish. He had a full beard and wore granny glasses."

Lee Gottschalk.

The address I got from the phone directory for Lee Gottschalk was on California Street not far from Twenty-fifth Avenue and only a couple of miles from where I'd first met the ranger at Fort Point. When I arrived there and parked at the opposite curb, I didn't need to check the mailboxes to see which apartment was his; the corner windows on the second floor were ablaze with light, and inside I could see Gottschalk, sitting in an armchair in what appeared to be his living room. He seemed to be alone but expecting company, because frequently he looked up from the book he was reading and checked his watch.

In case the company was Vanessa DiCesare, I didn't want to go barging in there. Gottschalk might find a way to warn her off, or simply not answer the door when she arrived. Besides, I didn't yet have a definite connection between the two of them; the "jerk in a soldier outfit" *could* have been someone else, someone in a rented costume that just happened to resemble the working uniform at the fort. But my suspicions were strong enough to keep me watching Gottschalk for well over an hour. The ranger *had* lied to me that afternoon.

The lies had been casual and convincing, except for two mistakes—such small mistakes that I hadn't caught them even when I'd later read the newspaper account of Vanessa's purported suicide. But now I recognized them for what they were: the paper had called Gary Stornetta a "political associate" of Vanessa's father, rather than his former campaign manager, as Lee had termed him. And while the paper mentioned the suicide note, it had not said it was *taped* inside the car. While Gottschalk conceivably could know about Gary managing Ernest's campaign for the Board of Supes from other newspaper accounts, there was no way he could have known how the note was secured—except from Vanessa herself.

Because of those mistakes, I continued watching Gottschalk, straining my eyes as the mist grew heavier, hoping Vanessa would show up or that he'd eventually lead me to her. The ranger appeared to be nervous: he got up a couple of times and turned on a TV, flipped through the channels, and turned it off again. For about ten minutes, he paced back and forth. Finally, around twelve-thirty, he checked his watch again, then got up and drew the draperies shut. The lights went out behind them.

I tensed, staring through the blowing mist at the door of the apartment building. Somehow Gottschalk hadn't looked like a man who was going to bed. And my impression was correct: in a few minutes he came through the door onto the sidewalk carrying a suitcase—pale leather like the one of Vanessa's Sylvia had described to me—and got into a dark-colored Mustang parked on his side of the street. The car started up and he made a U-turn, then went right on Twenty-fifth Avenue. I followed. After a few minutes, it became apparent he was heading for Fort Point.

When Gottschalk turned into the road to the fort, I kept going until I could pull over on the shoulder. The brake lights of the Mustang flared, and then Gottschalk got out and unlocked the low iron bar that blocked the road from sunset to sunrise; after he'd driven through he closed it again, and the car's lights disappeared down the road.

Had Vanessa been hiding at drafty, cold Fort Point? It seemed a strange choice of place, since she could have used a motel or Gottschalk's apartment. But perhaps she'd been afraid someone would recognize her in a public place, or connect her with Gottschalk and come looking, as I had. And while the fort would be a miserable place to hide during the hours it was open to the public—she'd have had to keep to one of the off-limits areas, such as the west side—at night she could probably avail herself of the heated employees' lounge.

Now I could reconstruct most of the ongoing scenario: Vanessa meets Lee; they talk about his work; she decides he is the person to help her fake her suicide. Maybe there's a romantic entanglement, maybe not; but for whatever reason, he agrees to go along with the plan. She leaves her car at Vista Point, walks across the bridge, and later he drives over there and picks up the suitcase . . . .

But then why hadn't he delivered it to her at the fort? And to go after the suitcase after she'd abandoned the car was too much of a risk; he might have been seen, or the people at the fort might have noticed him leaving for too long a break. Also, if she'd walked across the bridge, surely at least one of the people I'd talked with would have seen her—the maintenance crew near the north tower, for instance.

There was no point in speculating on it now, I decided. The thing to do was to follow Gottschalk down there and confront Vanessa before she disappeared again. For a moment I debated taking my gun out of the glovebox, but then decided against it. I don't like to carry it unless I'm going into a dangerous situation, and neither Gottschalk nor Vanessa posed any particular threat to me. I was merely here to deliver a message from Vanessa's parents asking her to come home. If she didn't care to respond to it, that was not my business—or my problem.

I got out of my car and locked it, then hurried across the road and down the narrow lane to the gate, ducking under it and continuing along toward the ranger station. On either side of me were tall, thick groves of eucalyptus; I could smell their acrid fragrance and hear the fog-laden wind rustle their brittle leaves. Their shadows turned the lane into a black winding alley, and the only sound besides distant traffic noises was my tennis shoes slapping on the broken pavement. The ranger station was dark, but ahead I could see Gottschalk's car parked next to the fort. The area was illuminated only by small security lights set at intervals on the walls of the structure. Above it the bridge arched, washed in fog-muted yellowish light; as I drew closer I became aware of the grumble and clank of traffic up there.

I ran across the parking area and checked Gottschalk's car. It was empty, but the suitcase rested on the passenger seat. I turned and started toward the sally port, noticing that its heavily studded door stood open a few inches. The low tunnel was completely dark. I felt my way along it toward the courtyard, one hand on its icy stone wall.

The doors to the courtyard also stood open. I peered through them into the gloom beyond. What light there was came from the bridge and more security beacons high up on the wooden watchtowers; I could barely make out the shapes of the construction equipment that stood near the west side. The clanking from the bridge was oppressive and eerie in the still night.

As I was about to step into the courtyard, there was a movement to my right. I drew back into the sally port as Lee Gottschalk came out of one of the ground-floor doorways. My first impulse was to confront him, but then I decided against it. He might shout, warn Vanessa, and she might escape before I could deliver her parents' message.

After a few seconds I looked out again, meaning to follow Gottschalk, but he was nowhere in sight. A faint shaft of light fell through the door from which he had emerged and rippled over the cobblestone floor. I went that way, through the door and along a narrow corridor to where an archway was illuminated. Then, realizing the archway led to the unrestored cell of the jail I'd seen earlier, I paused. Surely Vanessa wasn't hiding there . . . .

I crept forward and looked through the arch. The light came from a heavy-duty flashlight that sat on the floor. It threw macabre shadows on the waterstained walls, showing their streaked paint and graffiti. My gaze followed its beams upward and then down, to where the grating of the cistern lay out of place on the floor beside the hole. Then I moved over to the railing, leaned across it, and trained the flashlight down into the well.

I saw, with a rush of shock and horror, the dark hair and once-handsome features of Vanessa DiCesare.

She had been hacked to death. Stabbed and slashed, as if in a frenzy. Her clothing was ripped, there were gashes on her face and hands, she was covered with dark smears of blood. Her eyes were open, staring with that horrible flatness of death.

I came back on my heels, clutching the railing for support. A wave of dizziness swept over me, followed by an icy coldness. I thought: he killed her. And then I pictured Gottschalk in his Union Army uniform, the saber hanging from his belt, and I knew what the weapon had been.

"God!" I said aloud.

Why had he murdered her? I had no way of knowing yet. But the answer to why he'd thrown her into the cistern, instead of just putting her into the bay, was clear: she was supposed to have committed suicide; and while bodies that fall from the Golden Gate Bridge sustain a great many injuries, slash and stab wounds aren't among them. Gottschalk could not count on the body being swept out to sea on the current; if she washed up somewhere along the coast, it would be obvious she had been murdered—and eventually an investigation might have led back to him. To him and his soldier's saber.

It also seemed clear that he'd come to the fort tonight to move the body. But why not last night, why leave her in the cistern all day? Probably he'd needed to plan, to secure keys to the gate and fort, to check the schedule of the night patrols for the best time to remove her. Whatever his reason, I realized now that I'd walked into a very dangerous situation. Walked right in without bringing my gun. I turned quickly to get out of there . . . .

And came face-to-face with Lee Gottschalk.

His eyes were wide, his mouth drawn back in a snarl of surprise. In one hand he held a bundle of heavy canvas. "You!" he said. "What the hell are you doing here?"

I jerked back from him, bumped into the railing, and dropped the flashlight. It clattered on the floor and began rolling toward the mouth of the cistern. Gottschalk lunged toward me, and as I dodged, the light fell into the hole and the cell went dark. I managed to push past him and ran down the hallway to the courtyard.

Stumbling on the cobblestones, I ran blindly for the sally port. Its doors were shut now—he'd probably taken that precaution when he'd returned from getting the tarp to wrap her body in. I grabbed the iron hasp and tugged, but couldn't get it open. Gottschalk's footsteps were coming through the courtyard after me now. I let go of the hasp and ran again.

When I came to the enclosed staircase at the other end of the court, I started up. The steps were wide at the outside wall, narrow at the inside. My toes banged into the risers; a couple of times I teetered and almost fell backwards. At the first tier I paused, then kept going. Gottschalk had said something about unrestored rooms on the second tier; they'd be a better place to hide than in the museum.

Down below I could hear him climbing after me. The sound of his feet—clattering and stumbling—echoed in the close space. I could hear him grunt and mumble: low, ugly sounds that I knew were curses.

I had absolutely no doubt that if he caught me, he would kill me. Maybe do to me what he had done to Vanessa . . . .

I rounded the spiral once again and came out on the top floor gallery, my heart beating wildly, my breath coming in pants. To my left were archways, black outlines filled with dark-gray sky. To my right was blackness. I went that way, hands out, feeling my way.

My hands touched the rough wood of a door. I pushed, and it opened. As I passed through it, my shoulder bag caught on something; I yanked it loose and kept going. Beyond the door I heard Gottschalk curse loudly, the sound filled with surprise and pain; he must have fallen on the stairway. And that gave me a little more time.

The tug at my shoulder bag had reminded me of the small flashlight I keep there. Flattening myself against the wall next to the door, I rummaged through the bag and brought out the flash. Its beam showed high walls and arching ceilings, plaster and lathe pulled away to expose dark brick. I saw cubicles and cubbyholes opening into dead ends, but to my right was an arch. I made a small involuntary sound of relief, then thought, *Quiet!* Gottschalk's footsteps started up the stairway again as I moved through the archway.

The crumbling plaster walls beyond the archway were set at odd angles—an interlocking funhouse maze connected by small doors. I slipped through one and found an irregularly shaped room heaped with debris. There didn't seem to be an exit, so I ducked back into the first room and moved toward the outside wall, where gray outlines indicated small high-placed windows. I couldn't hear Gottschalk any more—couldn't hear anything but the roar and clank from the bridge directly overhead.

The front wall was brick and stone, and the windows had wide waist-high sills. I leaned across one, looked through the salt-caked glass, and saw the open sea. I was at the front of the fort, the part that faced beyond the Golden Gate; to my immediate right would be the unrestored portion. If I could slip over into that area, I might be able to hide until the other rangers came to work in the morning.

But Gottschalk could be anywhere. I couldn't hear his footsteps above the infernal noise from the bridge. He could be right here in the room with me, pinpointing me by the beam of my flashlight . . . .

Fighting down panic, I switched the light off and continued along the wall, my hands recoiling from its clammy stone surface. It was icy cold in the vast, echoing space, but my own flesh felt colder still. The air had a salt tang, underlaid by odors of rot and mildew. For a couple of minutes the darkness was unalleviated, but then I saw a lighter rectangular shape ahead of me.

When I reached it I found it was some sort of embrasure, about four feet tall, but only a little over a foot wide. Beyond it I could see the edge of the gallery where it curved and stopped at the chain link fence that barred entrance to the other side of the fort. The fence wasn't very high—only five feet or so. If I could get through this narrow opening, I could climb it and find refuge . . . .

The sudden noise behind me was like a firecracker popping. I whirled, and saw a tall figure silhouetted against one of the seaward windows. He lurched forward, tripping over whatever he'd stepped on. Forcing back a cry, I hoisted myself up and began squeezing through the embrasure.

Its sides were rough brick. They scraped my flesh clear through my clothing. Behind me I heard the slap of Gottschalk's shoes on the wooden floor.

My hips wouldn't fit through the opening. I gasped, grunted, pulling with my arms on the outside wall. Then I turned on my side, sucking in my stomach. My bag caught again, and I let go of the wall long enough to rip its strap off my elbow. As my hips squeezed through the embrasure, I felt Gottschalk grab at my feet. I kicked out frantically, breaking his hold, and fell off the sill to the floor of the gallery.

Fighting for breath, I pushed off the floor, threw myself at the fence, and began climbing. The metal bit into my fingers, rattled and clashed with my weight. At the top, the leg of my jeans got hung up on the spiked wire. I tore it loose and jumped down the other side.

The door to the gallery burst open and Gottschalk came through it. I got up from a crouch and ran into the darkness ahead of me. The fence began to rattle as he started up it. I raced, half-stumbling, along the gallery, the open archways to my right. To my left was probably a warren of rooms similar to those on the east side. I could lose him in there . . . .

Only I couldn't. The door I tried was locked. I ran to the next one and hurled my body against its wooden panels. It didn't give. I heard myself moan in fear and frustration.

Gottschalk was over the fence now, coming toward me, limping. His breath came in erratic gasps, loud enough to hear over the noise from the bridge. I twisted around, looking for shelter, and saw a pile of lumber lying across one of the open archways.

I dashed toward it and slipped behind, wedged between it and the pillar of the arch. The courtyard lay two dizzying stories below me. I grasped the end of the top two-by-four. It moved easily, as if on a fulcrum.

Gottschalk had seen me. He came on steadily, his right leg dragging behind him. When he reached the pile of lumber and started over it towards me, I yanked on the two-by-four. The other end moved and struck him on the knee.

He screamed and stumbled back. Then he came forward again, hands outstretched toward me. I pulled back further against the pillar. His clutching hands missed me, and when they did he lost his balance and toppled onto the pile of lumber. And then the boards began to slide toward the open archway.

He grabbed at the boards, yelling and flailing his arms. I tried to reach for him, but the lumber was moving like an avalanche now, pitching over the side and crashing down into the courtyard two stories below. It carried Gottschalk's thrashing body with it, and his screams echoed in its wake. For an awful few seconds the boards continued to crash down on him, and then everything was terribly still. Even the thrumming of the bridge traffic seemed muted.

I straightened slowly and looked down into the courtyard. Gottschalk lay unmoving among the scattered pieces of lumber. For a moment I breathed deeply to control my vertigo; then I ran back to the chain link fence, climbed it, and rushed down the spiral staircase to the courtyard.

When I got to the ranger's body, I could hear him moaning. I said, "Lie still. I'll call an ambulance."

He moaned louder as I ran across the courtyard and found a phone in the gift shop, but by the time I returned, he was silent. His breathing was so shallow that I thought he'd passed out, but then I heard mumbled words coming from his lips. I bent closer to listen.

"Vanessa," he said. "Wouldn't take me with her . . . ."

I said, "Take you where?"

"Going away together. Left my car . . . over there so she could drive across the bridge. But when she . . . brought it here she said she was going alone . . . ."

So you argued, I thought. And you lost your head and slashed her to death.

"Vanessa," he said again. "Never planned to take me . . . tricked me. . ."

I started to put a hand on his arm, but found I couldn't touch him. "Don't talk any more. The ambulance'll be here soon."

"Vanessa," he said. "Oh God, what did you do to me?"

I looked up at the bridge, rust red through the darkness and the mist. In the distance, I could hear the wail of a siren.

Deceptions, I thought.

Deceptions . . .

CACHE AND CARRY
A "Nameless Detective"/Sharon McCone Story
(With Bill Pronzini)

"HELLO?"

"Wolf? It's Sharon McCone."

"Well! Been a while, Sharon. How are you?"

"I've been better. Are you busy?"

"No, no, I just got home. What's up?"

"I've got a problem and I thought you might be able to help."

"If I can. Professional problem?"

"The kind you've run into before."

"Oh?"

"One of those things that *seem* impossible but that you know has to have a simple explanation."

" . . . ."

"Wolf, are you there?"

"I'm here. The poor man's Sir Henry Merrivale."

"Who's Sir Henry Merrivale?"

"Never mind. Tell me your tale of woe."

"Well, one of All Souls's clients is a small outfit in the Outer Mission called Neighborhood Check Cashing. You know, one of these places that cashes third-party or social-security checks for local residents who don't have bank accounts of their own or easy access to a bank. We did some legal work for them a year or so ago, when they first opened for business."

"Somebody rip them off?"

"Yes. For two thousand dollars."

"Uh-huh. When?"

"Sometime this morning."

"Why did you and All Souls get called in on a police matter?"

"The police were called first but they couldn't come up with any answers. So Jack Harvey, Neighborhood's owner and manager, contacted me. But I haven't come up with any answers either."

"Go ahead. I'm listening."

"There's no way anyone could have gotten the two thousand dollars out of Neighborhood's office. And yet, if the money is still hidden somewhere on the premises, the police couldn't find it and neither could I."

"Mmm."

"Only one of two people could have taken it—unless Jack Harvey himself is responsible, and I don't believe that. If I knew which one, I might have an idea of what happened to the money. Or vice versa. But I don't have a clue either way."

"Let's have the details."

"Well, cash is delivered twice a week—Mondays and Thursdays—by armored car at the start of the day's business. It's usually five thousand dollars, unless Jack requests more or less. Today it was exactly five thousand."

"Not a big operation, then."

"No. Jack's also an independent insurance broker; the employees help him out in that end of the business too."

"His employees are the two who could have stolen the money?"

"Yes. Art DeWitt, the bookkeeper, and Maria Chavez, the cashier. DeWitt's twenty-five, single, lives in Daly City. He's studying business administration nights at City College. Chavez is nineteen, lives with her family in the Mission. She's planning to get married next summer. They both seem to check out as solid citizens."

"But you say one of them has to be guilty. Why?"

"Opportunity. Let me tell you what happened this morning. The cash was delivered as usual, and Maria Chavez entered the amount in her daily journal, then put half the money in the till and half in the safe. Business for the first hour and a half was light; only one person came in to cash a small check: Jack Harvey's cousin, whom he vouches for."

"So Chavez couldn't have passed the money to him or another accomplice."

"No. At about ten-thirty a local realtor showed up wanting to cash a fairly large check: thirty-five hundred dollars. Harvey usually doesn't like to do that, because Neighborhood runs short before the next cash delivery. Besides, the fee for cashing a large check is the same as for a small one; he stands to lose on large transactions. But the realtor is a good friend, so he okayed it. When Chavez went in to cash the check, there was only five hundred dollars in the till."

"Did DeWitt also have access to the till?"

"Yes."

"Any way either of them could have slipped out of the office for even a few seconds?"

"No. Harvey's desk is by the back door and he was sitting there the entire time."

"What about through the front?"

"The office is separated from the customer area by one of those double Plexiglass security partitions and a locked security door. The door operates by means of a buzzer at Harvey's desk. He didn't buzz anybody in or out."

"Could the two thousand have been removed between the time the police searched and you were called in?"

"No way. When the police couldn't find it in the office, they body-searched DeWitt and had a matron do the same with Chavez. The money wasn't on either of the them. Then, after the cops left, Jack told his employees they couldn't take anything away from the office except Chavez's purse and DeWitt's briefcase, both of which he searched again, personally."

"Do either DeWitt or Chavez have a key to the office?"

"No."

"Which means the missing money is still there."

"Evidently. But *where*, Wolf?"

"Describe the office to me."

"One room, with an attached lavatory that doubles as a supply closet. Table, with a desktop copier, postage scale, postage meter. A big Mosler safe; only Harvey has the combination. Three desks: Jack's next to the back door; DeWitt's in the middle; Chavez's next to the counter behind the partition, where the till is. Desks have standard stuff on them—adding machines, a typewriter on Chavez's, family photos, stack trays, staplers, pen sets. Everything you'd expect to find."

"Anything you *wouldn't* expect to find?"

"Not unless you count some lurid romance novels that Chavez likes to read on her lunch break."

"Did anything unusual happen this morning, before the shortage was discovered?"

"Not really. The toilet backed up and ruined a bunch of supplies, but Jack says that's happened three or four times before. Old plumbing."

"Uh-huh."

"You see why I'm frustrated? There just doesn't seem to be any clever hidey-hole in that office. And Harvey's already started to tear his hair. Chavez and DeWitt resent the atmosphere of suspicion; they're nervous, too, and have both threatened to quit. Harvey doesn't want to lose the one that isn't guilty, anymore than he wants to lose his two thousand dollars."

"How extensive was the search you and the police made?"

"About as extensive as you can get."

"Desks gone over from top to bottom, drawers taken out?"

"Yes."

"Underside of the legs checked?"

"Yes."

"Same thing with all the chairs?"

"To the point of removing cushions and seat backs."

"The toilet backing up—any chance that could be connected?"

"I don't see how. Harvey and I both looked it over pretty carefully. The sink and the rest of the plumbing, too."

"What about the toilet paper roll?"

"I checked it. Negative."

"Chavez's romance novels—between the pages?"

"I thought of that. Negative."

"Personal belongings?"

"All negative. Including Jack Harvey's. I went through his on the idea that DeWitt or Chavez might have thought to use him as a carrier."

"The office equipment?"

"Checked and rechecked. Copier, negative. Chavez's typewriter, negative. Postage meter and scale, negative. Four adding machines, negative. Stack trays—"

"Wait a minute, Sharon. *Four* adding machines?"

"That's right."

"Why four, with only three people?"

"DeWitt's office machine jammed and he had to bring his own from home."

"When did that happen?"

"It jammed two days ago. He brought his own yesterday."

"Suspicious coincidence, don't you think?"

"I did at first. But I checked both machines, inside and out. Negative."

"Did either DeWitt or Chavez bring anything else to the office in recent days that they haven't brought before?"

"Jack says no."

"Then we're back to DeWitt's home adding machine."

"Wolf, I told you—"

"What kind is it? Computer type, or the old-fashioned kind that runs a tape?"

"The old-fashioned kind."

"Did you run a tape on it? Or on the office machine that's supposed to be jammed?"

"... No. No, I didn't."

"Maybe you should. Both machines are still in the office, right?"

"Yes."

"Why don't you have another look at them? Run tapes on both, see if the office model really is jammed—or if maybe it's DeWitt's home model that doesn't work the way it should."

"And if it's the home model, have it taken apart piece by piece."

"Right."

"I'll call Harvey and have him meet me at Neighborhood right away."

"Let me know, huh? Either way?"

"You bet I will."

"Wolf, hi. It's Sharon."

"You sound chipper. Good news?"

"Yes, thanks to you. You were right about the adding machines. I ran a tape on DeWitt's office model and it worked fine. But the one he brought from home didn't, for a damned good reason."

"Which is?"

"Its tape roll was a dummy. Hollow, made of metal and wood with just enough paper tape to make it look like the real thing. So real neither the police nor I thought to remove and examine it before. The missing money was inside."

"So DeWitt must have been planning the theft for some time."

"That's what he confessed to the police a few minutes ago. He made the dummy roll in his workshop at home; took him a couple of weeks. It was in his home machine when he brought that in yesterday. This morning he slipped the roll out and put it into his pocket. When Maria Chavez was in the lavatory and Jack Harvey was occupied on the phone, he lifted the money from the till and pocketed that too. He went into the john after Marie came out and hid the money in the dummy roll. Then, back at his desk, he put the fake roll into his own machine, which he intended to take home with him this evening. It was his bad luck—and Jack's good luck—that the realtor came in with such a large check to cash."

"I suppose he intended to doctor the books to cover the theft."

"So he said. You know, Wolf, it's too bad DeWitt didn't apply his creative talents to some legitimate enterprise. His cache-and-carry scheme was really pretty clever."

"What kind of scheme?"

"Cache and carry. C-a-c-h-e."

" . . . "

"Was that a groan I heard?"

"McCone, if you're turning into a rogue detective, call somebody else next time you come up against an impossible problem. Call Sir Henry Merrivale."

"What do you mean, a rogue detective?"

"The worse kind there is. A punslinger."

DEADLY FANTASIES

"MS. McCONE, I know what you're thinking. But I'm not paranoid. One of them—my brother or my sister—*is* trying to kill me!"

"Please, call me Sharon." I said it to give myself time to think. The young woman seated across my desk at All Souls Legal Cooperative certainly sounded paranoid. My boss, Hank Zahn, had warned me about that when he'd referred her for private investigative services.

"Let's go over what you've told me, to make sure I've got it straight," I said. "Six months ago you were living here in the Mission district and working as a counselor for emotionally disturbed teenagers. Then your father died and left you his entire estate, something in the neighborhood of thirty million dollars."

Laurie Newingham nodded and blew her nose. As soon as she'd come into my office she'd started sneezing. Allergies, she'd told me. To ease her watering eyes she'd popped out her contact lenses and stored them in their plastic case; in doing that she had spilled some of the liquid that the lenses soaked in over her fingers, then nonchalantly wiped them on her faded jeans. The gesture endeared her to me because I'm sloppy, too. Frankly, I couldn't imagine this freshly scrubbed young woman— she was about ten years younger than I, perhaps twenty-five—possessing a fortune. With her trim, athletic body, and tanned, snub-nosed face, and carelessly styled blond hair, she looked like a high school cheerleader. But Winfield Newingham had owned much of San Francisco's choice real estate, and Laurie had been the developer's youngest—and apparently favorite—child.

I went on, "Under the terms of the will, you were required to move back into the family home in St. Francis Wood. You've done so. The will stipulated that your brother Dan and sister Janet can remain there as long as they wish. So you've been living with them, and they've both been acting hostile because you inherited everything."

"Hostile? One of them wants to *kill* me! I keep having stomach cramps, throwing up—you know."

"Have you seen a doctor?"

"I *hate* doctors! They're always telling me there's nothing wrong with me, when I know there *is*."

"The police, then?"

"I like them a whole lot less than doctors. Besides, they wouldn't believe me." Now she took out an inhaler and breathed deeply from it.

Asthma, as well as allergies, I thought. Wasn't asthma sometimes psychosomatic? Could the vomiting and other symptoms be similarly rooted?

"Either Dan or Janet is trying to poison me," Laurie said, "because if I die, the estate reverts to them."

"Laurie," I said, "why did your father leave everything to you?"

"The will said it was because I'd gone out on my own and done something I believed in. Dan and Janet have always lived off him; the only jobs they've ever been able to hold down have been the ones Dad gave them."

"One more question: why did you come to All Souls?" My employer is a legal services plan for people who can't afford the going rates.

Laurie looked surprised. "I've *always* come here, since I moved to the Mission and started working as a counselor five years ago. I may be able to afford a downtown law firm, but I don't trust them, any more now than I did when I inherited the money. Besides, I talked it over with Dolph, and he said it would be better to stick with a known quantity."

"Dolph?"

"Dolph Edwards. I'm going to marry him. He's director of the guidance center where I used to work—still work, as a volunteer."

"That's the Inner Mission Self-Help Center?"

She nodded. "Do you know them?"

"Yes." The center offered a wide range of social services to a mainly Hispanic clientele—including job placement, psychological counseling, and short term financial assistance. I'd heard that recently their programs had been drastically cut back due to lack of funding—as all too often happens in today's arid political climate.

"Then you know what my father meant about my having done something I believed in," Laurie said. "The center's a hopeless mess, of course; it's never been very well organized. But it's the kind of project I'd like my money to work for. After I marry Dolph I'll help him realize his dreams effectively—and in the right way."

I nodded and studied her for a moment. She stared back anxiously. Laurie was emotionally ragged, I thought, and needed someone to look out for her. Besides, I identified with her in a way. At her age, I'd also been the cheerleader type, and I'd gone out of my own and done something I believed in, too.

"Okay," I said. "What I'll do is talk with your brother and sister, feel the situation out. I'll say you've applied for a volunteer position here, counseling clients with emotional problems, and that you gave their names as character references."

Her eyes brightened and some of the lines of strain smoothed. She gave me Dan's office phone number and Janet's private line at the St. Francis Wood house. Preparing to leave, she clumsily dropped her purse on the floor. Then she located her contact case and popped a lens into her mouth to clean it; as she fitted it into her right eye, her foot nudged the bag, and the inhaler and a bottle of time-release vitamin capsules rolled across the floor. We went for them at the same time, and our heads grazed each other's.

She looked at me apologetically. One of her eyes was now gray, the other a brilliant blue from the tint of the contact. It was like a physical manifestation of her somewhat schizoid personality: down to earth wholesomeness warring with what I had begun to suspect was a dangerous paranoia.

Dan Newingham said, "Why the hell does Laurie want to do that? She doesn't have to work any more, even as a volunteer. She controls all the family's assets."

We were seated in his office in the controller's department of Newingham Development, on the thirty-first floor of one of the company's financial district buildings. Dan was a big guy, with the same blond good looks as his sister, but they were spoiled by a petulant mouth and a body whose bloated appearance suggested an excess of good living.

"If she wants to work, " he added, "there're plenty of positions she could fill right here. It's her company, dammit, and she ought to take an interest in it."

"I gather her interests run more to social service."

"More to the low life, you mean."

"In what respect?"

Dan got up and went to look out the window behind the desk. The view of the bay was blocked by an upthrusting jumble of steel and plate glass—the legacy that firms such as Newingham Development had left a once old fashioned and beautiful town.

After a moment, Dan turned. "I don't want to offend you, Ms. . . McCone, is it? "

I nodded.

"I'm not putting down your law firm, or what you're trying to do," he went on, "but when you work on your end of the spectrum, you naturally have to associate with people who aren't quite . . . well, of our class. I wasn't aware of the kind of people Laurie was associating with during those years she didn't live at home, but now . . . her boyfriend, that Dolph, for instance. He's always around; I can't stand him. Anyway, my point is, Laurie should settle down now, come back to the real world, learn the business. Is that too much to ask in exchange for thirty million?"

"She doesn't seem to care about the money."

Dan laughed harshly. "Doesn't she? Then why did she move back into the house? She could have chucked the whole thing."

"I think she feels she can use the money to benefit people who really need it."

"Yes, and she'll blow it all. In a few years there won't *be* any New-ingham Development. Oh, I know what was going through my father's mind when he made that will: Laurie's always been the strong one, the dedicated one. He thought that if he forced her to move back home, she'd eventually become involved in the business and there'd be real leadership here. Laurie can be very single-minded when she wants things to go a certain way, and that's what it takes to run a firm like this. But the sad thing is, Dad just didn't realize how far gone she is in her bleeding heart sympathies."

"That aside, what do you think about her potential for counseling our disturbed clients?"

"If you really want to know, I think she'd be terrible. Laurie's a basket case. She has psychosomatic illnesses, paranoid fantasies. She needs counseling herself."

"Can you describe these fantasies?"

He hesitated, tapping his fingers on the window frame. "No, I don't think I care to. I shouldn't have brought them up."

"Actually, Mr. Newingham, I think I have an inkling of what they are. Laurie told her lawyer that someone's trying to poison her. She seemed obsessed with the idea, which is why we decided to check her references thoroughly."

"I suppose she also told her lawyer who the alleged poisoner is?"

"In a way. She said it was either you or your sister Janet."

"God, she's worse off than I realized. I suppose she claims one of us wants to kill her so he can inherent my father's estate. That's ridiculous—I don't need the damned money. I have a good job here, and I've invested profitably." Dan paused, then added, "I hope you can convince her to get into an intensive therapy program before she tries to counsel any of your clients. Her fantasies are starting to sound dangerous."

❖

Janet Newingham was the exact opposite of her sister: a tall brunette with a highly stylized way of moving and speaking. Her clothes were designer, her jewelry expensive, and her hair and nails told of frequent attention at the finest salons. We met at the St. Francis Wood house—a great pile of stone reminiscent of an Italian villa that sat on a double lot near the fountain that crowned the area's main boulevard. I had informed Laurie that I would be interviewing her sister, and she had agreed to absent herself from the house; I didn't want my presence to trigger an unpleasant scene between the two of them.

I needn't have worried, however. Janet Newingham was one of those cool, reserved women who may smolder under the surface but seldom display anger. She seated me in a formal parlor overlooking the strip of park that runs down the center of St. Francis Boulevard and served me coffee from a sterling silver pot. From all appearances, I might have been there to discuss the Junior League fashion show.

When I had gotten to the point of my visit, Janet leaned forward and extracted a cigarette from an ivory box on the coffee table. She took her time lighting it, then said, "*Another* volunteer position? It's bad enough she kept on working at that guidance center for nothing after they lost their federal funding last spring, but this . . . I'm surprised; I thought nothing would ever pry her away from her precious Dolph."

"Perhaps she feels it's not a good idea to stay on there, since they plan to be married."

"Did she tell you that? Laurie's always threatening to marry Dolph, but I doubt she ever will. She just keeps him around because he's her one claim to the exotic. He's one of these social reformers, you know. Totally devoted to his cause."

"And what is that?"

"Helping people. Sounds very sixties, doesn't it. That center is his *raison d'être*. He founded it, and he's going to keep it limping along no matter what. He plays the crusader role to the hilt, Dolph does: dresses in Salvation Army castoffs, drives a motorcycle. You know the type."

"That's very interesting," I said, "but it doesn't have much bearing on Laurie's ability to fill our volunteer position. What do you think of her potential as a counselor?"

"Not a great deal. On, I know that's what she's been doing these past five years, but recently Laurie's been . . . a very disturbed young woman. But you know that. My brother told me of your visit to his office, and that you had already heard of her fantasy that one of us is trying to kill her."

"Well, yes. It's odd—"

"It's not just odd, it's downright dangerous. Dangerous for her to walk around in such a paranoid state, and dangerous for Dan and me. It's our reputations she's smearing."

"Because on the surface you both appear to have every reason to want her out of the way."

Janet's lips compressed—a mild reaction, I thought, to what I'd implied. "On the surface, I suppose that is how it looks," she said. "But as far as I'm concerned Laurie is welcome to our father's money. I had a good job in the public relations department at Newingham Development; I saved and invested my salary well. After my father died, I quit working there, and I'm about to open my own public relations firm."

"Did the timing of your quitting have anything to do with Laurie's inheriting the company?"

Janet picked up a porcelain ashtray and carefully stubbed her cigarette out. "I'll be frank with you, Ms. McCone: it did. Newingham Development had suddenly become not a very good place to work; people were running scared—they always do when there's no clear managerial policy. Besides . . ."

"Besides?"

"Since I'm being frank, I may as well say it. I did not want to work for my spoiled little bitch of a sister who's always had things her own way. And if that makes me a potential murderer—"

She broke off as the front door opened. We both looked that way. A man wearing a shabby tweed coat and a shocking purple scarf and aviator sunglasses entered. His longish black hair was windblown, and his sharp features were ruddy from the cold. He pocketed a key and started for the stairway.

"Laurie's not here, Dolph," Janet said.

He turned. "Where is she?"

"Gone shopping."

"Laurie hates to shop."

"Well, that's where she is. You'd better come back in a couple of hours." Janet's tone did little to mask her dislike.

Nor did the twist of his mouth mask *his* dislike of his fiancée's sister. Without a word he turned and strode out the door.

I asked, "Dolph Edwards?"

"Yes. You can see what I mean."

Actually, I hadn't seen enough of him, and I decided to take the opportunity to talk to him while it was presented. I thanked Janet Newingham for her time and hurried out.

Dolph's motorcycle was parked at the curb near the end of the front walk, and he was just revving it up when I reached him. At first his narrow lips pulled down in annoyance, but when I told him who I was, he smiled and shut the machine off. He remained astride it while we talked.

"Yes, I told Laurie it would be better to stick with All Souls," he said when I mentioned the context in which I'd first heard of him. "You've got good people there, and you're more likely to take Laurie's problem seriously than someone in a downtown law firm."

"You think someone *is* trying to kill her, then?"

"I know what I see. The woman's sick a lot lately, and those two" —he motioned at the house—"hate her guts."

"You must see a great deal of what goes on here," I said. "I noticed you have a key."

"Laurie's my fiancée," he said with a puritanical stiffness that surprised me.

"So she said. When do you plan to be married?"

I couldn't make out his eyes behind the dark aviator glasses, but the lines around them deepened. Perhaps Dolph suspected what Janet claimed: that Laurie didn't really intend to marry him. "Soon," he said curtly.

We talked for a few minutes more, but Dolph could add little to what I'd already observed about the Newingham family. Before he started his bike he said apologetically, "I wish I could help, but I'm not around them very much. Laurie and I prefer to spend our time at my apartment."

I didn't like Dan or Janet Newingham, but I also didn't believe either was trying to poison Laurie. Still, I followed up by explaining the situation to my former lover and now good friend Greg Marcus, lieutenant with the SFPD homicide detail. Greg ran a background check on Dan for me, and came up with nothing more damning than a number of unpaid parking tickets. Janet didn't even have those to her discredit. Out of curiosity, I asked him to check on Dolph Edwards, too. Dolph had a record of two arrests involving political protests in the late seventies—just what I would have expected.

At that point I reported my findings to Laurie and advised her to ask her brother and sister to move out of the house. If they wouldn't, I said, she should talk to Hank about invalidating that clause of her father's will. And in any case she should also get herself some psychological counseling. Her response was to storm out of my office. And that, I assumed, ended my involvement with Laurie Newingham's problems.

But it didn't. Two weeks later Greg called to tell me that Laurie had been taken ill during a family cocktail party and had died at the St. Francis Wood house, an apparent victim of poisoning.

I felt terrible, thinking of how lightly I had taken her fears, how easily I'd accepted her brother and sister's claims of innocence, how I'd let Laurie down when she'd needed and trusted me. So I waited until Greg had the autopsy results and then went to the office at the Hall of Justice.

"Arsenic," Greg said when I'd seated myself on his visitor's chair. "The murderer's perfect poison: widely available, no odor, little if any taste. It takes the body a long time to eliminate arsenic, and a person can be fed small amounts over a period of two or three weeks, even longer, before he or she succumbs. According to the medical examiner, that's what happened to Laurie."

"But why small amounts? Why not just one massive dose?"

"The murderer was probably stupid enough that he figured if she'd been sick for weeks we wouldn't check for poisons. But why he went on with it after she started talking about someone trying to kill her . . ."

"He? Dan's your primary suspect, then?"

"I was using 'he' generically. The sister looks good, too. They both had extremely strong motives, but we're not going to be able to charge either until we can find out how Laurie was getting the poison."

"You say extremely strong motives. Is there something besides the money?"

"Something connected to the money; each of them seems to need it more badly than they're willing to admit. The interim management of Newingham Development has given Dan his notice; there'll be a hefty severance payment, of course, but he's deeply in debt—gambling debts, to the kind of people who won't accept fifty-dollars-a-week installments. The sister had most of her savings tied up in one of those real estate investment partnerships; it went belly up, and Janet needs to raise additional cash to satisfy outstanding obligations to the other partners."

"I wish I'd known about that when I talked with them. I might have prevented Laurie's death."

Greg held up a cautioning hand. "Don't blame yourself for something you couldn't know or foresee. That should be one of the cardinal rules of your profession."

"It's one of the rules, all right, but I seem to keep breaking it. Greg, what about Dolph Edwards?"

"He didn't stand to benefit by her death. Laurie hadn't made a will, so everything reverts to the brother and sister."

"No will? I'm surprised Hank didn't insist she make one."

"According to your boss, she had an appointment with him for the day after she died. She mentioned something about a change in circumstances, so I guess she was planning to make the will in favor of her future husband. Another reason we don't suspect Edwards."

I sighed. "So what you've got is a circumstantial case against one of two people."

"Right. And without uncovering the means by which the poison got to her, we don't stand a chance of getting an indictment against either."

"Well . . . the obvious means is in her food."

"There's a cook who prepares all the meals. She, a live-in maid, and the family basically eat the same things. On the night she died, Laurie, her brother and sister, and Dolph Edwards all had the same hors d'oeuvres with cocktails. The leftovers tested negative."

"And you checked what she drank, of course."

"It also tested negative."

"What about medications? Laurie probably took pills for her asthma. She had an inhaler—"

"We checked everything. Fortunately, I caught the call and remembered what you'd told me. I was more than thorough. Had the contents of the bedroom and bathroom inventoried, anything that could have contained poison was taken away for testing."

"What about this cocktail party? I know for a fact that neither Dan nor Janet liked Dolph. And according to Dolph, they both hated Laurie. He wasn't fond of them, either. It seems like an unlikely group for a convivial gathering."

"Apparently Laurie arranged the party. She said she had an announcement to make."

"What was it?"

"No one knows. She died before she could tell them."

Three days later Hank and I attended Laurie's funeral. It was in an old-fashioned churchyard in the little town of Tomales, near the bay of the same name northwest of San Francisco. The Newinghams had a summer home on the bay, and Laurie had wanted to be buried there.

It was one of those winter afternoons when the sky is clear and hard, and the sun is as pale as if it were filtered through water. Hank and I stood a little apart from the crowd of mourners on the knoll, near a windbreak of eucalyptus that bordered the cemetery. The people who had traveled from the city to lay Laurie to rest were an oddly assorted group: dark-suited men and women who represented San Francisco's business community; others who bore the unmistakable stamp of high society; shabbily dressed Hispanics who must have been clients of the Inner Mission Self-Help Center. Dolph Edwards arrived on his motorcycle; his inappropriate attire—the shocking purple scarf seemed several shades too festive—annoyed me.

Dan and Janet Newingham arrived in the limousine that followed the hearse and walked behind the flower-covered casket to the graveside. Their pious propriety annoyed me, too. As the service went on, the wind rose. It rustled the leaves of the eucalyptus trees and brought with it dampness and the odor of the nearby bay. During the final prayer, a strand of my hair escaped the knot I'd fastened it in and blew across my face. It clung damply there, and when I licked my lips to push it away, I tasted salt—whether from the sea air or tears, I couldn't tell.

As soon as the service was concluded, Janet and Dan went back to the limousine and were driven away. One of the Chicana women stopped to speak to Hank; she was a client, and he introduced us. When I looked around for Dolph, I found he had disappeared. By the time Hank finished chatting with his client, the only other person left at the graveside besides us and the cemetery workers was an old Hispanic lady who was placing a single rose on the casket.

Hank said, "I could use a drink." We started down the uneven stone walk, but I glanced back at the old woman, who was following us unsteadily.

"Wait," I said to Hank and went to take her arm as she stumbled.

The woman nodded her thanks and leaned on me, breathing heavily.

"Are you all right?" I asked. "Can we give you a ride back to the city?" My old MG was the only car left beyond the iron fence.

"Thank you, but no," she said. "My son brought me. He's waiting down the street, there's a bar. You were a friend of Laurie?"

"Yes." But not as good a friend as I might have been, I reminded myself. "Did you know her through the center?"

"Yes. She talked with my grandson many times and made him stay in school when he wanted to quit. He loved her, we all did."

"She was a good woman. Tell me, did you see her fiancé leave?" I had wanted to give Dolph my condolences.

The woman looked puzzled.

"The man she planned to marry—Dolph Edwards."

"I thought he was her husband."

"No, although they planned to marry soon."

The old woman sighed. "They were always together. I thought they were already married. But nowadays who can tell? My son—Laurie helped his own son, but is he grateful? No. Instead of coming to her funeral, he sits in a bar . . . ."

I was silent on the drive back to the city—so silent that Hank, who is usually oblivious to my moods, asked me twice what was wrong. I'm afraid I snapped at him, something to the effect of funerals not being my favorite form of entertainment, and when I dropped him at All Souls, I refused to have the drink he offered. Instead I went downtown to City Hall.

When I entered Greg Marcus's office a couple of hours later, I said without preamble, "The Newingham case: you told me you inventoried the contents of Laurie's bedroom and bathroom and had anything that could have contained poison taken away for testing?"

". . . Right."

"Can I see the inventory sheet?"

He picked up his phone and asked for the file to be brought in. While he waited, he asked me about the funeral. Over the years, Greg has adopted a wait-and-see attitude toward my occasional interference in his cases. I've never been sure whether it's because he doesn't want to disturb what he considers to be my shaky thought processes, or that he simply prefers to leave the hard work to me.

When the file came, he passed it to me. I studied the inventory sheet, uncertain exactly what I was looking for. But something was missing there. What? I flipped the pages, then wished I hadn't. A photo of Laurie looked up at me, brilliant blue eyes blank and lifeless. No more cheerleader out to save the world—

Quickly I flipped back to the inventory sheet. The last item was "1 handbag, black leather, & contents." I looked over the list of things from the bathroom again and focused on the word "unopened."

"Greg," I said, "what was in Laurie's purse?"

He took the file from me and studied the list. "It should say here, but it doesn't. Sloppy work—new man on the squad."

"Can you find out?"

Without a word he picked up the phone receiver, dialed, and made the inquiry. When he hung up he read off the notes he'd made. "Wallet. Checkbook. Inhaler, sent to lab. Vitamin capsules, also sent to lab. Contact lens case. That's all."

"That's enough. The contact lens case is a two-chambered plastic receptacle holding about half an ounce of fluid for the lenses to soak in. There was a brand-new, unopened bottle of the fluid on the inventory of Laurie's bathroom."

"So?"

"I'm willing to bet the contents of that bottle will test negative for arsenic; the surface of it might or might not show someone's fingerprints, but not Laurie's. That's because the murderer put it there *after* she died, but *before* your people arrived on the scene."

Greg merely waited.

"Have the lab test the liquid in that lens case for arsenic. I'm certain the results will be positive. The killer added arsenic to Laurie's soaking solution weeks ago, and then he removed that bottle and substituted the unopened one. We wondered why slow poisoning, rather than a massive dose; it was because the contact case holds so little fluid."

"Sharon, arsenic can't be ingested through the eyes—"

"Of course it can't! But Laurie had the habit, as lots of contact wearers do—you're not supposed to, of course; it can cause eye infections—of taking her lenses out of the case and putting them into her mouth to clean them before putting them on. She probably did it a lot because she had allergies and took the lenses off to rest her eyes. That's how he poisoned her, a little at a time over an extended period."

"Dan Newingham?"

"No. Dolph Edwards."

Greg waited, his expression neither doubting nor accepting.

"Dolph is a social reformer," I said. "He founded that Inner Mission Self-Help Center; it's his whole life. But its funding has been cancelled and it can't go on much longer. In Janet Newingham's words, Dolph is intent on keeping it going 'no matter what.'"

"So? He was going to marry Laurie. She could have given him plenty of money—"

"Not for the center. She told me it was a 'hopeless mess.' When she married Dolph, she planned to help him, but in the 'right way.' Laurie has been described to me by both her brother and sister as quite single-minded and always getting what she wanted. Dolph must have realized that too, and knew her money would never go for his self-help center."

"All right, I'll take your word for that. But Edwards still didn't stand to benefit. They weren't married, she hadn't made a will—"

"They *were* married. I checked that out at City Hall a while ago. They were married last month, probably at Dolph's insistence when he realized the poisoning would soon have a fatal effect."

Greg was silent for a moment. I could tell by the calculating look in his eyes that he was taking my analysis seriously. "That's another thing we slipped up on—just like not listing the contents of her purse. What made you check?"

"I spoke with an old woman who was at the funeral. She thought they were married and made the comment that nowadays you can't tell. It got me thinking . . . . Anyway, it doesn't matter about the will because under California's community property laws, Dolph inherits automatically in the absence of one."

"It seems stupid of him to marry her so soon before she died. The husband automatically comes under suspicion—"

"But the poisoning started long *before* they were married. That automatically threw suspicion on the brother and sister."

"And Dolph had the opportunity."

"Plenty. He even tried to minimize it by lying to me: he said he and Laurie didn't spend much time at the St. Francis Wood House, but Dan described Dolph as being around all the time. And even if he wasn't he could just as easily have poisoned her lens solution at his own apartment. He told another lie to you when he said he didn't know what the

the announcement Laurie was going to make at the family gathering was. It could only have been the announcement of their secret marriage. He may even have increased the dosage of poison, in the hope she'd succumb before she could reveal it."

"Why do you suppose they kept it secret?"

"I think Dolph wanted it that way. It would minimize the suspicion directed at him if he just let the fact of the marriage come out after either Dan or Janet had been charged with the murder. He probably intended to claim ignorance of the community property laws, say he'd assumed since there was no will he couldn't inherit. Why don't we ask him if I'm right?"

Greg's hand moved toward his phone. "Yes—why don't we?"

When Dolph Edwards confessed to Laurie's murder, it turned out that I'd been absolutely right. He also added an item of further interest: he hadn't been in love with Laurie at all, had had a woman on the Peninsula whom he planned to marry as soon as he could without attracting suspicion.

It was too bad about Dolph; his kind of social crusader had so much ego tied up in their own individual projects that they lost sight of the larger objective. Had Laurie lived, she would have applied her money to any number of worthy causes, but now it would merely go to finance the lifestyles of her greedy brother and sister.

But it was Laurie I felt worst about. And it was a decidedly bittersweet satisfaction that I took in solving her murder, in fulfilling my final obligation to my client.

ALL THE LONELY PEOPLE

"NAME, SHARON McCONE. Occupation . . . I can't put private investigator. What should I be?" I glanced over my shoulder at Hank Zahn, my boss at All Souls Legal Cooperative. He stood behind me, his eyes bemused behind thick horn-rimmed glasses.

"I've heard you tell people you're a researcher when you don't want to be bothered with stupid questions like 'What's a nice girl like you. . .'"

"*Legal* researcher." I wrote it on the form. "Now—'About the person you are seeking.' Age—does not matter. Smoker—does not matter. Occupation—does not matter. I sound excessively eager for a date, don't I?"

Hank didn't answer. He was staring at the form. "The things they ask. Sexual preference." He pointed at the item. "Hetero, bi, lesbian, gay. There's no place for 'does not matter.'"

As he spoke, he grinned wickedly. I glared at him. "You're enjoying this!"

"Of course I am. I never thought I'd see the day you'd fill out an application for a dating service."

I sighed and drummed my fingertips on the desk. Hank is my best male friend, as well as my boss. I love him like a brother—sometimes. But he harbors an overactive interest in my love life and delights in teasing me about it. I would be hearing about the dating service for years to come. I asked, "What should I say I want the guy's cultural interests to be? I can't put 'does not matter' for everything."

"I don't think burglars *have* cultural interests."

"Come on, Hank. Help me with this!"

"Oh, put film. Everyone's gone to a movie."

"Film." I checked the box.

The form was quite simple, yet it provided a great deal of information about the applicant. The standard questions about address, income level, whether the individual shared a home or lived alone, and hours free for dating were enough in themselves to allow an astute burglar to weed out prospects—and pick times to break in when they were not likely to be on the premises.

And that apparently was what had happened at the big singles complex down near the San Francisco–Daly City line, owned by Hank's client, Dick Morris. There had been three burglaries over the past five months, beginning not long after the place had been leafleted by All the Best People Introduction Service. Each of the people whose apartments had been hit were women who had filled out application forms; they had had from two to ten dates with men with whom the service had put them in touch. The burglaries had taken place when one renter was at work, another away for the weekend, and the third out with a date whom she had also met through Best People.

Coincidence, the police had told the renters and Dick Morris. After all, none of the women had reported having dates with the same man. And there were many other common denominators among them besides their use of the service. They lived in the same complex. They all knew one another. Two belonged to the same health club. They shopped at the same supermarket, shared auto mechanics, hairstylists, dry cleaners, and two of them went to the same psychiatrist.

Coincidence, the police insisted. But two other San Francisco area members of Best People had also been burglarized—one of them male—and so they checked the service out carefully.

What they found was absolutely no evidence of collusion in the burglaries. It was no fly-by-night operation. It had been in business ten years—a long time for that type of outfit. Its board of directors included a doctor, psychologist, a rabbi, a minister, and a well-known author of somewhat weird but popular novels. It was respectable—as such things go.

But Best People was still the strongest link among the burglary victims. And Dick Morris was a good landlord who genuinely cared about his tenants. So he put on a couple of security guards, and when the police couldn't run down the perpetrator(s) and backburnered the cases, he came to All Souls for legal advice.

It might seem unusual for the owner of a glitzy singles complex to come to a legal services plan that charges its clients on a sliding-fee scale, but Dick Morris was cash-poor. Everything he'd saved during his long years as a journeyman plumber had gone into the complex, and it was barely turning a profit as yet. Wouldn't be turning any profit at all if the burglaries continued and some of his tenants got scared and moved out.

Hank could have given Dick the typical attorney's spiel about leaving things in the hands of the police and continuing to pay the guards out of his dwindling cash reserves, but Hank is far from typical. Instead he referred Dick to me. I'm All Souls's staff investigator, and assignments like this one—where there's a challenge—are what I live for.

They are, that is, unless I have to apply for membership in a dating service, plus set up my own home as a target for a burglar. Once I started "dating," I would remove anything of value to All Souls, plus Dick would station one of his security guards at my house during the hours I was away from there, but it was still a potentially risky and nervous-making proposition.

Now Hank loomed over me, still grinning. I could tell how much he was going to enjoy watching me suffer through an improbable, humiliating, *asinine* experience. I smiled back—sweetly.

"'Your sexual preference.' Hetero." I checked the box firmly. "Except for inflating my income figure, so I'll look like I have a lot of good stuff to steal, I'm filling this out truthfully," I said. "Who knows—I might find someone wonderful."

When I looked back up at Hank, my evil smile matched his earlier one. He, on the other hand, looked as if he'd swallowed something the wrong way.

✧

My first "date" was a chubby little man named Jerry Hale. Jerry was *very* into the singles scene. We met at a bar in San Francisco's affluent Marina district, and while we talked, he kept swiveling around in his chair and leering at every woman who walked by. Most of them ignored him but a few glared; I wanted to hang a big sign around my neck saying, "I'm not really with him, it's only business." While I tried to find out about his experiences with All the Best People Introduction Service, plus impress him with the easily fenceable items I had at home, he tried to educate me on the joys of being single.

"I used to be into the bar scene pretty heavily," he told me. "Did all right too. But then I started to worry about herpes and AIDS—I'll let you see the results of my most recent test if you want—and my drinking was getting out of hand. Besides, it was expensive. Then I went the other way—a health club. Did all right there too. But goddamn, it's *tiring*. So I then joined a bunch of church groups—you meet a lot of horny women there. But churches encourage matrimony, and I'm not into that."

"So you applied to All the Best People. How long have you—?"

"Not right away. First I thought about joining AA, even went to a meeting. Lots of good-looking women are recovering alcoholics, you know. But I like to drink too much to make the sacrifice. Dear Abby's always saying you could enroll in courses, so I signed up for a couple at U. C. Extension. Screenwriting and photography."

My mouth was stiff from smiling politely, and I had just about written Jerry off as a possible suspect—he was too busy to burglarize anyone. I took a sip of wine and looked at my watch.

Jerry didn't notice the gesture. "The screenwriting class was terrible—the instructor actually wanted you to write stuff. And photography—how can you see women in the darkroom, let alone make any moves when you smell like chemicals?"

I had no answer for that. Maybe my own efforts at photography accounted for my not having a lover at the moment . . . .

"Finally I found All the Best People," Jerry went on. "Now I really do all right. And it's opened up a whole new world of dating to me—eighties-style. I've answered ads in the paper, placed my own ads too. You've always got to ask that they send a photo, though, so you can screen out the dogs. There's Weekenders, they plan trips. When I don't want to go out of the house, I use the Intro Line—there's a phone club you can join, where you call in for three bucks and either talk to one person or on a party line. There's a video exchange where you can make tapes and trade them with people so you'll know you're compatible before you set up a meeting. I do all right."

He paused expectantly, as if he thought I was going to ask how I could get in on all these eighties-style deals.

"Jerry," I said, "have you read any good books lately?"

"Have I . . . *what*?"

"What do you do when you're not dating?"

"I work. I told you, I'm in sales—"

"Do you ever spend time alone?"

"Doing what?"

"Oh, just being alone. Puttering around the house or working at hobbies. Just thinking."

"Are you crazy? What kind of a computer glitch are you, anyway?" He stood, all five-foot-three of him quivering indignantly. "Believe me, I'm going to complain to Best People about setting me up with you. They described you as 'vivacious,' but you've hardly said a word all evening!"

Morton Stone was a nice man, a sad man. He insisted on buying me dinner at his favorite Chinese restaurant. He spent the evening asking me questions about myself and my job as a legal researcher; while he listened, his fingers played nervously with the silverware. Later, over a brandy in a nearby bar, he told me how his wife had died the summer before, of cancer. He told me about his promise to her that he would get on with his life, find someone new, and be happy. This was the first date he'd arranged through All the Best People; he'd never done anything like that in his life. He'd only tried them because he wasn't good at meeting people. He had a good job, but it wasn't enough. He had money to travel, but it was no fun without someone to share the experience with. He would have liked to have children, but he and his wife had put it off until they'd be financially secure, and then they found out about the cancer . . . .

I felt guilty as hell about deceiving him, and for taking his time, money, and hope. But by the end of the evening I'd remembered a woman friend who was just getting over a disastrous love affair. A nice, sad woman who wasn't good at meeting people; who had a good job, loved to travel, and longed for children . . .

Bob Gillespie was a sailing instructor on a voyage of self-discovery. He kept prefacing his remarks with statements such as, "You know, I had a great insight into myself last week." That was nice; I was happy for him. But I would rather have gotten to know his surface persona before probing into his psyche. Like the two previous men, Bob didn't fit any of the recognizable profiles of the professional burglar, nor had he any great insight into how All the Best People worked.

Ted Horowitz was a recovering alcoholic, which was admirable. Unfortunately, he was also the confessional type. He began every anecdote with the admission that it had happened "back when I was drinking." He even felt compelled to describe how he used to throw up on his ex-wife. His only complaint about Best People—this with a stern look at my wineglass—was that they kept referring him to women who drank.

✧

Jim Rogers was an adman who wore safari clothes and was into guns. I refrained from telling that I own two .38 Specials and am a highly qualified marksman, for fear it would incite him to passion. For a little while I considered him seriously for the role of burglar, but when I probed the subject by mentioning a friend having recently been ripped off, Jim became enraged and said the burglar ought to be hunted down and shot.

✧

"I'm going about this all wrong," I said to Hank.

It was ten in the morning, and we were drinking coffee at the big round table in All Souls's kitchen. The night before I'd spent hours on the phone with an effervescent insurance underwriter who was going on a whale-watching trip with Weekenders, the group that god-awful Jerry had mentioned. He'd concluded our conversation by saying he'd be sure to note in his pocket organizer to call me the day after he returned. Then I'd been unable to sleep and had sat up hours longer, drinking too much and listening for burglars and brooding about loneliness.

I wasn't involved with anyone at the time—nor did I particularly want to be. I'd just emerged from a long-term relationship and was reordering my life and getting used to doing things alone again. I was fortunate in that my job and my little house—which I'm constantly remodeling—filled most of the empty hours. But I could still understand what Morton and Bob and Ted and Jim and even that dreadful Jerry were suffering from.

It was the little things that got to me. Like the times I went to the supermarket and everything I felt like having for dinner was packaged for two or more, and I couldn't think of anyone I wanted to have over to share it with. Or the times I'd be driving around a curve in the road and come upon a spectacular view, but have no one in the passenger seat to point it out to. And then there were the cold sheets on the other side of a wide bed on a foggy San Francisco night.

But I got through it, because I reminded myself that it wasn't going to be that way forever. And when I couldn't convince myself of that, I thought about how it was better to be totally alone than alone *with* some-one. That's how *I* got through the cold, foggy nights. But I was discovering there was a whole segment of the population that availed itself of dating services and telephone conversation clubs and video exchanges. Since I'd started using Best People, I'd been inundated by mail solicitations and found that the array of services available to singles was astonishing.

Now I told Hank, "I simply can't stand another evening making polite chitchat in a bar. If I listen to another ex-wife story, I'll scream. I don't want to know that these guys' parents did to them at age ten that made the whole rest of their lives a mess. And besides, having that security guard on my house is costing Dick Morris a bundle he can ill afford."

Helpfully Hank said, "So change your approach."

"Thanks for your great suggestion." I got up and went out to the desk that belongs to Ted Smalley, our secretary, and dug out a phone directory. All the Best People wasn't listed. My file on the case was on the kitchen table. I went back there—Hank had retreated to his office—and checked the introductory letter they'd sent me; it showed nothing but a post-office box. The zip code told me it was the main post office at Seventh and Mission streets.

I went back and borrowed Ted's phone book again, then looked up the post office's number. I called it, got the mail-sorting supervisor, and identified myself as Sharon from Federal Express. "We've got a package here for All the Best People Introduction Service," I said, and read off the box number. "That's all I've got—no contact phone, no street address."

"Assholes," she said wearily. "Why do they send them to a P. O. box when they know you can't deliver to one? For that matter, why do you accept them when they're addressed like that?"

"Damned if I know. I only work here."

"I can't give out the street address, but I'll supply the contact phone." She went away, came back, and read it to me.

"Thanks." I depressed the disconnect button and redialed.

A female voice answered with only the phone number. I went into my Federal Express routine. The woman gave me the address without hesitation, in the 200 block of Gough Street near the Civic Center. After I hung up I made one more call: to a friend on the *Chronicle*. J. D. Smith was in the city room and agreed to leave a few extra business cards with the security guard in the newspaper building's lobby.

All the Best People's offices took up the entire second floor of a renovated Victorian. I couldn't imagine why they needed so much space, but they seemed to be doing a landslide business, because phones in the offices on either side of the long corridor were ringing madly. I assumed it was because the summer vacation season was approaching and San

Francisco singles were getting anxious about finding someone to make travel plans with.

The receptionist was more or less what I expected to find in the office of that sort of business: petite, blond, sleekly groomed, and expensively dressed, with an elegant manner. She took J. D.'s card down the hallway to see if their director was available to talk with me about the article I was writing on the singles scene. I paced around the tiny waiting room, which didn't even have chairs. When the young woman came back, she said Dave Lester would be happy to see me and led me to an office at the rear.

The office was plush, considering the attention that had been given to decor in the rest of the suite. It had a leather couch and chairs, a wet bar, and an immense mahogany desk. There wasn't so much as a scrap of paper or a file folder to suggest anything resembling work was done there. I couldn't see Dave Lester, because he had swiveled his high-backed chair around toward the window and was apparently contemplating the wall of the building next door. The receptionist backed out the door and closed it. I cleared my throat, and the chair turned toward me.

The man in the chair was god-awful Jerry Hale.

Our faces must have been mirror images of shock. I said, "What are *you* doing here?"

He said, "You're not J. D. Smith. You're Sharon McCone!" Then he frowned down at the business card he held. "Or is Sharon McCone really J. D. Smith?"

I collected my scattered wits and said, "Which are you—Dave Lester or Jerry Hale?" I added, "I'm a reporter doing a feature article on the singles scene."

"So Marie said. How did you get this address? We don't publish it because we don't want all sorts of crazies wandering in. This is an exclusive service; we screen our applicants carefully."

They certainly hadn't screened me; otherwise they'd have uncovered numerous deceptions. I said, "Oh, we newspaper people have our sources."

"Well, you certainly misrepresented yourself to us."

"And you misrepresented yourself to *me*."

He shrugged. "It's all part of the screening process, for our clients' protection. We realize most applicants would shy away from a formal interview situation, so we have the first date take the place of that."

"You yourself go out with *all* the women who apply?"

"A fair amount, using a different name every time, of course, in case any of them know each other and compare notes." At my astonished look he added, "What can I say? I like women. But naturally I have help. And Marie"—he motioned at the closed door—"and one of the secretaries check out the guys."

No wonder Jerry had no time to read. "Then none of the things you told me were true? About being into the bar scene and the church groups and the health club?"

"Sure they were. My previous experiences were what led me to buy Best People from its former owners. They hadn't studied the market, didn't know how to make a go of it in the eighties."

"Well, you're certainly a good spokesman for your own product. But how come you kept referring me to other clients? We didn't exactly part on amiable terms."

"Oh, that was just a ruse to get out of there. I had another date. I'd seen enough to know you weren't my type. But I decided you were still acceptable; we get a lot of men looking for your kind."

The "acceptable" rankled. "What exactly is my kind?"

"Well, I'd call you . . . introspective. Bookish? No, not exactly. A little offbeat? Maybe intense? No. It's peculiar . . . you're peculiar—"

"Stop right there!"

Jerry—who would always be god-awful Jerry and never Dave Lester to me—stood up and came around the desk. I straightened my posture. From my five-foot-six vantage point I could see the beginnings of a bald spot under his artfully styled hair. When he realized where I was looking, his mouth tightened. I took a perverse delight in his discomfort.

"I'll have to ask you to leave now," he said stiffly.

"But don't you want Best People featured in a piece on singles?"

"I do not. I can't condone the tactics of a reporter who misrepresents herself."

"Are you sure that's the reason you don't want to talk with me?"

"Of course. What else—"

"Is there something about Best People that you'd rather not see publicized?"

Jerry flushed. When he spoke, it was in a flat, deceptively calm manner. "Get out of here," he said, "or I'll call your editor."

Since I didn't want to get J. D. in trouble with the *Chron*, I went.

Back at my office at All Souls, I curled up in my ratty armchair—my favorite place to think. I considered my visit to All the Best People; I considered what was wrong with the setup there. Then I got out my list of burglary victims and called each of them. All three gave me similar answers to my questions. Next I checked the phone directory and called my friend Sandy in the billing office at Pacific Bell.

"I need an address for a company that's only listed by number in the directory," I told her.

"Billing address, or location where the phone's installed?"

"Both, if they're different."

She tapped away on her computer keyboard. "Billing and location are the same: two-eleven Gough. Need anything else?"

"That's it. Thanks—I owe you a drink."

In spite of my earlier determination to depart the singles scene, I spent the next few nights on the phone, this time assuming the name of Patsy Newhouse, my younger sister. I talked to various singles about my new VCR; I described the sapphire pendant my former boyfriend had given me and how I planned to have it reset to erase old memories. I babbled happily about the trip to Las Vegas I was taking in a few days with Weekenders, and promised to make notes in my pocket organizer to call people as soon as I got back. I mentioned—in seductive tones— how I loved to walk barefoot over my genuine Persian rugs. I praised the merits of my new microwave oven. I described how I'd gotten into collecting costly jade carvings. By the time the Weekenders trip was due to depart for Vegas, I was constantly sucking on throat lozenges and wondering how long my voice would hold out.

Saturday night found me sitting in my kitchen sharing ham sandwiches and coffee by candlelight with Dick Morris's security guard, Bert Jankowski. The only reason we'd chanced the candles was that we'd taped the shades securely over the windows. There was something about eating in total darkness that put us both off.

Bert was a pleasant-looking man of about my age, with sandy hair and a bristly mustache and a friendly, open face. We'd spent a lot of time together—Friday night, all day today—and I'd pretty much heard his life story. We had a lot in common: he was from Oceanside, not far from where I'd grown up in San Diego; like me, he had a degree in the social sciences and hadn't been able to get a job in his field. Unlike me, he'd been working for the security service so long that he was making a decent wage, and he liked it. It gave him more time, he said, to read and to fish. I'd told him life story, too: about my somewhat peculiar family, about my blighted romances, even about the man I'd once had to shoot. By Saturday night I sensed both of us were getting bored with examining our pasts, but the present situation was even more stultifying.

I said, "Something has *got* to happen soon."

Bert helped himself to another sandwich. "Not necessarily. Got any more of those pickles?"

"No, we're out."

"Shit. I don't suppose if this goes on that there's any possibility of cooking breakfast tomorrow? Sundays I always fix bacon."

In spite of my having wolfed down some ham, my mouth began to water. "No," I said wistfully. "Cooking smells, you know. This house is supposed to be vacant for the weekend."

"So far no one's come near it, and nobody seems to be casing it. Maybe you're wrong about the burglaries."

"Maybe . . . No, I don't think so. Listen: Andie Wyatt went to Hawaii; she came back to a cleaned-out apartment. Janie Roos was in Carmel with a lover; she lost everything fenceable. Kim New was in Vegas, where I'm supposed to be—"

"But maybe you're wrong about the way the burglar knows—"

There was a noise toward the rear of the house, past the current construction zone on the back porch. I held up my hand for Bert to stop talking and blew out the candles.

I sensed Bert tensing. He reached for his gun at the same time I did mine.

The noise came louder—the sound of an implement probing the back-porch lock. It was one of those useless toy locks that had been there when I bought the cottage; I'd left the dead bolt unlocked since Friday.

Rattling sounds. A snap. The squeak of the door as it moved inward.

I touched Bert's arm. He moved over into the recess by the pantry, next to the light switch. I slipped up next to the door to the porch. The outer door shut, and footsteps came toward the kitchen, then stopped.

A thin beam of light showed under the inner door between the kitchen and the porch—the burglar's flashlight. I smiled, imagining his surprise at the sawhorses and wood scraps and exposed wiring that make up my own personal urban-renewal project.

The footsteps moved toward the kitchen door again. I took the safety off the .38.

The door swung toward me. A half-circle of light from the flash illuminated the blue linoleum. It swept back and forth, then up and around the room. The figure holding the flash seemed satisfied that the room was empty; it stepped inside and walked toward the hall.

Bert snapped on the overhead light.

I stepped forward, gun extended, and said, "All right, Jerry. Hands above your head and turn around—slowly."

The flash clattered to the floor. The figure—dressed all in black—did as I said.

But it wasn't Jerry.

It was Morton Stone—the nice, sad man I'd had the dinner date with. He looked as astonished as I felt.

I thought of the evening I'd spent with him, and my anger rose. All that sincere talk about how lonely he was and how much he missed his dead wife. And now he turned out to be a common crook!

"You son of a bitch!" I said. "And I was going to fix you up with one of my friends!"

He didn't say anything. His eyes were fixed nervously on my gun.

Another noise on the back porch. Morton opened his mouth, but I silenced him by raising the .38.

Footsteps clattered across the porch, and a second figure in black came through the door. "Morton, what's wrong? Why'd you turn the lights on?" a woman's voice demanded.

It was Marie, the receptionist from All the Best People. Now I knew how she could afford her expensive clothes.

"So I was right about *how* they knew when to burglarize people, but wrong about *who* was doing it," I told Hank. We were sitting at the bar in the Remedy Lounge, our favorite Mission Street watering hole.

"I'm still confused. The Intro Line is part of All the Best People?"

"It's owned by Jerry Hale, and the phone equipment is located in the same offices. But as Jerry—Dave Lester, whichever incarnation you prefer—told me later, he doesn't want the connection publicized because the Intro Line is kind of sleazy, and Best People's supposed to be high-toned. Anyway, I figured it out because I noticed there were an awful lot of phones ringing at their offices, considering their number isn't published. Later I confirmed it with the phone company and started using the line myself to set the burglar up."

"So this Jerry wasn't involved at all?"

"No. He's the genuine article—a born-again single who decided to put his knowledge to turning a profit."

Hank shuddered and took a sip of Scotch.

"The burglary scheme," I went on, "was all Marie Stone's idea. She had access to the addresses of the people who joined the Intro Line club, and she listened in on the phone conversations and scouted out good prospects. Then, when she was sure their homes would be vacant for a period of time, her brother, Morton Stone, pulled the job while she kept watch outside."

"How come you had a date with Marie's brother? Was he looking you over as a burglary prospect?"

"No. They didn't use All the Best People for that. It's Jerry's pride and joy; he's too involved with the day-to-day workings and might have realized something was wrong. But the Intro Line is just a profit-making arm of the business to him—he probably uses it to subsidize his dating. He'd virtually turned the operation of it over to Marie. But he did allow Marie to send out mail solicitations for it to Best People clients, as well as mentioning it to the women he 'screened,' and that's how the burglary victims heard of it."

"But it still seems too great a coincidence that you ended up going out with this Morton."

I smiled. "It wasn't a coincidence at all. Morton also works for Best People, helping Jerry screen the female clients. When I had my date with Jerry, he found me . . . well, he said I was peculiar."

Hank grinned and started to say something, but I glared. "Anyway, he sent Mort out with me to render a second opinion"

"Ye gods, you were almost rejected by a dating service."

"What really pisses me off is Morton's grieving-widower story. I really fell for the whole tasteless thing. Jerry told me Morton gets a lot of women with it—they just can't resist a man in pain."

"But not McCone." Hank drained his glass and gestured at mine. "You want another?"

I looked at my watch. "Actually, I've got to be going."

"How come? It's early yet."

"Well, uh . . . I have a date."

He raised his eyebrows. "I thought you were through with the singles scene. Which one is it tonight—the gun nut?"

I got off the bar stool and drew myself up in a dignified manner. "It's someone I met on my own. They always tell you that you meet the most compatible people when you're just doing what you like to do and not specifically looking."

"So where'd you meet this guy?"

"On a stakeout."

Hank waited. His eyes fairly bulged with curiosity.

I decided not to tantalize him any longer. I said, "It's Bert Jankowski, Dick Morris's security guard."

THE PLACE THAT TIME FORGOT

IN SAN FRANCISCO'S Glen Park district there is a small building with the words GREENGLASS 5 & 10¢ STORE painted in faded red letters on its wooden facade. Broadleaf ivy grows in planter boxes below its windows and partially covers their dusty panes. Inside is a counter with jars of candy and bubble gum on top and cigars, cigarettes, and pipe tobacco down below. An old-fashioned jukebox—the kind with colored glass tubes—hulks against the opposite wall. The rest of the room is taken up by counters laden with merchandise that has been purchased at fire sales and manufacturers' liquidations. In a single shopping spree, it is possible for a customer to buy socks, playing cards, off-brand cosmetics, school supplies, kitchen utensils, sports equipment, toys and light bulbs—all at prices of at least ten years ago.

It is a place forgotten by time, a fragment of yesterday in the midst of today's city.

I have now come to know the curious little store well, but up until one rainy Wednesday last March, I'd done no more than glance inside while passing. But that morning Hank Zahn, my boss at All Souls Legal Cooperative, had asked me to pay a call on its owner, Jody Greenglass. Greenglass was a client who had asked if Hank knew an investigator who could trace a missing relative for him. It didn't sound like a particularly challenging assignment, but my assistant, who usually handles routine work, was out sick. So at ten o'clock, I put on my raincoat and went over there.

When I pushed open the door I saw there wasn't a customer in sight. The interior was gloomy and damp; a fly buzzed fitfully against one of the windows. I was about to call out, thinking the proprietor must be beyond the curtained doorway at the rear, when I realized a man was sitting on a stool behind the counter. That was all he was doing—just sitting, his eyes fixed on the wall above the jukebox.

He was a big man, elderly, with a belly that bulged out under his yellow shirt and black suspenders. His hair and beard were white and luxuriant, his eyebrows startlingly black by contrast. When I said, "Mr.

Greenglass?" he looked at me, and I saw an expression of deep melancholy.

"Yes?" he asked politely.

"I'm Sharon McCone, from All Souls Legal Cooperative."

"Ah, yes. Mr. Zahn said he would send someone."

"I understand you want to locate a missing relative."

"My granddaughter."

"If you'll give me the particulars, I can get on it right away." I looked around for a place to sit, but didn't see any chair.

Greenglass stood. "I'll get you a stool." He went toward the curtained doorway, moving gingerly, as if his feet hurt him. They were encased in floppy slippers.

While I waited for him, I looked up at the wall behind the counter and saw it was plastered with faded pieces of slick paper that I first took to be playbills. Upon closer examination I realized they were sheet music, probably of forties and fifties vintage. Their artwork was of that era anyway: formally dressed couples performing intricate dance steps; showgirls in extravagant costumes; men with patent-leather hair singing their hearts out; perfectly coiffed women showing plenty of even, pearly white teeth. Some of the song titles were vaguely familiar to me: "Dreams of You," "The Heart Never Lies," "Sweet Mystique." Others I had never heard of.

Jody Greenglass came back with a wooden stool and set it on my side of the counter. I thanked him and perched on it, then took a pencil and notebook from my bag. He hoisted himself onto his own stool, sighing heavily.

"I see you were looking at my songs," he said.

"Yes. I haven't really seen any sheet music since my piano teacher gave up on me when I was about twelve. Some of those are pretty old, aren't they?"

"Not nearly as old as I am." He smiled wryly. "I wrote the first in thirty-nine, the last in fifty-three. Thirty-seven of them in all. A number were hits."

"*You* wrote them?"

He nodded and pointed to the credit line on the one closest to him: "Words and Music by Jody Greenglass."

"Well, for heaven's sake." I said. "I've never met a songwriter before. Were these recorded too?"

"Sure. I've got them all on the jukebox. Some good singers performed them—Como, Crosby." His smile faded. "But then, in the fifties, popular music changed. Presley, Holly, those fellows—that's what did it. I couldn't change with it. Luckily, I'd always had the store; music was more of a hobby for me. 'My Little Girl'"—he indicated a sheet with a picture-pretty toddler on it—"was the last song I ever sold. Wrote it for my granddaughter when she was born in fifty-three. It was *not* a big hit."

"This is the granddaughter you want me to locate?"

"Yes. Stephanie Ann Weiss. If she's still alive, she's thirty-seven now."

"Let's talk about her. I take it she's your daughter's daughter?"

"My daughter Ruth's. I only had the one child."

"Is your daughter still living?"

"I don't know." His eyes clouded. "There was a . . . an estrangement. I lost track of both of them a couple of years after Stephanie was born."

"If it's not too painful, I'd like to hear about that."

"It's painful, but I can talk about it." He paused, thoughtful. "It's funny. For a long time it didn't hurt, because I had my anger and disappointment to shield myself. But those kinds of emotions can't last without fuel. Now that they're gone, I hurt as much as if it happened yesterday. That's what made me decide to try to make amends to my granddaughter."

"But not your daughter too?"

He made a hand motion as if to erase the memory of her. "Our parting was too bitter; there are some things that can't be atoned for, and frankly, I'm afraid to try. But Stephanie—if her mother hasn't completely turned her against me, there might be a chance for us."

"Tell me about this parting."

In a halting manner that conveyed exactly how deep his pain went, he related his story.

Jody Greenglass had been widowed when his daughter was only ten and had raised the girl alone. Shortly after Ruth graduated from high school, she married the boy next door. The Weiss family had lived in the house next to Greenglass's Glen Park cottage for close to twenty years, and their son, Eddie, and Ruth were such fast childhood friends that a gate was installed in the fence between their adjoining backyards. Jody, in fact, thought of Eddie as his own son.

After their wedding the couple moved north to the small town of Petaluma, where Eddie had found a good job in the accounting department of one of the big egg hatcheries. In 1953, Stephanie Ann was born. Greenglass didn't know exactly when or why they began having marital problems; perhaps they hadn't been ready for parenthood, or perhaps the move from the city to the country didn't suit them. But by 1955, Ruth had divorced Eddie and taken up with a Mexican national named Victor Rios.

"I like to think I'm not prejudiced," Greenglass said to me. "I've mellowed with the years, I've learned. But you've got to remember that this was the mid-fifties. Divorce wasn't all that common in my circle. And people didn't marry outside our faith, much less form relationships out of wedlock with those of a different race. Rios was an illiterate laborer, not even an American citizen. I was shocked that Ruth was living with this man, exposing her child to such a situation."

"So you tried to stop her."

He nodded wearily. "I tried. But Ruth wasn't listening to me anymore. She'd always been such a good girl. Maybe that was the problem—she'd been *too* good and it was her time to rebel. We quarreled bitterly, more than once. Finally I told her that if she kept on living with Rios, she and her child would be dead to me. She said that was just fine with her. I never saw or heard from her again."

"Never made any effort to contact her?"

"Not until a couple of weeks ago. I nursed my anger and bitterness, nursed them well. But then in the fall I had some health problems—my heart—and realized I'd be leaving this world without once seeing my grown-up granddaughter. So when I was back on my feet again, I went up to Petaluma, checked the phone book, asked around their old neighborhood. Nobody remembered them. That was when I decided I needed a detective."

I was silent, thinking of the thirty-some years that had elapsed. Locating Stephanie Ann Weiss—or whatever name she might now be using—after all that time would be difficult. Difficult, but not impossible, given she was still alive. And certainly more challenging than the job I'd initially envisioned.

Greenglass seemed to interpret my silence as pessimism. He said, "I know it's been a very long time, but isn't there something you can do for me? I'm seventy-eight years old; I want to make amends before I die."

I felt the prickle of excitement that I often experience when faced with an out-of-the-ordinary problem. I said, "I'll try to help you. As I said before, I can get on it right away."

I gathered more information from him—exact spelling of names, dates—then asked for the last address he had for Ruth in Petaluma. He had to go in the back of the store where, he explained, he now lived, to look it up. While he did so, I wandered over to the jukebox and studied the titles of the 78s. There was a basket of metal slugs on top of the machine, and on a whim I fed it one and punched out selection E–3, "My Little Girl." The somewhat treacly lyrics boomed forth in a smarmy baritone; I could understand why the song hadn't gone over in the days when America was gearing up to feverishly embrace the likes of Elvis Presley. Still, I had to admit the melody was pleasing—downright catchy, in fact. By the time Greenglass returned with the address, I was humming along.

Back in my office at All Souls, I set a skiptrace in motion, starting with an inquiry to my friend Tracy at the Department of Motor Vehicles regarding Ruth Greenglass, Ruth Weiss, Ruth Rios, Stephanie Ann Rios, or any variant thereof. A check with directory assistance revealed that neither woman currently had a phone in Petaluma or the surrounding communities. The Petaluma Library had nothing on them in their reverse street directory. Since I didn't know either woman's occupation, professional affiliations, doctor, or dentist, those avenues were closed to me. Petaluma High School would not divulge information about graduates, but the woman in records with whom I spoke assured me that no one named Stephanie Weiss or Stephanie Rios had attended during the mid- to late-sixties. The county's voter registration had a similar lack of information. The next line of inquiry to pursue while waiting for a reply from the DMV was vital statistics—primarily marriage licenses and death certificates—but for those I would need to go to the Sonoma County Courthouse in Santa Rosa. I checked my watch, saw it was only a little after one, and decided to drive there.

Santa Rosa, some fifty miles north of San Francisco, is a former country town that has risen to the challenge of migrations from the crowded communities of the Bay Area and become a full-fledged city with a population nearing a hundred thousand. Testimony to this is the new County Administration Center on its outskirts, where I found the Recorder's Office housed in a building on the aptly named Fiscal Drive.

My hour-and-a-half journey up there proved well worth the time: the clerk I dealt with was extremely helpful, the records easily accessed. Within half an hour, for a nominal fee, I was in possession of a copy of Ruth Greenglass Weiss's death certificate. She had died of cancer at Petaluma General Hospital in June of 1974; her next of kin was shown as Stephanie Ann Weiss, at an address on Bassett Street in Petaluma. It was a different address from the last one Greenglass had had for them.

The melody of "My Little Girl" was still running through my head as I drove back down the freeway to Petaluma, the southernmost community in the county. A picturesque river town with a core of nineteenth-century business buildings, Victorian homes, and a park with a bandstand, it is surrounded by little hills—which is what the Indian word *Petaluma* means. The town used to be called the Egg Basket of the World, because of the proliferation of hatcheries such as the one where Eddie Weiss worked, but since the decline of the egg- and chicken-ranching business, it has become a trendy retreat for those seeking to avoid the high housing costs of San Francisco and Marin. I had friends there—people who had moved up from the city for just that reason—so I knew the lay of the land fairly well.

Bassett Street was on the older west side of town, far from the bland, treeless tracts that have sprung up to the east. The address I was seeking turned out to be a small white frame bungalow with a row of lilac bushes planted along the property line on either side. Their branches hung heavy with as yet unopened blossoms; in a few weeks the air would be sweet with their perfume.

When I went up on the front porch and rang the bell, I was greeted by a very pregnant young woman. Her name, she said, was Bonita Clark; she and her husband Russ had bought the house two years before from some people named Berry. The Berrys had lived there for at least ten years and had never mentioned anyone named Weiss.

I hadn't really expected to find Stephanie Weiss still in residence, but I'd hoped the present owner could tell me where she had moved. I said, "Do you know anyone on the street who might have lived here in the early seventies?"

"Well, there's old Mrs. Caubet. The pink house on the corner with all the rosebushes. She's lived here forever."

I thanked her and went down the sidewalk to the house she'd indicated. Its front yard was a thicket of rosebushes whose colors ranged from yellows to reds to a particularly beautiful silvery purple. The rain had stopped before I'd reached town, but not all that long ago; the roses' velvety petals were beaded with droplets.

Mrs. Caubet turned out to be a tall, slender woman with sleek gray hair, vigorous-looking in a blue sweatsuit and athletic shoes. I felt a flicker of amusement when I first saw her, thinking of how Bonita Clark had called her "old," said she'd lived there "forever." Interesting, I thought, how one's perspective shifts. . . .

Yes, Mrs. Caubet said after she'd examined my credentials, she remembered the Weisses well. They'd moved to Bassett Street in 1970. "Ruth was already ill with the cancer that killed her," she added. "Steff was only seventeen, but so grown-up, the way she took care of her mother."

"Did either of them ever mention a man named Victor Rios?"

The woman's expression became guarded. "You say you're working for Ruth's father?"

"Yes."

She looked thoughtful, then motioned at a pair of white wicker chairs on the wraparound porch. "Let's sit down."

We sat. Mrs. Caubet continued to look thoughtful, pleating the ribbing on the cuff of her sleeve between her fingers. I waited.

After a time she said, "I wondered if Ruth's father would ever regret disowning her."

"He's in poor health. It's made him realize he doesn't have much longer to make amends."

"A pity that it took until now. He's missed a great deal because of his stubbornness. I know; I'm a grandparent myself. And I'd like to put him in touch with Steff, but I don't know what happened to her. She left Petaluma six months after Ruth died."

"Did she say where she planned to go?"

"Just something about getting in touch with relatives. By that I assumed she meant her father's family in the city. She promised to write, but she never did, not even a Christmas card."

"Will you tell me what you remember about Ruth and Stephanie? It may give me some sort of lead, and besides, I'm sure my client will want to know about their lives after his falling-out with Ruth."

She shrugged. "It can't hurt. And to answer your earlier question, I have heard of Victor Rios. He was Ruth's second husband; although the marriage was a fairly long one, it was not a particularly good one. When she was diagnosed as having cancer, Rios couldn't deal with her illness, and he left her. Ruth divorced him, took back her first husband's name. It was either that, she once told me, or Greenglass, and she was even more bitter toward her father than toward Rios."

"After Victor Rios left, what did Ruth and Stephanie live on? I assume Ruth couldn't work."

"She had some savings—and, I suppose, alimony."

"It couldn't have been much. Jody Greenglass told me Rios was an illiterate laborer."

Mrs. Caubet frowned. "That's nonsense! He must have manufactured the idea, out of prejudice and anger at Ruth for leaving her first husband. He considered Eddie Weiss a son you know. It's true that when Ruth met Rios, he didn't have as good a command of the English language as he might, but he did have a good job at Sunset Line and Twine. They weren't rich, but I gather they never lacked for the essentials."

It made me wonder what else Greenglass had manufactured. "Did Ruth ever admit to living with Rios before their marriage?"

"No, but it wouldn't have surprised me. She always struck me as a nonconformist. And that, of course, would better explain her father's attitude."

"One other thing puzzles me," I said. "I checked with the high school, and they have no record of Stephanie attending."

"That's because she went to parochial school. Rios was Catholic, and that's what he wanted. Ruth didn't care either way. As it was, Steff dropped out in her junior year to care for her mother. I offered to arrange home care so she might finish her education—I was once a social worker and know how to go about it—but Steff said no. The only thing she really missed about school, she claimed, was choir and music class. She had a beautiful singing voice."

So she'd inherited her grandfather's talent, I thought. A talent I was coming to regard as considerable, since I still couldn't shake the lingering melody of "My Little Girl."

"How did Stephanie feel about her grandfather? And Victor Rios?" I asked.

"I think she was fond of Rios, in spite of what he'd done to her mother. Her feelings toward her grandfather I'm less sure of. I do remember that toward the end Steff had become very like her mother; observing that alarmed me somewhat."

"Why?"

"Ruth was a very bitter woman, totally turned in on herself. She had no real friends, and she seemed to want to draw Steff into a little circle from which the two of them could fend off the world together. By the time Steff left Petaluma she'd closed off, too, withdrawn from what few friends she'd been permitted. I'd say such bitterness in so young a woman is cause for alarm, wouldn't you?"

"I certainly would. And I suspect that if I do find her, it's going to be very hard to persuade her to reconcile with her grandfather."

Mrs. Caubet was silent for a moment, then said, "She might surprise you."

"Why do you say that?"

"It's just a feeling I have. There was a song Mr. Greenglass wrote in celebration of Steff's birth. Do you know about it?"

I nodded.

"They had a record of it. Ruth once told me that it was the only thing he'd ever given them, and she couldn't bear to take that away from Steff. Anyway, she used to play it occasionally. Sometimes I'd go over there, and Steff would be humming the melody while she worked around the house."

That didn't mean much, I thought. After all, I'd been mentally humming it since that morning.

❖

When I arrived back in the city I first checked at All Souls to see if there had been a response to my inquiry from my friend at the DMV. There hadn't. Then I headed for Glen Park to break the news about his daughter's death to Jody Greenglass, as well as to get some additional information.

This time there were a few customers in the store: a young couple poking around in Housewares; an older woman selecting some knitting yarn. Greenglass sat at his customary position behind the counter. When I gave him the copy of Ruth's death certificate, he read it slowly, then folded it carefully and placed it in his shirt pocket. His lips trembled inside their nest of fluffy white beard, but otherwise he betrayed no emotion. He said, "I take it you didn't find Stephanie Ann at that address."

"She left Petaluma about six months after Ruth died. A neighbor thought she might have planned to go to relatives. Would that be the Weisses, do you suppose?"

He shook his head. "Norma and Al died within months of each other in the mid-sixties. They had a daughter, name of Sandra, but she married and moved away before Eddie and Ruth did. To Los Angeles, I think. I've no idea what her husband's name might be."

"What about Eddie Weiss—what happened to him?"

"I didn't tell you?"

"No."

"He died a few months after Ruth divorced him. Auto accident. He'd been drinking. Damned near killed his parents, following so close on the divorce. That was when Norma and Al stopped talking to me; I guess they blamed Ruth. Things got so uncomfortable there on the old street that I decided to come to live here at the store."

The customer who had been looking at yarn came up, her arms piled high with heather-blue skeins. I stepped aside so Greenglass could ring up the sale, glanced over my shoulder at the jukebox, then went up to it and played "My Little Girl" again. As the mellow notes poured from the machine, I realized that what had been running through my head all day was not quite the same. Close, very close, but there were subtle differences.

And come to think of it, why should the song have made such an impression, when I'd only heard it once? It was catchy, but there was no reason for it to haunt me as it did.

Unless I'd heard something like it. Heard it more than once. And recently . . .

I went around the counter and asked Greenglass if I could use his phone. Dialed the familiar number of radio KSUN, the Light of the Bay. My former lover, Don Del Boccio, had just come into the studio for his six-to-midnight stint as disc jockey, heartthrob, and hero to half a million teenagers who have to be either hearing-impaired or brain-damaged, and probably both. Don said he'd be glad to provide expert assistance, but not until he got off work. Why didn't I meet him at his loft around twelve-thirty?

I said I would and hung up, thanking the Lord that I somehow managed to remain on mostly good terms with the men from whom I've parted.

✧

Don said, "Hum it again."

"You know I'm tone-deaf."

"You have no vocal capabilities. You can distinguish tone, though. And I can interpret your warbling. Hum it."

We were seated in his big loft in the industrial district off Third Street, surrounded by his baby grand piano, drums, sound equipment, books, and—a recent acquisition—a huge aquarium of tropical fish. I'd taken a nap after going home from Greenglass's and felt reasonably fresh. Don—a big, easygoing man who enjoys his minor celebrity status and also keeps up his serious musical interests—was reasonably wired. We were drinking red wine and picking at a plate of antipasto he'd casually thrown together.

"Hum it," he said again.

I hummed, badly, my face growing hot as I listened to myself.

He imitated me—on key. "It's definitely not rock, not with that tempo. Soft rock? Possibly. There's something about it . . . that sextolet—"

"That what?"

"An irregular rhythmic grouping. One of the things that makes it stick in your mind. Folk? Maybe country. You say you think you've been hearing it recently?"

"That's the only explanation I can come up with for it sticking in my mind the way it has."

"Hmm. There's been some new stuff coming along recently, out of L.A. rather than Nashville, that might . . . You listen to a country station?"

"KNEW, when I'm driving sometimes."

"Disloyal thing."

"I never listened to KSUN much, even when we . . ."

Our eyes met and held. We were both remembering, but I doubted if the mental images were the same. Don and I are too different; that was what ultimately broke us up.

After a moment he grinned and said, "Well, no one over the mental age of twelve does. Listen, what I guess is that you've been hearing a song that's a variation on the melody of the original one: which is odd, because it's an uncommon one to begin with."

"Unless the person who wrote the new song knew the old one."

"Which you tell me isn't likely, since it wasn't very popular. What is it you're investigating—a plagiarism case?"

I shook my head. If Jody Greenglass's last song had been plagiarized, I doubted it was intentional—at least not on the conscious level. I said, "Is it possible to track down the song, do you suppose?"

"Sure. Care to run over to the studio? I can do a scan on our library, see what we've got."

"But KSUN doesn't play anything except hard rock."

"No, but we get all sorts of promos, new releases. Let's give it a try."

"There you are," Don said. "'It Never Stops Hurting.' Steff Rivers. Atlas Records. Released last November."

I remembered it now, half heard as I'd driven the city streets with my old MG's radio tuned low. Understandable that for her professional name she'd Anglicized that of the only father figure she'd ever known.

"Play it again," I said.

Don pressed the button on the console and the song flooded the sound booth, the woman's voice soaring and clean. The lyrics were about grieving for a lost lover, but I thought I knew other experiences that had gone into creating the naked emotion behind them: the scarcely known father who had died after the mother left him; the grandfather who had rejected both mother and child; the stepfather who had been unable to cope with fatal illness and had run away.

When the song ended and silence filled the little booth, I said to Don, "How would I go about locating her?"

He grinned. "One of the Atlas reps just happens to be a good friend of mine. I'll give her a call in the morning, see what I can do."

The rain started again early the next morning. It made the coastal road that wound north on the high cliffs above the Pacific highway dangerously slick. By the time I arrived at the village of Gualala, just over the Mendocino County line, it was close to three and the cloud cover was beginning to break up.

The town, I found, was just a strip of homes and businesses between the densely forested hills and the sea. A few small shopping centers, some unpretentious eateries, the ubiquitous realty offices, a new motel, and a hotel built during the logging boom of the late 1800s—that was about it. It would be an ideal place, I thought, for retirees or starving artists, as well as a young woman seeking frequent escape from the pressures of a career in the entertainment industry.

Don's record-company friend had checked with someone she knew in Steff Rivers's producer's office to find out her present whereabouts, had sworn me to secrecy about where I'd received the information and given me an address. I'd pinpointed the turnoff from the main highway on a county map. It was a small lane that curved off toward the sea about a half mile north of town; the house at its end was actually a pair of A frames, weathered gray shingle, connected by a glassed-in walkway. Hydrangeas and geraniums bloomed in tubs on either side of the front door; a stained glass oval depicting a sea gull in flight hung in the window. I left the MG next to a gold Toyota sports car parked in the drive.

There was no answer to my knock. After a minute I skirted the house and went around back. The lawn there was weedy and uneven; it sloped down toward a low grapestake fence that guarded the edge of the ice-plant-covered bluff. On a bench in front of it sat a small figure wearing a red rain slicker, the hood turned up against the fine mist. The person was motionless, staring out at the flat, gray ocean.

When I started across the lawn, the figure turned. I recognized Steff Rivers from the publicity photo Don had dug out of KSUN's files the night before. Her hair was black and cut very short, molded to her head like a bathing cap; her eyes were large, long-lashed, and darkly luminous. In her strong features I saw traces of Jody Greenglass's.

She called out, "Be careful there. Some damn rodent has dug the yard up."

I walked cautiously the rest of the way to the bench.

"I don't know what's wrong with it," she said, gesturing at a hot tub on a deck opening off the glassed-in walkway of the house. "All I can figure is something's plugging the drain."

"I'm sorry?"

"Aren't you the plumber?"

"No."

"Oh. I knew she was a woman, and I thought . . . Who are you then?"

I took out my identification and showed it to her. Told her why I was there.

Steff Rivers seemed to shrink inside her loose slicker. She drew her knees up and hugged them with her arms.

"He needs to see you," I concluded. "He wants to make amends."

She shook her head. "It's too late for that."

"Maybe. But he *is* sincere."

"Too bad." She was silent for a moment, turning her gaze back toward the sea. "How did you find me? Atlas and my agent know better than to give out this address."

"Once I knew Stephanie Weiss was Steff Rivers, it was easy."

"And how did you find *that* out?"

"The first clue I had was 'It Never Stops Hurting.' You adapted the melody of 'My Little Girl' for it."

"I what?" She turned her head toward me, features frozen in surprise. Then she was very still, seeming to listen to the song inside her head. "I guess I did. My God . . . I *did*."

"You didn't do it consciously?"

"No. I haven't thought of that song in years. I . . . I broke the only copy of the record that I had the day my mother died." After a moment she added, "I suppose the son of a bitch will want to sue me."

"You know that's not so." I sat down beside her on the wet bench, turned my collar up against the mist. "The lyrics of that song say a lot about you, you know."

"Yeah—that everybody's left me or fucked me over as long as I've lived."

"Your grandfather wants to change that pattern. He wants to come back to you."

"Well, he can't. I don't want him."

A good deal of her toughness was probably real—would have to be, in order for her to survive in her business—but I sensed some of it was armor that she could don quickly whenever anything threatened the vulnerable core of her persona. I remained silent for a few minutes, wondering how to get through to her, watching the waves ebb and flow on the beach at the foot of the cliff. Eroding the land, giving some of it back again. Take and give, take and give . . .

Finally I asked, "Why were you sitting out here in the rain?"

"They said it would clear around three. I was just waiting. Waiting for something good to happen."

"A lot of good things must happen to you. Your career's going well. This is a lovely house, a great place to escape to."

"Yeah, I've done all right. 'It Never Stops Hurting' wasn't my first hit, you know."

"Do you remember a neighbor of yours in Petaluma—a Mrs. Caubet?"

"God! I haven't thought of her in years either. How is she?"

"She's fine. I talked with her yesterday. She mentioned your talent."

"Mrs. Caubet. Petaluma. That all seems so long ago."

"Where did you go after you left there?"

"To my Aunt Sandra, in L.A. She was married to a record-company flack. It made breaking in a little easier."

"And then?"

"Sandra died of a drug overdose. She found out that the bastard she was married to had someone else."

"What did you do then?"

"What do you think? Kept on singing and writing songs. Got married."

"And?"

"What the hell is this and-and-and? Why am I even talking to you?"

I didn't reply.

"All right. Maybe I need to talk to somebody. That didn't work out—the marriage, I mean—and neither did the next one. Or about a dozen other relationships. But things just kept clicking along with my career. The money kept coming in. One weekend a few years ago I was up here visiting friends at Sea Ranch. I saw this place while we were just driving around, and . . . now I live here when I don't have to be in L.A. Alone. Secure. Happy."

"Happy, Steff?"

"Enough." She paused, arms tightening around her drawn-up knees. "Actually, I don't think much about being happy anymore."

"You're a lot like your grandfather."

She rolled her eyes. "Here we go again!"

"I mean it. You know how he lives? Alone in the back of his store. He doesn't think much about being happy either."

"He still has that store?"

"Yes." I described it, concluding, "It's a place that's just been forgotten by time. *He's* been forgotten. When he dies there won't be anybody to care—unless you do something to change that."

"Well, it's too bad about him, but in a way he had it coming."

"You're pretty bitter toward someone you don't even know."

"Oh, I know enough about him. Mama saw to that. You think *I'm* bitter? You should have known her. She'd been thrown out by her own father, had two rotten marriages, and then she got cancer. Mama was a very bitter, angry woman."

I didn't say anything, just looked out at the faint sheen of the sunlight that had appeared on the gray water.

Steff seemed to be listening to what she'd just said. "I'm turning out exactly like my mother, aren't I?"

"It's a danger."

"I don't seem to be able to help it. I mean, it's all there in that song. It never *does* stop hurting."

"No, but some things can ease the pain."

"The store—it's in the Glen Park district, isn't it?"

"Yes. Why?"

"I get down to the city occasionally."

"How soon can you be packed?"

She looked over her shoulder at the house, where she had been secure in her loneliness. "I'm not ready for that yet."

"You'll never be ready. I'll drive you, go to the store with you. If it doesn't work out, I'll bring you right back here."

"Why are you doing this? I'm a total stranger. Why didn't you just turn my address over to my grandfather, let him take it from there?"

"Because you have a right to refuse comfort and happiness. We all have that."

Steff Rivers tried to glare at me but couldn't quite manage it. Finally—as a patch of blue sky appeared offshore and the sea began to glimmer in the sun's rays—she unwrapped her arms from her knees and stood.

"I'll go get my stuff," she said.

SOMEWHERE IN THE CITY

At 5:04 p. m. on October 17, 1989, the city of San Francisco was jolted by an earthquake that measured a frightening 7.1 on the Richter Scale. The violent tremors left the Bay Bridge impassable, collapsed a double-decker freeway in nearby Oakland, and toppled or severely damaged countless homes and other buildings. From the Bay Area to the seaside town of Santa Cruz some 100 miles south, 65 people were killed and thousands left homeless. And when the aftershocks subsided, San Francisco entered a new era—one in which things would never be quite the same. As with all cataclysmic events, the question "Where were you when?" will forever provoke deeply emotional responses in those of us who lived through it . . . .

WHERE I WAS WHEN: the headquarters of the Golden Gate Crisis Hotline in the Noe Valley district. I'd been working a case there—off and on, and mostly in the late afternoon and evening hours, for over two weeks—with very few results and with a good deal of frustration.

The hotline occupied one big windowless room behind a rundown coffeehouse on Twenty-fourth Street. The location, I'd been told, was not so much one of choice as of convenience (meaning the rent was affordable), but had I not known that, I would have considered it a stroke of genius. There was something instantly soothing about entering through the coffeehouse, where the aromas of various blends permeated the air and steam rose from huge stainless-steel urns. The patrons were unthreatening—mostly shabby and relaxed, reading or conversing with their feet propped up on chairs. The pastries displayed in the glass case were comfort food at its purest—reminders of the days when calories and cholesterol didn't count. And the round face of the proprietor, Lloyd Warner, was welcoming and kind as he waved troubled visitors through to the crisis center.

On that Tuesday afternoon I arrived at about twenty to five, answering Lloyd's cheerful greeting and trying to ignore the chocolate-covered doughnuts in the case. I had a dinner date at seven-thirty, had been promised some of the best French cuisine on Russian Hill, and was unwilling to spoil my appetite. The doughnuts called out to me, but I turned a deaf ear and hurried past.

The room beyond the coffeehouse contained an assortment of mismatched furniture: several desks and chairs of all vintages and materials; phones in colors and styles ranging from standard black touchtone to a shocking turquoise princess; three tattered easy chairs dating back to the fifties; and a card table covered with literature on health and psychological services. Two people manned the desks nearest the door. I went to the desk with the turquoise phone, plunked my briefcase and bag down on it, and turned to face them.

"He call today?" I asked.

Pete Lowry, a slender man with a bandit's mustache who was director of the center, took his booted feet off the desk and swiveled to face me. "Nope. It's been quiet all afternoon."

"Too quiet." This came from Ann Potter, a woman with dark frizzed hair who affected the aging-hippie look in jeans and flamboyant over-blouses. "And this weather—I don't like it one bit."

"Ann's having one of her premonitions of gloom and doom," Pete said. "Evil portents and omens lurk all around us—although most of them went up front for coffee a while ago."

Ann's eyes narrowed to a glare. She possessed very little sense of humor, whereas Pete perhaps possessed too much. To forestall the inevitable spat, I interrupted. "Well, I don't like the weather much myself. It's muggy and too warm for October. It makes me nervous."

"Why?" Pete asked.

I shrugged. "I don't know, but I've felt edgy all day."

The phone on his desk rang. He reached for the receiver. "Golden Gate Crisis Hotline, Pete speaking."

Ann cast one final glare at his back as she crossed to the desk that had been assigned to me. "It has been too quiet," she said defensively. "Hardly anyone's called, not even to inquire about how to deal with a friend or a family member. That's not normal, even for a Tuesday."

"Maybe all the crazies are out enjoying the warm weather."

Ann half-smiled, cocking her head. She wasn't sure if what I'd said was funny or not, and didn't know how to react. After a few seconds her attention was drawn to the file I was removing from my briefcase. "Is that about our problem caller?"

"Uh-huh." I sat down and began rereading my notes silently, hoping she'd go away. I'd meant it when I'd said I felt on edge, and was in no mood for conversation.

The file concerned a series of calls that the hotline had received over the past month—all from the same individual, a man with a distinctive raspy voice. Their content had been more or less the same: an initial plaint of being all alone in the world with no one to care if he lived or died; then a gradual escalating from despair to anger, in spite of the trained counselors' skillful responses; and finally the declaration that he had an assault rifle and was going to kill others and himself. He always ended with some variant on the statement, "I'm going to take a whole lot of people with me."

After three of the calls, Pete had decided to notify the police. A trace was placed on the center's lines, but the results were unsatisfactory; most of the time the caller didn't stay on the phone long enough, and in the instances that the calls could be traced, they turned out to have originated from booths in the Marina district. Finally, the trace was taken off, the official conclusion being that the calls were the work of a crank—and possibly one with a grudge against someone connected with the hotline.

The official conclusion did not satisfy Pete, however. By the next morning he was in the office of the hotline's attorney at All Souls Legal Cooperative, where I am chief investigator. And a half an hour after that, I was assigned to work the phones at the hotline as often as my other duties permitted, until I'd identified the caller. Following a crash course from Pete in techniques for dealing with callers in crisis—augmented by some reading of my own—they turned me loose on the turquoise phone.

✧

After the first couple of rocky, sweaty-palmed sessions, I'd gotten into it: become able to distinguish the truly disturbed from the fakers or the merely curious; learned to gauge the responses that would work best with a given individual; succeeded at eliciting information that would permit a crisis team to go out and assess the seriousness of the situation in person. In most cases, the team would merely talk the caller into getting counseling. However, if they felt immediate action was warranted, they would contact the SFPD, who had the authority to have the individual held for evaluation at S. F. General Hospital for up to seventy-two hours.

During the past two weeks the problem caller had been routed to me several times, and with each conversation I became more concerned about him. While his threats were melodramatic, I sensed genuine disturbance and desperation in his voice; the swift escalation of panic and anger seemed much out of proportion to whatever verbal stimuli I offered. And, as Pete had stressed in my orientation, no matter how theatrical or frequently made, any threat of suicide or violence toward others was to be taken with the utmost seriousness by the hotline volunteers.

Unfortunately I was able to glean very little information from the man. Whenever I tried to get him to reveal concrete facts about himself, he became sly and would dodge my questions. Still, I could make several assumptions about him: he was youngish, reasonably well-educated, and Caucasian. The traces to the Marina indicated he probably lived in that bayside district—which meant he had to have a good income. He listened to classical music (three times I'd heard it playing in the background) from a transistor radio, by the tinny tonal quality. Once I'd caught the call letters of the FM station—one with a wide-range signal in the Central Valley town of Fresno. Why Fresno? I'd wondered. Perhaps he was from there? But that wasn't much to go on; there were probably several Fresno transplants in his part of the city.

When I looked up from my folder, Ann had gone back to her desk. Pete was still talking in low, reassuring tones with his caller. Ann's phone rang, and she picked up the receiver. I tensed, knowing the next call would cycle automatically to my phone.

When it rang some minutes later, I glanced at my watch and jotted down the time while reaching over for the receiver. Four-fifty-eight. "Golden Gate Crisis Hotline, Sharon speaking."

The caller hung up—either a wrong number or, more likely, someone who lost his nerve. The phone rang again about twenty seconds later and I answered it in the same manner.

"Sharon. It's me." The greeting was the same as the previous times, the raspy voice unmistakable.

"Hey, how's it going?"

A long pause, labored breathing. In the background I could make out the strains of music—Brahms, I thought. "Not so good. I'm really down today."

"You want to talk about it?"

"There isn't much to say. Just more of the same. I took a walk a while ago, thought it might help. But the people, out there flying their kites, I can't take it."

"Why is that?"

"I used to . . . ah, forget it."

"No, I'm interested."

"Well, they're always in couples, you know."

When he didn't go on, I made an interrogatory sound.

"The whole damn world is in couples. Or families. Even here inside my little cottage I can feel it. There are these apartment buildings on either side, and I can feel them pressing in on me, and I'm here all alone."

He was speaking rapidly now, his voice rising. But as his agitation increased, he'd unwittingly revealed something about his living situation. I made a note about the little cottage between the two apartment buildings.

"This place where the people were flying kites," I said, "do you go there often?"

"Sure—it's only two blocks away." A sudden note of sullenness now entered his voice—a part of the pattern he'd previously exhibited. "Why do you want to know about that?"

"Because . . . I'm sorry, I forgot your name."

No response.

"It would help if I knew what to call you."

"Look, bitch, I know what you're trying to do."

"Oh?"

"Yeah. You want to get a name, an address. Send the cops out. Next thing I'm chained to the wall at S. F. General. I've been that route before. But I know my rights now; I went down the street to the Legal Switchboard, and they told me . . ."

I was distracted from what he was saying by a tapping sound—the stack trays on the desk next to me bumped against the wall. I looked over there, frowning. What was causing that . . . ?

". . . gonna take the people next door with me . . ."

I looked back at the desk in front of me. The lamp was jiggling.

"What the hell?" the man on the phone exclaimed.

My swivel chair shifted. A coffee mug tipped and rolled across the desk and into my lap.

Pete said, "Jesus Christ, we're having and earthquake!"

". . . The ceiling's coming down!" The man's voice was panicked now.

"Get under a door frame!" I clutched the edge of the desk, ignoring my own advice.

I heard a crash from the other end of the line. The man screamed in pain. "Help me! Please help—" And then the line went dead.

For a second or so I merely sat there—longtime San Franciscan, frozen by my own disbelief. All around me formerly inanimate objects were in motion. Pete and Ann were scrambling for the archway that led to the door of the coffeehouse.

"Sharon, get under the desk!" she yelled at me.

And then the electricity cut out, leaving the windowless room in blackness. I dropped the dead receiver, slid off the chair, crawled into the kneehole of the desk. There was a cracking, a violent shifting, as if a giant hand had seized the building and twisted it. Tremors buckled the floor beneath me.

This is a bad one. Maybe the big one that they're always talking about.

The sound of something wrenching apart. Pellets of plaster rained down on the desk above me. Time had telescoped; it seemed as if the quake had been going on for many minutes, when in reality it could not have been more than ten or fifteen seconds.

Make it stop! Please make it stop!

And then, as if whatever powers-that-be had heard my unspoken plea, the shock waves diminished to shivers, and finally ebbed.

Blackness. Silence. Only bits of plaster bouncing off the desks and the floor.

"Ann?" I said. "Pete?" My voice sounded weak, tentative.

"Sharon?" It was Pete. "You okay?"

"Yes. You?"

"We're fine."

Slowly I began to back out of the kneehole. Something blocked it— the chair. I shoved it aside, and emerged. I couldn't see a thing, but I could feel fragments of plaster and other unidentified debris on the floor. Something cut into my palm; I winced.

"God, it's dark," Ann said. "I've got some matches in my purse. Can you—"

"No matches," I told her. "Who knows what shape the gas mains are in."

". . . Oh, right."

Pete said, "Wait, I'll open the door to the coffeehouse."

On hands and knees I began feeling my way toward the sound of their voices. I banged into one of the desks, overturned a wastebasket, then finally reached the opposite wall. As I stood there, Ann's cold hand reached out to guide me. Behind her I could hear Pete fumbling at the door.

I leaned against the wall. Ann was close beside me, her breathing erratic. Pete said, "Goddamned door's jammed." From behind it came voices of the people in the coffeehouse.

Now that the danger was over—at least until the first of the after-shocks—my body sagged against the wall, giving way to tremors of its own manufacture. My thoughts turned to the lover with whom I'd planned to have dinner: where had he been when the quake hit? And what about my cats, my house? My friends and my co-workers at All Souls? Other friends scattered throughout the Bay Area?

And what about a nameless, faceless man somewhere in the city who had screamed for help before the phone went dead?

The door to the coffeehouse burst open, spilling weak light into the room. Lloyd Warner and several of his customers peered anxiously through it. I prodded Ann—who seemed to have lapsed into lethargy—toward them.

The coffeehouse was fairly dark, but late afternoon light showed beyond the plate-glass windows fronting on the street. It revealed a floor that was awash in spilled liquid and littered with broken crockery. Chairs were tipped over—whether by the quake or the patrons' haste to get to shelter I couldn't tell. About ten people milled about, talking noisily.

Ann and Pete joined them, but I moved forward to the window. Outside, Twenty-fourth Street looked much as usual, except for the lack of traffic and pedestrians. The buildings still stood, the sun still shone, the air drifting through the open door of the coffeehouse was still warm and muggy. In this part of the city, at least, life went on.

Lloyd's transistor radio had been playing the whole time—tuned to the station that was carrying the coverage of the third game of the Bay Area World Series, due to start at five-thirty. I moved closer, listening.

The sportscaster was saying, "Nobody here knows *what's* going on. The Giants have wandered over to the A's dugout. It looks like a softball game where somebody forgot to bring the ball."

Then the broadcast shifted abruptly to the station's studios. A newswoman was relaying telephone reports from the neighborhoods. I was relieved to hear that Bernal Heights, where All Souls is located, and my own small district near Glen Park were shaken up but for the most part undamaged. The broadcaster concluded by warning listeners not to use their phones except in cases of emergency. Ann snorted and said, "Do as I say but not . . . "

Again the broadcast made an abrupt switch—to the station's traffic helicopter. "From where we are," the reporter said, "it looks as if part of the upper deck on the Oakland side of the Bay Bridge has collapsed onto the bottom deck. Cars are pointing every whichway, there may be some in the water. And on the approaches—" The transmission broke, then resumed after a number of static-filled seconds. "It looks as if the Cypress Structure on the Oakland approach to the bridge has also collapsed. Oh my God, there are cars and people—" This time the transmission broke for good.

It was very quiet in the coffeehouse. We all exchanged looks—fearful, horrified. This was an extremely bad one, if not the catastrophic one they'd been predicting for so long.

Lloyd was the first to speak. He said, "I'd better see if I can insulate the urns in some way, keep the coffee hot as long as possible. People'll need it tonight." He went behind the counter, and in a few seconds a couple of the customers followed.

The studio newscast resumed. ". . . fires burning out of control in the Marina district. We're receiving reports of collapsed buildings there, with people trapped inside . . . "

The Marina district. People trapped.

I thought again of the man who had cried out for help over the phone. Of my suspicion, more or less confirmed by today's conversation, that he lived in the Marina.

Behind the counter Lloyd and the customers were wrapping the urns in dishtowels. Here—and in other parts of the city, I was sure—people were already overcoming their shock, gearing up to assist in the relief effort. There was nothing I could do in my present surroundings, but . . .

I hurried to the back room and groped until I found my purse on the floor beside the desk. As I picked it up, an aftershock hit—nothing like the original trembler, but strong enough to make me grab the chair for support. When it stopped, I went shakily out to my car.

Twenty-fourth Street was slowly coming to life. People bunched on the sidewalks, talking and gesturing. A man emerged from one of the shops, walked to the center of the street and surveyed the facade of his building. In the parking lot of nearby Bell Market, employees and customers gathered by the grocery carts. A man in a butcher's apron looked around, shrugged, and headed for a corner tavern. I got into my MG and took a city map from the side pocket.

✧

The Marina area consists mainly of early twentieth-century stucco homes and apartment buildings built on fill on the shore of the bay—which meant the quake damage there would naturally be bad. The district extends roughly from the Fisherman's Wharf area to the Presidio—not large, but large enough, considering I had few clues as to where within its boundary my man lived. I spread out the map against the steering wheel and examined it.

The man had said he'd taken a walk that afternoon, to a place two blocks from his home where people were flying kites. That would be the Marina Green near the Yacht Harbor, famous for the elaborate and often fantastical kites flown there in fine weather. Two blocks placed the man's home somewhere on the far side of Northpoint Street.

I had one more clue: in his anger at me he'd let it slip that the Legal Switchboard was "down the street." The switchboard, a federally-funded assistance group, was headquartered in one of the piers at Fort Mason, at the east end of the Marina. While several streets in that vicinity ended at Fort Mason, I saw that only two—Beach and Northpoint—were within two blocks of the Green as well.

Of course, I reminded myself, "down the street" and "two blocks" could have been generalizations or exaggerations. But it was somewhere to start. I set the map aside and turned the key in the ignition.

The trip across the city was hampered by near-gridlock traffic on some streets. All the stoplights were out; there were no police to direct the panicked motorists. Citizens helped out: I saw men in three-piece suits, women in heels and business attire, even a ragged man who looked to be straight out of one of the homeless shelters, all playing traffic cop. Sirens keened, emergency vehicles snaked from lane to lane. The car radio kept reporting further destruction; there was another aftershock, and then another, but I scarcely felt them because I was in motion.

As I inched along a major crosstown arterial, I asked myself why I was doing this foolhardy thing. The man was nothing to me, really— merely a voice on the phone, always self-pitying, and often antagonistic and potentially violent. I ought to be checking on my house and the folks at All Souls; if I wanted to help people, my efforts would have been better spent in my own neighborhood or Bernal Heights. But instead I was traveling to the most congested and dangerous part of the city in search of a man I'd never laid eyes on.

As I asked the question, I knew the answer. Over the past two weeks the man had told me about his deepest problems. I'd come to know him in spite of his self-protective secretiveness. And he'd become more to me than just the subject of an investigation; I'd begun to care whether he lived or died. Now we had shared a peculiarly intimate moment—that of being together, if only in voice, when the catastrophe that San Franciscans feared the most had struck. He had called for help; I had heard his terror and pain. A connection had been established that could not be broken.

After twenty minutes and little progress, I cut west and took a less-traveled residential street through Japantown and over the crest of Pacific Heights. From the top of the hill I could see and smell the smoke over the Marina; as I crossed the traffic-snarled intersection with Lombard, I could see the flames. I drove another block, then decided to leave the MG and continue on foot.

All around I could see signs of destruction now: a house was twisted at a tortuous angle, its front porch collapsed and crushing a car parked at the curb; on Beach Street an apartment building's upper story had slid into the street, clogging it with rubble; three bottom floors of another building were flattened, leaving only the top intact.

I stopped at a corner, breathing hard, nearly choking on the thickening smoke. The smell of gas from broken lines was vaguely nauseating—frightening, too, because of the potential for explosions. To my left the street was cordoned off; fire-department hoses played on the blazes—weakly, because of damaged water mains. People congregated everywhere, staring about with horror-struck eyes; they huddled together, clinging to one another; many were crying. Firefighters and police were telling people to go home before dark fell. "You should be looking after your property," I heard one say. "You can count on going seventy-two hours without water or power."

"Longer than that," someone said.

"It's not safe here," the policeman added. "Please go home."

Between sobs, a woman said, "What if you've got no home to go to any more?"

The cop had no answer for her.

Emotions were flying out of control among the onlookers. It would have been easy to feed into it—to weep, even panic. Instead, I turned my back to the flaming buildings, began walking the other way, toward Fort Mason. If the man's home was beyond the barricades, there was nothing I could do for him. But if it lay in the other direction, where there was a lighter concentration of rescue workers, then my assistance might save his life.

I forced myself to walk slower, to study the buildings on either side of the street. I had one last clue that could lead me to the man: he'd said he lived in a little cottage between two apartment buildings. The homes in this district were mostly of substantial size; there couldn't be too many cottages situated in just that way.

Across the street a house slumped over to one side, its roof canted at a forty-five-degree angle, windows from an apartment house had popped out of their frames, and its iron fire escapes were tangled and twisted like a cat's cradle of yarn. Another home was unrecognizable, merely a heap of rubble. And over there, two four-story apartment buildings leaned together, forming an arch over a much smaller structure . . . .

I rushed across the street, pushed through a knot of bystanders. The smaller building was a tumble-down mass of white stucco with a smashed red tile roof and a partially flattened iron fence. It had been a Mediterranean-style cottage with grillwork over high windows; now the grills were bent and pushed outward; the collapsed windows resembled swollen-shut eyes.

The woman standing next to me was cradling a terrified cat under her loose cardigan sweater. I asked, "Did the man who lives in the cottage get out okay?"

She frowned, tightened her grip on the cat as it burrowed deeper. "I don't know who lives there. It's always kind of deserted-looking."

A man in front of her said, "I've seen lights, but never anybody coming or going."

I moved closer. The cottage was deep in the shadows of the leaning buildings, eerily silent. From above came a groaning sound, and then a piece of wood sheared off the apartment house to the right, crashing onto what remained of the cottage's roof. I looked up, wondering how long before one or the other of the buildings toppled. Wondering if the man was still alive inside the compacted mass of stucco . . . .

A man in jeans and a sweatshirt came up and stood beside me. His face was smudged and abraded; his clothing was smeared with dirt and what looked to be blood; he held his left elbow gingerly in the palm of his hand. "You were asking about Dan?" he said.

So that was the anonymous caller's name. "Yes. Did he get out okay?"

"I don't think he was at home. At least, I saw him over at the Green around quarter to five."

"He was at home. I was talking with him on the phone when the quake hit."

"Oh, Jesus." The man's face paled under the smudges. "My name's Mel; I live . . . lived next door. Are you a friend of Dan's?"

"Yes," I said, realizing it was true.

"That's a surprise." He stared worriedly at the place where the two buildings leaned together.

"Why?"

"I thought Dan didn't have any friends left. He's pushed us away ever since the accident."

"Accident?"

"You must be a new friend, or else you'd know. Dan's woman was killed on the freeway last spring. A truck crushed her car."

The word "crushed" seemed to hang in the air between us. I said, "I've got to try to get him out of there," and stepped over the flattened portion of the fence.

Mel said, "I'll go with you."

I looked skeptically at his injured arm.

"It's nothing, really," he told me. "I was helping an old lady out of my building, and a beam grazed me."

"Well—" I broke off as a hail of debris came from the building to the left.

Without further conversation, Mel and I crossed the small front yard, skirting fallen bricks, broken glass, and jagged chunks of wallboard. Dusk was coming on fast now; here in the shadows of the leaning buildings it was darker than on the street. I moved toward where the cottage's front door should have been, but couldn't locate it. The windows, with their protruding grillwork, were impassable.

I said, "Is there another entrance?"

"In the back, off a little service porch."

I glanced to either side. The narrow passages between the cottage and the adjacent buildings were jammed with debris. I could possibly scale the mound at the right, but I was leery of setting up vibrations that might cause more debris to come tumbling down.

Mel said, "You'd better give it up. The way the cottage looks, I doubt he survived."

But I wasn't willing to give it up—not yet. There must be a way to at least locate Dan, see if he was alive. But how?

And then I remembered something else from our phone conversations . . . .

I said, "I'm going back there."

"Let me."

"No, stay here. That mound will support my weight, but not yours." I moved toward the side of the cottage before Mel could remind me of the risk I was taking.

The mound was over five feet high. I began to climb cautiously, testing every hand- and foothold. Twice jagged chunks of stucco cut my fingers; a piece of wood left a line of splinters on the back of my hand. When I neared the top, I heard the roar of a helicopter, its rotors flapping overhead. I froze, afraid that the air currents would precipitate more debris, then scrambled down the other side of the mound into a weed-choked backyard.

As I straightened, automatically brushing dirt from my jeans, my foot slipped on the soft, spongy ground, then sank into a puddle, probably a water main was broken nearby. The helicopter still hovered overhead; I couldn't hear a thing above its racket. Nor could I see much: it was even darker back here. I stood still until my eyes adjusted.

The cottage was not so badly damaged at its rear. The steps to the porch had collapsed and the rear wall leaned inward, but I could make out a door frame opening into blackness inside. I glanced up in irritation at the helicopter, saw it was going away. Waited, and then listened . . .

And heard what I had been hoping to. The music was now Beethoven—his third symphony, the *Eroica*. Its strains were muted, tinny. Music played by an out-of-area FM station, coming from a transistor radio. A transistor whose batteries were functioning long after the electricity had cut out. Whose batteries might have outlived its owner.

I moved quickly to the porch, grasped the iron rail beside the collapsed steps, and pulled myself up. I still could see nothing inside the cottage. The strains of the *Eroica* continued to pour forth, close by now.

Reflexively I reached into my purse for the small flashlight I usually kept there, then remembered it was at home on the kitchen counter—a reminder for me to replace its weak batteries. I swore softly, then started through the doorway, calling out to Dan.

No answer.

"Dan!"

This time I heard a groan.

I rushed forward into the blackness, following the sound of the music. After a few feet I came up against something solid, banging my shins. I lowered a hand, felt around. It was a wooden beam, wedged crosswise.

"Dan?"

Another groan. From the floor—perhaps under the beam. I squatted and made a wide sweep with my hands. They encountered a wool-clad arm; I slid my fingers down it until I touched the wrist, felt for the pulse. It was strong, although slightly irregular.

"Dan," I said, leaning closer, "it's Sharon, from the hotline. We've got to get you out of here."

"Unh, Sharon?" His voice was groggy, confused. He'd probably been drifting in and out of consciousness since the beam fell on him.

"Can you move?" I asked.

". . . Something on my legs."

"Do they feel broken?"

"No, just pinned."

"I can't see much, but I'm going to try to move this beam off you. When I do, roll out from under."

". . . Okay."

From the position at which the beam was wedged, I could tell it would have to be raised. Balancing on the balls of my feet, I got a good grip on it and shoved upward with all my strength. It moved about six inches and then slipped from my grasp. Dan grunted.

"Are you all right?"

"Yeah. Try it again."

I stood, grasped it, and pulled this time. It yielded a little more, and I heard Dan slide across the floor. "I'm clear," he said—and just in time, because I once more lost my grip. The beam crashed down, setting up a vibration that made plaster fall from the ceiling.

"We've got to get out of here fast," I said. "Give me your hand."

He slipped it into mine—long-fingered, work-roughened. Quickly we went through the door, crossed the porch, jumped to the ground. The radio continued to play forlornly behind us. I glanced briefly at Dan, couldn't make out much more than a tall, slender build and a thatch of pale hair. His face turned from me, toward the cottage.

"Jesus," he said in an awed voice.

I tugged urgently at his hand. "There's no telling how long those apartment buildings are going to stand."

He turned, looked up at them, said "Jesus" again. I urged him toward the mound of debris.

This time I opted for speed rather than caution—a mistake, because as we neared the top, a cracking noise came from high above. I gave Dan a push, slid after him. A dark, jagged object hurtled down, missing us only by inches. More plaster board—deadly at that velocity.

For a moment I sat straddle-legged on the ground, sucking in my breath, releasing it tremulously, gasping for more air. Then hands pulled me to my feet and dragged me across the yard toward the sidewalk—Mel and Dan.

Night had fallen by now. A fire had broken out in the house across the street. Its red-orange flickering showed the man I'd just rescued: ordinary-looking, with regular features that were now marred by dirt and a long cut on the forehead, from which blood had trickled and dried. His pale eyes were studying me; suddenly he looked abashed and shoved both hands into his jeans pocket.

After a moment he asked, "How did you find me?"

"I put together some of the things you'd said on the phone. Doesn't matter now."

"Why did you even bother?"

"Because I care."

He looked at the ground.

I added, "There never was any assault rifle, was there?"

He shook his head.

"You made it up, so someone would pay attention."

". . . Yeah."

I felt anger welling up—irrational, considering the present circumstances, but nonetheless justified. "You didn't have to frighten the people at the hotline. All you had to do was ask them for help. Or ask friends like Mel. He cares. People do, you know."

"Nobody does."

"Enough of that! All you have to do is look around to see how much people care about each other. Look at your friend here." I gestured at Mel, who was standing a couple feet away, staring at us. "He hurt his arm rescuing an old lady from his apartment house. Look at those people over by the burning house—they're doing everything they can to help the firefighters. All over this city people are doing things for one another. Goddamn it, I'd never laid eyes on you, but I risked my life anyway!"

Dan was silent for a long moment. Finally he looked up at me. "I know you did. What can I do in return?"

"For me? Nothing. Just pass it on to someone else."

Dan stared across the street at the flaming building, looked back into the shadows where his cottage lay in ruins. Then he nodded and squared his shoulders. To Mel he said, "Let's go over there, see if there's anything we can do."

He put his arm around my shoulders and hugged me briefly, then he and Mel set off at a trot.

✧

The city is recovering now, as it did in 1906, and as it doubtless will when the next big quake hits. Resiliency is what disaster teaches us, I guess—along with the preciousness of life, no matter how disappointing or burdensome it may often seem.

Dan's recovering, too: he's only called the hotline twice, once for a referral to a therapist, and once to ask for my home number so he could invite me to dinner. I turned the invitation down, because neither of us needs to dwell on the trauma of October seventeenth, and I was fairly sure I heard a measure of relief in his voice when I did so.

I'll never forget Dan, though—or where I was when. And the strains of Beethoven's Third Symphony will forever remind me of the day after which things would never be the same again.

FINAL RESTING PLACE

THE VOICES of the well-dressed lunch crowd reverberated off the chromium and formica of Max's Diner. Busy waiters made their way through the room, trays laden with meatloaf, mashed potatoes with gravy, and hot turkey sandwiches. The booths and tables and counter seats of the trendy restaurant—one of the forerunners of San Francisco's fifties revival—were all taken, and a sizable crowd awaited their turn in the bar. What I waited for was Max's famous onion rings, along with the basket of sliders—little burgers—I'd just ordered.

I was seated in one of the window booths overlooking Third Street with Diana Richards, an old friend from college. Back in the seventies, Diana and I had shared a dilapidated old house a few blocks from the U.C. Berkeley campus with a fluctuating group of anywhere from five to ten other semi-indigent students, but nowadays we didn't see much of each other. We had followed very different paths since graduation: she'd become a media buyer for the city's top ad agency, drove a new Mercedes, and lived graciously in one of the new condominium complexes near the financial district; I'd become a private investigator with a law cooperative, drove a beat-up MG, and lived chaotically in an old cottage that was constantly in the throes of renovation. I still liked Diana, though—enough that when she'd called that morning and asked to meet with me to discuss a problem, I'd dropped everything and driven downtown to Max's.

Milkshakes—the genuine article—arrived. I poured a generous dollop into my glass from the metal shaker. Diana just sat there, staring out at the passersby on the sidewalk. We'd exchanged the usual small talk while waiting for a table and scanning the menu ("Have you heard from any of the old gang?" "Do you still like your job?" "Any interesting men in your life?"), but then she'd grown uncharacteristically silent. Now I sipped and waited for her to speak.

After a moment she sighed and turned her yellow eyes toward me. I've never known anyone with eyes so much like a cat's; their color always startles me when we meet to renew our friendship. And they are her best feature, lending her heart-shaped face an exotic aura and perfectly complementing her wavy light brown hair.

She said, "As I told you on the phone, Sharon, I have a problem."

"A serious one?"

"Not serious so much as . . . nagging."

"I see. Are you consulting me on a personal or a professional basis?"

"Professional, if you can take on something for someone who's not an All Souls client." All Souls is the legal cooperative where I work; our clients purchase memberships, much as they would in a health plan, and pay fees that are scaled to their incomes.

"Then you actually want to hire me?"

"I'd pay whatever the going rate is."

I considered. At the moment my regular caseload was exceptionally light. And I could certainly use some extra money; I was in the middle of a home-repair crisis that threatened to drain my checking account long before payday. "I think I can fit it in. Why don't you tell me about the problem."

Diana waited while our food was delivered, then began: "Did you know that my mother died two months ago?"

"No, I didn't. I'm sorry."

"Thanks. Mom died in Cabo San Lucas, at a second home she and my father have down there. Dad had the cause of death hushed up; she'd been drinking a lot and passed out and drowned in the hot tub."

"God."

"Yes." Diana's mouth pulled down grimly. "It was a horrible way to go. And so unlike my mother. Dad naturally wanted to keep it from getting into the papers, so it wouldn't damage his precious reputation."

The bitterness and thinly veiled anger in her voice brought me a vivid memory of Carl Richards: a severe, controlling man, chief executive with a major insurance company. When we'd been in college, he and his wife, Teresa, had crossed the Bay Bridge from San Francisco once a month to take Diana and a few of her friends to dinner. The evenings were not great successes; the restaurants the Richardses chose were too elegant for our preferred jeans and t-shirts, the conversations stilted to the point of strangulation. Carl Richards made no pretense of liking any of us; he used the dinners as a forum for airing his disapproval of the liberal political climate at Berkeley, and boasted that he had refused to pay more than Diana's basic expenses because she'd insisted on enrolling there. Teresa Richards tried hard, but her ineffectual social flutterings reminded me of a bird trapped in a confined space. Her husband often mocked what she said, and it was obvious she was completely dominated by him. Even with the nonwisdom of nineteen, I sensed they were a couple who had grown apart, as the man made his way in the world and the woman tended the home fires.

Diana plucked a piece of fried chicken from the basket in front of her, eyed it with distaste, then put it back. I reached for an onion ring.

"Do you know what the San Francisco Memorial Columbarium is?" she asked.

I nodded. The Columbarium was the old Odd Fellows mausoleum for cremated remains, in the Inner Richmond district. Several years ago it had been bought and restored by the Neptune Society—a sort of All Souls of the funeral industry, specializing in low-cost cremations and interments, as well as burials at sea.

"Well, Mom's ashes are interred there, in a niche on the second floor. Once a week, on Tuesday, I have to consult with a major client in South San Francisco, and on the way back I stop in over the noon hour and . . . visit. I always take flowers—carnations, they were her favorite. There's a little vaselike thing attached to the wall next to the niche where you can put them. There were never any other flowers in it until three weeks ago. But then carnations, always white ones with a dusting of red, started to appear."

I finished the onion ring and started in on the little hamburgers. When she didn't go on, I said, "Maybe your father left them."

"That's what I thought. It pleased me, because it meant he missed her and had belatedly come to appreciate her. But I had my monthly dinner with him last weekend." She paused, her mouth twisting ruefully. "Old habits die hard. I suppose I do it to keep up the illusion we're a family. Anyway, at dinner I mentioned how glad I was he'd taken to visiting the Columbarium, and he said he hadn't been back there since the interment."

The man certainly didn't trouble with sentiment, I thought. "Well, what about another relative? Or a friend?"

"None of our relatives live in the area, and I don't know of any close friend Mom might have had. Social friends, yes. The wives of other executives at Dad's company, the neighbors on Russian Hill, the ladies she played bridge with at her club. But no one who would have cared enough to leave flowers."

"So you want me to find out who is leaving them."

"Yes."

"Why?"

"Because since they've started appearing it's occurred to me that I never really knew my mother. I loved her, but in my own way I dismissed her almost as much as my father did. If Mom had that good a friend, I want to talk with her. I want to see my mother through the eyes of someone who *did* know her. Can you understand that?"

"Yes, I can," I said, thinking of my own mother. I would never dismiss Ma—wouldn't *dare* dismiss the hundred-and-five pound dynamo who warms and energizes the McCone homestead in San Diego—but at the same time I didn't really know much about her life, except as it related to Pa and us kids.

"What about the staff at the Columbarium?" I asked. "Could they tell you anything?"

"The staff occupy a separate building. There's hardly ever anyone in the mausoleum, except for occasional visitors, or when they hold a memorial service."

"And you've always gone on Tuesday at noon?"

"Yes."

"Are the flowers you find there fresh?"

"Yes. And that means they'd have to be left that morning, since the Columbarium's not open to visitors on Monday."

"Then it means this friend goes there before noon on Tuesdays."

"Yes. Sometime after nine, when it opens."

"Why don't you spend a Tuesday morning there and wait for her?"

"As I said, I have regular meetings with a major client then. Besides, I'd feel strange, just approaching her and asking to talk about Mom. It would be better if I knew something about her first. That's why I thought of you. You could follow her, find out where she lives and something about her. Knowing a few details would make it easier for me."

I thought for a moment. It was an odd request, something she really didn't need a professional investigator for, and not at all the kind of job I'd normally take on. But Diana was a friend, so for old times' sake . . .

"Okay," I finally said. "Today's Monday. I'll go to the Columbarium at nine tomorrow morning and check it out."

❖

Tuesday dawned gray, with a slowly drifting fog that provided a perfect backdrop for a visit to the dead. Foghorns moaned a lament as I walked along Loraine Court, a single block of pleasant stucco homes that deadended at the gates of the park surrounding the Columbarium. The massive neoclassical building loomed ahead of me, a poignant reminder of the days when the Richmond district was mostly sand dunes stretching toward the sea, when San Franciscans were still laid to rest in the city's soil. That was before greed gripped the real-estate market in the early decades of the century, and developers decided the limited acreage was too valuable to be wasted on cemeteries. First cremation was outlawed within the city, then burials, and by the late 1930s the last bodies were moved south to the necropolis of Colma. Only the Columbarium remained, protected from destruction by the Homestead Act.

When I'd first moved to the city I'd often wondered about the verdigrised copper dome that could be glimpsed when driving along Geary Boulevard, and once I'd detoured to investigate the structure it topped. What I'd found was a decaying rotunda with four small wings jutting off. Cracks and water stains marred its facade; weeds grew high around it; one stained-glass window had buckled with age. The neglect it had suffered since the Odd Fellows had sold it to an absentee owner some forty years before had taken its full toll.

But now I saw the building sported a fresh coat of paint: a medley of lavender, beige, and subdued green highlighted its ornate architectural details. The lawn was clipped, the surrounding fir trees pruned, the names and dates on the exterior niches newly lettered and easily readable. The dome still had a green patina, but somehow it seemed more appropriate than shiny copper.

As I followed the graveled path toward the entrance, I began to feel as if I were suspended in a shadow world between the past and the present. A block away Geary was clogged with cars and trucks and buses, but here their sounds were muted. When I looked to my left I could see the side wall of the Coronet Theater, splattered with garish, chaotic graffiti; but when I turned to the right, my gaze was drawn to the rich colors and harmonious composition of a stained-glass window. The modern-day city seemed to recede, leaving me not unhappily marooned on this small island in time.

The great iron doors to the building stood open, inviting visitors. I crossed a small entry and stepped into the rotunda itself. Tapestry-cushioned straight chairs were arranged in rows there, and large floral offerings stood next to a lectern, probably for a memorial service. I glanced briefly at them and then allowed my attention to be drawn upward, toward the magnificent round stained-glass window at the top of the dome. All around me soft, prismatic light fell from it and the other windows.

The second and third floors of the building were galleries—circular mezzanines below the dome. The interior was fully as ornate as the exterior and also freshly painted, in restful blues and white and tans and gilt that highlighted the bas-relief flowers and birds and medallions. As I turned and walked toward an enclosed staircase to my left, my heels clicked on the mosaic marble floor; the sound echoed all around me. Otherwise the rotunda was hushed and chill; as near as I could tell, I was the only person there.

Diana had told me I would find her mother's niche on the second floor, in the wing called Kepheus—named, as the others were, after one of the four Greek winds. I climbed the curving staircase and began moving along the gallery. The view of the rotunda floor, through railed archways that were banked with philodendrons, was dizzying from their height; the wall opposite the arches was honeycombed with niches. Some of them were covered with plaques engraved with people's names and dates of birth and death; others were glass-fronted and afforded a view of the funerary urns. Still others were vacant, a number marked with red tags—meaning, I assumed, that the niche had been sold.

I found the name Kepheus in sculpted relief above an archway several yards from the entrance to the staircase. Inside was a smallish room—no more than twelve by sixteen feet—containing perhaps a hundred niches. At its front were two marble pillars and steps leading up to a large niche containing a coffin-shaped box; the ones on the walls to either side of it were backed with stained-glass windows. Most of the other niches were smaller and contained urns of all types—gold, silver, brass, ceramics. Quickly I located Teresa Richards': at eye level near the entry, containing a simple jar of handthrown blue pottery. There were no flowers in the metal holder attached to it.

Now what? I thought, shivering from the sharp chill and glancing around the room. The reason for the cold was evident: part of the leaded-glass skylight was missing. Water stains were prominent on the vaulted ceiling and walls; the pillars were chipped and cracked. Diana had mentioned that the restoration work was being done piecemeal, because the Neptune Society—a profitmaking organization—was not eligible for funding usually available to those undertaking projects of historical significance. While I could appreciate the necessity of starting on the ground floor and working upward, I wasn't sure I would want my final resting place to be in a structure that—up here, at least—reminded me of Dracula's castle.

And then I thought, just listen to yourself. It isn't as if you'd be peering through the glass of your niche at your surroundings! And just think of being here with all the great San Franciscans—Adolph Sutro, A. P. Hotaling, the Stanfords and Folgers and Magnins. Of course, it isn't as if you'd be creeping out of your niche at night to hold long, fascinating conversations with them, either . . . .

I laughed aloud. The sound seemed to be sucked from the room and whirled in an inverted vortex toward the dome. Quickly I sobered and considered how to proceed. I couldn't just be standing here when Teresa Richards' friend paid her call—*if* she paid her call. Better to move about on the gallery, pretending to be a history buff studying the niches out there.

I left the Kepheus room and walked around the gallery, glancing at the names, admiring the more ornate or interesting urns, peering through archways. Other than the tapping of my own heels on the marble, I heard nothing. When I leaned out and looked down at the rotunda floor, then up at the gallery above me, I saw no one. I passed a second staircase, wandered along, glanced to my left, and saw familiar marble pillars . . . .

What is this? I wondered. How far have I walked? Surely I'm not already back where I started.

But I was. I stopped, puzzled, studying what I could discern of the Columbarium's layout.

It was a large building, but by virtue of its imposing architecture it seemed even larger. I'd had the impression I'd only traveled partway around the gallery, when in reality I'd made the full circle.

I ducked into the Kepheus room to make sure no flowers had been placed in the holder at Teresa Richards' niche during my absence. Disoriented as I'd been, it wouldn't have surprised me to find that someone had come and gone. But the little vase was still empty.

Moving about, I decided, was a bad idea in this place of illusion and filtered light. Better to wait in the Kepheus room, appearing to pay my respects to one of the other persons whose ashes were interred there.

I went inside, chose a niche belonging to someone who had died the previous year, and stood in front of it. The remains were those of an Asian man—one of the things I'd noticed was the ethnic diversity of the people who had chosen the Columbarium as their resting place—and his urn was of white porcelain, painted with one perfect, windblown tree. I stared at it, trying to imagine what the man's life had been, its happiness and sorrows. And all the time I listened for a footfall.

After a while I heard voices, down on the rotunda floor. They boomed for a moment, then there were sounds as if the tapestried chairs were being rearranged. Finally all fell as silent as before. Fifteen minutes passed. Footsteps came up the staircase, slow and halting. They moved along the gallery and went by. Shortly after that there were more voices, women's that came close and then faded.

Was it always this deserted? I wondered. Didn't anyone visit the dead who rested all alone?

More sounds again, down below. I glanced at my watch, was surprised to see it was ten-thirty.

Footsteps came along the gallery—muted and squeaky this time, as if the feet were shod in rubber soles. Light, so light I hadn't heard them on the staircase. And close, coming through the archway now.

I stared at the windbent tree on the urn, trying to appear reverent, oblivious to my surroundings.

The footsteps stopped. According to my calculations, the person who had made them was now in front of Teresa Richards' niche.

For a moment there was no sound at all. Then a sigh. Then noises as if someone was fitting flowers into the little holder. Another sigh. And more silence.

After a moment I shifted my body ever so slightly. Turned my head. Strained my peripheral vision.

A figure stood before the niche, head bowed as if in prayer. A bunch of carnations blossomed in the holder—white, with a dusting as red as blood. The figure was clad in a dark blue windbreaker, faded jeans, and worn athletic shoes. Its hands were clasped behind its back.

It wasn't the woman Diana had expected I would find. It was a man, slender and tall, with thinning gray hair. And he looked very much like a grieving lover.

At first I was astonished, but I had to control the urge to laugh at Diana's and my joint naïveté. A friend of mine has coined a phrase for that kind of childlike thinking: "teddy bears on the brain." Even the most cynical of us occasionally falls prey to it, especially when it comes to relinquishing the illusion that our parents—while they may be flawed— are basically infallible. Almost everyone seems to have difficulty setting that idea aside, probably because we fear that acknowledging their human frailty will bring with it a terrible and final disappointment. And that, I supposed, was what my discovery would do to Diana.

But maybe not. After all, didn't this mean that someone had not only failed to dismiss Teresa Richards, but actually loved her? Shouldn't Diana be able to take comfort from that?

Either way, now was not the time to speculate. My job was to find out something about this man. Had it been the woman I'd expected, I might have felt free to strike up a conversation with her, mention that Mrs. Richards had been acquaintance. But with this man, the situation was different: he might be reluctant to talk with a stranger, might not want his association with the dead woman known. I would have to follow him, use indirect means to glean my information.

I looked to the side again; he stood in the same place, staring silently at the blue pottery urn. His posture gave me no clue as to how long he would remain there. As near as I could tell, he'd given me no more than a cursory glance upon entering, but if I departed at the same time he did, he might become curious. Finally I decided to leave the room and wait on the opposite side of the gallery. When he left, I'd take the other staircase and tail him at a safe distance.

I went out and walked halfway around the rotunda, smiling politely at two old ladies who had just arrived laden with flowers. They stopped at one of the niches in the wall near the Kepheus room and began arguing about how to arrange the blooms in the vase, in voices loud enough to raise the niche's occupant. Relieved that they were paying no attention to me, I slipped behind a philodendron on the railing and trained my eyes on the opposite archway. It was ten minutes or more before the man came through it and walked toward the staircase.

I straightened and looked for the staircase on this side. I didn't see one.

That can't be! I thought, then realized I was still a victim of my earlier delusion. While I'd gotten it straight as to the distance around the rotunda and the number of small wings jutting off it, I hadn't corrected my false assumption that there were two staircases instead of one.

I hurried around the gallery as fast as I could without making a racket. By the time I reached the other side and peered over the railing, the man was crossing toward the door. I ran down the stairs after him.

Another pair of elderly women were entering. The man was no-where in sight. I rushed toward the entry, and one of the old ladies glared at me. As I went out, I made mental apologies to her for offending her sense of decorum.

There was no one near the door, except a gardener digging in a bed of odd, white-leafed plants. I turned left toward the gates to Loraine

Court. The man was just passing through them. He walked unhurriedly, his head bent, hands shoved in the pockets of his windbreaker.

I adapted my pace to his, went through the gates, and started along the opposite sidewalk. He passed the place where I'd left my MG and turned right on Anza Street. He might have parked his car there, or he could be planning to catch a bus or continue on foot. I hurried to the corner, slowed, and went around it.

The man was unlocking the door of a yellow VW bug three spaces down. When I passed, he looked at me with that blank, I'm-not-really-seeing-you expression that we city dwellers adopt as protective coloration. His face was thin and pale, as if he didn't spend a great deal of time outdoors; he wore a small beard and mustache, both liberally shot with gray. I returned the blank look, then glanced at his license plate and consigned its number to memory.

"It's a man who's been leaving the flowers," I said to Diana. "Gordon DeRosier, associate professor of art at S. F. State. Fifty-three years old. He owns a home on Ninth Avenue, up the hill from the park in the area near Golden Gate Heights. Lives alone; one marriage, ending in divorce eight years ago, no children. Drives a 1979 VW bug, has a good driving record. His credit's also good—he pays his bills in full, on time. A friend of mine who teaches photography at State says he's a likable enough guy, but hard to get to know. Shy, doesn't socialize. My friend hasn't heard of any romantic attachments."

Diana slumped in her chair, biting her lower lip, her yellow eyes troubled. We were in my office at All Souls—a big room at the front of the second floor, with a bay window that overlooks the flat Outer Mission district. It had taken me all afternoon and used up quite a few favors to run the check on Gordon DeRosier; at five Diana had called wanting to know if I'd found anything, and I'd asked her to come there so I could report my findings in person.

Finally she said, "You, of course, are thinking what I am. Otherwise you wouldn't have asked your friend about this DeRosier's romantic attachments."

I nodded, keeping my expression noncommittal.

"It's pretty obvious, isn't it?" she added. "A man wouldn't bring a woman's favorite flowers to her grave three weeks running if he hadn't felt strongly about her."

"That's true."

She frowned. "But why did he start doing it now? Why not right after her death?"

"I think I know the reason for that: he's probably done it all along, but on a different day. State's summer class schedule just began; DeRosier is probably free at different times than he was in the spring."

"Of course." She was silent a moment, then muttered, "So that's what it came to."

"What do you mean?"

"My father's neglect. It forced her to turn to another man." Her eyes clouded even more, and a flush began to stain her cheeks. When she continued, her voice shook with anger. "He left her alone most of the time, and when he was there he ignored or ridiculed her. She'd try so hard—at being a good conversationalist, a good hostess, an interesting person—and then he'd just laugh at her efforts. The bastard!"

"Are you planning to talk with Gordon DeRosier?" I asked, hoping to quell the rage I sensed building inside her.

"God, Sharon, I can't. You know how uncomfortable I felt about approaching a woman friend of Mom's. This . . . the *implications* of this make it impossible for me."

"Forget it, then. Content yourself with the fact that someone loved her."

"I can't do that, either. This DeRosier could tell me so much about her."

"Then call him up and ask to talk."

"I don't think . . . Sharon, would you—"

"Absolutely not."

"But you know how to approach him tactfully, so he won't resent the intrusion. You're so good at things like that. Besides I'd pay a bonus."

Her voice had taken on a wheedling, pleading tone that I remembered from the old days. I recalled one time she'd convinced me that I really *wanted* to get out of bed and drive her to Baskin-Robbins at midnight for a gallon of pistachio ice cream. And I don't even like ice cream much, especially pistachio.

"Diana—"

"It would mean so much to me."

"Dammit—"

"*Please.*"

I sighed. "All right. But if he's willing to talk with you, you'd better follow up on it."

"I will, I promise."

Promises, I thought. I knew all about promises . . . .

"We met when she took an art class from me at State," Gordon DeRosier said. "An oil painting class. She wasn't very good. Afterwards we laughed about that. She said that she was always taking classes in things she wasn't good at, trying to measure up to her husband's expectations."

"When was that?"

"Two years ago last April."

Then it hadn't been a casual affair, I thought.

We were seated in the living room of DeRosier's small stucco house on Ninth Avenue. The house was situated at the bottom of a dip in the road, and the evening fog gathered there; the branches of an overgrown plane tree shifted in a strong wind and tapped at the front window. Inside, however, all was warm and cozy. A fire burned on the hearth, and DeRosier's paintings—abstracts done in reds and blues and golds—enhanced the comfortable feeling. He'd been quite pleasant when I'd shown up on his doorstep, although a little puzzled because he remembered seeing me at the Columbarium that morning. When I'd explained my mission, he'd agreed to talk with me and graciously offered me a glass of an excellent zinfandel.

I asked, "You saw her often after that?"

"Several times a week. Her husband seldom paid any attention to her comings and goings, and when he did she merely said she was pursuing her art studies."

"You must have cared a great deal about her."

"I loved her," he said simply.

"Then you won't mind talking with her daughter."

"Of course not. Teresa spoke of Diana often. Knowing her will be a link to Teresa—something more tangible than the urn I visit every week."

I found myself liking Gordon DeRosier. In spite of his ordinary appearance, there was an impressive dignity about the man, as well as a warmth and genuineness. Perhaps he could be a friend to Diana, someone who would make up in part for losing her mother before she really knew her.

He seemed to be thinking along the same lines, because he said, "It'll be good to finally meet Diana. All the time Teresa and I were together I'd wanted to, but she was afraid Diana wouldn't accept the situation. And then at the end, when she'd decided to divorce Carl, we both felt it was better to wait until everything was settled."

"She was planning to leave Carl?"

He nodded. "She was going to tell him that weekend, in Cabo San Lucas, and move in here the first of the week. I expected her to call on Sunday night, but she didn't. And she didn't come over as she'd promised she would on Monday. On Tuesday I opened the paper and found her obituary."

"How awful for you!"

"It was pretty bad. And I felt so . . . shut out. I couldn't even go to her memorial service—it was private. I didn't even know how she had died—the obituary merely said 'suddenly.'"

"Why didn't you ask someone? A mutual friend? Or Diana?"

"We didn't have any mutual friends. Perhaps that was the bond between us; neither of us made friends easily. And Diana . . . I didn't see any reason for her ever to know about her mother and me. It might have caused her pain, colored her memories of Teresa."

"That was extremely caring of you."

He dismissed the compliment with a shrug and asked, "Do you know how she died? Will you tell me, please?"

I related the circumstances. As I spoke DeRosier shook his head as if in stunned denial.

When I finished, he said, "That's impossible."

"Diana said something similar—how unlike her mother it was. I gather Teresa didn't drink much—"

"No, that's not what I mean." He rose and began to pace, extremely agitated now. "Teresa did drink too much. It started during all those years when Carl alternately abused her and left her alone. She was learning to control it, but sometimes it would still control her."

"Then I imagine that's what happened during that weekend down in Cabo. It would have been a particularly stressful time, what with having to tell Carl she was getting a divorce, and it's understandable that she might—"

"That much is understandable, yes. But Teresa would *not* have gotten into that hot tub—not willingly."

I felt a prickly sense of foreboding. "Why not?"

"Teresa had eczema, a severe case, lesions on her wrists and knees and elbows. She'd suffered from it for years, but shortly before her death it had spread and become seriously aggravated. Water treated with chemicals, as it is in hot tubs and swimming pools, makes eczema worse and causes extreme pain."

"I wonder why Diana didn't mention that."

"I doubt she knew about it. Teresa was peculiar about illness—it stemmed from having been raised a Christian Scientist. Although she wasn't religious anymore, she felt physical imperfection was shameful and wouldn't talk about it."

"I see. Well, about her getting into the hot tub—don't you think if she was drunk, she might have anyway?"

"No. We had a discussion about hot tubs once, because I was thinking of installing one here. She told me not to expect her to use it, that she had tried the one in Cabo just once. Not only had it aggravated her skin condition, but it had given her heart palpitations, made her feel she was suffocating. She hated that tub. If she really did drown in it, she was put in against her will. Or after she passed out from too much alcohol."

"If that was the case, I'd think the police would have caught on and investigated."

DeRosier laughed bitterly. "In Mexico? When the victim is the wife of a wealthy foreigner with plenty of money to spread around, and plenty of influence?" He sat back down, pressed his hands over his face, as if to force back tears. "When I think of her there, all alone with him, at his mercy .... I never should have let her go. But she said the weekend was planned, that after all the years she owed it to Carl to break the news gently." His fist hit the arm of the chair. "*Why* didn't I stop her?"

"You couldn't know." I hesitated trying to find a flaw in his logic. "Mr. DeRosier, why would Carl Richards kill his wife? I know he's a proud man, and conscious of his position in the business and social communities, but divorce really doesn't carry any stigma these days."

"But a divorce would have denied him the use of Teresa's money. Carl had done well in business, and they lived comfortably. But the month before she died, Teresa inherited a substantial fortune from an uncle. The inheritance was what made her finally decide to leave Carl; she didn't want him to get his hands on it. And, as she told me in legalese, she hadn't commingled it with what she and Carl held jointly. If she divorced him immediately, it wouldn't fall under the community property laws."

I was silent, reviewing what I knew about community property and inheritances. What Teresa had told him was valid—and it gave Carl Richards a motive for murder.

DeRosier was watching me. "We could go to the police. Have them investigate."

I shook my head. "It happened on foreign soil; the police down there aren't going to admit they were bribed, or screwed up, or whatever happened. Besides, there's not hard evidence."

"What about Teresa's doctor? He could substantiate that she had eczema and wouldn't have gotten into that tub voluntarily."

"That's not enough. She was drunk; drunks do irrational things."

"Teresa wasn't an irrational woman, drunk or sober. Anyone who knew her would agree with me."

"I'm sure they would. But that's the point: you knew her; the police didn't."

DeRosier leaned back, deflated and frustrated. "There's got to be some way to get the bastard."

"Perhaps there is," I said, "through some avenue other than the law."

"How do you mean?"

"Well, consider Carl Richards: he's very conscious of his social position, his business connections. He's big on control. What if all that fell apart—either because he came under suspicion of murder or if he began losing control because of psychological pressure?"

DeRosier nodded slowly. "He *is* big on control. He dominated Teresa for years, until she met me."

"And he tried to dominate Diana. With her it didn't work so well."

"Diana . . ." De Rosier half-rose from his chair.

"What about her?"

"Shouldn't we tell her what we suspect? Surely she'd want to avenge her mother somehow. And she knows her father and his weak points better than you or I."

I hesitated, thinking of the rage Diana often displayed toward Carl Richards. And wondering if we wouldn't be playing a dangerous game by telling her. Would her reaction to our suspicions be a rational one? Or would she strike out at her father, do something crazy? Did she really need to know any of this? Or did she have a right to the knowledge? I was ambivalent: on the one hand, I wanted to see Carl Richards punished in some way; on the other, I wanted to protect my friend from possible ruinous consequences.

DeRosier's feelings were anything but ambivalent, however; he waited, staring at me with hard, glittering eyes. I knew he would embark on some campaign of vengeance, and there was nothing to stop him from contacting Diana if I refused to help. Together their rage at Richards might flare out of control, but if I exerted some sort of leavening influence . . .

After a moment I said, "All right, I'll call Diana and ask her to come over here. But let me handle how we tell her."

It was midnight when I shut the door of my little brown-shingled cottage and leaned against it, sighing deeply. When I'd left Gordon DeRosier's house, Diana and he still hadn't decided what course of action to pursue in regard to Carl Richards, but I felt certain it would be a sane and rational one.

A big chance, I thought. That's what you took tonight. Did you really have a right to gamble with your friend's life that way? What if it had turned out the other way?

But then I pictured Diana and Gordon standing in the doorway of his house when I'd left. Already I sensed a bond between them, knew they'd forged a united front against a probable killer. Old Carl would get his, one way or the other.

Maybe their avenging Teresa's death wouldn't help her rest more easily in her niche at the Columbarium, but it would certainly salve the pain of the two people who remembered and loved her.

SILENT NIGHT

"LARRY, I hardly know what to say!"

What I *wanted* to say was, "What am I supposed to do with this?" The object I'd just liberated from its gay red-and-gold Christmas wrappings was a plastic bag, about eight by twelve inches, packed firm with what looked suspiciously like sawdust. I turned it over in my hands, as if admiring it, and searched for some clue to its identity.

When I looked up, I saw Larry Koslowski's brown eyes shining expectantly; even the ends of his little handlebar mustache seemed to bristle as he awaited my reaction. "It's perfect," I said lamely.

He let his bated breath out in a long sigh. "I thought it would be. You remember how you were talking about not having much energy lately? I told you to try whipping up my protein drink for breakfast, but you said you didn't have that kind of time in the morning."

The conversation came back to me—vaguely. I nodded.

"Well," he went on, "put two tablespoons of that mixture in a tall glass, add water, stir, and you're in business."

Of course—it was an instant version of his infamous protein drink. Larry was the health nut on the All Souls Legal Cooperative staff; his fervent exhortations for the rest of us to adopt better nutritional standards often fell upon deaf ears—mine included.

"Thank you," I said. "I'll try it first thing tomorrow."

Larry ducked his head, his lips turning up in shy pleasure beneath his straggly little mustache.

It was late in the afternoon of Christmas Eve, and the staff of All Souls was engaged in the traditional gift exchange between members who had drawn each other's names earlier in the month. The yearly ritual extends back to the days of the co-op's founding, when most people were too poor to give more than one present; the only rule is Keep It Simple.

The big front parlor of the co-op's San Francisco Victorian was crowded. People perched on the furniture or, like Larry and me, sat cross-legged on the floor, oohing and aahing over their gifts. Next to the Christmas tree in the bay window, my boss, Hank Zahn, sported a new cap and muffler, knitted for him—after great deliberation and consultation as to colors—by my assistant, Rae Kelleher. Rae, in turn, wore the scarf and cap I'd purchased (because I can't knit to save my life) for her in the hope she would consign relics from her days at U. C. Berkeley to the trash can. Other people had homemade cookies and sinful fudge, special bottles of wine, next year's calendars, assorted games, plants, and paperback books.

And I had a bag of instant health drink that looked like sawdust.

The voices in the room created such a babble that I barely heard the phone ring in the hall behind me. Our secretary, Ted Smalley, who is a compulsive answerer, stepped over me and went out to where the instrument sat on his desk. A moment later he called, "McCone, it's for you."

My stomach did a little flip-flop, because I was expecting news of a personal nature that could either be very good or very bad. I thanked Larry again for my gift, scrambled to my feet, and went to take the receiver from Ted. He remained next to the desk; I'd confided my family's problem to him earlier that week, and now, I knew, he would wait to see if he could provide air or comfort.

"Shari?" My youngest sister Charlene's voice was composed, but her use of the diminutive of Sharon, which no one but my father calls me unless it's a time of crisis, made my stomach flip.

"I'm here," I said.

"Shari, somebody's seen him. A friend of Ricky's saw Mike!"

"Where? When?"

"Today around noon. Up there—in San Francisco."

I let out my breath in a sigh of relief. My fourteen-year-old nephew, oldest of Charlene and Ricky's six kids, had run away from their home in Pacific Palisades five days ago. Now, it appeared, he was alive, if not exactly safe.

The investigator in me counseled caution, however. "Was this friend sure it was Mike he saw?"

"Yes. He spoke to him. Mike said he was visiting you. But afterward our friend got to thinking that he looked kind of grubby and tired, and that you probably wouldn't have let him wander around that part of town, so he called us to check it out."

A chill touched my shoulder blades. "What part of town?"

". . . Somewhere near City Hall, a sleazy area, our friend said."

A very sleazy area, I thought. Dangerous territory to which runaways are often drawn, where boys and girls alike fall prey to pimps and pushers . . .

Charlene said, "Shari?"

"I'm still here, just thinking."

"You don't suppose he'll come to you?"

"I doubt it, if he hasn't already. But in case he does, there's some-body staying at my house—an old friend who's here for Christmas—and she knows to keep him there and call me immediately. Is there anybody else he knows here in the city?"

". . . I can't think of anybody."

"What about that friend you spent a couple of Christmases with—the one with the two little girls who lived on Sixteenth Street across from Mission Dolores?"

"Ginny Shriber? She moved away about four years ago." There was a noise as if Charlene was choking back a sob. "He's really just a little boy yet. So little, and so stubborn."

But stubborn little boys grow up fast on the rough city streets. I didn't want that kind of coming-of-age for my nephew.

"Look at the up side of this Charlene," I said, more heartily than I felt. "Mike's come to the one city where you have your own private investigator. I'll start looking for him right away."

It had begun with, of all things, a moped that Mike wanted for Christmas. Or maybe it had started a year earlier, when Ricky Savage finally hit it big.

During the first fourteen years of his marriage to my sister, Ricky had been merely another faceless country-and-western musician, playing and singing backup with itinerant bands, dreaming seemingly improbable dreams of stardom. He and Charlene had developed a reproductive pattern (and rate) that never failed to astound me, in spite of its regu-larity: he'd get her pregnant, go out on tour, return after the baby was born; then he'd go out again when the two o'clock feedings got to him, return when the kid was weaned, and start the whole cycle all over. Finally, after the sixth child, Charlene had wised up and gotten her tubes tied. But Ricky still stayed on the road more than at home, and still dreamed his dreams.

But then, with money borrowed from my father on the promise that if he didn't make it within one more year he'd give up music and go into my brother John's housepainting business, Ricky had cut a demo of a song he'd written called "Cobwebs in the Attic of My Mind." It was about a lovelorn fellow who, besides said cobwebs, had a "sewer that's backed up in the cellar of his soul" and "a short in the wiring of his heart." When I first heard it, I was certain that Pa's money had washed down that same pipe before it clogged, but fate—perverse creature that it is—would have it otherwise. The song was a runaway hit, and more Ricky Savage hits were to follow.

In true *nouveau* style, Ricky and Charlene quickly moved uptown— or in this case up the coast, from West Los Angeles to affluent Pacific Palisades. There were new cars, new furniture and clothes, a house with a swimming pool, and toys and goodies for the children. *Lots* of goodies, anything they wanted—until this Christmas when, for reasons of safety, Charlene had balked at letting Mike have the moped. And Mike, head-strong little bastard that he was, had taken his life's savings of some fifty-five dollars and hitched away from home on the Pacific Coast Highway.

It was because of a goddamned moped that I was canceling my Christmas Eve plans and setting forth to comb the sleazy streets and alleys of the area known as Polk Gulch for a runaway . . . .

The city was strangely subdued on this Christmas Eve, the dark streets hushed, although not deserted. Most people had been drawn inside to the warmth of family and friends; others, I suspected, had re-treated to nurse the loneliness that is endemic to this season. The pedes-trians I passed moved silently, as if reluctant to call attention to their presence; occasionally I heard laughter from the bars as I went by, but even that was muted. The lost, drifting souls of the city seemed to collec-tively hold their breath as they waited for life to resume its everyday pattern.

I had started at Market Street and worked my way northwest, through the Tenderloin to Polk Gulch. Before I'd started out, I'd had a photographer friend who likes to make a big fee more than he likes to celebrate holidays run off a hundred copies of my most recent photo of Mike. Those I passed out, along with my card, to clerks in what liquor stores, corner groceries, cheap hotels, and greasy spoon restaurants I found open. The pictures drew no response other than indifference or sympathetic shakes of the head and promises to keep an eye out for him. By the time I reached Polk Street, where I had an appointment in a gay bar at ten, I was cold, footsore, and badly discouraged.

Polk Gulch, so called because it is in a valley that has an under-ground river running through it, long ago was the hub of gay life in San Francisco. In the seventies, however, most of the action shifted up Market Street to the Castro district, and the vitality seemed to drain out of the Gulch. Now parts of it, particularly those bordering the Tenderloin, are depressingly sleazy. As I walked along, examining the face of each young man I saw, I became aware of the hopelessness and resignation in the eyes of the street hustlers and junkies and winos and homeless people.

A few blocks from my destination was a vacant lot surrounded by a chain link fence. Inside gaped a huge excavation, the cellar of the building that had formerly stood there, now open to the elements. People had scaled the fence and taken up residence down in it; campfires blazed, in defiance of the NO TRESPASSING signs. The homeless could rest easy—at least for this one night. No one was going to roust them on Christmas Eve.

I went to the fence and grasped its cold mesh with my fingers, staring down into the shifting light and shadows, wondering if Mike was among the ragged and hungry ranks. Many of the people were middle-aged to elderly, but there were also families with children and a scattering of young people. There was no way to tell, though, without scaling the fence and climbing down there. Eventually I turned away, realizing I had only enough time to get to the gay bar by ten.

The transvestite's name was Norma and she—he? I never know what to call them—was coldly beautiful. The two of us sat at a corner table in the bar, sipping champagne because Norma had insisted on it. ("After all, it's Christmas Eve, darling!") The bar, in spite of winking colored lights on its tree and flickering bayberry candles on each table, was gloomy and semideserted; Norma's brave velvet finery and costume jewelry had about it more than a touch of the pathetic. She'd been sitting alone when I'd entered and had greeted me eagerly.

I'd been put in touch with Norma by Ted Smalley, who is gay and has a wide-ranging acquaintance among all the segments of the city's homosexual community. Norma, he'd said, knew everything there was to know about what went on it Polk Gulch; if anyone could help me, it was she.

The photo of Mike didn't look familiar to Norma. "There are so many runaways on the street at this time of year," she told me. "Kids get their hopes built up at Christmas time. When they find out Santa isn't the great guy he's cracked up to be, they take off. Like your nephew."

"So what would happen to a kid like him? Where would he go?"

"Lots of places. There's a hotel—the Vinton. A lot of runaways end up there at first, until their money runs out. If he's into drugs, try any flophouse, doorway, or alley. If he's connected with a pimp, look for him hustling."

My fingers tightened involuntarily on the stem of my champagne glass. Norma noticed and shook her elaborately coiffed head in sympathy. "Not a pretty thought, is it? But what do you see around here that's pretty—except for me?" As she spoke the last words, her smile became self-mocking.

"He's been missing five days now," I said, "and he only had fifty-some dollars on him. That'll be gone by now, so he probably won't be at the hotel, or any other. He's never been into drugs. His father's a musician, and a lot of his cronies are druggies; the kid actually disapproves of them. The other I don't even want to think about—though I probably will have to, eventually."

"So what are you going to do?"

"Try the hotel. Go back and talk to the people at that vacant lot. Keep looking at each kid who walks by."

Norma stared at the photo of Mike that lay face up on the table between us. "It's a damned shame, a nice-looking kid like that. He ought to be home with his family, trimming the tree, roasting chestnuts on the fire, or whatever other things families do."

"The American Christmas dream, huh?"

"Yeah." She smiled bleakly, raised her glass. "Here's to the American Christmas dream—and to all the people it's eluded."

I touched my glass to hers. "Including you and me."

"Including you and me. Let's just hope it doesn't elude young Mike forever."

The Vinton Hotel was a few blocks away, around the corner on Eddy Street. Its lobby was a flight up, over a closed sandwich shop, and I had to wait and be buzzed in before I could climb carpetless stairs that stank strongly of disinfectant and faintly of urine. Lobby was a misnomer, actually: it was more a narrow hall with a desk to one side, behind which sat a young black man with a tall afro. The air up there was thick with the odor of marijuana; I guess he'd been spending his Christmas Eve with a joint. His eyes flashed panic when I reached in my bag for my identification. Then he realized it wasn't a bust and relaxed somewhat.

I took out another photo of Mike and laid it on the counter. "You seen this kid?"

He barely glanced at it. "Nope, can't help you."

I shoved it closer. "Take another look."

He did, pushed it back toward me. "I said no."

There was something about his tone that told me he was lying—would lie out of sheer perversity. I could get tough with him, make noises about talking to the hotel's owners, mentioning how the place reeked of grass. The city's fleabags had come under a good bit of media scrutiny recently; the owners wouldn't want me to cause any trouble that would jeopardize this little goldmine that raked in outrageously high rents from transients, as well as government subsidized payments for welfare recipients. Still, there had to be a better way . . . .

"You work here every night?" I asked.

"Yeah."

"Rough, on Christmas Eve."

He shrugged.

"Christmas night, too?"

"Why do you care?"

"I understand what a rotten deal that is. You don't think I'm running around here in the cold because I like it, do you?"

His eyes flickered to me, faintly interested. "You got no choice, either?"

"Hell, no. The client says find a kid, I go looking. Not that it matters. I don't have anything better to do."

"Know what you mean. Nothing for me at home, either."

"Where's home?"

"My real home, or where I live?"

"Both, I guess."

"Where I live's up there." He gestured at the ceiling. "Room goes with the job. Home's not there no more. Was in Motown, back before my ma died and things got so bad in the auto industry. I came out here thinking I'd find work." He smiled ironically. "Well, I found it, didn't I?"

"At least it's not as cold here as in Detroit."

"No, but it's not home either." He paused, then reached for Mike's picture. "Let me see that again." Another pause. "Okay. He stayed here. Him and this blond chick got to be friends. She's gone, too."

"Do you know the blond girl's name?"

"Yeah. Jane Smith. Original, huh?"

"Can you describe her?"

"Just a little blond, maybe five-two. Long hair. Nothing special about her."

"When did they leave?"

"They were gone when I came on last night. The owner don't put up with the ones that can't pay, and the day man, he likes tossing their asses out on the street."

"How did the kid seem to you? Was he okay?"

The man's eyes met mine, held them for a moment. "Thought this was just a job to you."

". . . He's my nephew."

"Yeah, I guessed it might be something like that. Well, if you mean was he doing drugs or hustling, I'd say no. Maybe a little booze, that's all. The girl was the same. Pretty straight kids. Nobody's gotten to them yet."

"Let me ask you this: what would kids like that do after they'd been thrown out of here? Where would they hang out?"

He considered. "There's a greasy spoon on Polk, near O'Farrell. Owner's an old guy, Iranian. He feels sorry for the kids, feeds them when they're about to starve, tries to get them to go home. He might of seen those two."

"Would he be open tonight?"

"Sure. Like I said, he's Iranian. It's not his holiday. Come to think of it, it's not mine anymore, either."

"Why not?"

Again the ironic smile. "Can't celebrate peace-on-earth-good-will-to-men when you don't believe in it anymore, now can you?"

I reached into my bag and took out a twenty-dollar bill, slid it across the counter to him. "Peace on earth, and thanks."

He took it eagerly, then looked at it and shook his head. "You don't have to."

"I *want* to. That makes a difference."

The "greasy spoon" was called The Coffee Break. It was small—just five tables and a lunch counter, old green linoleum floors, Formica and molded plastic furniture. A slender man with thinning gray hair sat behind the counter smoking a cigarette. A couple of old women were hunched over coffee at a corner table. Next to the window was a dirty-haired blond girl; she was staring through the glass with blank eyes—another of the city's casualties.

I showed Mike's picture to the man behind the counter. He told me Mike looked familiar, thought a minute, then snapped his fingers and said, "Hey, Angie."

The girl by the window turned. Full-face, I could see she was red-eyed and tear-streaked. The blankness of her face was due to misery, not drugs.

"Take a look at the picture this lady has. Didn't I see you with this kid yesterday?"

She got up and came to the counter, self-consciously smoothing her wrinkled jacket and jeans. "Yeah," she said after glancing at it, "that's Michael."

"Where's he now? The lady's his aunt, wants to help him."

She shook her head. "I don't know. He was at the Vinton, but he got kicked out the same time I did. We stayed down at the cellar in the vacant lot last night, but it was cold and scary. These drunks kept bothering us. Mr. Ahmeni, how long do you think it's going to take my dad to get here?"

"Take it easy. It's a long drive from Oroville. I only called him an hour ago." To me, Mr. Ahmeni added, "Angie's going home for Christmas."

I studied her. Under all that grime, a pretty, conventional girl hid. I said, "Would you like a cup of coffee? Something to eat?"

"I wouldn't mind a Coke. I've been sponging off Mr. Ahmeni for hours." She smiled faintly. "I guess he'd appreciate it if I sponged off somebody else for a change."

I bought us both Cokes and sat down with her. "When did you meet Mike?"

"Three days ago, I guess. He was at the hotel when I got into town. He kind of looked out for me. I was glad; that place is pretty awful. A lot of addicts stay there. One OD'd in the stairwell the first night. But it's cheap and they don't ask questions. A guy I met on the bus coming down here told me about it."

"What did Mike do here in the city, do you know?"

"Wandered around, mostly. One afternoon we went out to Ocean Beach and walked on the dunes."

"What about drugs or—"

"Michael's not into drugs. We drank some wine, is all. He's . . . I don't know how to describe it, but he's not like a lot of the kids on the streets."

"How so?"

"Well, he's kind of . . . sensitive, deep."

"This sensitive soul ran away from home because his parents wouldn't buy him a moped for Christmas."

Angie sighed. "You really don't know anything about him, do you? You don't even know he wants to be called Michael, not Mike."

That silenced me for a moment. It was true: I really didn't know my nephew, not as a person. "Tell me about him."

"What do you want to know?"

"Well, this business with the moped—what was that all about?"

"It didn't really have anything to do with the moped. At least not much. It had to do with the kids at school."

"In what way?"

"Well, the way Michael told it, his family used to be kind of poor. At least there were some months when they worried about being able to pay the rent."

"That's right."

"And then his father became a singing star and they moved to this awesome house in Pacific Palisades, and all of a sudden Michael was in school with all these rich kids. But he didn't fit in. The kids, he said, were really into having things and doing drugs and partying. He couldn't relate to it. He says it's really hard to get into that kind of stuff when you've spent your life worrying about real things."

"Like if your parents are going to be able to pay the rent."

Angie nodded, her fringe of limp blond hair falling over her eyes. She brushed it back and went on. "I know about that; my folks don't have much money, and my mom's sick a lot. The kids, they sense you're different and they don't want to have anything to do with you. Michael was lonely at the new school, so he tried to fit in—tried too hard, I guess, by having the latest stuff, the most expensive clothes. You know."

"And the moped was part of that."

"Uh-huh. But when his mom said he couldn't have it, he realized what he'd been doing. And he also realized that the moped wouldn't have done the trick anyway. Michael's smart enough to know that people don't fall all over you just because you've got another new toy. So he decided he'd never fit in, and he split. He says he feels more comfortable on the streets, because life here is real." She paused, eyes filling, and looked away at the window. "God, is it *real.*"

I followed the direction of her gaze: beyond the plate glass a girl of perhaps thirteen stumbled by. Her body was emaciated, her face blank, her eyes dull—the look of a far-gone junkie.

I said to Angie, "When did you last see Mike . . . Michael?"

"Around four this afternoon. Like I said, we spent the night in that cellar in the vacant lot. After that I knew I couldn't hack it anymore, and I told him I'd decided to go home. He got pissed at me and took off."

"Why?"

"Why do you think? I was abandoning him. I could go home, and he couldn't."

"Why not?"

"Because Michael's . . . God, you don't know a thing about him! He's proud. He couldn't admit to his parents that he couldn't make it on his own. Any more than he could admit to them about not fitting in at school."

What she said surprised me and made me ashamed. Ashamed for Charlene, who had always referred to Mike as stubborn or bullheaded, but never as proud. And ashamed for myself, because I'd never really seen him, except as the leader of a pack jokingly referred to in family circles as "the little savages."

"Angie," I said, "do you have any idea where he might have gone after he left you?"

She shook her head. "I wish I did. It would be nice if Michael could have a Christmas. He talked about how much he was going to miss it. He spent the whole time we were walking around on the dunes telling me about the Christmases they used to have, even though they didn't have much money: the tree trimming, the homemade presents, the candlelit masses on Christmas Eve, the cookie decorating and the turkey dinners. Michael absolutely loves Christmas."

I hadn't known that either. For years I'd been too busy with my own life to do more than send each of the Savage kids a small check. Properly humbled, I thanked Angie for talking with me, wished her good luck with her parents, and went back out to continue combing the dark, silent streets.

✧

On the way back down Polk Street toward the Tenderloin, I stopped again at the chain link fence surrounding the vacant lot. I was fairly sure

Mike was not among the people down there—not after his and Angie's experience of the night before—but I was curious to see the place where they had spent that frightening time.

The campfires still burned deep in the shelter of the cellar. Here and there drunks and addicts lay passed out on the ground; others who had not yet reached that state passed bottles and shared joints and needles; one group raised inebriated voices in a chorus of "Rudolph, the Red-Nosed Reindeer." In a far corner I saw another group—two women, three children, and a man—gathered around a scrawny Christmas tree.

The tree had no ornaments, wasn't really a tree at all, but just a top that someone had probably cut off and tossed away after finding that the one he'd bought was too tall for the height of his ceiling. There was no star atop it, no presents under it, no candy canes or popcorn chains, and there was certain to be no turkey dinner tomorrow. The people had nonetheless gathered around it and stood silently, their heads bowed in prayer.

My throat tightened and I clutched at the fence, fighting back tears. Even though I spent a disproportionate amount of my professional life probing into events and behavior that would make the average person gag, every now and then the indestructible courage of the human spirit absolutely stuns me.

I watched the scene for a moment longer, then turned away, glancing at my watch. Its hands told me why the people were praying: Christmas Day was upon us. This was their midnight service.

And then I realized that those people, who had nothing in the world with which to celebrate Christmas except somebody's cast-off treetop, may have given me a priceless gift. I thought I knew now where I would find my nephew.

When I arrived at Mission Dolores, the neoclassical facade of the basilica was bathed in floodlights, the dome and towers gleaming against the post-midnight sky. The street was choked with double-parked vehicles, and from within I heard voices raised in a joyous chorus. Beside the newer early twentieth-century structure, the small adobe church built in the late 1700s seemed dwarfed and enveloped in deep silence. I hurried up the wide steps to the arching wooden doors of the basilica, then took a moment to compose myself before entering.

Like many of my generation, it had been years since I'd been even nominally a Catholic, but the old habit of reverence had never left me.

I couldn't just blunder in there and creep about, peering into every worshipper's face, no matter how great my urgency. I waited until I felt relatively calm before pulling open the heavy door and stepping over the threshold.

The mass was candlelit; the robed figures of the priest and altar boys moved slowly in the flickering, shifting light. The stained glass window behind the altar and those on the side walls gleamed richly. In contrast, the massive pillars reached upward to vaulted arches that were deeply shadowed. As I moved slowly along one of the side aisles, the voices of the choir swelled to a majestic finale.

The congregants began to go forward to receive Communion. As they did, I was able to move less obtrusively, scanning the faces of the young people in the pews. Each time I spotted a teenaged boy, my heart quickened. Each time I felt a sharp stab of disappointment.

I passed behind the waiting communicants, then moved unhurriedly up the nave and crossed to the far aisle. The church was darker and sparsely populated toward the rear; momentarily a pillar blocked my view of the altar. I moved around it.

He was there in the pew next to the pillar, leaning wearily against it. Even in the shadowy light, I could see that his face was dirty and tired, his jacket and jeans rumpled and stained. His eyes were half-closed, his mouth slack; his hands were shoved between his thighs, as if for warmth.

Mike—no, Michael—had come to the only safe place he knew in the city, the church where on two Christmas Eves he'd attended mass with his family and their friends, the Shribers, who had lived across the street.

I slipped into the pew and sat down next to him. He jerked his head toward me, stared in openmouthed surprise. What little color he had drained from his face; his eyes grew wide and alarmed.

"Hi, Michael." I put my hand on his arm.

He looked at me as if he wanted to shake it off. "How did you. . . ?"

"Doesn't matter. Not now. Let's just sit quietly till mass is over."

He continued to stare at me. After a few seconds he said, "I bet Mom and Dad are really mad at me."

"More worried than anything else."

"Did they hire you to find me?"

"No, I volunteered."

"Huh." He looked away at the line of communicants.

"You still go to church?" I asked.

"Not much. None of us do anymore. I kind of miss it."

"Do you want to take Communion?"

He was silent. Then, "No. I don't think that's something I can do right now. Maybe never."

"Well, that's okay. Everybody expresses his feelings for . . . God, or whatever, in different ways." I thought of the group of homeless worshippers in the vacant lot. "What's important is that you believe in something."

He nodded, and then we sat silently, watching people file up and down the aisle. After a while he said, "I guess I do believe in something. Otherwise I couldn't have gotten through this week. I learned a lot, you know."

"I'm sure you did."

"About me, I mean."

"I know."

"What're you going to do now? Send me home?"

"Do you want to go home?"

"Maybe. Yes. But I don't want to be sent there. I want to go on my own."

"Well, nobody should spend Christmas Day on a plane or a bus anyway. Besides, I'm having ten people to dinner at four this afternoon. I'm counting on you to help me stuff the turkey."

Michael hesitated, then smiled shyly. He took one hand from between his thighs and slipped it into mine. After a moment he leaned his tired head on my shoulder, and we celebrated the dawn of Christmas together.

BENNY'S SPACE

AMORFINA ANGELES was terrified, and I could fully empathize with her. Merely living in the neighborhood would have terrified me—all the more so had I been harassed by members of one of its many street gangs.

Hers was a rundown side street in the extreme southeast of San Francisco, only blocks from the crime- and drug-infested Sunnydale public housing projects. There were bars over the windows and grilles on the doors of the small stucco houses; dead and vandalized cars stood at the broken curbs; in the weed-choked yard next door, a mangy guard dog of indeterminate breed paced and snarled. Fear was written on this street as plainly as the graffiti on the walls and fences. Fear and hopelessness and a dull resignation to a life that none of its residents would willingly have opted to lead.

I watched Mrs. Angeles as she crossed her tiny living room to the front window, pulled the edge of the curtain aside a fraction, and peered out at the street. She was no more than five feet tall, with rounded shoulders, sallow skin, and graying black hair that curled in short, unruly ringlets. Her shapeless flower-printed dress did little to conceal a body made soft and fleshy by bad food and too much childbearing. Although she was only forty, she moved like a much older woman.

Her attorney and my colleague, Jack Stuart of All Souls Legal Cooperative, had given me a brief history of his client when he'd asked me to undertake an investigation on her behalf. She was a Filipina who had emigrated to the states with her husband in search of their own piece of the good life that was reputed to be had here. But as with many of their countrymen and -women, things hadn't worked out as the Angeleses had envisioned: first Amorfina's husband had gone into the import-export business with a friend from Manila; the friend absconded two years later with Joe Angeles's life savings. Then, a year after that, Joe was killed in a freak accident at a construction site where he was working. Amorfina and their six children were left with no means of support, and in the years since Joe's death their circumstances had gradually been reduced to this two-bedroom rental cottage in one of the worst areas of the city.

Mrs. Angeles, Jack told me, had done the best she could for her family, keeping them off the welfare rolls with a daytime job at the Mission district sewing factory and nighttime work doing alterations. As they grew older, the children helped with part-time jobs. Now there were only two left at home: sixteen-year-old Alex and fourteen-year-old Isabel. It was typical of their mother, Jack said, that in the current crisis she was more concerned for them than for herself.

She turned from the window now, her face taut with fear, deep lines bracketing her full lips. I asked, "Is someone out there?"

She shook her head and walked wearily to the worn recliner opposite me. I occupied the place of honor on a red brocade sofa encased in the same plastic that had doubtless protected it long ago upon delivery from the store. "I never see anybody," she said. "Not till it's too late."

"Mrs. Angeles, Jack Stuart told me about your problem, but I'd like to hear it in your own words—from the beginning, if you would."

She nodded, smoothing her bright dress over her plump thighs. "It goes back a long time, to when Benny Crespo was . . . they called him the Prince of Omega Street, you know."

Hearing the name of her street spoken made me aware of its ironic appropriateness: the last letter of the Greek alphabet is symbolic of endings, and for most of the people living here, Omega Street was the end of a steady decline into poverty.

Mrs. Angeles went on, "Benny Crespo was Filipino. His gang controlled the drugs here. A lot of people looked up to him; he had power, and that don't happen much with our people. Once I caught Alex and one of my older boys calling him a hero. I let them have it pretty good, you bet, and there wasn't any more of *that* kind of talk around this house. I got no use for the gangs—Filipino or otherwise."

"What was the name of Benny Crespo's gang?"

"The *Kabalyeros*. That's Tagalog for Knights."

"Okay—what happened to Benny?"

"The house next door, the one with the dog—that was where Benny lived. He always parked his fancy Corvette out front, and people knew better than to mess with it. Late one night he was getting out of the car and somebody shot him. A drug burn, they say. After that the *Kabalyeros* decided to make the parking space a shrine to Benny. They roped it off, put flowers there every week. On All Saints Day and the other fiestas, it was something to see."

"And that brings us to last March thirteenth," I said.

Mrs. Angeles bit her lower lip and smoothed her dress again.

When she didn't speak, I prompted her. "You'd just come home from work."

"Yeah. It was late, dark. Isabel wasn't here, and I got worried. I kept looking out the window, like a mother does."

"And you saw . . . ?"

"The guy who moved into the house next door after Benny got shot, Reg Dawson. He was black, one of a gang called the Victors. They say he moved into that house to show the *Kabalyeros* that the Victors were taking over their turf. Anyway, he drives up and stops a little way down the block. Waits there, revving his engine. People start showing up; the word's been put out that something's gonna go down. And when there's a big crowd, Reg Dawson guns his car and drives right into Benny's space, over the rope and the flowers.

"Well, that started one hell of a fight—Victors and *Kabalyeros* and folks from the neighborhood. And while it's going on, Reg Dawson just stands there in Benny's space acting macho. That's when it happened, what I saw."

"And what was that?"

She hesitated, wet her lips. "The leader of the *Kabalyeros*, Tommy Dragón—the Dragon, they call him—was over by the fence in front of Reg Dawson's house, where you couldn't see him unless you were really looking. I was, 'cause I was trying to see if Isabel was anyplace out there. And I saw Tommy Dragón point this gun at Reg Dawson and shoot him dead."

"What did you do then?"

"Ran and hid in the bathroom. That's where I was when the cops came to the door. Somebody'd told them I was in the window when it all went down and then ran away when Reg got shot. Well, what was I supposed to do? I got no use for the *Kabalyeros* or the Victors, so I told the truth. And now here I am in this mess."

Mrs. Angeles had been slated to be the chief prosecution witness at Tommy Dragón's trial this week. But a month ago the threats had started: anonymous letters and phone calls warning her against testifying. As the trial date approached this had escalated into blatant intimidation: a fire was set in her trash can; someone shot out her kitchen window; a dead dog turned up on her doorstep. The previous Friday, Isabel had been accosted on her way home from the bus stop by two masked men with guns. And that had finally made Mrs. Angeles capitulate; in court yesterday, she'd refused to take the stand against Dragón.

The state needed her testimony; there were no other witnesses, Dragón insisted on his innocence, and the murder gun had not been found. The judge had tried to reason with Mrs. Angeles, then cited her for contempt—reluctantly, he said. "The court is aware that there have been threats made against you and your family," he told her, "but it is unable to guarantee your protection." Then he gave her forty-eight hours to reconsider her decision.

As it turned out, Mrs. Angeles had a champion in her employer. The owner of the sewing factory was unwilling to allow one of his long-term workers to go to jail or to risk her own and her family's safety. He brought her to All Souls, where he held a membership in our legal-services plan, and this morning Jack Stuart asked me to do something for her.

What? I'd asked. What could I do that the SFPD couldn't to stop vicious harassment by a street gang?

Well, he said, get proof against whoever was threatening her so that they could be arrested and she'd feel free to testify.

Sure, Jack, I said. And exactly why *hadn't* the police been able to do anything about the situation?

His answer was not surprising: lack of funds. Intimidation of prosecution witnesses in cases relating to gang violence was becoming more and more prevalent and open in San Francisco, but the city did not have the resources to protect them. An old story nowadays—not enough money to go around.

Mrs. Angeles was watching my face, her eyes tentative. As I looked back at her, her gaze began to waver. She'd experienced too much disappointment in her life to expect much in the way of help from me.

I said, "Yes, you certainly are in a mess. Let's see if we can get you out of it."

We talked for a while longer, and I soon realized that Amor—as she asked me to call her—held the misconception that there was some way I could get the contempt citation dropped. I asked her if she'd known beforehand that a balky witness could be sent to jail. She shook her head. A person had a right to change her mind, hadn't she? When I set her straight on that, she seemed to lose interest in the conversation; it was difficult to get her to focus long enough to compile a list of people I should talk with. I settled for enough names to keep me occupied for the rest of the afternoon.

I was ready to leave when angry voices came from the front steps. A young man and woman entered. They stopped speaking when they saw the room was occupied, but their faces remained set in lines of contention. Amor hastened to introduce them as her son and daughter, Alex and Isabel. To them she explained that I was a detective "helping with the trouble with the judge."

Alex, a stocky youth with a tracery of mustache on his upper lip, seemed disinterested. He shrugged out of his high school letter jacket and vanished through a door to the rear of the house. Isabel studied me with frank curiosity. She was a slender beauty, with black hair that fell in soft curls to her shoulders; her features had a delicacy lacking in those of her mother and brother. Unfortunately, bright blue eyeshadow and garish orange lipstick detracted from her natural good looks, and she wore an imitation leather outfit in a particularly gaudy shade of purple. However, she was polite and well-spoken as she questioned me about what I could do to help her mother. Then, after a comment to Amor about an assignment that was due the next day, she left through the door her brother had used.

I turned to Amor, who was fingering the leaves of a philodendron plant that stood in a stand near the front window. Her posture was stiff, and when I spoke to her she didn't meet my eyes. Now I was aware of a tension in her that hadn't been there before her children returned home. Anxiety, because of the danger her witnessing the shooting had placed them in? Or something else? It might have had to do with the quarrel they'd been having, but weren't arguments between siblings fairly common? They certainly had been in my childhood home in San Diego.

I told Amor I'd be back to check on her in a couple of hours. Then, after a few precautionary and probably unnecessary reminders about locking doors and staying clear of windows, I went out into the chill November afternoon.

The first name on my list was Madeline Dawson, the slain gang leader's widow. I glanced at the house next door and saw with some relief that the guard dog no longer paced in its yard. When I pushed through the gate in the chain link fence, the creature's whereabouts became apparent: a bellowing emanated from the small, shabby cottage.

I went up a broken walk bordered by weeds, climbed the sagging front steps, and pressed the bell. A woman's voice yelled for the dog to shut up, then a door slammed somewhere within, muffling the barking. Footsteps approached, and the woman called, "Yes, who is it?"

"My name's Sharon McCone, from All Soul's Legal Cooperative. I'm investigating the threats your neighbor, Mrs. Angeles, has been receiving."

A couple of locks turned and the door opened on its chain. The face that peered out at me was very thin and pale, with wisps of red hair straggling over the high forehead; the Dawson marriage had been an interracial one, then. The woman stared at me for a moment before she asked, "What threats?"

"You don't know that Mrs. Angeles and her children have been threatened because she's to testify against the man who shot your husband?"

She shook her head and stepped back, shivering slightly—whether from the cold outside or the memory of the murder, I couldn't tell. "I . . . don't get out much these days."

"May I come in, talk with you about the shooting?"

She shrugged, unhooked the chain, and opened the door. "I don't know what good it will do. Amor's a damned fool for saying she'd testify in the first place."

"Aren't you glad she did? The man killed your husband."

She shrugged again and motioned me into a living room the same size as that in the Angeles house. All resemblance stopped there, however. Dirty glasses and dishes, full ashtrays, piles of newspapers and magazines covered every surface; dust balls the size of rats lurked under the shabby Danish furniture. Madeline Dawson picked up a heap of tabloids from the couch and dumped it on the floor, then indicated I should sit there and took a hassock for herself.

I said, "You *are* glad that Mrs. Angeles was willing to testify, aren't you?"

"Not particularly."

"You don't care if your husband's killer is convicted or not?"

"Reg was asking to be killed. Not that I wouldn't mind seeing the Dragon get the gas chamber—he may not have killed Reg, but he killed plenty of other people—"

"What did you say?" I spoke sharply, and Madeline Dawson blinked in surprise. It made me pay closer attention to her eyes; they were glassy, their pupils dilated. The woman, I realized, was high.

"I said the Dragon killed plenty of other people."

"No, about him not killing Reg."

"Did I say that?"

"Yes."

"I can't imagine why. I mean, Amor must know. She was up there in the window watching for sweet Isabel like always."

"You don't sound as if you like Isabel Angeles."

"I'm not fond of flips in general. Look at the way they're taking over this area. Daly City's turning into another Manila. All they do is buy, buy, buy—houses, cars, stuff by the truckload. You know, there's a joke that the first three words their babies learn are 'Mama, Papa, and Serramonte.'" Serramonte was a large shopping mall south of San Francisco.

The roots of the resentment she voiced were clear to me. One of our largest immigrant groups today, the Filipinos are highly westernized and by and large better educated and more affluent than other recently arrived Asians—or many of their neighbors, black or white. Isabel Angeles, for all her bright, cheap clothing and excessive makeup, had behind her a tradition of industriousness and upward mobility that might help her to secure a better place in the world than Madeline Dawson could aspire to.

I wasn't going to allow Madeline's biases to interfere with my line of questioning. I said, "About Dragón not having shot your husband—"

"Hey, who knows? Or cares? The bastard's dead, and good riddance."

"Why good riddance?"

"The man was a pig. A pusher who cheated and gouged people— people like me who need the stuff to get through. You think I was always like this, lady? No way. I was a nice Irish Catholic girl from the Avenues when Reg got his hands on me. Turned me on to coke and a lot of other things when I was only thirteen. Likes his pussy young, Reg did. But then I got old—I'm all of nineteen now—and I needed more and more stuff just to keep going, and all of a sudden Reg didn't even *see* me anymore. Yeah, the man was a pig, and I'm glad he's dead."

"But you don't think Dragón killed him."

She sighed in exasperation. "I don't know what I think. It's just that I always supposed that when Reg got it it would be for something more personal than driving his car into a stupid shrine in a parking space. You know what I mean? But what does it matter who killed him, anyway?"

"It matters to Tommy Dragón, for one."

She dismissed the accused man's life with a flick of her hand. "Like I said, the Dragon's a killer. He might as well die for Reg's murder as for any of the others. In a way, it'd be the one good thing Reg did for the world."

Perhaps in a certain primitive sense she was right, but her off-handedness made me uncomfortable. I changed the subject. "About the threat to Mrs. Angeles—which of the *Kabalyeros* would be behind them?"

"All of them. These guys in the gangs, they work together."

But I knew about the structure of street gangs—my degree in sociology from U. C. Berkeley hadn't been totally worthless—to be reasonably sure that wasn't so. There is usually one dominant personality, supported by two or three lieutenants; take away these leaders, and the followers become ineffectual, purposeless. If I could turn up enough evidence against the leaders of the *Kabalyeros* to have them arrested, the harassment would stop.

I asked, "Who took over the *Kabalyeros* after Dragón went to jail?"

"Hector Bulis."

It was a name that didn't appear on my list; Amor had claimed not to know who was the current head of the Filipino gang. "Where can I find him?"

"There's a fast-food joint over on Geneva, near the Cow Palace. Fat Robbie's. That's where the *Kabalyeros* hang out."

The second person I'd intended to talk with was the young man who had reportedly taken over the leadership of the Victors after Dawson's death, Jimmy Willis. Willis could generally be found at a bowling alley, also on Geneva Avenue near the Cow Palace. I thanked Madeline for taking the time to talk with me and headed for the Daly City line.

The first of the two establishments that I spotted was Fat Robbie's, a cinderblock-and-glass relic of the early sixties whose specialties appeared to be burgers and chicken-in-a-basket. I turned into a parking lot that was half-full of mostly shabby cars and left my MG beside one of the defunct drive-in speaker poles.

The interior of the restaurant took me back to my high school days: orange leatherette booths beside the plate glass windows, a long Formica counter with stools, laminated color pictures of disgusting-looking food on the wall above the pass-through counter from the kitchen. Instead of a jukebox there was a bank of video games along one wall. Three

Filipino youths in jeans and denim jackets gathered around one called "Invader!". The *Kabalyeros*, I assumed.

I crossed to the counter with only a cursory glance at the trio, sat, and ordered coffee from a young woman who looked to be Eurasian. The *Kabalyeros* didn't conceal their interest in me; they stared openly, and after a moment one of them said something that sounded like "tick-tick," and they all laughed nastily. Some sort of Tagalog obscenity, I supposed. I ignored them, sipping the dishwater-weak coffee, and after a bit they went back to their game.

I took out the paperback that I keep in my bag for protective coloration and pretended to read, listening to the few snatches of conversation that drifted over from the three. I caught the names of two: Sal and Hector—the latter presumably Bulis, the gang's leader. When I glanced covertly at him, I saw he was tallish and thin, with long hair caught back in a ponytail; his features were razor-sharp and slightly skewed, creating the impression of a perpetual sneer. The trio kept their voices low, and although I strained to hear, I could make out nothing of what they were saying. After about five minutes Hector turned away from the video machine. With a final glance at me he motioned to his companions, and they all left the restaurant.

I waited until they'd driven away in an old green Pontiac before I called the waitress over and showed her my identification. "The three men who just left," I said. "Is the tall one Hector Bulis?"

Her lips formed a little "O" as she stared at the I. D. Finally she nodded.

"May I talk with you about them?"

She glanced toward the pass-through to the kitchen. "My boss, he don't like me talking with the customers when I'm supposed to be working."

"Take a break. Just five minutes."

Now she looked nervously around the restaurant. "I shouldn't—"

I slipped a twenty-dollar bill from my wallet and showed it to her. "Just five minutes."

She still seemed edgy, but fear lost out to greed. "Okay, but I don't want anybody to see me talking to you. Go back to the restroom—it's through that door by the video games. I'll meet you there as soon as I can."

I got up and found the ladies' room. It was tiny, dimly lit, with a badly cracked mirror. The walls were covered with a mass of graffiti;

some of it looked as if it had been painted over and had later worked its way back into view through the fading layers of enamel. The air in there was redolent of grease, cheap perfume, and stale cigarette and marijuana smoke. I leaned against the sink as I waited.

The young Eurasian woman appeared a few minutes later. "Bastard gave me a hard time," she said. "Tried to tell me I'd already taken my break."

"What's your name?"

"Anna Smith."

"Anna, the three men who just left—do they come in here often?"

"Uh-huh"

"Keep pretty much to themselves, do they?"

"It's more like other people stay away from them." She hesitated. "They're from one of the gangs; you don't mess with them. That's why I wanted to talk with you back here."

"Have you ever heard them say anything about Tommy Dragón?"

"The Dragon? Sure. He's in jail; they say he was framed."

Of course they would claim that. "What about a Mrs. Angeles— Amorfina Angeles?"

". . . Not that one, no."

"What about trying to intimidate someone? Setting fires, going after someone with a gun?"

"Uh-uh. That's gang business; they keep it pretty close. But it wouldn't surprise me. Filipinos—I'm part Filipina myself, my mom met my dad when he was stationed at Subic Bay—they've got this saying, *kumukuló ang dugó.* It means, 'the blood is boiling.' They can get pretty damn mad 'specially the men. So stuff like what you said—sure they do it."

"Do you work on Fridays?"

"Yeah, two to ten."

"Did you see any of the *Kabalyeros* in here last Friday around six?" That was the time when Isabel had been accosted.

Anna Smith scrunched up her face in concentration. "Last Friday . . . oh, yeah, sure. That was when they had the big meeting all of them."

"*All* of them?"

"Uh-huh. Started around five-thirty, went on a couple of hours. My boss, he was worried something heavy was gonna go down, but the way it turned out, all he did was sell a lot of food."

"What was the meeting about?"

"Had to do with the Dragon, who was gonna be character witnesses at the trial, what they'd say."

The image of the three I'd seen earlier—or any of their ilk—as character witnesses was somewhat ludicrous, but I supposed in Tommy Dragón's position you took what you could get. "Are you sure they were all there?"

"Uh-huh."

"And no one at the meeting said anything about trying to keep Mrs. Angeles from testifying?"

"No. That lawyer the Dragon's got, he was there too."

Now that was odd. Why had Dragón's public defender chosen to meet with his witnesses in a public place? I could think of one good reason: he was afraid of them, didn't want them in his office. But what if the *Kabalyeros* had set the time and place—as an alibi for when Isabel was to be assaulted?

"I better get back to work," Anna Smith said. "Before the boss comes looking for me."

I gave her the twenty dollars. "Thanks for your time."

"Sure." Halfway out the door she paused, frowning. "I hope I didn't get any of the *Kabalyeros* in trouble."

"You didn't."

"Good. I kind of like them. I mean, they push dope and all, but these days, who doesn't?"

These days, who doesn't? I thought. *Good Lord . . .*

The Starlight Lanes was an old-fashioned bowling alley girded by a rough cliff face and an auto dismantler's yard. The parking lot was crowded, so I left the MG around back by the garbage cans. Inside, the lanes were brightly lit and noisy with the sound of crashing pins, rumbling balls, shouts, and groans. I paused by the front counter and asked where I might find Jimmy Willis. The woman behind it directed me to a lane at the far end.

Bowling alleys—or lanes, as the new upscale bowler prefers to call them—are familiar territory to me. Up until a few years ago my favorite uncle Jim was a top player on the pro tour. The Starlight Lanes reminded me of the ones where Jim used to practice in San Diego—from the racks full of tired-looking rental shoes to the greasy-spoon coffeeshop smells to the molded plastic chairs and cigarette-burned scorekeeping consoles. I walked along it, soaking up the ambience—some people would say lack of it—until I came to lane 32 and spotted an agile young black man bowling alone. Jimmy Willis was a left-hander, and his ball hooked out until it hung on the edge of the channel, then hooked back with deadly accuracy and graceful form. His concentration was so great that he didn't notice me until he'd finished the last frame and retrieved his ball.

"You're quite a bowler," I said. "What's your average?"

He gave me a long look before he replied, "Two hundred."

"Almost good enough to turn pro."

"That's what I'm looking to do."

Odd, for the head of a street gang that dealt in drugs and death. "You ever heard of Jim McCone?" I asked.

"Sure. Damned good in his day."

"He's my uncle."

"No kidding." Willis studied me again, now as if looking for a resemblance.

Rapport established, I showed him my ID and explained that I wanted to talk about Reg Dawson's murder. He frowned, hesitated, then nodded. "Okay, since you're Jim McCone's niece, but you'll have to buy me a beer."

"Deal."

Willis toweled off his ball, stowed it and his shoes in their bag, and led me to a typical smoke-filled, murkily lighted bowling alley bar. He took one of the booths while I fetched us a pair of Buds.

As I slid into the booth I said, "What can you tell me about the murder?"

"The way I see it, Dawson was asking for it."

So he and Dawson's wife were of a mind about that. "I can understand what you mean, but it seems strange, coming from you. I hear you were his friend, that you took over the Victors after his death."

"You heard wrong on both counts. Yeah, I was in the Victors, and when Dawson bought it, they tried to get me to take over. But by then I'd figured out—never mind how, doesn't matter—that I wanted out of that life. Ain't nothing in it but what happened to Benny Crespo and Dawson—or what's going to happen to the Dragon. So I decided to put my hand to something with a future." He patted the bowling bag that sat on the banquette beside him. "Got a job here now—not much, but my bowling's free and I'm on my way."

"Good for you. What about Dragón—do you think he's guilty?"

Willis hesitated, looking thoughtful. "Why do you ask?"

"Just wondering."

". . . Well, to tell you the truth, I never did believe the Dragon shot Reg."

"Who did, then?"

He shrugged.

I asked him if he'd heard about the *Kabalyeros* trying to intimidate the chief prosecution witness. When he nodded, I said, "They also threatened the life of her daughter last Friday."

He laughed mirthlessly. "Wish I could of seen that. Kind of surprises me, though. That lawyer of Dragón's, he found out what the *Kabalyeros* were up to, read them the riot act. Said they'd put Dragón in the gas chamber for sure. So they called it off."

"When was this?"

"Week, ten days ago."

Long before Isabel had been accosted. Before the dead dog and the shooting incidents, too. "Are you sure?"

"It's what I hear. You know, in a way I'm surprised that they'd go after Mrs. Angeles at all."

"Why?"

"The Filipinos have this macho tradition. 'Specially when it comes to their women. They don't like them messed with, 'specially by non-Filipinos. So how come they'd turn around and mess with one of their own?"

"Well, her testimony *would* jeopardize the life of one of their fellow gang members. It's an extreme situation."

"Can't argue with that."

Jimmy Willis and I talked a bit more, but he couldn't—or wouldn't—offer any further information. I bought him a second beer, then went out to where I'd left my car.

And came face-to-face with Hector Bulis and the man called Sal.

Sal grabbed me by the arm, twisted it behind me, and forced me up against the latticework fence surrounding the garbage cans. The stench from them filled my nostrils; Sal's breath rivaled it in foulness. I struggled, but he got hold of my other arm and pinned me tighter. I looked around, saw no one, nothing but the cliff face and the high board fence of the auto dismantler's yard. Bulis approached, flicking open a switchblade, his twisty face intense. I stiffened, went very still, eyes on the knife.

Bullis placed the tip of the knife against my jawbone, then traced a line across my cheek. "Don't want to hurt you, bitch," he said. "You do what I say, I won't have to mess you up."

The Tagalog phrase that Anna Smith had translated for me—*kumukuló ang dugó*—flashed through my mind. *The blood is boiling.* I sensed Bullis's was—and dangerously so.

I wet my dry lips, tried to keep my voice from shaking as I said, "What do you want me to do?"

"We hear you're asking around about Dawson's murder, trying to prove the Dragon did it."

"That's not—"

"We want you to quit. Go back to your own part of town and leave our business alone."

"Whoever told you that is lying. I'm only trying to help the Angeles family."

"They wouldn't lie." He moved the knife's tip to the hollow at the base of my throat. I felt it pierce my skin—a mere pinprick, but frightening enough.

When I could speak, I did so slowly, phrasing my words carefully. "What I hear is that Dragón is innocent. And that the *Kabalyeros* aren't behind the harassment of the Angeleses—at least not for a week or ten days."

Bullis exchanged a look with his companion—quick, unreadable.

"Someone's trying to frame you," I added. "Just like they did Dragón."

Bullis continued to hold the knife to my throat, his hand firm. His gaze wavered, however, as if he was considering what I'd said. After a moment he asked, "All right—who?"

"I'm not sure, but I think I can find out."

He thought a bit longer, then let his arm drop and snapped the knife shut. "I'll give you till this time tomorrow," he said. Then he stuffed the knife into his pocket, motioned for Sal to let go of me, and the two quickly walked away.

I sagged against the latticework fence, feeling my throat where the knife had pricked it. It had bled a little, but the flow already was clotting. My knees were weak and my breath came fast, but I was too caught up in the possibilities to panic. There were plenty of them—and the most likely was the most unpleasant.

Kumukuló ang dugó. The blood is boiling . . . .

✧

Two hours later I was back at the Angeles house on Omega Street. When Amor admitted me, the tension I'd felt in her earlier had drained. Her body sagged, as if the extra weight she carried had finally proved to be too much for her frail bones; the skin of her face looked flaccid, like melting putty; her eyes were sunken and vague. After she shut the door and motioned for me to sit, she sank into the recliner, expelling a sigh. The house was quiet—too quiet.

"I have a question for you," I said. "What does 'tick-tick' mean in Tagalog?"

Her eyes flickered with dull interest. "*Tiktík.*" She corrected my pronunciation. "It's a word for detective."

Ever since Hector Bulis and Sal had accosted me I'd suspected as much.

"Where did you hear that?" Amor asked.

"One of the *Kabalyeros* said it when I went to Fat Robbie's earlier. Someone had told them I was a detective, probably described me. Whoever it was said I was trying to prove Tommy Dragón killed Reg Dawson."

"Why would—"

"More to the point, *who* would? At the time, only four people knew that I'm a detective."

She wet her lips, but remained silent.

"Amor, the night of the shooting, you were standing in your front window, watching for Isabel."

"Yes."

"Do you do that often?"

". . . Yes."

"Because Isabel is often late coming home. Because you're afraid she may have gotten into trouble."

"A mother worries—"

"Especially when she's given good cause. Isabel is running out of control, isn't she?"

"No, she—"

"Amor, when I spoke with Madeline Dawson, she said you were standing in the window watching for 'sweet Isabel, like always.' She didn't say 'sweet' in a pleasant way. Later, Jimmy Willis implied that your daughter is not . . . exactly a vulnerable young girl."

Amor's eyes sparked. "The Dawson woman is jealous."

"Of course she is. There's something else: when I asked the waitress at Fat Robbie's if she'd ever overheard the *Kabalyeros* discussing you, she said, 'No, not that one.' It didn't register at the time, but when I talked to her again a little while ago, she told me Isabel is the member of your family they discuss. They say she's wild, runs around with the men in the gangs. You know that, so does Alex. And so does Madeline Dawson. She just told me the first man Isabel became involved with was her husband."

Amor seemed to shrivel. She gripped the arms of the chair, white-knuckled.

"It's true, isn't it?" I asked more gently.

She lowered her eyes, nodding. When she spoke her voice was ragged. "I don't know what to do with her anymore. Ever since that Reg Dawson got to her, she's been different, not my girl at all."

"Is she on drugs?"

"Alex says no, but I'm not so sure."

I let it go; it really didn't matter. "When she came home earlier," I said, "Isabel seemed very interested in me. She asked questions, looked me over carefully enough to be able to describe to the *Kabalyeros*. She was afraid of what I might find out. For instance, that she wasn't accosted by any men with guns last Friday."

"She was!"

"No, Amor. That was just a story, to make it look as if your life—and your children's—were in danger if you testified. In spite of what you said early on, you haven't wanted to testify against Tommy Dragón from the very beginning.

"When the *Kabalyeros* began harassing you a month ago, you saw that as the perfect excuse not to take the stand. But you didn't foresee that Dragón's lawyer would convince the gang to stop the harassment. When that happened, you and Isabel, and probably Alex, too, manufactured incidents—the shot-out window, the dead dog on the doorstep, the men with the guns—to make it look as if the harassment was still going on."

"Why would I? They're going to put me in jail."

"But at the time you didn't know they could do that—or that your employer would hire me. My investigating poses yet another danger to you and your family."

"This is . . . why would I do all that?"

"Because basically you're an honest woman, a good woman. You didn't want to testify because you knew Dragón didn't shoot Dawson. It's my guess you gave the police his name because it was the first one that came to mind."

"I had no reason to—"

"You had the best reason in the world: a mother's desire to protect her child."

She was silent, sunken eyes registering despair and defeat.

I kept on, even though I hated to inflict further pain on her. "The day he died, Dawson had let the word out that he was going to desecrate Benny's space. The person who shot him knew there would be fighting and confusion, counted on that as a cover. The killer hated Dawson—"

"Lots of people did."

"But only one person you'd want to protect so badly that you'd accuse an innocent man."

"Leave my mother alone. She's suffered enough on account of what I did."

I turned. Alex had come into the room so quietly I hadn't noticed. Now he moved midway between Amor and me, a Saturday night special clutched in his right hand.

The missing murder weapon.

I tensed, but one look at his face told me he didn't intend to use it. Instead he raised his arm and extended the gun, grip first.

"Take this," he said. "I never should of bought it. Never should of used it. I hated Dawson on account of what he did to my sister. But killing him wasn't worth what we've all gone through since."

I glanced at Amor; tears were trickling down her face.

Alex said, "Mama, don't cry. I'm not worth it."

When she spoke, it was to me. "What will happen to him?"

"Nothing like what might have happened to Dragón; Alex is a juvenile. You, however—"

"I don't care about myself, only my children."

Maybe that was the trouble. She was the archetypal selfless mother: living only for her children, sheltering them from the consequences of their actions—and in the end doing them irreparable harm.

There were times when I felt thankful that I had no children. And there were times when I was thankful that Jack Stuart was a very good criminal lawyer. This was a time I was thankful on both counts. I went to the phone, called Jack, and asked him to come over here. At least I could leave the Angeles family in good legal hands.

After he arrived, I went out into the gathering dusk. An old yellow VW was pulling out of Benny's space. I walked down there and stood on the curb. Nothing remained of the shrine to Benny Crespo. Nothing remained to show that blood had boiled and been shed here. It was merely a stretch of cracked asphalt, splotched with oil drippings, littered with the detritus of urban life. I stared at it for close to a minute, then turned away from the bleak landscape of Omega Street.

THE LOST COAST

CALIFORNIA'S Lost Coast is at the same time one of the most desolate and beautiful of shorelines. Northerly winds whip the sand into dust-devil frenzy; eerie, stationary fogs hang in the trees and distort the drift-wood until it resembles the bones of prehistoric mammals; bruised clouds hover above the peaks of the distant King Range, then blow down to sea level and dump icy torrents. But on a fair day the sea and sky show in-finite shadings of blue, and the wildflowers are a riot of color. If you wait quietly, you can spot deer, peregrine falcons, foxes, otters, even black bears and mountain lions.

A contradictory and oddly compelling place, this seventy-three-mile stretch of coast southwest of Eureka, where—as with most worthwhile things or people—you must take the bad with the good.

Unfortunately, on my first visit there I was taking mostly the bad. Strong winds pushed my MG all over the steep, narrow road, making hairpin turns even more perilous. Early October rain cut my visibility to a few yards. After I crossed the swollen Bear River, the road continued to twist and wind, and I began to understand why the natives had dubbed it The Wildcat.

Somewhere ahead, my client had told me, was the hamlet of Petrolia—site of the first oil well drilled in California, he'd irrelevantly added. The man was a conservative politician, a former lumber-company attorney, and given what I knew of his voting record on the environ-ment, I was certain we disagreed on the desirability of that event, as well as any number of similar issues. But the urgency of the current situation dictated that I keep my opinions to myself, so I'd simply written down the directions he gave me—omitting his travelogue-like asides—and gotten under way.

I drove through Petrolia—a handful of new buildings, since the village had been all but leveled in the disastrous earthquake of 1992—and turned toward the sea on an unpaved road. After two miles I began looking for the orange post that marked the dirt track to the client's cabin.

The whole time I was wishing I was back in San Francisco. This wasn't my kind of case; I didn't like the client, Steve Shoemaker; and even though the fee was good, this was the week I'd scheduled to take off a few personal business days from All Souls Legal Cooperative, where I'm chief investigator. But Jack Stuart, our criminal specialist, had asked me to take on the job as a favor to him. Steve Shoemaker was Jack's old friend from college in Southern California, and he'd asked for a referral to a private detective. Jack owed Steve a favor; I owed Jack several, so there was no way I could gracefully refuse.

But I couldn't shake the feeling that something was wrong with this case. And I couldn't help wishing that I'd come to the Lost Coast in summertime, with a backpack and in the company of my lover—instead of on a rainy fall afternoon, with a .38 Special and soon to be in the company of Shoemaker's disagreeable wife, Andrea.

The rain was sheeting down by the time I spotted the orange post. It had turned the hard-packed earth to mud, and my MG's tires sank deep in the ruts, its undercarriage scraping dangerously. I could barely make out the stand of live oaks and sycamores where the track ended; no way to tell if another vehicle had traveled over it recently.

When I reached the end of the track I saw one of those boxy four-wheel-drive wagons—Bronco? Cherokee?—drawn in under the drooping branches of an oak. Andrea Shoemaker's? I'd neglected to get a description from her husband of what she drove. I got out of the MG, turning the hood of my heavy sweater up against the downpour; the wind promptly blew it off. So much for what the catalog had described as "extra protection on those cold nights." I yanked the hood up again and held it there, went around and took my .38 from the trunk and shoved it into the outside flap of my purse. Then I went over and tried the door of the four-wheel drive. Unlocked. I opened it, slipped into the driver's seat.

Nothing identifying its owner was on the seats or in the side pockets, but in the glove compartment I found a registration in the name of Andrea Shoemaker. I rummaged around, came up with nothing else of interest. Then I got out and walked through the trees, looking for the cabin.

Shoemaker had told me to follow a deer track through the grove. No sign of it in this downpour; no deer, either. Nothing but wind-lashed trees, the oaks pelting me with acorns. I moved slowly through them, swiveling my head from side to side, until I made out a bulky shape tucked beneath the farthest of the sycamores.

As I got closer, I saw the cabin was of plain weathered wood, rudely constructed, with the chimney of a woodstove extending from its composition shingle roof. Small—two or three rooms—and no light showing in its windows. And the door was open, banging against the inside wall . . . .

I quickened my pace, taking the gun from my purse. Alongside the door I stopped to listen. Silence. I had a flashlight in my bag; I took it out. Moved to where I could see inside, then turned the flash on and shone it through the door.

All that was visible was rough board walls, an oilcloth-covered table and chairs, an ancient woodstove. I stepped inside, swinging the light around. Unlit oil lamp on the table; flower-cushioned wooden furniture of the sort you always find in vacation cabins; rag rugs; shelves holding an assortment of tattered paperbacks, seashells, and driftwood. I shifted the light again, more slowly.

A chair on the far side of the table was tipped over, and a woman's purse lay on the edge of the woodstove, its contents spilling out. When I got over there I saw a .32 Iver Johnson revolver lying on the floor.

Andrea Shoemaker owned a .32. She'd told me so the day before.

Two doors opened off the room. Quietly I went to one and tried it. A closet, shelves stocked with staples and canned goods and bottled water. I looked around the room again, listening. No sound but the wail of wind and the pelt of rain on the roof. I stepped to the other door.

A bedroom, almost filled wall-to-wall by a king-sized bed covered with a goosedown comforter and piled with colorful pillows. Old bureau pushed in one corner, another unlit oil lamp on the single nightstand. Small travel bag on the bed.

The bag hadn't been opened. I examined its contents. Jeans, a couple of sweaters, underthings, toilet articles. Package of condoms. Uh-huh. She'd come here, as I'd found out, to meet a man. The affairs usually began with a casual pickup; they were never of long duration; and they all seemed to culminate in a romantic weekend in the isolated cabin.

Dangerous game, particularly in these days when AIDS and the prevalence of disturbed individuals of both sexes threatened. But Andrea Shoemaker had kept her latest date with an even larger threat hanging over her: for the past six weeks, a man with a serious grudge against her husband had been stalking her. For all I knew, he and the date were one and the same.

And where was Andrea now?

❖

This case had started on Wednesday, two days ago, when I'd driven up to Eureka, a lumbering and fishing town on Humboldt Bay. After I passed the Humboldt County line I began to see huge logging trucks toiling through the mountain passes, shredded curls of redwood bark trailing in their wakes. Twenty-five miles south of the city itself was the company-owned town of Scotia, mill stacks belching white smoke and filling the air with the scent of freshly cut wood. Yards full of logs waiting to be fed to the mills lined the highway. When I reached Eureka itself, the downtown struck me as curiously quiet; many of the stores were out of business, and the sidewalks were mostly deserted. The recession had hit the lumber industry hard, and the earthquake hadn't helped the area's strapped economy.

I'd arranged to meet Steve Shoemaker at his law offices in Old Town, near the waterfront. It was a picturesque area full of renovated warehouses and interesting shops and restaurants, tricked up for tourists with the inevitable horse-and-carriage rides and t-shirt shops, but still pleasant. Shoemaker's offices were off a cobblestoned courtyard containing a couple of antique shops and a decorator's showroom.

When I gave my card to the secretary, she said Assemblyman Shoemaker was in conference and asked me to wait. The man, I knew, had lost his seat in the state legislature this past election, so the term of address seemed inappropriate. The appointments of the waiting room struck me as a bit much: brass and mahogany and marble and velvet, plenty of it, the furnishings all antiques that tended to the garish. I sat on a red velvet sofa and looked for something to read. *Architectural Digest, National Review, Foreign Affairs*—that was it, take it or leave it. I left it. My idea of waiting-room reading material is *People*; I love it, but I'm too embarrassed to subscribe.

The minutes ticked by: ten, fifteen, twenty. I contemplated the issue of *Architectural Digest*, then opted instead for staring at a fake Rembrandt on the far wall. Twenty-five, thirty. I was getting irritated now. Shoemaker had asked me to be here by three; I'd arrived on the dot. If this was, as he'd claimed, a matter of such urgency and delicacy that he couldn't go into it on the phone, why was he in conference at the appointed time?

Thirty-five minutes. Thirty-seven. The door to the inner sanctum opened and a woman strode out. A tall woman, with long chestnut hair, wearing a raincoat and black leather boots. Her eyes rested on me in passing—a cool gray, hard with anger. Then she went out, slamming the door behind her.

The secretary—a trim blond in a tailored suit—started as the door slammed. She glanced at me and tried to cover with a smile, but its edges were strained, and her fingertips pressed hard against the desk. The phone at her elbow buzzed; she snatched up the receiver. Spoke into it, then said to me, "Ms. McCone, Assemblyman Shoemaker will see you now." As she ushered me inside, she again gave me her frayed-edge smile.

Tense situation in this office, I thought. Brought on by what? The matter Steve Shoemaker wanted me to investigate? The client who had just made her angry exit? Or something else entirely . . . ?

Shoemaker's office was even more pretentious than the waiting room: more brass, mahogany, velvet, and marble; more fake Old Masters in heavy gilt frames; more antiques; more of everything. Shoemaker's demeanor was not as nervous as his secretary's, but when he rose to greet me, I noticed a jerkiness in his movements, as if he was holding himself under tight control. I clasped his outstretched hand and smiled, hoping the familiar social rituals would set him more at ease.

Momentarily they did. He thanked me for coming, apologized for making me wait, and inquired after Jack Stuart. After I was seated in one of the clients' chairs, he offered me a drink; I asked for mineral water. As he went to a wet bar tucked behind a tapestry screen, I took the opportunity to study him.

Shoemaker was handsome: dark hair, with the gray so artfully interwoven that it must have been professionally dyed. Chiseled features; nice, well-muscled body, shown off to perfection by an expensive blue suit. When he handed me my drink, his smile revealed white, even teeth that I, having spent the greater part of the previous month in the company of my dentist, recognized as capped. Yes, a very good-looking man, politician handsome. Jack's old friend or not, his appearance and manner called up my gut-level distrust.

My client went around his desk and reclaimed his chair. He held a drink of his own—something dark amber—and he took a deep swallow before speaking. The alcohol replenished his vitality some; he drank again, set the glass on a pewter coaster, and said, "Ms. McCone, I'm glad you could come up here on such short notice."

"You mentioned on the phone that the case is extremely urgent—and delicate."

He ran his hand over his hair—lightly, so as not to disturb its styling. "Extremely urgent and delicate," he repeated, seeming to savor the phrase.

"Why don't you tell me about it?"

His eyes strayed to the half-full glass on the coaster. Then they moved to the door through which I'd entered. Returned to me. "You saw the woman who just left?"

I nodded.

"My wife, Andrea."

I waited.

"She's very angry with me for hiring you."

"She did act angry. Why?"

Now he reached for the glass and belted down its contents. Leaned back and rattled the ice cubes as he spoke. "It's a long story. Painful to me. I'm not sure where to begin. I just . . . don't know what to make of the things that are happening."

"That's what you've hired me to do. Begin anywhere. We'll fill in the gaps later." I pulled a small tape recorder from my bag and set it on the edge of his desk. "Do you mind?"

Shoemaker eyed it warily, but shook his head. After a moment's hesitation, he said, "Someone is stalking my wife."

"Following her? Threatening her?"

"Not following, not that I know of. He writes notes, threatening to kill her. He leaves . . . things at the house. At her place of business. Dead things. Birds, rats, one time a cat. Andrea loves cats. She . . ." He shook his head, went to the bar for a refill.

"What else? Phone calls?"

"No. One time, a floral arrangement—suitable for a funeral."

"Does he sign the notes?"

"John. Just John."

"Does Mrs. Shoemaker know anyone named John who has a grudge against her?"

"She says no. And I . . ." He sat down, fresh drink in hand. "I have reason to believe that this John has a grudge against me, is using this harassment of Andrea to get at me personally."

"Why do you think that?"

"The wording of the notes."

"May I see them?"

He looked around, as if he were afraid someone might be listening. "Later. I keep them elsewhere."

Something, then, I thought, that he didn't want his office staff to see. Something shameful, perhaps even criminal.

"Okay," I said, "how long has this been going on?"

"About six weeks."

"Have you contacted the police?"

"Informally. A man I know on the force, Sergeant Bob Wolfe. But after he started looking into it, I had to ask him to drop it."

"Why?"

"I'm in a sensitive political position."

"Excuse me if I'm mistaken, Mr. Shoemaker, but it's my understanding that you're no longer serving in the state legislature."

"That's correct, but I'm about to announce my candidacy in a special election for a senate seat that's recently been vacated."

"I see. So after you asked your contact on the police force to back off, you decided to use a private investigator, and Jack recommended me. Why not use someone local?"

"As I said, my position is sensitive. I don't want word of this getting out in the community. That's why Andrea is so angry with me. She claims I value my political career more than her life."

I waited, wondering how he'd attempt to explain that away.

He didn't even try, merely went on, "In our . . . conversation just prior to this, she threatened to leave me. This coming weekend she plans to go to a cabin on the Lost Coast that she inherited from her father to, as she put it, sort things through. Alone. Do you know that part of the coast?"

"I've read some travel pieces on it."

"Then you're aware how remote it is. The cabin's very isolated. I don't want Andrea going there while this John person is on the loose."

"Does she go there often?"

"Fairly often. I don't; it's too rustic for me—no running water, phone, or electricity. But Andrea likes it. Why do you ask?"

"I'm wondering if John—whoever he is—knows about the cabin. Has she been there since the harassment began?"

"No. Initially she agreed that it wouldn't be a good idea. But now . . ." He shrugged.

"I'll need to speak with Mrs. Shoemaker. Maybe I can reason with her, persuade her not to go until we've identified John. Or maybe she'll allow me to go along as her bodyguard."

"You can speak with her if you like, but she's beyond reasoning with. And there's no way you can stop her or force her to allow you to accompany her. My wife is a strong-willed woman; that interior decorating firm across the courtyard is hers, she built it from the ground up. When Andrea decides to do something, she does it. And asks permission from no one."

"Still, I'd like to try reasoning. This trip to the cabin—that's the urgency you mentioned on the phone. Two days to find the man behind the harassment before she goes out there and perhaps makes a target of herself."

"Yes."

"Then I'd better get started. That funeral arrangement—what florist did it come from?"

Shoemaker shook his head. "It arrived at least five weeks ago, before either of us noticed a pattern to the harassment. Andrea just shrugged it off, threw the wrappings and card away."

"Let's go look at the notes, then. They're my only lead."

Vengeance will be mine. The sudden blow. The quick attack. Vengeance is the price of silence.

Mute testimony paves the way to an early grave. The rest is silence.

A freshly turned grave is silent testimony to an old wrong and its avenger.

There was more in the same vein—slightly biblical-flavored and stilted. But chilling to me, even though the safety-deposit booth at Shoemaker's bank was overly warm. If that was my reaction, what had these notes done to Andrea Shoemaker? No wonder she was thinking of leaving a husband who cared more for the electorate's opinion than his wife's life and safety.

The notes had been typed without error on an electric machine that had left no such obvious clues as chipped or skewed keys. The paper and envelopes were plain and cheap, purchasable at any discount store. They had been handled, I was sure, by nothing more than gloved hands. No signature—just the typed name "John."

But the writer had wanted the Shoemakers—one of them, anyway—to know who he was. Thus the theme that ran through them all: silence and revenge.

I said, "I take it your contact at the E.P.D. had their lab go over these?"

"Yes. There was nothing. That's why he wanted to probe further—something I couldn't permit him to do."

"Because of this revenge-and-silence business. Tell me about it."

Shoemaker looked around furtively. My God, did he think bank employees had nothing better to do with their time than to eavesdrop on our conversation?

"We'll go have a drink," he said. "I know a place that's private."

We went to a restaurant a few blocks away, where Shoemaker had another bourbon and I toyed with a glass of iced tea. After some prodding, he told me his story; it didn't enhance him in my eyes.

Seventeen years ago Shoemaker had been interviewing for a staff attorney's position at a large lumber company. While on a tour of the mills, he witnessed an accident in which a worker named Sam Carding was severely mangled while trying to clear a jam in a bark-stripping machine. Shoemaker, who had worked in the mills summers to pay for his education, knew the accident was due to company negligence, but accepted a handsome job offer in exchange for not testifying for the plaintiff in the ensuing lawsuit. The court ruled against Carding, confined to a wheelchair and in constant pain; a year later, while the case was still under appeal, Carding shot his wife and himself. The couple's three children were given token settlements in exchange for dropping the suit and then were adopted by relatives in a different part of the country.

"It's not a pretty story, Mr. Shoemaker," I said, "and I can see why the wording of the notes might make you suspect there's a connection between it and this harassment. But who do you think John is?"

"Carding's oldest boy. Carding and his family knew I'd witnessed the accident; one of his coworkers saw me watching from the catwalk and told him. Later, when I turned up as a senior counsel . . ." He shrugged.

"But why, after all this time—?"

"Why not? People nurse grudges. John Carding was sixteen at the time of the lawsuit; there were some ugly scenes with him, both at my home and my office at the mill. By now he'd be in his forties. Maybe it's his way of acting out some sort of midlife crisis."

"Well, I'll call my office and have my assistant run a check on all three Carding kids. And I want to speak with Mrs. Shoemaker—preferably in your presence."

He glanced at his watch. "It can't be tonight. She's got a meeting of her professional organization, and I'm dining with my campaign manager."

A potentially psychotic man was threatening Andrea's life, yet they both carried on as usual. Well, who was I to question it? Maybe it was their way of coping.

"Tomorrow, then," I said. "Your home. At the noon hour."

Shoemaker nodded. Then he gave me the address, as well as the names of John Carding's siblings.

I left him on the sidewalk in front of the restaurant: a handsome man whose shoulders now slumped inside his expensive suitcoat, shivering in the brisk wind off Humboldt Bay. As we shook hands, I saw that shame made his gaze unsteady, the set of his mouth less than firm.

I knew that kind of shame. Over the course of my career, I'd committed some dreadful acts that years later woke me in the deep of the night to sudden panic. I'd also *not* committed certain acts—failures that woke me to regret and emptiness. My sins of omission were infinitely worse than those of commission, because I knew that if I'd acted, I could have made a difference. Could even have saved a life.

I wasn't able to reach Rae Kelleher, my assistant at All Souls, that evening, and by the time she got back to me the next morning—Thursday—I was definitely annoyed. Still, I tried to keep a lid on my irritation. Rae is young, attractive, and in love; I couldn't expect her to spend her evenings waiting to be of service to her workaholic boss.

I got her started on a computer check on all three Cardings, then took myself to the Eureka P.D. and spoke with Shoemaker's contact, Sergeant Bob Wolfe. Wolfe—a dark-haired, sharp-featured man whose appearance was a good match for his surname—told me he'd had the notes processed by the lab, which had turned up no useful evidence.

"Then I started to probe, you know? When you got a harassment case like this, you look into the victims' private lives."

"And that was when Shoemaker told you to back off."

"Uh-huh."

"When was this?"

"About five weeks ago."

"I wonder why he waited so long to hire me. Did he, by any chance, ask you for a referral to a local investigator?"

Wolfe frowned. "Not this time."

"Then you'd referred him to someone before?"

"Yeah, guy who used to be on the force—Dave Morrison. Last April."

"Did Shoemaker tell you why he needed an investigator?"

"No, and I didn't ask. These politicians, they're always trying to get something on their rivals. I didn't want any part of it."

"Do you have Morrison's address and phone number handy?"

Wolfe reached into his desk drawer, shuffled things, and flipped a business card across the blotter. "Dave gave me a stack of these when he set up shop," he said. "Always glad to help an old pal."

Morrison was out of town, the message on his answering machine said, but would be back tomorrow afternoon. I left a message of my own, asking him to call me at my motel. Then I headed for the Shoemakers' home, hoping I could talk some common sense into Andrea.

But Andrea wasn't having any common sense.

She strode around the parlor of their big Victorian—built by one of the city's lumber barons, her husband told me when I complimented them on it—arguing and waving her arms and making scathing statements punctuated by a good amount of profanity. And knocking back martinis, even though it was only a little past noon.

Yes, she was going to the cabin. No, neither her husband nor I was welcome there. No, she wouldn't postpone the trip; she was sick and tired of being cooped up like some kind of zoo animal because her husband had made a mistake years before she'd met him. All right, she realized this John person was dangerous. But she'd taken self-defense classes and owned a .32 revolver. Of course she knew how to use it. Practiced frequently, too. Women had to be prepared these days, and she was.

But, she added darkly, glaring at her husband, she'd just as soon not have to shoot John. She'd rather send him straight back to Steve and let them settle this score. May the best man win—and she was placing bets on John.

As far as I was concerned, Steve and Andrea Shoemaker deserved each other.

I tried to explain to her that self-defense classes don't fully prepare you for a paralyzing, heart-pounding encounter with an actual violent stranger. I tried to warn her that the ability to shoot well on a firing range doesn't fully prepare you for pumping a bullet into a human being who is advancing swiftly on you.

I wanted to tell her she was being an idiot.

Before I could, she slammed down her glass and stormed out of the house.

Her husband replenished his own drink and said, "Now do you see what I'm up against?"

I didn't respond to that. Instead I said, "I spoke with Sergeant Wolfe earlier."

"And?"

"He told me he referred you to a local private investigator, Dave Morrison, last April."

"So?"

"Why didn't you hire Morrison for this job?"

"As I told you yesterday, my—"

"Sensitive position, yes."

Shoemaker scowled.

Before he could comment, I asked, "What was the job last April?"

"Nothing to do with this matter."

"Something to do with politics?"

"In a way."

"Mr. Shoemaker, hasn't it occurred to you that a political enemy may be using the Carding case as a smoke screen? That a rival's trying to throw you off balance before this special election?"

"It did, and . . . well, it isn't my opponent's style. My God, we're civilized people. But those notes . . . they're the work of a lunatic."

I wasn't so sure he was right—both about the notes being the work of a lunatic and politicians being civilized people—but I merely said, "Okay, you keep working on Mrs. Shoemaker. At least persuade her to let me go to the Lost Coast with her. I'll be in touch." Then I headed for the public library.

✧

After a few hours of ruining my eyes at the microfilm machine, I knew little more than before. Newspaper accounts of the Carding accident, lawsuit, and murder-suicide didn't differ substantially from what my client had told me. Their coverage of the Shoemakers' activities was only marginally interesting.

Normally I don't do a great deal of background investigation on clients, but as Sergeant Wolfe had said, in a case like this where one or both of them was a target, a thorough look at careers and lifestyles was mandatory. The papers described Steve as a straightforward, effective assemblyman who took a hard, conservative stance on such issues as welfare and the environment. He was strongly pro-business, particularly the lumber industry. He and his "charming and talented wife" didn't share many interests: Steve hunted and golfed; Andrea was a "generous supporter of the arts" and a "lavish party-giver." An odd couple, I thought, and odd people to be friends of Jack Stuart, a liberal who'd chosen to dedicate his career to representing the underdog.

Back at the motel, I put in a call to Jack. Why, I asked him, had he remained close to a man who was so clearly his opposite?

Jack laughed. "You're trying to say politely that you think he's a pompous, conservative ass."

"Well . . ."

"Okay, I admit it: he is. But back in college, he was a mentor to me. I doubt I would have gone into the law if it hadn't been for Steve. And we shared some good times, too: one summer we took a motorcycle trip around the country, like something out of *Easy Rider* without the tragedy. I guess we stay in touch because of a shared past."

I was trying to imagine Steve Shoemaker on a motorcycle; the picture wouldn't materialize. "Was he always so conservative?" I asked.

"No, not until he moved back to Eureka and went to work for that lumber company. Then . . . I don't know. Everything changed. It was as if something had happened that took all the fight out of him."

What had happened, I thought, was trading another man's life for a prestigious job.

Jack and I chatted for a moment longer, and then I asked him to transfer me to Rae. She hadn't turned up anything on the Cardings yet, but was working on it. In the meantime, she added, she'd taken care of what correspondence had come in, dealt with seven phone calls, entered next week's must-do's in the call-up file she'd created for me, and found a remedy for the blight that was affecting my rubber plant.

With a pang, I realized that the office ran just as well—better, perhaps—when I wasn't there. It would keep functioning smoothly without me for weeks, months, maybe years.

Hell, it would probably keep functioning smoothly even if I were dead.

In the morning I opened the Yellow Pages to Florists and began calling each that was listed. While Shoemaker had been vague on the date his wife received the funeral arrangement, surely a customer who wanted one sent to a private home, rather than a mortuary, would stand out in the order-taker's mind. The listing was long, covering a relatively wide area; it wasn't until I reached the R's and my watch showed nearly eleven o'clock that I got lucky.

"I don't remember any order like that in the past six weeks," the clerk at Rainbow Florists said, "but we had one yesterday, was delivered this morning."

I gripped the receiver harder. "Will you pull the order, please?"

"I'm not sure I should—"

"Please. You could help to save a woman's life."

Quick intake of breath, then his voice filled with excitement; he'd become part of a real-life drama. "One minute. I'll check." When he came back on the line, he said, "Thirty-dollar standard condolence arrangement, delivered this morning to Mr. Steven Shoemaker—"

"*Mister?* Not Mrs. or Ms.?"

"Mister, definitely. I took the order myself." He read off the Shoemakers' address.

"Who placed it?"

"A kid. Came in with cash and written instructions."

Standard ploy—hire a kid off the street so nobody can identify you.

"Thanks very much."

"Aren't you going to tell me—"

I hung up and dialed Shoemaker's office. His secretary told me he was working at home today. I dialed the home number. Busy. I hung up, and the phone rang immediately. Rae, with information on the Cardings.

She'd traced Sam Carding's daughter and younger son. The daughter lived near Cleveland, Ohio, and Rae had spoken with her on the phone. John, his sister had told her, was a drifter and an addict; she hadn't seen or spoken to him in more than ten years. When Rae reached the younger brother at his office in L.A., he told her the same, adding that he assumed John had died years ago.

I thanked Rae and told her to keep on it. Then I called Shoemaker's home number again. Still busy; time to go over there.

Shoemaker's Lincoln was parked in the drive of the Victorian, a dusty Honda motorcycle beside it. As I rang the doorbell I again tried to picture a younger, free-spirited Steve bumming around the country on a bike with Jack, but the image simply wouldn't come clear. It took Shoemaker a while to answer the door, and when he saw me, his mouth pulled down in displeasure.

"Come in, and be quick about it," he told me. "I'm on an important conference call."

I was quick about it. He rushed down the hallway to what must be a study, and I went into the parlor where we'd talked the day before. Unlike his offices, it was exquisitely decorated, calling up images of the days of the lumber barons. Andrea's work, probably. Had she also done his offices? Perhaps their gaudy decor was her way of getting back at a husband who put his political life ahead of their marriage?

It was at least half an hour before Shoemaker finished with his call. He appeared in the archway leading to the hall, somewhat disheveled, running his fingers through his hair. "Come with me," he said. "I have something to show you."

He led me to a large kitchen at the back of the house. A floral arrangement sat on the granite-topped center island: white lilies with a single red rose. Shoemaker handed me the card: "My sympathy on your wife's passing." It was signed "John."

"Where's Mrs. Shoemaker?" I asked.

"Apparently she went out to the coast last night. I haven't seen her since she walked out on us at the noon hour."

"And you've been home the whole time?"

He nodded. "Mainly on the phone."

"Why didn't you call me when she didn't come home?"

"I didn't realize she hadn't until mid-morning. We have separate bedrooms, and Andrea comes and goes as she pleases. Then this arrangement arrived, and my conference call came through . . . ." He shrugged, spreading his hands helplessly.

"All right," I said, "I'm going out there whether she likes it or not. And I think you'd better clear up whatever you're doing here and follow. Maybe your showing up there will convince her you care about her safety, make her listen to reason."

As I spoke, Shoemaker had taken a fifth of Tanqueray gin and a jar of Del Prado Spanish olives from a Lucky sack that sat on the counter. He opened a cupboard, reached for a glass.

"No," I said. "This is no time to have a drink."

He hesitated, then replaced the glass, and began giving me directions to the cabin. His voice was flat, and his curious travelogue-like digressions made me feel as if I were listening to a tape of a *National Geographic* special. Reality, I thought, had finally sunk in, and it had turned him into an automaton.

✧

I had one stop to make before heading out to the coast, but it was right on my way. Morrison Investigations had its office in what looked to be a former motel on Highway 101, near the outskirts of the city. It was a neighborhood of fast-food restaurants and bars, thrift shops and marginal businesses. Besides the detective agency, the motel's cinderblock units housed an insurance brokerage, a secretarial service, two accountants, and a palm reader. Dave Morrison, who was just arriving as I pulled into the parking area, was a bit of a surprise: in his mid-forties, wearing one small gold earring and a short ponytail. I wondered what Steve Shoemaker had made of him.

Morrison showed me into a two-room suite crowded with computer equipment and file cabinets and furniture that looked as if he might have hauled it down the street from the nearby Thrift Emporium. When he noticed me studying him, he grinned easily. "I know, I don't look like a former cop. I worked undercover Narcotics my last few years on the force. Afterwards I realized I was comfortable with the uniform." His gesture took in his lumberjack's shirt, work-worn jeans and boots.

I smiled in return, and he cleared some files off a chair so I could sit.

"So you're working for Steve Shoemaker," he said.

"I understand you did, too."

He nodded. "Last April and again around the beginning of August."

"Did he approach you about another job after that?"

He shook his head.

"And the jobs you did for him were—"

"You know better than to ask that."

"I was going to ask, were they completed to his satisfaction?"

"Yes."

"Do you have any idea why Shoemaker would go to the trouble of bringing me up from San Francisco when he had an investigator here whose work satisfied him?"

Headshake.

"Shoemaker told me the first job you did for him had to do with politics."

The corner of his mouth twitched. "In a matter of speaking." He paused, shrewd eyes assessing me. "How come you're investigating your own client?"

"It's that kind of case. And something feels wrong. Did you get that sense about either of the jobs you took on for him?"

"No." Then he hesitated, frowning. "Well, maybe. Why don't you just come out and ask what you want to? If I can, I'll answer."

"Okay—did either of the jobs have to do with a man named John Carding?"

That surprised him. After a moment he asked a question of his own. "He's still trying to trace Carding?"

"Yes."

Morrison got up and moved toward the window, stopped and drummed his fingers on top of a file cabinet. "Well, I can save you further trouble. John Carding is untraceable. I tried every way I know—and that's every way there is. My guess is that he's dead, years dead."

"And when was it you tried to trace him?"

"Most of August."

Weeks before Andrea Shoemaker had begun to receive the notes from "John." Unless the harassment had started earlier? No, I'd seen all the notes, examined their postmarks. Unless she'd thrown away the first ones, as she had the card that came with the funeral arrangement?

"Shoemaker tell you why he wanted to find Carding?" I asked.

"Uh-uh."

"And your investigation last April had nothing to do with Carding?"

At first I thought Morrison hadn't heard the question. He was looking out the window; then he turned, expression thoughtful, and opened one of the drawers of the filing cabinet beside him. "Let me refresh my memory," he said, taking out a couple of folders. I watched as he flipped through them, frowning.

Finally he said, "I'm not gonna ask about your case. If something feels wrong, it could be because of what I turned up last spring—and that I don't want on my conscience." He closed one file, slipped it back in the cabinet, then glanced at his watch. "Damn! I just remembered I've got to make a call." He crossed to the desk, set the open file on it. "I better do it from the other room. You stay here, find something to read."

I waited until he'd left, then went over and picked up the file. Read it with growing interest and began putting things together. Andrea had been discreet about her extramarital activities, but not so discreet that a competent investigator like Morrison couldn't uncover them.

When Morrison returned, I was ready to leave for the Lost Coast.

"Hope you weren't bored," he said.

"No, I'm easily amused. And, Mr. Morrison, I owe you a dinner."

"You know where to find me. I'll look forward to seeing you again."

✧

And now that I'd reached the cabin, Andrea had disappeared. The victim of violence, all signs indicated. But the victim of whom? John Carding—a man no one had seen or heard from for over ten years? Another man named John, one of her cast-off lovers? Or . . . ?

What mattered now was to find her.

I retraced my steps, turning up the hood of my sweater again as I went outside. Circled the cabin, peering through the lashing rain. I could make out a couple of other small structures back there: outhouse and shed. The outhouse was empty. I crossed to the shed. Its door was propped open with a log, as if she'd been getting fuel for the stove.

Inside, next to a neatly stacked cord of wood, I found her.

She lay facedown on the hard-packed dirt floor, blue-jeaned legs splayed, plaid-jacketed arms flung above her head, chestnut hair cascading over her back. The little room was silent, the total silence that surrounds the dead. Even my own breath was stilled; when it came again, it sounded obscenely loud.

I knelt beside her, forced myself to perform all the checks I've made more times than I could have imagined. No breath, no pulse, no warmth to the skin. And the rigidity . . .

On the average—although there's a wide variance—rigor mortis sets in to the upper body five to six hours after death; the whole body is usually affected within eighteen hours. I backed up and felt the lower portion of her body. Rigid; rigor was complete. I straightened, went to stand in the doorway. She'd probably been dead since midnight. And the cause? I couldn't see any wounds, couldn't further examine her without disturbing the scene. What I should be doing was getting in touch with the sheriff's department.

Back to the cabin. Emotions tore at me: anger, regret, and—yes—guilt that I hadn't prevented this. But I also sensed that I *couldn't* have prevented it. I, or someone like me, had been an integral component from the first.

In the front room I found some kitchen matches and lit the oil lamp. Then I went around the table and looked down at where her revolver lay on the floor. More evidence; don't touch it. The purse and its spilled contents rested near the edge of the stove. I inventoried the items visually: the usual makeup, brush, comb, spray perfume; wallet, keys, roll of postage stamps; daily planner that had flopped open to show pockets for business cards and receipts. And a loose piece of paper . . .

Lucky Food Center, it said at the top. Perhaps she'd stopped to pick up supplies before leaving Eureka; the date and time on this receipt might indicate how long she'd remained in town before storming out on her husband and me. After I picked it up. At the bottom I found yesterday's date and the time of purchase: 9:14 p. m.

"KY SERV DELI . . .CRABS . . .WINE . . . DEL PRAD OLIVE . . . LG RED DEL . . . ROUGE ET NOIR . . . BAKERY. . . TANQ GIN—"

A sound outside. Footsteps slogging through the mud. I stuffed the receipt into my pocket.

Steve Shoemaker came through the open door in a hurry, rain hat pulled low on his forehead, droplets sluicing down his chiseled nose. He stopped when he saw me, looked around. "Where's Andrea?"

I said, "I don't know."

"What do you mean you don't know? Her Bronco's outside. That's her purse on the stove."

"And her weekend bag's on the bed, but she's nowhere to be found."

Shoemaker arranged his face into lines of concern. "There's been a struggle here."

"Appears that way."

"Come on, we'll go look for her. She may be in the outhouse or the shed. She may be hurt—"

"It won't be necessary to look." I had my gun out of my purse now, and I leveled it at him. "I know you killed your wife, Shoemaker."

"What!"

"Her body's where you left it last night. What time did you kill her? How?"

His faked concern shaded into panic. "I didn't—"

"You did."

No reply. His eyes moved from side to side—calculating, looking for a way out.

I added, "You drove her here in the Bronco, with your motorcycle inside. Arranged things to simulate a struggle, put her in the shed, then drove back to town on the bike. You shouldn't have left the bike outside the house where I could see it. It wasn't muddy out here last night, but it sure was dusty."

"Where are these baseless accusations coming from? John Carding—"

"Is untraceable, probably dead, as you know from the check Dave Morrison ran."

"He told you— What about the notes, the flowers, the dead things—"

"Sent by you."

"Why would I do that?"

"To set the scene for getting rid of a chronically unfaithful wife who had potential to become a political embarrassment."

He wasn't cracking, though. "Granted, Andrea had her problems. But why would I rake up the Carding matter?"

"Because it would sound convincing for you to admit what you did all those years ago. God knows it convinced me. And I doubt the police would ever have made the details public. Why destroy a grieving widower and prominent citizen? Particularly when they'd never find Carding or bring him to trial. You've got one problem, though: me. You never should have brought me in to back up your scenario."

He licked his lips, glaring at me. Then he drew himself up, leaned forward aggressively—a posture the attorneys at All Souls jokingly refer to as their "litigator's mode."

"You have no proof of this," he said firmly, jabbing his index finger at me. "No proof whatsoever."

"Deli items, crabs, wine, apples," I recited. "Del Prado Spanish olives, Tanqueray gin."

"What the hell are you talking about?"

"I have Andrea's receipt for the items she bought at Lucky yesterday, before she stopped home to pick up her weekend bag. None of those things is here in the cabin."

"So?"

"I know that at least two of them—the olives and the gin—are at your house in Eureka. I'm willing to bet they all are."

"What if they are? She did some shopping for me yesterday morning—"

"The receipt is dated yesterday *evening*, nine-fourteen p.m. I'll quote you, Shoemaker: 'Apparently she went out to the coast last night. I haven't seen her since she walked out on us at the noon hour.' But you claim you didn't leave home after noon."

That did it; that opened the cracks. He stood for a moment, then half collapsed into one of the chairs and put his head in his hands.

The next summer, after I testified at the trial in which Steve Shoemaker was convicted of the first-degree murder of his wife, I returned to the Lost Coast—with a backpack, without the .38, and in the company of my lover. We walked sand beaches under skies that showed infinite shadings of blue; we made love in fields of wildflowers; we waited quietly for the deer, falcons, and foxes.

I'd already taken the bad from this place; now I could take the good.

FILE CLOSED

THE MOVERS had come for my office furniture. All that remained was for me to haul a few cartons to McCone Investigations' nearly new van. I hefted one and carried it down to the foyer of All Souls's big Victorian, then made three round trips for the others. Before I went downstairs for the last time I let my gaze wander around the front room that for years had been my home away from home. Empty, it looked battle-scarred and shabby: the wallpaper was peeling; the ceiling paint had blistered; the hardwood floors were scraped; there were gouges in the mantel of the nonworking fireplace.

A far cry from the new offices on the waterfront, I thought, but still I'd miss this room. Would miss sitting in my swivel chair in the window bay and contemplating the sagging rooflines of the Outer Mission district or the weedy triangular park below. Would miss pacing the faded Oriental carpet while talking on the phone. But most of all I would miss the familiar day-to-day sounds of the co-op that had assured me that I was among friends.

Only in the end friends here had been damned few. Now none were left. Time to say goodbye. Time to move on to McCone Investigations' new offices on one of the piers off the Embarcadero, next to the equally new offices of Altman & Zahn, Attorneys-at-Law.

I took the last carton downstairs.

Ted's old desk still stood in the foyer, but without his personal possessions—particularly the coffee mug shaped like Gertrude Stein's head and the campy lamp fashioned from a mesh-stockinged mannequin's leg—it was a slate wiped clean of the years he had presided there. Already he'd be arranging those treasures down at the pier. I set the box with the others and, both out of curiosity and nostalgia, went along the hall to the converted closet under the stairs that had been my first office.

Rae Kelleher, its recent occupant, had already taken her belongings to McCone Investigations. With relief I saw she'd left the ratty old armchair. For a moment I stood in the door looking at each familiar crack in the walls; then I stepped inside and ran my hand over the chair's back where stuffing sprouted. How many hours had I sat there, honing my fledgling investigator's skills?

A cardboard box tucked under the angle of the staircase caught my eye. I peered at it, wondering why Rae had left it behind, and saw lettering in her hand: "McCone Files." Early ones, they must be. I'd probably neglected to remove them from the cabinet when I transferred my things upstairs. I pulled the box toward me, sat down in the armchair, and lifted the lid. A dry, dusty odor wafted up. On the files' tabs I saw names: Albritton, DiCesare, Kaufmann, Morrison, Smith, Snelling, Whelan, and many more. Some I recognized immediately, others were only vaguely familiar, and about the rest I hadn't a clue. I scanned them, remembering—

Morrison! That damned case! It was the only file I hadn't been able to close in all my years at All Souls.

I pulled it from the box and flipped through. Interesting case. Marnie Morrison, the naive young woman with Daddy's American Express card. Jon Howard, the "financier" who had used her to help him scam half the merchants in San Francisco. And Hank in turn had used the case's promise to lure me into taking the job here.

But I hadn't been able to solve it.

Could I solve it now?

Well, maybe. I was a far better investigator than when I'd operated out of this tiny office. The hundreds of hours spent honing my skills had paid off; so had my life experiences, good and bad. I picked up on facts that I might not have noticed back then, could interpret them more easily, had learned to trust my gut-level instincts, no matter how far-fetched they might seem.

I turned my attention to the file.

Well, there was one thing right off—the daily phone calls Jon Howard had made to the car dealership in Walnut Creek. When I'd driven out there and talked with its manager, neither he nor his salesmen could remember the memorable young couple.

I took a pen from my purse, made a note of the dealership's name, address, and phone number, then read on.

And there was something else—the conversation I'd had with the salesman at European Motors here in the city. My recent experience with buying a "pre-owned" van for the agency put a new light on his comments.

My office phone had been disconnected the day before, and the remaining partners would frown on me placing toll calls on All Souls's line. Quickly I hauled the file box out to where my other cartons sat, threw on my jacket, and headed downhill to the Remedy Lounge on Mission Street.

The Remedy had long been a favorite watering hole for the old-timers at All Souls. Brian, the owner, extended us all sorts of courtesies—excluding table service for anyone but Rae, who reminded him of his dead sister, and including running tabs and letting us use his office phone. When I got there the place was empty and the big Irishman was watching his favorite soap opera on the TV mounted above the bar.

"Sure," he said in answer to my request, "use the phone all you want. Yours is turned off already?"

"Right. It's moving day."

Brian's fleshy face grew melancholy. He picked up a rag and began wiping down the already polished surface of the bar. "Guess I won't be seeing much of you guys any more."

"Why not? The bar's on a direct line between the new offices and the Safeway where we all shop."

He shrugged. "People always say stuff like that, but in the end they drift away."

"We'll prove you wrong," I told him, even though I suspected he was right.

"We'll see." He pressed the button that unlocked the door to his office.

At his desk I opened my notebook and dialed the number of Ben Rudolph Chevrolet in Walnut Creek. I reached their used-car department. The salesman's answer to my first question confirmed what I already suspected. His supervisor, who had worked there since the late seventies, was out to lunch, he told me, but would be back around two.

Five minutes later I was in the van and on my way to the East Bay.

Walnut Creek is a suburb of San Francisco, but a city in its own right, sprawling in a broad valley in the shadow of Mount Diablo. When I'd traveled there on the Morrison case more than a decade earlier, it still had a small-town flavor: few trendy shops and restaurants in the downtown district; only one office building over two stories; tracts and shopping centers, yes, but also semi-rural neighborhoods where the residents still kept horses and chickens. Now it was a hub of commerce, with tall buildings whose tinted and smoked glass glowed in the afternoon sun. There was a new cultural center, a restaurant on nearly every corner, and the tracts went on forever.

Ben Rudolph Chevrolet occupied the same location on North Main Street, although its neighbors squeezed more tightly against it. As I parked in the customer lot I wondered why years ago I had neglected to call the phone number the SFPD had supplied me. If I'd phoned ahead rather than just driven out here, I'd have discovered that the dealership maintained separate lines for its new- and used-car departments. And I'd have known that Jon Howard's daily calls weren't made because he was hot on the trail of a snappy new Corvette.

I went directly to the manager of the used-car department, a ruddy-faced, prosperous-looking man named Dave Swenson. Yes, he confirmed, he'd worked there since seventy-eight. "Only way to survive in this business is you stick with one dealership, dig in, create your own clientele."

"I'm looking for someone who might've been a salesman here in the late seventies and early eighties." I showed him my I. D. "Handsome man, dark hair and mustache, late twenties. Good build. Below average height. His name may have been Jon Howard."

"No, it wasn't."

"I'm sorry?"

"I know the fella you're talking about, but you got it backwards. His name was Howard John."

Howard John—simple transposition. The salesman at European Motors had told me he knew enough about used cars to sell them, and he'd been correct. "John's not working here any more?"

"Hell, no. He was fired over a dozen years ago. I don't recall exactly when." Swenson tapped his temple. "Sorry, the old memory's going."

"But you remembered him right off."

"Well, he was that kind of guy. A real screw-up, always talking big and never doing anything about it, but you couldn't help liking him."

"Talking big, how?"

"Ah, the usual. He was studying nights, gonna get his MBA, set up some financial company, be somebody. He'd have a big house in the city, a limo, boats and planes, hobnob with all the right people—you know. All smoke and no fire, Howie was, but you had to hand it to him, he could be an entertaining fellow."

"And then he was fired."

"Yeah. It was stupid, it didn't have to happen. The guy was producing; he made sales when nobody else could. What Howie did, he took a vacation to Mammouth to ski. When his week was up, he started calling in, saying he was sick with some bug he caught down there. This went on for weeks, and the boss got suspicious, so he checked out Howie's apartment. The manager said he hadn't been back since he drove off with his ski gear the month before. So a few days after that when Howie strolled in here all innocent and business-as-usual, the boss had no choice but to can him."

"What happened to him? Do you know where he's working now?"

Swenson stared thoughtfully at me. "You know, I meant it when I said I liked the guy."

"I don't mean him any harm, Mr. Swenson."

"No?" He waited.

Quickly I considered several stories, rejected all of them, and told Swenson the truth. He reacted with glee, laughing loudly and slapping his hand on his desk. "Good for Howie! At least he got a few weeks of the good life before everything went down the sewer."

"So will you tell me where I can find him?"

"I still don't know why you want him."

I hesitated, unsure myself as to why I did. No one was looking for Howard John any more, and the organization that had assigned me to find him had ceased to exist. Finally I said, "When you have a sale pending that you think is a sure thing and then it falls through, does it nag at you afterwards?"

"Sure, for years, sometimes. I wonder what I did wrong, why it didn't fly."

"I'm the same way about my cases. This is my last open file from the law firm where I used to work. Closing it will tie off some loose ends."

"Well . . ." Swenson considered some more. "Okay. I don't know if Howie's still there, but I saw him working another lot about three months ago—Roy's motors, up in Concord."

Concord was a city to the north. I thanked Swenson and hurried out to the van.

Concord, like Walnut Creek, had developed into a metropolis since I once worked a case at its performing arts pavilion, but the windswept frontage road where Roy's Motors was located was a throwback to the early sixties. An aging shopping center with a geodesic dome-type cinema and dozens of mostly dead stores adjoined the used-car lot; both were almost devoid of customers. Faded plastic flags fluttered limply above Roy's stock, which consisted mainly of vehicles that looked as though they'd welcome a trip to the auto dismantler's; a sign proclaiming it HOME OF THE BEST DEALS IN TOWN creaked disconsolately. I could make out the figure of a man sitting inside the small sales shack, but his features were obscured by the dirty window glass.

A young couple were wandering through the lot, stopping here and there to examine pick-up trucks. After a few minutes they displayed more than passing interest in a canary-yellow Ford, and the man got up and came out of the shack. He was on the short side and running to paunch, with thinning dark hair, a brushy mustache, and a face that once had been handsome. Howard John?

As he approached the couple, the salesman held himself more erect and sucked in his stomach; his step took on a jaunty rhythm and a charismatic smile lit up his face. He shook hands with the couple, began expounding on the truck. He laughed; they laughed. He helped the woman into the cab, urged the man in on the driver's side. The chemistry was working, the magic flowing. This, I was sure, was the man who years before had scammed the greedy merchants of San Francisco.

A few short weeks of living like the high rollers, I thought, then dismissal from a good job and a series of steps down to this. How did he go on, with the memory of those weeks ever in the back of his mind? How did he come to this windswept lot every day and put himself through the paces?

Well, maybe his dreams—improbable as they might seem—had survived intact. He'd done it once, his reasoning might go, and he could do it again. Maybe Howard John still believed that he was only occupying a waystation on the road to the top.

But what about Marnie Morrison?

I found Howard John's residence by a method whose simplicity and effectiveness have never ceased to amaze me: a look-see into the phone book. The listing was in two names, and the wife's was Marnie.

The shabby residential street was not far from the used-car lot: a two-block row of identical shoebox-style tract homes of the same vintage as the shopping center. The pavement was potholed and the houses on the west side backed up on a concrete viaduct, but big poplars arched over the street and, in spite of the hum of nearby freeway traffic, it had an aura of tranquillity. The house I was looking for was painted mint green and surrounded by a low chain link fence. A sign on its gate said SUNNYSIDE DAYCARE CENTER, and in the yard beyond it sat an assortment of brightly colored playground equipment.

It was close to five o'clock; for the next hour I watched a steady stream of parents arrive and depart with their offspring. Ten minutes after the last had left a woman came out of the house and began collecting the playthings strewn in the yard. I peered through my shade-dappled windshield and recognized an older, heavier version of Marnie Morrison. Clad in an oversized sweatshirt and leggings that strained over her ample thighs, she moved slowly, stopping now and then to wipe sweat from her brow. When she finished she trudged inside.

So this was what Marnie had become since I'd last seen her: the over-worked, prematurely aged wife of an unsuccessful used-car salesman, who operated a daycare center to make ends meet. And one of those ends was her periodic hundred-dollar atonement to her parents' favorite charity for the credit-card binge that had bought her a few weeks of high living and dreams.

Unsure as to why I was doing it, I continued to watch the mint green house. I'd found Marnie. Why didn't I give up and go back to the city? There were things I should be doing at the new offices, things I should be doing at home.

But I wanted an end to the story, so I stayed where I was.

Half an hour later a Ford Bronco passed me and pulled into the Johns's driveway. Howard got out carrying a bouquet of pink car-nations. He let himself into the yard, stopping to pick up a stuffed bear that Marnie had missed. He held the bear at arm's length, gave it a jaunty grin, and tucked it under his arm. His step was light as he moved toward the door. Before he got it open his wife appeared, now dressed in a gauzy caftan, and enveloped him in a welcoming embrace.

I'd reached the end of the tale. Leaving Marnie and Howard to their surviving dreams and illusions, I drove back to All Souls for the last time.

The big Victorian was mostly dark and totally silent. Only the porchlight and another far back in the kitchen shone. It was about eight o'clock; none of the remaining partners lived in the building, and they rarely spent more time there than was necessary. The new corporation they'd formed had the property up for sale and would move downtown as soon as a buyer was found.

Moving on, all of us.

I was about to haul the cartons I'd left in the foyer down to the van when I heard a sound in the kitchen—the familiar creak of the refrigerator door. Curiosity aroused, I went back there, walking softly. The room was dim, the light coming from a single bulb in the sconce over the sink. A figure turned from the fridge, glass of wine in hand. Hank.

He started, nearly dropping the glass. "Jesus, Shar!"

"Sorry. I'm not up to talking to any of the new guard tonight, so I tiptoed. Why aren't you down at the pier helping everybody shove the new furniture around?"

"I was, but nobody could make up their mind where it should go, and I foresaw a long and unpleasant relationship with a chiropractor."

"So you came *here*?"

He shrugged. "Why not? You want some wine?"

"Sure. For old times' sake."

Hank went to the fridge and poured the last of the so-so jug variety that had been an All Souls staple. He handed it to me and motioned for me to sit at the round table by the window. As we took our places I realized that they were identical to those we'd occupied the first afternoon I'd come here.

I said, "You still haven't told me why you're here."

"You haven't told me why *you're* here."

"I meant to be gone hours ago, but wait till you hear my news!" I explained about closing the Morrison file.

He shook his head. "You *do* believe in tying up loose ends. So what about those two—do you think they're happy?"

I hesitated. "What's happy? It's all relative. The guy still brings her flowers. She still dresses up for him. Maybe that's enough."

"But after the scams they pulled, the style they lived?"

"It only lasted a few weeks. Maybe that was enough, too."

"Maybe." He took a long pull at his wine, took a longer look around the kitchen. His expression grew melancholy. This room and this table had been a big part of Hank's life since leaving law school.

"Don't," I said, "or you'll get me going."

His eyes moved to the window, scanning the lights of downtown. After a moment they stopped and his lips curved into a smile. I knew he was looking at the section of waterfront where the law firm of Altman & Zahn had recently rented offices next to McCone Investigations on a renovated pier.

"File closed," he said.

We finished our wine in silence. Around us the big house creaked and groaned, as it did every evening when the day's warmth faded. I felt my eyes sting, blinked hard. Only an incurable romantic would find significance in tonight's particular creaks and groans. And I, of course, had not a romantic bone in my body.

So why had that last creak sounded like "goodbye"?

Hank drained his glass and stood. Carried both to the sink, where he rinsed them carefully and set them on the drainboard. "In answer to your earlier question," he said, "I'm here because I forgot something."

"Oh? What?"

He came over and rapped his knuckles on the table where we'd eaten and drunk, played games and talked, celebrated and commiserated, fought and made up, and—now—let go. "This table and chairs're mine. Marin County Flea Market, the week after we founded All Souls. They're going along."

"To our joint conference room?"

"Mind reader. Is that okay with you?"

I nodded.

"Then give me a hand with them, will you?"

I stood, grinning. "Sure, but only if . . ."

"If what?"

It was a stupid, sentimental decision—one I was sure to regret. "Only if you'll give me a hand with that ratty armchair in my former office. I can't imagine why Rae forgot it."

❖

ACKNOWLEDGMENTS

❖

"The Last Open File," an original story published here for the first time. Copyright 1995 by Marcia Muller.

"Merrill-Go-Round," first published in *The Arbor House Treasury of Mystery and Suspense.* Copyright © 1981 by Marcia Muller. Revised version, copyright © 1995 by Marcia Muller.

"Wild Mustard," first published in *The Eyes Have It.* Copyright © 1984 by Marcia Muller.

"The Broken Men," first published in *Women Sleuths.* Copyright © 1985 by Marcia Muller.

"Deceptions," first published in *A Matter of Crime #1.* Copyright © 1987 by Marcia Muller.

"Cache and Carry," first published in *Small Felonies.* Copyright © 1988 by Marcia Muller and Bill Pronzini.

"Deadly Fantasies," first published in *Alfred Hitchcock's Mystery Magazine,* April 1989. Copyright © 1989 by Marcia Muller.

"All the Lonely People," first published in *Sisters in Crime.* Copyright © 1989 by Marcia Muller.

"The Place That Time Forgot," first published in *Sisters in Crime 2,* copyright © 1990 by Marcia Muller.

"Somewhere in the City," first published in *The Armchair Detective,* Spring 1990. Copyright © 1990 by Marcia Muller.

"Final Resting Place," first published in *Justice for Hire.* Copyright © 1990 by Marcia Muller.

"Silent Night," first published in *Mistletoe Mysteries*. Copyright © 1990 by Marcia Muller.

"Benny's Space," first published in *A Woman's Eye*. Copyright © 1992 by Marcia Muller.

"The Lost Coast," first published in *Deadly Allies II*. Copyright © 1994 by Marcia Muller.

"File Closed," an original story published here for the first time. Copyright © 1995 by Marcia Muller.

THE McCONE FILES

The McCone Files by Marcia Muller, with cover painting by Carol Heyer, is set in 11 point Garamond Antiqua and printed on 50 pound Glatfelter Supple Opaque (recycled) acid-free paper. The book was printed by Thomson-Shore, Inc., Dexter, Michigan. The first edition comprises eight hundred and eighty-three copies in trade paper and two hundred and seventeen copies in Roxite-B Linen cloth, signed and numbered by the author Each of the clothbound copies contains a tipped-in page of the author's type-script, or a page of galley proofs (with corrections by the author), or a photocopied page of the original appearance of one of the stories (with corrections by the author). *The McCone Files* was published in May 1995 by Crippen & Landru Publishers, Norfolk, Virginia. The second printing of five hundred copies was published in November 1995. The third printing of seven hundred and fifty copies was published in September 1996.